PRAISE ... TER

"Angela Slatter's newest collection is an exemplary specimen of that endangered genre: fairytale re-tellings that read as something wholly original and fresh. Dark, bold, visceral, and sly, full of smart fierce girls and women saving each other; all in all reminiscent of nothing so much as Angela Carter's best. One of the strongest thematic undercurrents here is that of transformation, as expected of most folklore worth its salt. These, however, are transformations couched in a metafictional nesting-doll of source material. Here are heroines who are aware not only of the well-worn paths they tread, not only of the dark woods of which they are on all sides beset, but also that some paths are meant to be strayed from, and that new paths are made in so doing."

~ Nicole Kornher-Stace, author of *Archivist Wasp*

"A Slatter story collection is both an unforgettable feast and a welcome inspiration."

~ Marianne de Pierres, author of *Peacemaker*
and the Parrish Plessis series

"An evocative, mysterious, and memorable collection of stories told with wit, wisdom and humour; combined with a perfect pinch of dread and darkness."

~ Garth Nix, author of *The Old Kingdom*
and The Keys to the Kingdom series

"Earthy yet wis~~~~~~~~~~~~~~~~~~emonstrates clearly the glori~~~~~~~~~~~~~~~~~~tting heir to Angela Carter a~~~~~~~~~~~~~~~~~~

~ Jeff VanderMeer, author of
The Southern Reach trilogy

MORE PRAISE FOR ANGELA SLATTER

"Angela Slatter's new collection is full of heart-breaking fairy tales—not in the sanitized modern sense, but in the original style which used compelling stories to mask warnings. They combine timeless peril and beauty."

~ Mary Robinette Kowal, author of
The Glamourist Histories series

"Angela Slatter's stories, like the fairy tales of old, are steeped in blood and darkness. To step into them is to immediately feel the presence of old energies, to hear the whisper of dreadful warnings. Building upon the foundations of the fairy tales, these stories are layered with character, narratively sophisticated, and galvanized by a beleaguered wisdom. With this wide release of stories previously only available in limited editions, the world at large is about to discover what some of us have known for years: Angela Slatter writes some of the darkest, most beautiful stories in the world today."

~ Nathan Ballingrud, author of
North American Lake Monsters

A Feast of Sorrows: Stories

A FEAST OF SORROWS: STORIES

Angela Slatter

Prime Books

Prime Books
Germantown, MD
www.prime-books.com

Print ISBN: 978-1-60701-474-4
Ebook ISBN: 978-1-60701-479-9

To my beloved sister, Michelle, who still dreams

~

Thank you:
*To Nicole Korhner-Stace, Marianne de Pierres, Garth Nix, Mary
Robinette Kowal, Nathan Ballingrud, and Jeff VanderMeer
for their kind words.
To Theodora Goss for the lovely introduction.
To Sean Wallace and Paula Guran for publishing* A Feast of Sorrows.
*To the Katharine Susannah Prichard Writers Centre
for the time and place to complete the edits,
and to the Copyright Agency for assistance with funding.
To those who first published these tales.
The warmest and deepest of thanks to my family—Betty, Peter, Michelle,
and Matthew—who keep me grounded when I'm wandering.
And, as always, the last and best is for David, whose heart I never doubt.*

CONTENTS

Stories from Angelia:
an Introduction

Angela Slatter is a sorceress.

I thought I should warn you before you start reading this book. Unless you've already read it and are coming back to read the introduction? In which case you already know. You've been through the dark, dangerous woods, where women turn into bears and the Erl-King roams. You've already been transformed into something different from what you were.

If you meet Angela, maybe at your neighbourhood bookstore signing books or at a literary festival, and she looks like you or me or anyone else, that's because sorceresses are clever. They know how to disguise themselves. But if you follow her home to what probably looks like a perfectly normal house (but isn't) and peek through her kitchen window, you will see her standing at the stove in a robe of mist and cobwebs, which is a sorceress' version of sweat pants. She will be brewing potions in an alembic and making conversation with her pet griffin (probably named Fluff). She will pause to look up recipes in a silver mirror, which is the sorceress' version of checking *Wikipedia* on her iPhone.

What is she making? you will ask. Stories, of course. That is how sorceresses make stories. (Revisions, however, are still done on a computer.)

Just like the stories you will read, or have perhaps already read, here. For these stories are spells . . .

What a funny word, "spell." According to the *Oxford English Dictionary*, that most magical of grimoires, to spell is to "set down in order the letters of (a word or syllable)," but that's actually the third meaning listed. The first is to "utter, declare, relate, tell," like telling a story. The second is to "make out, understand, decipher, or comprehend," which is what you're doing by reading this book. So a spell is something you and the author make together: she utters the story, you decipher it, and the result is magic. Otherwise known as reading, although for some reason that definition does not appear in the *OED*.

What you have here is a book that takes you to imaginary lands, including Australia, where the jacaranda trees grow. If you have not seen a jacaranda, I will tell you it is a mass of purple blossoms, like a tree in a fairy tale. Australia itself is a magical country bordering on Fairyland that seems utterly fantastical unless you have grown up there, and perhaps even then. (In Australia, griffins are marsupial.) Most of these stories do not take place in Australia, but rather a country I think of as Angelia. I made that up of course: it's equal parts Angela and Anglia (the medieval Latin for England, because so many of these stories are inflected with an English sensibility). But in all of them, there is a touch of Australia, particularly in repeated references to ships and ports and the sea. Angelia has its displaced queens and impoverished merchants, its mad seamstresses and coffin-makers' daughters. Its ghosts. I believe there must be an atlas of it inside Angela's head, and wouldn't that be an interesting map to study?

According to her official biography, Angela is Australian and has graduate degrees in Creative Writing, but I wonder. This is of course the cleverness of the typical sorceress (to the extent sorceresses are ever typical, for to be a sorceress is by definition to be atypical, out of the ordinary). I'm quite sure she lives primarily in Angelia, in one of the neighbourhoods with tall, narrow houses close to the Cathedral, although she probably has a pied-à-terre in Brisbane when she needs to stay in our world for a while, like for bookstore signings. There must be a secret trans-dimensional passage leading from one house to the other. And I suspect her MA and PhD are actually in Sorceressing. At any rate, I'm sure she has passports from both countries. The one from Angelia is probably stamped with gilt letters and a crown.

All author-sorceresses have their themes, the issues and concerns they explore most often. In this book you will find, above all, stories of women: in love, out of love, trying to find and make their way in the world. They will search for esoteric knowledge, turn feminine arts such as sewing and baking to magical purposes. They will leave home, find home, create homes for their families. They are, above all, different and individual. Whether students at St Dymphna's School for Poison Girls or Bluebeard's daughter, they are each utterly themselves.

These stories are also deeply informed by the structure of fairy tales. In some you will find three dresses, in some an apple, but such objects will appear in different contexts than you might expect, take on different meanings than they had for Charles Perrault or the Brothers Grimm. The action takes place in the moral world of fairy tales, where right conduct is situational: sometimes you must give an old woman bread, sometimes you must push her into the oven. Both old women are witches, but only one is trying to eat you. These are stories in which the characters must do the best they can with the information they are given; they must learn to trust their instincts, take what is offered when they can get it. And these are stories of metamorphosis: by the end, everything will be different, everyone will have changed, like a boy into a bear or a girl into a woman realizing what she wants for the first time, growing up before our eyes. Like fairy tales, they are often stories of revenge, which can be another word for justice. Endings may be harsh, but they are usually fair. They are also usually conditional: the end of a tale is never entirely the end. We get the sense that characters live on; more will happen after we stop reading about them. These are also stories about home: how we lose or create it, where we might find it again. They are about outcasts and misfits, some with aristocratic titles, and about the condition of homelessness. This, I think, makes them deeply Australian, no matter where they take place.

Finally, these are stories about storytelling itself, about the joy of the other kind of spelling: the making of words. They are told in language that is both beautiful and precise, that holds two things in equipoise, like the cameo described in "By the Weeping Gate": "engraved with the head of a Medusa, lovely and serpentine." Today we think of the Greek figure of Medusa as a monster, but she was cursed with snakes for hair precisely because she was so lovely she incurred the wrath of the gods. She is a visual contradiction, holding two things in tension and therefore balance. That sort of tension, between love and death, beauty and decay, desire and loss, homecoming and exile, is what gives these stories their strength. They would not be so beautiful if they were not also infused with darkness, if we could not see the skeletal bones beneath the lyricism. They are sad stories, and joyful stories, but most of all they are ultimately satisfying stories, like the loaves of bread baked by Emmeline into fancy shapes in "Sourdough." Angela is also skilled at making fancy shapes. Just be careful not to get the loaf with poison at its heart, unless you're prepared with an antidote.

I started this introduction with a warning. If you've already read this book, you should be all right. After all, you made it through the dark, dangerous woods once already. You know to watch out for huntsmen, to avoid any houses made of marzipan, chocolate ganache, and caramel spun into a delicate bird's nest. You know that you must either find your fortune or make it yourself. There are no fairy godmothers out there, or if there are, you should not trust them. This is a world you will need to navigate with intelligence and as much kindness as possible under the circumstances. If you've survived to return and read this introduction, so far so good.

But if you're about to read this book for the first time, watch out. All I can tell you is to keep your head and trust your luck. There's magic and danger ahead . . .

Theodora Goss
11 April 2016
Boston, Massachusetts, USA

SOURDOUGH

MY FATHER DID NOT KNOW that my mother knew about his other wives, but she did.

It didn't seem to bother her, perhaps because, of them all, she had the greater independence and a measure of prosperity that was all her own. Perhaps that's why he loved her best.

Mother baked very fine bread, black and brown for the poor and shining white for the affluent. We were by no means rich, but we had more than those around us, and there was enough money spare for occasional gifts: a book for George, a toy train for Artor, and a thin silver ring for me, engraved with flowers and vines.

The sight of other children in other squares, with Father's uniquely gleaming red hair, did not bother Mother at all. After he died, I think she found it comforting, to be reminded of him by all those bright little heads.

Our home was in one of the squares at the edge of the merchants' quarter—the town was divided into "quarters" that weren't really quarters. Seen from above, the town was a large square, made up of groups of much smaller squares (tall houses built around a common courtyard); in the centre of the town was the Cathedral, high up on a hill, then spreading around it in an orderly fashion were rows and rows of city blocks, the richest ones nearest the Cathedral, then the further out you got, the poorer the blocks. We sat just before the poorest houses, not quite good enough to be in the middle of the merchants' rows, but still not in among the places where rats shared cradles with babies. We had several large rooms mid-way up one of the tall houses, and Mother leased out the big ground-floor kitchen for her business.

From the time I could walk I would follow Mother around the kitchen, learning her art. For a while she was simply annoyed by my constant presence, as I got under foot, but when I learnt to sit on the bench next to the huge wooden table on which she kneaded the bread, and be quiet, she decided to share her knowledge. I was her firstborn, after all, and her only daughter.

When I could see over the top of the table, I started to help her. Baking tiny child's loaves at first for practice, much to Mother's amusement, then making the dark, "poor" bread for those who could not afford refined flour. Finally, I was allowed to create white bread to grace the tables of the rich: those born to wealth and knowing nothing else, the higher merchants, the bishop and his like. I began to create complicated twists of dough to look like artworks. At first Mother laughed, but the orders kept coming for them, so she watched and imitated me.

One morning, after we'd finished baking for the day, I began to play with the leftover dough on the board in front of me. Soon a child formed, a baby perfectly copied to the life, with tiny hands and feet, an angel's smile and a sculpted lick of hair on its forehead.

Mother came up behind me and stared. She reached past me and squashed her fists down on the dough-child, pushing and kneading until it was once again a featureless lump.

"Never do that. Never make an image of a person or a child. They bring bad luck, Emmeline, or things you don't want. We don't need any of that."

I should have remembered the dough-child, but memory is a traitor to good sense.

There was to be a wedding, arranged, a fine society "do," and we were to supply the bread.

The parents of the groom—or rather, his mother—insisted on being involved in every decision pertaining to the wedding, so there was a power struggle in train between her and the bride's mother (two titans in boned bodices). Things were getting tense, apparently—this information we had from Madame Fifine (about as French as Yorkshire pudding), the confectioner who was to supply the bonbons for the wedding feast. We were to appear at the groom's parents' house, goods in tow, to show our wares.

Mother and I tidied ourselves as well as we could, pulling flour-free dresses from chests and piling our hair high. Artor and George were press-ganged into carrying the wooden trays of our finest white breads to the big house near the Cathedral. We were shown into a drawing room almost as big as our ground-floor kitchen.

As soon as the boys gingerly laid the trays on the big table, Mother shooed them out. I knew they'd be in the stableyard, bumming cigarillos from the stable and kitchen lads, eyeing the horses longingly, waiting for the day when Mother could afford a horse and carriage (that day was a long way off, but they hoped the proceeds from the wedding would speed up the process).

The drawing room was awash with boredom. The parents sat stiffly across from each other on heavily embroidered chairs whose legs were so finely carved it seemed that they should not be able to support the weight of anyone, let alone these four who almost dripped with the fat of their prosperity. The bride, conversely, was thin as a twig, nervous and sallow, but pretty, with darting dark eyes and tightly pulled hair sitting in a thick, dark red bun at the base of her neck. The groom did not face the room: he had removed himself to the large French window and was staring at the courtyard below (probably watching my brothers watching his horses). He had dark hair, curly, that kissed the collar of his jacket, and he was tall but that was all I could tell. Madame Fifine had said he was called Peregrine.

Mother nodded to me and I took the first loaf from one of the trays, showed it to the clients so they could observe its clever shape (a church bell with bows), then placed it on a platter and cut six slices for them to taste. The two mothers, the two fathers, the bride all took their slices and the room was silent but for their well-bred chewing. I crossed the room and offered the groom the last slice. He didn't turn, merely raised his hand in a "no" and shook his head. I noticed his hand bore the stain of a port-wine birthmark.

"It would be a shame, sir, to waste something so fine."

Perhaps struck by the fact that I spoke to him, he looked at me and broke into a smile.

"Yes. You're right. It would be a shame." He took the bread, green eyes bright. "What hair you have, miss."

I blushed.

"Emmeline." Mother called me and I began my task over again: now the loaf shaped like a flower, now the one like an angel, now all the animal shapes (rabbits, doves, kittens, a horse), the one like a church. Each time I saved his slice until last and we spoke in low voices, he asked me about my life and laughed at my pert answers. When the tasting was finished, the mothers began to argue; the design to choose was the cause of combat. Finally, they turned to the girl, Sylvia, and made her decide. She had the look of a trapped animal and I felt sorry for her.

"Perhaps . . ." I began and all eyes turned to me, the mothers' brimming with affront, the fathers' with boredom, the groom's with amusement, my own mother's with something like dread, and the bride's with hope of rescue. "Perhaps Miss Sylvia has a favourite animal or flower. We could make the bread to her choice if she does not like what we have brought today."

"A fox!" she cried, clapping her hands to her mouth as if she had said something a'wrong or too bold. I smiled and she said more firmly, "Yes, a fox. That would please me."

"As you wish, Miss Sylvia." Mother's voice was a relieved breeze. "My Emmeline can make anything with her hands; she has great skill."

So it was settled. The bride had spoken, and defied both her mother and future mother-in-law. Mother and I hefted the wooden trays scattered with the remains of butchered loaves and made for the door. The groom was there before the footman and ushered us through. He smiled and I felt as warm as bread fresh from the oven.

In the months before the wedding he came to me many times.

The first time I was alone in the kitchen—Mother was ill, spending half her time sleeping the other half shouting delirious orders (which

I ignored) from her bed. Artor and George took turns delivering the bread and sitting by her side, while I kept the kitchen running.

I dropped the tray when I saw him at the door. I was covered in flour, my hair covered by a scarf, and barefoot because I loved the feel of the kitchen flags cool and covered with a light dusting of flour. He laughed and held out the largest bunch of flowers I had ever seen. I examined it as he picked up the fallen tray and placed it on one of the benches. This was no posy picked from the fields outside the town, these were exotic blooms, blossoms grown in hothouses and afforded only by the rich.

"Hello, Miss Emmeline. Are you baking for my wedding yet?"

"That's months off, young sir, as you well know. How would it look to serve stale bread at your wedding feast?"

"It would be appropriate, more appropriate than you know. My fox bride might even tell you that herself, if she were truthful." He touched one of the florid roses in the bouquet and smiled. "Do you like these?"

"They are very fine, sir. Fit for your bride."

"But I think you will like them best."

"Yes."

We did nothing more, that first time, than talk. Subsequent times were very different, but that first visit, I think, made us friends and stood us in good stead. He brought gifts, even though I told him not to; something for me always, sometimes things for Mother and the boys. Artor and George, hostile and suspicious at first, were won over when he brought the horses. Two of the finest creatures I've ever seen, with a red-gold fleck to their coats and white stars on their foreheads. Peregrine told me later that their colouring reminded him of our bright hair. The most beautiful thing he gave me was a ring, rose-gold with a square-cut emerald.

"A dangerous stone," I told him.

"What do you mean?"

"An emerald will crack, if given by a lover whose heart is unfaithful," I replied. He laughed and dragged me down.

"Yours will be safe."

I had no expectation of marriage—I was friend and mistress. He would marry his fox bride, as he called Sylvia, and I knew it. I only expected constancy and for many months I had it.

When my belly began to swell, he laughed with delight, his fingers lightly dancing over my taut skin, stroking the curls at the apex of my thighs, and gently showing me how pleased he was at what we had made together. I thought then, briefly, of the dough-child, but put it from my mind.

One day, a fortnight before his wedding, he ceased to visit. Instead, the fox bride came one morning as I kneaded dough in the kitchen.

She was different to the nervous girl I had met months ago. She eyed the kitchen—and me—with disdain, as if she might somehow find some uncleanness clinging to her silken skirts from the mere proximity of such a place and personage. I put my hands to my stomach. She snorted, a brief, sharp laugh that cut.

"You will not have him anymore," she said. "He will be my husband."

"You do not love him," I replied. It had not occurred to me that the fox bride would not *share*.

"But I want this marriage. I want to be away from my parents. I want to be mistress of my own house. But if he keeps running to you, keeps loving you more and more then he may decide not to marry me." She glared. "I will not allow that to happen."

"Stay away from here. Stay away from me. I will tell him."

"He does not remember you." She laughed, came close, and showed her sharp white teeth in a smile. "Why do you think he isn't here? With his love, watching what he's planted grow? You're not the only one who can make things; potions are more powerful than bread, little Emmeline."

Her hand shot out and she laid her palm against my belly. I moved back, almost falling over an uneven flag. "Watch nothing goes into your food, Emmeline. You wouldn't want to lose this last piece of Peregrine."

I heard her laughter even as she walked down the street. I thought only to run to Peregrine, but my nose began to bleed and my belly contracted so hard that I did fall this time, and mercifully found the dark balm of sleep.

~

Their wedding day dawned grey and overcast as summer slipped into autumn. The weather kept all but the most enthusiastic of wedding goers at home—the old women who wait outside the church, knitting and yammering, commenting on all aspects of the event: how the bride looked, how well her dress suited (or not), if she was glowing and if so, why (*honeymoon baby, my sainted aunt!*), and how long the marriage would last.

It was with these ancient birds that I waited on the first day I had managed to leave my bed.

The child had come too soon, a little boy, looking not unlike the dough-child, and leaving me bereft. Mother had barely left my side, worrying that I would not speak, would not touch the still little body before she took it away. Artor and George brought me posies but they only made me cry. I missed the brief funeral that was held for my son, confined to bed by a bleeding the sad, gentle little doctor could not stop. Mother brought an old woman one night who gave me something foul to drink and applied a sweet-smelling poultice of moss between my legs. My body started to repair itself then.

Mother told me that the boys had tried to speak to Peregrine; he had simply looked at them in bewilderment, saying he did not know who they were. They had hidden the horses he had given them in a stable at the outer edges of town, in case someone accused them of theft. Mother had presented herself at the big house, ostensibly to discuss the wedding bread, and Peregrine simply looked through her. She felt that she must be a ghost, so empty was his face. The old woman who had tended to me told her there were things that could bewitch a man's mind and make him forget his dearest desire.

The fox bride was more than she seemed.

I watched her as she left the Cathedral on her husband's arm. I would have let her have this; it had never been my intent to take it from her, but she had stolen my lover and my child was dead. She stepped into a puddle of mud as she headed toward the carriage, and shrieked her distaste as her silk shoes and white lace hem turned the colour of dirty chocolate. I smiled in spite of myself and slid the hood from my head, my bright hair shining out in the dimness of the day. Peregrine looked up from his wife's distress and saw me. His face twisted, distracted and uncertain, but he did not know me. His attention turned back to his bride and I slipped away before she could see me and triumph.

In my kitchen, I found the remnants of the wedding bread dough and began to sculpt another dough-child. I fashioned it as cunningly as the first but this time with intent and not a little malice. Such magic requires only intent and ill-will but no great skill.

I drew from my finger the ring Peregrine had given me. The emerald gleamed at me, intact, unbroken; his heart was never unfaithful, only his memory. The ring was pushed into the dough-child's belly. I made a bellybutton to cover its ingress.

When it came from the oven, it had a fine golden crust and looked like a cherub. I delivered it to the cook at the house the newlyweds were to share; she was a friend of Mother's and took the dough-child gladly.

"Tell them it's for fertility, to bless them with a child."

She nodded. "They shall have it for supper this very eve, Emmeline."

He told me later how the dough-child had been served to them on a silver tray, with butter and a selection of jams. Sylvia had ooh-ed and aah-ed over the silly little thing and happily cut herself a thick slice, slathering it with sugary conserve. Peregrine ate the bread dry and unadorned. When the sourdough touched his tongue his memory returned.

The fox bride continued to eat as he railed at her. She greedily chewed and swallowed great bites of bread, laughing at his rage and talking around her food, telling him she would do it again, too. Then she began to choke. Her face went red, then blue around the lips as she struggled to draw in air. She pointed at her throat, threw things at him as he stood, staring in horror. When she was finally still, he called for a doctor.

The little doctor, the one who had attended me so unsuccessfully, found the emerald ring lodged in her throat. He, I'm sure, recognised it and placed it in Peregrine's hand, closing the young widower's fingers around the piece of jewellery. "Someone will be looking for that, young man."

I no longer wear it very often, knowing what I did with it, although I do bring it out now and then to remind myself of his constant heart. We live in another house, as far away from his parents as he could get, but still in one of the nicer squares. My mother runs her business out of a real shop not far from us, and has two young girls apprenticed to her.

"They don't have your touch, Emmeline," she sometimes says but she knows why I will no longer bake, why my hands will never again knead dough. She is happy, for she knows her grandchild comes. I am content to visit the small grave where my first child lies. I speak with him often and tell him about his father and sister, who comes to us soon. I tell him I am sorry I could not protect him and that I will never forget him. My memory is true.

Dresses, three

I LIVE, NOW, IN ONE ROOM.

The rest of the huge house is quiet around me; nothing runs along its artery-like corridors, no life. Perhaps that is why it seems to be dying. There is only me and I have taken up residence in the library, napping on the once-resplendent but now lumpen couch when sleep will no longer be denied. I bathe once a week, just before the woman from the village, who comes to "do" for me, arrives. I, myself, don't find the smell of an aging man offensive, but Mrs Morgan made it clear *she* did, so for her sake I weekly wake the plumbing, and the pipes screech their protest. The water runs pale russet into the claw-footed bathtub; I lower my carcass down, and splash about in the lukewarm fluid for a time, like an ancient bird.

Mrs Morgan does the laundry, tidies the house, and dusts the furniture with such enthusiasm that some days I fear she will dust me if I stay in one place too long. She admires the many, many pieces of fancywork, embroidery, doilies, runners, littering the house. She makes enough meals for a week. I feed most of it to the stray, once-scrawny cat who is now very fine indeed, fat, shiny, contented. It's not that I don't like her cooking, but why feed a body that has no desire to go on?

Over the past months, I have moved methodically through the house, gathering all the bits-and-bobs pertaining to my life: reacquainting myself with them, reminiscing and, finally, systematically destroying them in the library fireplace.

I found, this morning, the last of the oddments to which my memories cling. From the upended envelope floated a peacock feather; a pair of butterfly wings; and a piece of paper, a list of words embedded into its onion-skin fineness with a calligraphy pen, traced in a very fine hand.

Three things, three things upon which once hung life, freedom, and quite possibly a soul.

Finn watches his mother, her head bent over a piece of fabric; a paper-thin woman, and not quite right. Cerridwen has white fluff-hair that belies her youth, and pale blue eyes; she barely strings two words together, but sings in a sweet, sad voice that doesn't seem to belong to her. Her sole skill, her only resource, is her talent as seamstress. Cerridwen can spin a dress from air and spider silk if need be, and this is how she keeps them fed, clothed, and housed. They do not travel by her volition, but are passed from hand to hand by rich women, wives of mighty men who can afford their helpmeets' expensive tastes for exotic frocks. The women offer each other ridiculous bribes for use of Cerridwen; she is, essentially, *purchased.* The boy wonders, some days, if she wishes for freedom, either for herself or for him, for a chance to not be passed from hand to hand like a strange pet.

He remembers no other kind of life, having been born into the erratic flow of his mother's travels. They have always been in "big houses," she sewing and he wandering through halls and wings, attics, and cellars. An old governess in the big house before last, freed of nursery duties and with time on her hands, taught him to read, and so he added libraries to his stock of places to haunt.

Cerridwen is eighteen when they come to the De Freitas townhouse in Russell Square; the boy, Finn, is nudging seven. They are installed in an attic room that is better than it should be for an itinerant seamstress and her fatherless son: the room is wide and high with tall windows through which pours pure white light. There are two feather beds, three trunks for clothes (they need only one), a place to wash up, and a large multicoloured Turkish rug, like a fallen stained-glass window, on the floor to keep the cold out of the bare boards.

Finn and Cerridwen come when Aurora De Freitas turns seventeen. One of her great-aunts hands them on—Aurora had demanded three special dresses for her Season and no one but the little Welsh seamstress could create them. Cerridwen makes sure she and Finn stay out of sight, sticking to their rooms as much as possible. Sometimes Finn slips away to explore when his mother is caught up in her work, her mind elsewhere.

Aurora De Freitas is different from other women. In fact, she simply strikes Finn as being not quite like anyone else, female or male. She has long black hair, straight and sleek as an Oriental, and heavy-lidded, slanted, pale green eyes. She does not walk, glide, prance, dance, or float; Aurora stalks. She has the gait of a hunting animal and a habit of flicking her eyes side to side, so she never misses a thing. It will be many years before it occurs to Finn that this was a survival mechanism. She is tall and straight-backed, but fine-boned and pale.

Aurora lives with her guardian, Master Justin De Freitas, a paternal uncle. They are in the Russell Square house for the Season; for the rest of the year, they reside in a grey stone manor down in Kent. Master Justin is obsessed with his niece. A portrait of Aurora's mother, Celeste, hangs in the library; Aurora looks very like her and one wonders if the obsession has merely been transferred from mother to daughter. Finn hears the whispers of the scullery maids that, although Master Justin has kept her to himself in the grey stone house, he has held himself in check. But she is seventeen now and has demanded a Season. They mutter darkly as they conjecture how she convinced him, what she promised him, how he will be rewarded after her time in London. He would never, everyone knew, let her leave him and marry.

Master Justin is not an ugly man. On the contrary, he shares Aurora's intense beauty, the raven-black hair and pale skin, but his eyes are darkest blue. His niece is the same height as him, and perhaps this has contributed to his patience, his caution: the fact that she is not a tiny girl who can be easily overcome. Perhaps it is important to him that she surrender.

They whisper that she does not lock her doors at night, but sometimes, when sleep does not come, Finn wanders the shadowed corridors and finds Justin at her door, whispering at the heavy wood, trying to convince her to let him in, let him in, only for a moment, only for a hug, a sweet avuncular kiss, only to smell the lavender of her hair, to feel its silk against his palm, only for a moment and then he will leave her in peace.

She does not open the door, at least not on the nights when Finn watches from the darkness, tucked behind a suit of armour, an old chair or chest, the long velvet curtains. She does not answer her uncle, merely lets him chew on her silence until he leaves, empty-handed, empty-hearted.

"You worked for my mother, didn't you?" Aurora's voice, if a voice could be said to do so, stalks the listener. Cerridwen dips her head but does not answer. Aurora continues, "Seven years ago, was it not?" Her eyes flick to Finn, sitting on the edge of his bed, legs swinging, shadowy blue eyes fixed on her; she takes in his tousled black hair.

Cerridwen says nothing except, "What kind of dresses would you like, miss?"

"The first dress—and understand this, I must have precisely the dresses I ask for or my bargain will not be fulfilled." She waits until Cerridwen nods her slight bobbing nod. "And so, I will make a bargain with you. If you give me exactly what I ask for, I will give you your freedom. A house, money, everything to live, and you will never need to sew again."

Cerridwen's eyes are wide and she forgets to hide behind her dullard's stare. Finn ponders his mother, knowing she's not as fey or as stupid as people think. He wonders how she can bear to be thought of this way.

Aurora smiles and nods. "So."

The first dress she demands is to be made of peacock feathers. Aurora cares not at all for the design, only that it be made of the specified feathers. Cerridwen, who never sketches anything, never uses a pattern, sees the dress in her mind, finds it fully formed. She does not take Aurora's measurements; she has seen the girl and that will be sufficient.

The dress lies like a second skin. The eyes of the peacock feathers are everywhere; they bow and sway, viewing everything around them, seeming to move even when Aurora is still. Above her head soars a great spray of feathers, the fan of a peacock's tail, stitched just above the curve of her buttocks and just below the small of her back, on a band of whalebone to hold it firm. When she moves, it sways in time with her steps, dips as if nodding. The green in the feathers picks out the green in her eyes and makes them glow. She is fantastical, exotic, bizarre, unique, bewitching. She regards herself in the mirror, almost grudging in her approval.

"It's perfect, Cerridwen. Utterly perfect. Thank you."

She sweeps out of the room, down to join the sounds of the ball, swathed in her outrageous dress that will briefly stop all movement, talk, and time when she appears. She will create a scandal. Her uncle will burn with desire, jealousy, but he must not reveal himself. It's bad enough the servants whisper about him; it would not do for people of his own class to know the truth.

He does, however, take his niece's arm for the first dance, holding her close, mesmerized by the feathered eyes of her dress that seem to watch him constantly.

Finn, sitting at one of the library windows, a book open but unattended to in his lap, watches Aurora through the thick glass. At her insistence, three targets are lined up behind the house, in a space too small, really, for archery practice. She has been besting three of her suitors for the past hour and they still seem to find it charming—she is beautiful and rich, after all, and a man can briefly forgive many things when these two virtues are so in evidence.

A hard hand clamps down on Finn's shoulder. He starts, the book falls from his lap and onto the foot of Master Justin, who does not let the boy go. He glares, his mouth set in a hard line, Finn's in a trembling one. In the ghostly mirror of the window, they look rather alike.

"You. You belong to that little Welsh bitch?" Justin spits, turning the boy this way and that, examining him like something to be held up to the light.

"Cerridwen is my mother. She is Welsh," says the boy obliquely, wishing himself big enough to hurt this man.

"How old are you?"

"Seven."

Justin lets him go, dropping him as a dog does a bone it suddenly finds boring. "Stay out of my library."

Finn scrambles to the door, opens it, is stopped by Justin's next question. "What is your name?"

Finn does not answer, knowing there is power in names, and escapes down the corridor as fast as he can. Justin doesn't follow. He stands at the window, watching his niece torment her beaux.

"Butterfly wings," says Aurora. "A dress of butterfly wings, Cerridwen?"

Cerridwen nods slowly, formulates one of her rare sentences. "I will need a net."

"The housekeeper is to give you whatever you need." Aurora smiles at Finn as he huddles on the bed, not calmly sitting on the edge this time, but curled against the wall, as if this is safest. "Did he scare you much?"

Finn shakes his head, wonders how she knows.

"You look like us, that's all," she says. "It scares *him*." She turns again to Cerridwen. "Doesn't he, Cerridwen? Doesn't he look like a De Freitas?"

Cerridwen chooses not to answer, opens her box of threads to select the bobbin of her finest silk. She pulls at the loose end, reels it out a little and holds it up, examining the minuscule thread. Aurora contemplates the pale fluff of hair for a moment, then, flicking Finn a strange smile, she mouths *little cousin* and leaves.

In his short life, Finn has occasionally speculated about his father's identity, about how Cerridwen came to have a child so young. He doesn't ask her, so she never tells.

Finn marvels at his mother; he cannot even begin to think how she gathered so many butterflies and persuaded them to give up their wings, let alone how she coaxed them all into the dress that now drapes Aurora's tall form. It hangs like silk, an empire waist this time, and a foot-long train that seems not to touch the floor, but float above it, carried by still-fluttering wings.

Aurora's black hair has been piled onto her head, then teased out on either side. Jewelled butterflies from London's finest jeweller nestle there, catching the light and throwing it back out.

"Thank you, Cerridwen. Once again, it's perfect. Goodnight. Goodnight, Finn."

Finn awakes to the sound of a struggle. A figure leans over his mother's bed and he can make out in the moonlight his tiny mother, fighting fiercely.

"Give it up. Give it up, little whore, you didn't fight this much last time!" The voice is lustful, frustrated. Finn throws himself at the shadow-man. Justin curses and kicks him aside, but Finn surges forward once again, fiercely determined, ignoring the pain of Justin's blows.

Justin gives up, shakes the boy off and backs away from the bed, re-buttoning his trousers. He points at Cerridwen, bathed in moonlight and so pale she might be a ghost. "I can take him away any time. Remember that! Any time!"

He slams the door behind him and Finn climbs into his mother's bed. She holds him tightly, rocking; neither of them falls asleep.

Aurora asks for her final dress, a dress made only of words. Cerridwen shakes, balks, refuses to meet the girl's eyes. Aurora drops to her knees beside the seamstress. She takes the tiny, needle-scarred hand, and whispers, "They say the Welsh witches are the most dangerous, because it's so hard to tell who they are."

She stands. "A dress of words, Cerridwen. Everything hangs on this, for both of us. You know the words but I shall write them down for you, so you do not forget."

In the deepest part of the Common, far away from the house in Russell Square, Cerridwen sits on the night-damp ground with a piece of parchment beside her. She has collected thistles, spider webs, and a bottle filled with moonlight from a night long ago. She piles the three ingredients onto a small pyre of twigs and kindling, and lights them with a tinderbox. She begins to sing, her voice light, beautiful, fine as the spider webs, bright as the moonlight, and sharp as the thistles. She knows the words by heart, barely looks at the piece of parchment as she sings, conjuring the dress from air and moonlight and words. It forms like a ghost, coalescing above the tiny fire, eddying in the evening breeze.

Finn, having crept out of the house to follow her, watches from behind a tree trunk as she takes a thin knife from her pocket, draws it across her palm and sprinkles blood over the already-dying fire. The dress solidifies, hangs in the air over the smouldering coals as if caught on an invisible hook. It shimmers like gossamer and, if he concentrates, Finn thinks he can see words flying around inside it, whirling like stars being born and dying, creating a universe all within the warp and weft of the dress.

Cerridwen seems smaller; this has cost her much.

The newspaper reports of what happened that night vary, but they agree that Master Justin De Freitas died horribly.

His niece entered the ballroom, all eyes upon her. She wore a strange gown, grey and shimmering, a fabric seemingly alive, but it was hard to tell; the dress defied the eye. Many of the guests had simply wanted to see what she would wear next; tales of her dresses had echoed throughout Society, and they found this one strangely disappointing. All most witnesses could say was that it was grey.

Aurora stood at the top of the great curved staircase, smiling down at the assembly. Master Justin waited at the bottom of the stairs, staring up at his niece in a manner some described as "adoring," others as "inappropriate." She began to descend and by the time she was mid-way down the staircase, those nearest him noticed smoke coming from Master Justin's jacket. At first it seemed to be steam but then the odour of smoke (of sulphur, some said) began to tickle noses. It took Master Justin himself some time to notice, but when the first flames licked from the tongues of his shoes, then up his trousers, shirt, and frock coat and finally reached his cravat, it most certainly had his attention.

His screams were awful, as was the smell, overpoweringly brimstone, and, some said, something even less savoury: the scent of spilled seed.

The immolation happened all too quickly, there was nothing anyone could do. The guests departed rapidly, so there was no one to see the tiny Welsh seamstress and her fragile son creep down the stairs behind Aurora and peer at the smouldering heap of charred humanity and once-fine green velvet frock coat.

"Was he my father?" I asked, but Cerridwen did not answer—she no longer had words. She used them all in the making of Aurora's dress.

That night, Aurora spirited us away, to the grey stone house in Kent. The same Aurora who came to us ten years later, tired of her travels and eager for a quiet place to rest. Cerridwen, worn out by her spell and spending her final years on endless fancywork and embroidery, succumbed and died soon after. The same Aurora who, although my cousin by some counts, stayed with me and lived as my wife these past seventy years.

The very same Aurora De Freitas who died six months ago and left me alone in the grey stone house with only my memories, a peacock feather, butterfly wings, and a scrap of parchment.

BLUEBEARD'S DAUGHTER

"HERE," SHE SAYS, "HAVE AN APPLE."

Yeah, right. As if I know nothing about stepmothers. As if I know nothing about apples. But I'm polite and I'm not stupid, so I put the green orb in my bag, and thank her.

"Now, don't forget: you'll need to be careful and cunning. You'll need your wits about you. It's hidden deep, the treasure, and there will be all kinds of obstacles." Hands on hips, Orienne surveys me critically. "It's a long journey, but you've got the most fat on you of all of us. You'll be fine; the exercise will do you good. Don't forget that apple, Rosaline; no cakes or pastries."

As if I'm likely to forget that bloody apple; I know what she's done to it. Trust her to manage a dig at my weight—I come from a long line of women who eat their grief, but my father's fifth wife is of thin stock. Busy, busy, busy all the time, bustling and fidgeting, organising and ordering, burning away everything she eats, hating anyone to be idle; she's got the energy of a hummingbird and a heart that softens for her own child alone. Gods forbid anyone should spend an afternoon sitting on their arse, reading a good book. That was how I got caught; sitting on my arse, buried in a book, oblivious to the world. The rest of the family had made themselves scarce, knowing she was on a tear about too little food, too many mouths; as if we were poor, as if my father didn't provide for all the children he'd sired, and all those that had been brought by previous wives and left here when said wives had gone.

As if it wasn't just an excuse to cull the herd.

As if she hadn't done it before.

As if a horrifyingly large number of my siblings—full, half, and step—haven't ended badly.

35

"Here's the map, but you won't need a compass, you've got a wonderful sense of direction." We both know I get lost in the library sometimes, but it's no use contradicting her; she'll just raise her voice and talk right over the top of me, pretending this is a serious task. A journey from which I'll return. "Remember to be polite and biddable to any creature you meet on the way. Try to be home before winter . . . of course, your natural insulation should keep you warm. We're all counting on you, Rosaline. And don't forget that apple, if you're peckish."

She finishes adjusting the strap of my satchel and stands back, surveying me with the resigned disappointment of a woman who knows she's done her best with second-rate materials. "Well, that's you taken care of then."

Or so she bloody well hopes.

My father likes being married and, despite everything, he's apparently catnip for women, whether for his fortune, castle, or the great virile bushy beard, who can say.

Matrimony's never worked out too well for his wives, however, but they all appear to think it's a good idea at the time. None of them ever seems to think he'll turn on them. None of them ever seems to consider *not* entering the locked room, even when he makes it very clear that possession of the key comes with responsibilities and consequences. None of them ever seems to think they'll get caught. Eventually, they all go—even my own mother—and open the door to take a peek inside.

All of them until *her*.

I have to give Orienne credit, she's smart. If she has ever entered that room—whether by witchcraft or dint of the same skill I've used: lockpicking—she's managed to keep it a secret from my father. Whenever he returns from a voyage, she'll hand him back the keys, and he looks carefully at the smallest one—he always has the wives' copies made of gold because it's so soft and there's no hiding if it's been used, even once—and without fail, he nods with a kind of satisfied surprise. He'll give her a resounding kiss, before carrying her up to their bedchamber. Maybe that's why he's so wilfully blind to the dwindling number of children in his house.

Dispatched to get water, Zipporah and Judith both met an old woman by a well. The former, sweet-natured, helped her without complaint, and was rewarded with diamonds, pearls, and roses falling from her lips each time she spoke. She vomited such things for three days before she died, spitting blood and spewing slivers of her own torn flesh. Judith, wary of her sister's fate, let her sharp tongue have rein when the very same old woman asked for assistance—she threw herself from a cliff when toads and vipers began to accompany her words. Ada and Beatrice, Sara and Lizzie, were sent with charity baskets to help the less-fortunate who lived deep in the woods, but none of the girls was ever seen again, although it was observed on several occasions that the wolves looked particularly well-fed that winter. Minette, Anya, and Louise were crushed in an unfortunate mattress-stacking accident whilst setting up a test for a potential bride for Armand, my stepmother's son; come to think of it, the bride died, too. Leticia, playing with matches, trying to stay warm in the icy attic to which Orienne had banished her, managed to self-immolate. Gabriella was scalded to death when a vat of boiling broth mysteriously tipped from the hob. Susannah was carried away by a kelpie while crossing a river she'd been assured was *perfectly safe*. And Lucy . . . Lucy, was turned into a hare, somehow, and torn apart by our stepmother's pack of brachet hounds. After each and every misfortune, Orienne wept cold, glittering tears and proclaimed "How dreadful!" in most convincing tones, at least in Father's hearing.

Six daughters remain, of whom I am one and, apparently, the next to be shuffled aside in Orienne's quest to secure her own future: no other heirs will be tolerated. I thought I was safe, and for a long while I was, being Father's favourite . . . but after Lucy I thought, *Enough's enough*. I complained to Father and discovered I'd made a mistake; favourite or no, not a word against his beloved, trusted wife would be tolerated. So I've been in the dog house for a few weeks and, with my parent having departed on yet another trip, Orienne's decided it's time to move against me. I should have known better. The only one who's secure is Armand, her very own boy, her sole offspring whom she loves to distraction, and the single good thing she brought into this house.

He looks a little like her, slender and pale, with blackest of black hair and blue eyes, though where hers are ashen-frost, his are summer-sky. He's tall and broad-shouldered, and beautiful my stepbrother, so beautiful that even I can't ignore him, no matter how I feel about his mother. And he's been kind to me, even though Orienne never has been. He likes books and we talk about them, and one time we almost . . . I'll miss him, talking to him, staring at him, and almost-ing him.

I'd set off from the castle nice and early into a morning that was already puffing out wintry breath, waved off by those who cared or simply wished to make sure I was gone. Orienne watched longer than the others—I kept looking over my shoulder to see if she was still there, and she was so I couldn't do what I wanted, which was to go left at the fork in the road, not right. But she was still staring, so I gave one last wave and stoically traipsed onwards as if I had every intention of going where she wants me to go. As if I was going to do what she wants me to do, which is die horribly either whilst trying to find objects that probably don't exist or eating the poisoned apple she's pressed on me as a snack. And even if the items in question are real, they won't be where she claims. But there'll be ogres and trolls and witches—the bad kind—or robber bridegrooms who've got more in common with my father than I'd like to think. But the things I'm supposed to look for, specifically a loaf of bread you can never entirely devour and a bottle of wine that never runs out? They'll not be there.

After hours of walking the path through the forest isn't too bad. The road is wide and not terribly rutted, and the leafy canopy above isn't so thick that it blocks the sun, creating a darkness that might encourage predators to come and bid me welcome. My boots are sturdy and comfortable, well-worn; it should be a while before blisters appear, but I can feel my thighs chaffing under my skirts as I walk, *oosh, oosh, oosh*. I should have insisted on grabbing a pair of trews before I left, no matter how fast she was hustling me out of the castle; I barely had time to pin my long hair back. I'll find a pair of britches as soon as I can, whether I have to beg, borrow, or steal them from someone's washing line.

Which may be an opportunity that will present itself sooner rather than later: there's a little trail winding off the roadway, compressed by soft shoes and leather-padded paws. Through the fat tree trunks I can see where it leads: to a cottage that looks small and neat, but odd. The tones are all wrong, the textures . . . I squint. It should be wood . . . wattle and daub; it should be thatch and glass and stone . . . but all I can make out is a riot of colours that don't naturally occur in woodland architecture. I can't resist: I *must* investigate. If there's a chance of satisfying my curiosity and need for trousers, I'll risk it.

I creep along the path, and then pause before stepping into the clearing. The place doesn't look dangerous. There's a lot of brown but it's a cinnamon-sprinkle kind of brown; there's frosting of blue and green and yellow and rose along the eaves and around the window frames. I stare a little longer. The garden inside the fence is full of flowers but they don't move in the breeze like proper ones should; they stay stiff, quite rigid as if made of sterner stuff, like liquorice and marzipan, with leaves of sugared mint. The windowpanes look like clear-blown toffee. It's one of the most bizarre things I've ever seen and that's saying something.

I'm about to commit to the glade when a hand grabs my arm and clamps tight. I bite down on a scream purely because it won't help matters at all, and I remember I put the kitchen knife I stole inside my pack, so there's no getting to it now. I swing about and see blue, blue eyes, high cheekbones, and pouting lips, hair as black as ebony. My heart, embarrassingly enough, steps up its rhythm, kicks out a little tarantella.

"Hello," says Armand. "What are you doing here?"

"What am *I* doing?" I hiss. "I'm supposed to be here. *Your* mother sent me away."

He ignores the tone and says, "Not here, though, you're meant to be on the main road, heading towards the mountains so you can complete your quest and come back to us."

"I've been walking for hours. I need somewhere to rest. And to find breeches." I peer at him. "Why are *you* here?"

"I wanted to help." He shrugs and I can see it's the truth, plain and simple. Sweet boy just wanted to render assistance in a princely fashion. "Come on, let's get a move on."

"No," I begin, and am interrupted by a weak shriek coming from inside the weird little cottage. Then there's a cry for help, a woman's voice cracked with age and fear. "Well, that settles it," I say, and head off at a run, through the gate in the white picket fence that smells like peppermint, along the path made of humbugs, towards the Turkish Delight window boxes bloom-full of icing-sculpted flowers in a riot of hues.

I knock on the door, which is sturdy yet peculiarly pliant; it thuds nicely beneath my hand, but gives a little too, like a firm sponge. It smells like gingerbread.

"Are you all right?" I call, and the wail comes again, trickling to a whimper as Armand thunders up behind me. I turn the lemon sherbet door handle and shove.

A pink cloud that smells like musk and dreams puffs around us as we collapse over the threshold. Any queries as to anyone's safety or otherwise expire on our lips as we fall immediately into a deep slumber.

I wake up overheated and flushed, the smell of warm sugar in my nostrils. My face is pressed against something tacky on the floor . . . no, not the floor. The bottom of a cage, a cage made of candy canes shaped and melded into a box, not big enough for me to stand, but I can sit if I slouch. I roll up, pulling painfully away from the gluey surface. My head feels as if candyfloss, blown in one ear, has chosen not to go out the other, but rather take up residence in my skull.

I look around, blinking. My satchel, with the kitchen knife in it—not to mention my little roll of lockpicks—lies on the flags beside the door, for all the good it will do me. Idly, I wonder how long it would take for me to chew my way out.

There's all the usual furniture you'd expect of a little old lady's cottage, although made of substances not generally associated with furniture: marshmallow armchairs with antimacassars of fondant lace; tables of fudge; rugs of pulled taffy; paintings with wafer picture frames; jelly bean footstools; a peanut brittle bedstead, with chocolate brownie pillows and a coverlet that looks like woven ribbon candy, atop which lies Armand, still unconscious. It all looks adorable and, in spite of everything, my stomach rumbles, and that's what attracts the attention of the little old lady herself, who's diligently stoking the fire beneath the enormous oven in one corner. She's wizened and ancient, shoulders rounded and back bent. She limps over to me, fingers thin and twigish, hair like steel wool, nose crooked.

"Ah!" She cackles. "Awake, awake, awake!"

"I rushed in to help you, you know," I tell her with reproach. "You tricked me."

"Well, I'd never get a meal otherwise. People are very particular about not getting eaten. Do all sorts of things to avoid it." She shakes her head. "Good meals are few and far between for the likes of me."

"Bad witch."

"We're all bad witches at some point, dearie. Have you not worked that out yet?"

I don't say anything because I know she's right, more or less.

"Anyway, though you won't appreciate this, it's pleased I am to see you. Far too many skinny girls nowadays, not enough for a filling repast." She eyes my well-padded flanks. "I'll have you salted and smoked and put away for the cold months! Meatloaf! Steaks! Chops and ribs! Ah, the soups your bones will make—I've got the best pearl barley and dried peas set by. Oh, and black pudding! I've not had that in so long." She fairly salivates.

"What have you done to Armand?"

"Nothing. Yet." She grins lasciviously and she's missing teeth here and there. I notice the shackle around Armand's ankle, a genuine iron item in this place of sugar and spice. "He's a heavy sleeper, still under for now, but I'll be on top of him soon and that'll wake him up."

I think my jaw drops at that.

"What? I've got needs! I get lonely."

"Didn't anyone ever teach you that fulfilling your own needs at the cost of others is not okay?"

"Do you think anyone ever bothered teaching me anything?" she sneers, and glares at me for long moments. "Those of us who are on our own, with no one to care for us, we make our own way, our own rules as and how we must."

And though part of that makes sense, I can't see how it justifies turning me into a five-course feast and Armand into a sex slave. I'm about to tell her so when there's a groan from the bed.

"Ah. Time to change into something a little less comfortable." She draws herself up, pats at her dark grey skirts, her iron-sky hair, and begins to whisper a spell. The words come out as a mist, slowly falling and encircling her as it goes, until she's enveloped in a minty-fresh fog that thickens and thickens until she at last steps out of the cloud of it, thoroughly changed.

She's tall and blond; her squinty raisin eyes are large and limpid and green, furrowed lips are full and ripe as cherries, her age-spotted skin is milky and smooth, her cloth of gold dress is a thing to cause Orienne to turn jade.

"Neat trick," I say, more than a little envious that someone can change their shape so easily.

She pulls a swathe of cloth from a shelf and says, "Thank you. Now, I like a little privacy, so don't take this personally," and wraps the cloth around my cage as if I'm a bird being put to sleep for the night.

I hear her move away, begin to coo sweet nothings to the rousing man.

I examine the lock on my prison: it's made of metal and I can work with that. My lockpicks might be out of reach, but there are more than enough pins in my hair to make up for it. It takes me a little longer than usual—I'm less skilled with a clip, and I have to try to block out the sounds of her seduction and Armand's drowsy responses—but eventually I hear a *snick*. The door cracks open without too much noise, while I, on the other hand, make a racket and a half getting out of the cage. I leave skin behind, my legs are all pins and needles, and don't want to hold me up as I wobble about, flailing at the draped sheet.

All of which gives the witch time to struggle off the bed, bodice unhooked, hair dishevelled, skirts getting in the way. Although she's magicked herself a young woman's body, she still moves like an old one, and that gives me the chance to grab a metal poker from beside the oven, just as she's coming towards me, just as she's raising her hands, just as she's moving her lips to spill out some curse, some hex, some enchantment that will turn me into a toad or a goose or an entrée.

I'm faster with the poker than she is with her words, and I split her skull like an egg. The spell shatters as easily as her head does, and both spill out grey and red. In a moment, she's shrunk to fairy dust and floss, fine and silver as spider webs. I wait for the cottage to dissolve around us, to melt and drip into a sugary apocalypse, that's generally the way things go, but no. It stays. It sticks. It's not connected to her like so many magic things are to their masters. Perhaps she didn't make it, perhaps she just wandered in, found it. Perhaps it just grew up around her, made strange on its own.

"Rosaline," mumbles Armand, stretched out on the bed, his shirt lacings loose, his trousers disturbed in more ways than one. "Are you all right?"

"Uh huh. Nothing a good bath won't cure." I move towards him, throwing one final suspicious look at the witchy mess on the floor. Into the oven with that as soon as I get my stepbrother free. I'm faster with the hairpin this time, and have him unfettered in a trice. "There."

"Thank you." He pulls me up to lie beside him, strokes my face, my hair, my lips, my throat, my chest, oh my! Part of me thinks *This isn't for you, this is just what the witch started*, but the other part, the hopeful part says *He followed you, he came after you, he wanted to keep you safe—and for the love of all that's holy, this has got to be better than those spotty stableboys!*

When he kisses me my heart feels as if it's unfurling like the petals of a flower blooming in the sun.

We can, I think, be together. We can make a future, untethered from our pasts, from our family. *We can be happy.*

"We can be happy," I say aloud, curled around Armand. "We can stay here."

"Oh, no," he answers, blinking. "We have to go. You have to find the loaf of bread that can't be eaten up and the bottle of wine that never runs out. It's the only way we'll make it through winter."

"What?" I ask stupidly, all the glowing feelings that were surging through me, thudding happily in my chest, warming my flesh, buzzing between my legs with a lovely throbbing pulse . . . all of them stop, freeze over, feel like a coating of ice on my sweaty skin.

"We have to bring them back to Mother. She'll be waiting." He smiles. "She said you'd never make it, that you'd never return home again. That's why I came after you, to keep you motivated." He slaps my ample backside as if I'm an ornery horse he's been obliged to ride.

"Your mother wants me to die out here, Armand, the way all the other sisters have on their fool's errands." *You stupid bastard, you'll die too—whatever will Mother say to that?*

He sits up, stares down at me. "Don't be silly. Mother wouldn't do that. Mother loves her stepdaughters. It's not her fault you're all so unfortunate."

He wanted to help *her*, not me. He's too thick to realise I'm not meant to succeed. He'll never believe it of her, has never suspected her of any ill intent towards the children that aren't her own—no more than my father will. And as I stare into his eyes I can see her there, as a white dot in the pupils, an unmelting ice queen, a woman who'll always be there before me. Someone he'll never let go; someone he'll always love best. I'll never hold him as tightly as she does. My heart tightens, curls in upon itself, and I realise this is what my father feels every damned time one of the wives lets him down. He allows himself love, to care, and to trust . . . and they requite him so badly. I think I understand him at last.

"I'm hungry," says Armand. Armand who's clueless, who's blind to what's beneath his nose; who'll happily drive me to my doom all to please his murderous mater.

And I think about secret chambers and poisoned hearts, and lackwits who can't be trusted. I roll out of bed, find my satchel by the door, and fish out a green orb, crisp and sweet-looking, tempting as can be.

"Here," I say, "have an apple."

The Jacaranda Wife

Sometimes, not very often, but sometimes when the winds blow right, the summer heat is kind, and the rain trickles down just-so, a woman is born of a jacaranda tree.

The indigenous inhabitants leave these women well alone. They know them to be foreign to the land for all that they spring from the great tree deeply embedded in the soil. White-skinned as the moon, violet-eyed, they bring only grief.

So when, in 1849, James Willoughby found one such woman sleeping beneath the spreading boughs of the old jacaranda tree in his house yard, members of the Birbai tribe who had once quite happily come to visit the kitchens of the station, disappeared. As they went, they told everyone they encountered, both black and white, that one of the pale women had come to Rollands Plain station and there would be no good of her. Best to avoid the place for a long, long time.

Willoughby, the younger son of an old Sussex family, had fought with his father, migrated to Australia, and made his fortune, in that order. His property stretched across ten thousand acres, and the Merino sheep he'd purchased from John McArthur thrived on the green, rolling pastures spotted with eucalypts and jacarandas. He had a house built from buttery sandstone, on a slight rise, surrounded on three sides by trees and manicured lawns, a turning circle out the front for carriages. Willoughby made sure the windows were wide enough to drink in the bright Australian light, and filled its rooms with all the finest things that reminded him of England. His one lack was that of a wife.

He had in his possession, it must be said, a large collection of miniatures sent by the parents of potential brides. Some were great beauties—and great beauties did not wish to live in the Colonies. Some were obviously plain, in spite of efforts the portraitists had gone to imbue them with some kind of charm; these girls were quite happy to make the arduous journey to a rich, handsome, dark-haired husband, but *he* did not want a plain wife. He had not made his way in the world to ornament this place with a plain-faced woman, no matter how sweet her nature might be.

The silver-haired girl he found early one morning was beyond even his dreams and demands. Long-limbed, delicate, with skin so pale he could see blue veins pulsing beneath her skin—for she was naked, sleeping on a bed of brilliant purple jacaranda flowers, crushed by the weight and warmth of her body. As he leaned over her, she opened her eyes and he was lost in their violet depths.

Ever the gentleman, he wrapped his proper Englishman's coat about her shoulders, speaking to her in the low, gentle voice he reserved for skittish horses, and steered her inside. He settled her on his very own bed, the place he had always hoped to bring a suitable wife, and called for his housekeeper. The broad, red-faced Mrs Flynn bustled in. She was a widow, living now with Willoughby's overseer in a fine arrangement that suited both of them. In Ireland, her three sons had been hung for treason against the British, and the judge who sentenced them decided that a woman who had produced three such anarchists must herself have strong anti-English sympathies. She was arrested, charged, tried, and sent to live in this strange land with an arid centre and a wet green edge. She'd been allocated to Willoughby, and although her heart would always have a hole in it where her sons had been torn away, she had, in some measure, come to feel maternal about her master and directed her energies to making him happy as only a mother could.

The sight of the girl on the bed, lids shut once again, and the mooncalf look in her master's eyes troubled her but she held her tongue, pushed her greying red hair back under its white cap, and began to bustle around the girl. Willoughby sat and stared.

"She's perfect, Martha. Don't you think?"

"Beautiful for sure, Master James, for all she's underdressed. Who is she? Where's she from?" Mrs Flynn surreptitiously sniffed at the girl's mouth for a whiff of gin. Finding nothing, her suspicions shifted; surely the girl was addle-pated. Or a tart, left adrift by a client of the worst sort. Or a convict on the run. Or a good girl who'd had something unspeakable visited upon her. She'd check later, to see if there was any bleeding. "Perhaps the doctor . . . "

"Is she hurt?" The urgency in his voice pierced her heart and she winced, like a good mother.

"Not that I can see, but we'd best be sure. Send for Dr Abrams. Go on now." She urged him from the room, her hands creating a small breeze as she flapped at him. Turning back to the girl, she found the violet eyes open once more, staring around her, without fear, and with only a mild curiosity.

"And what's your name, little miss?" Mrs Flynn asked, adjusting the blanket she'd laid over the girl. The eyes widened, the mouth opened but the only thing that came out was a noise like the breeze rushing through leaves.

Martha Flynn felt cold all over. Her bladder threatened to betray her and she had to rush from the room and relieve herself outside. She wore her sweat like a coat when she returned (it had taken all of her courage to step back inside). The girl eyed her mildly, a little sadly perhaps, but something in her gaze told Martha Flynn that she had been *entrusted* with a secret. It moved her fear to pity.

"Now then, the doctor will be here soon. You make yourself comfortable, *mavourneen*."

"She's a mute, you see," explained Willoughby to the parson. "No family that we can find. Someone has to look after her."

The Reverend St John Clare cleared his throat, playing for time before he had to answer. Willoughby saved him for a moment.

"She seems fond enough of me," he lied a little. She *seemed* not to hate him, nor anyone else. Even "fond" was too strong a term, but he didn't want to say "She seems slightly less than indifferent to me." Sometimes she smiled, but mostly when she was outdoors, near the tree he'd found her under. She was neither grateful for his rescue, nor ungrateful; she simply took whatever was offered, be it protection, affection, or food (she preferred vegetables to meat, screwing her nose up at the plates of lamb and mutton). She did, however, take some joy in the new lambs, helping Mrs Flynn to care for them, feeding the motherless ones by hand, and they would follow her.

He'd named her Emily, after his grandmother. She had taken up painting; Willoughby had presented her with a set of watercolours, thinking it would be a lady-like way for her to pass the time. She sat outside and painted the jacaranda tree over and over, her skill growing with each painting, until she had at last produced a finely detailed, subtly rendered image, which Willoughby had framed. It hung over the fireplace in his study; he would stare it for hours, knowing there was something he was missing, some construction of line and curve, some intersection of colour he had failed to properly see. She would smile whenever she found him thus engaged, lightly drop her hand to his shoulder and finally leave as quietly as she had come.

"Does she want to marry you?" asked the parson.

"I think so. It's . . . " struggled Willoughby, "it's just so damned inappropriate to have her under my roof like this! She's not a relative, she's not a ward, she's a woman and I . . . "

"You love her," finished St John. Mrs Flynn had spoken to him quietly upon his arrival. "There's always a charitable institution? I could find her a position with one of the ladies in Sydney Town, as a maid or companion?"

"No! I won't let her go!" Willoughby wiped the sweat from his brow, felt his shirt sticking to the skin of his back. "I can't let her go. I want to look after her. I want her to wife."

St John Clare released a heavy sigh. He was, to a large extent, dependent on Willoughby's good will—what mind did it make to him if Willoughby wished to marry a mute who'd appeared from nowhere? Younger sons were still kidnapping brides in England—this was marginally less reprehensible. "Very well. I will conduct the ceremony. Next Sunday?"

"Tomorrow."

"Ah, yes, tomorrow. Very well." He did not use the phrase "unseemly haste," although he knew others would. What Willoughby wanted, Willoughby would have, and if it benefited the Reverend Clare in the long and short term then so much the better.

~

The ceremony was short, the groom radiant and the bride silent.

Mrs Flynn had dressed the girl in the prettiest of the new frocks James ordered made for her. It was pink—Willoughby had wanted white, but Mrs Flynn insisted it would wash-out someone so pale and she had carried the day, on territory too uncertain for a male to risk insistence.

The ring was not a plain yellow band, but something different, white gold set with an enormous amethyst. She seemed to like the stone, staring at it throughout the ceremony, smiling at the parson when he asked if she agreed to the marriage. Willoughby saw only a smile but heard a resounding "Yes," and convinced himself that she loved him.

She didn't seem to care what he did to her body—having no experience of men, either good or bad, having no concept of her body as her own, she accepted whatever he did to her. For his part, he laboured over her trying to elicit a response, some sign of love or lust, some desire to *be* with him. Never finding it, he became frustrated, at first simply slaking his own lust, quickly. Gradually, he became a little cruel, pinching, biting, hoping to inflict on her a little of the hurt his love caused him. For all the centuries men have dreamed of the joy of a silent wife, Willoughby discovered that the reality of one was entirely unsatisfactory.

It was Mrs Flynn who first noticed the changes in her. Not her husband who stripped her bare each night and used her body as he wished. It was Martha, with her unerring woman's instinct, who pulled him aside and told him the girl was pregnant. Willoughby became gentle once again, no longer insisting upon his conjugal rights, but sleeping wrapped around her, his hands wandering to the slowly swelling belly, praying that what he had planted there would stay, and would in turn, keep her by his side.

More and more, he found her under the jacaranda tree. She sat silently for hours, no longer interested in painting, but stroking her growing belly as if soothing the child inside. Whenever he arrived back at the house at the end of the day he would go straight to the tree, for he knew that was where he would find his wife.

~

"Where's Sally?" demanded Willoughby. On one of his infrequent trips to the kitchen, he found Martha alone; no sign of the indigenous girl (re-named "Sally" in spite of her protests) who helped around the kitchen.

"Gone. They're all gone, all the natives. They won't come here anymore," said Mrs Flynn, her skin shining, hair trying to escape the cotton cap as usual.

Willoughby paused, astounded. "Why not? Haven't I always been good to them? I've never abused them or punished them unduly. I don't understand."

Mrs Flynn was silent for a moment, weighing her words, wishing she's not opened her mouth in the first place. How to explain? "It's Emily. They're scared of her," she said reluctantly.

"Scared of Emily?" His laugh was sharp. "How the hell can anyone be scared of Emily?"

"She's . . . different, Master James. Leave it at that. It scares them. They have their legends and she scares them."

"What bloody legends? What are you talking about?" He gripped her upper arm tightly, squeezing a slight squeal from her as the flesh began to pinch between his knuckles. She could smell the sour brandy on his breath. He let her go, but insisted, "What legends, damn it?"

"Sally said they come from the trees. They don't belong anywhere. They bring grief and eventually they go back to the trees." Mrs Flynn batted away tears with the back of her hand.

Willoughby stared at her. "And you? What do you think?"

"There are superstitions and then there are things we cannot under-stand, Master James." She bent her head, new tears fell onto the dough she was kneading; she folded them into the rubbery mixture and refused to look at him again. He left the kitchen, swearing and shaking his head.

Willoughby rounded the corner of the house, raised his eyes and saw his wife, her curved belly seeming to defy gravity, walking slowly towards the jacaranda tree. She stood before its thick trunk and placed one hand against the rough bark. As he watched, the slender pale limb seemed to sink deeply into the wood, and the rest of her arm looked sure to follow.

With a yell, he charged at her, pulled her away with a force driven by anger and despair. She was flung about like a leaf in the wind. Finally settling, she stared at him with something approaching fear, something approaching anger. He was too furious to see it and he ranted at her, finger pointed like a blade. "Never, never, never. You will never go near those trees again. You will never leave me!"

He locked her in their bedroom, then gave orders to his station hands.

"Get rid of all the jacarandas. Cut them down, burn them. Destroy them all, all the ones you can find."

So all the jacarandas within the bounds of Rollands Plain were razed; he even sent some of his men to walk three days beyond the boundaries and destroy any offending tree they found there.

He let her out only when he was certain they were all gone.

Her scream, when she found the dead stump of the tree, was the sound of every violated, outraged thing.

Mrs Flynn ushered the child into the world that evening. Emily did not stop screaming the entire birth, but Mrs Flynn could not help but feel that the screams were more for rage, than for any pain the tearing child caused, for there was very little blood. Strangely little blood. The milk that dripped from Emily's nipples smelled strongly of sap. The child made a face at her first taste, then settled to empty the breast, her face constantly twisted in an expression of dissatisfaction.

Willoughby came to visit his wife and daughter, his contrite face having no effect on Emily. She opened her mouth and a noise came like that of a tree blasted by storm winds. Having not heard his wife utter a sound before, he was stunned; having not heard anything like this, ever, he was appalled. He backed out of the room, and retreated to his study and the bottle of brandy with which he'd become very familiar since his marriage.

Late one evening, a few weeks after the birth, Mrs Flynn saw Emily, standing slender and silver in the moonlight, motionless beside the stump of her tree. She held the baby at her breast; the child was quiet.

Martha was minded, though she knew not why, of selkie wives, women stripped of their seal skin by husbands afraid to lose them, by men who feared them more than they could love them. She called quietly to Emily and gestured for her to follow.

She led her to a stand of eucalypts not far from the house.

Within the circle of gum trees stood a lone jacaranda, the one she knew Willoughby had missed, the one she kept to herself. The silver woman needed to be able to go back to her place or she'd haunt them forever.

Martha shivered. She was terrified of this ghostly creature, but she hoped she loved Emily more than she feared her, loved her enough to show her the way back. She watched Emily's face as she recognised the jacaranda, smiled, leaned against the trunk, and a sound like a leaves laughing blew around the clearing. Martha backed away. She watched the woman's hands slide into the trunk, saw her move forward, then stop.

The child would not go into the tree. Her diluted flesh and blood tied her to her father and his kind. Martha watched as the pale woman kissed the child's forehead and laid her gently on the ground. Emily pushed her way into the tree, disappearing until the brown bark was visible again, undisturbed for all intents and purposes. The tree shook itself and let fall an unseasonal shower of purple flowers, to cover Martha and the baby she scooped up and held tightly.

Willoughby drinks; Mrs Flynn often pours for him. She is strangely disappointed in him each time he swallows back the brandy decanted by her own hand. Most of her time she spends with his daughter, who has her father's dark curls and her mother's violet eyes.

She is a quiet child, but on the occasions when her cries have a certain tone, a certain pitch, Martha catches her up and takes her for a walk, to the stand of eucalypts. Rollands Plain's sole remaining jacaranda will release a purple blanket no matter what the weather, and the child stares up at the tree as if she finds it very lovely indeed.

LIGHT AS MIST, HEAVY AS HOPE

"MY DAUGHTER," BREATHED MILLER, "my daughter can spin gold out of straw."

This sudden boast struck his fellow-drinkers as interesting, if stupid. Miller had a tendency to open his mouth unwisely when ale had passed his lips. The bragging was, however, astonishingly egregious. Their king, after all, finding himself in something of a hole, financially speaking, was wont to do anything to refill the kingdom's coffers. Those with wiser minds shook their heads; Miller was asking for trouble.

The Taverner, sensing the man was finely balanced between merely making noise and starting a fight, thought it best to send him on his way. He heaved Miller to his feet. The odour of flour that clung to the man crept into the Taverner's nostrils. It was the smell of his profession, of his world; had he been asked, Miller would have denied the existence of any smell. Miller swayed, peered at the Taverner, and raised his voice so that all in the tavern could hear. "My Alice can spin gold from straw," he bellowed.

Looking around, taking in the disbelieving looks with a bleary stare, he began to mutter. "A good girl, my Alice. Good, beautiful, industrious. Better than her bitch of a mother."

Noticing the three soldiers in the corner, the Taverner propped one shoulder under Miller's arm and manoeuvred the sot away. He felt eyes upon his back and sensed danger.

He sensed danger, too, in the way Miller spoke of his daughter's beauty. The Taverner suspected when Miller got that look he was somehow confusing Alice with her dead mother in the most base of manners. Sometimes he feared for the girl; most of the time he decided she was her father's property, like all daughters. And Alice was smart. She could take care of herself.

Miller stumbled into the night, muttering. A few moments after the door swung shut, a soldier detached himself from the huddle in the corner and approached the Taverner.

The sound of the front door thudding against the wall made Alice open her eyes. It didn't wake her, for she never slept when her father was out drinking, or when he came home, drunk and reeking of ale. She never answered when he came to her door.

At first he would scratch quietly, as if ashamed, then the knocking would grow louder, until he was hammering at the door and shouting, calling her by a name not her own. He would stay until he remembered who she was, and then sob for a while before going away.

For a whole month after her mother's death he stayed away from the drink. A whole month when he was her father and nothing more, not a monster or a nightmare or a beast. Weak, like all his kind, he succumbed soon enough and the visits to Alice's door resumed. Thus far she had remained safe.

A loud crash hammered her nerves before she heard Miller's voice, calling her down, calling for help. Tightly wrapping a robe around herself Alice unlocked the door and made her way downstairs.

Her father was crumpled near the kitchen table, blood flowing from a wound on his head. He looked up at her, pale eyes unfocused as they caught at her, taking in the tumble of golden curls, the eyes so darkly blue that they seemed almost black, the crushed strawberry lips and the swell of her breasts under the robe. He reached out, the gesture unfinished when he passed out.

Unhurriedly, Alice left the house to draw water from the well. When she returned, she knelt by Miller's fallen bulk and wiped away the blood, gently wrapped his head with a bandage, and turned away. His hand found her, kneading her thigh like dough, then clawing upward to her breast. She scrambled backward, falling in her haste to escape him.

He was asleep, but even in his sleep he craved her flesh. She took two swift steps and sunk her foot into his ribs. A loud gasp of air escaped him but still he slept; he would ache in the morning without knowing why.

In the safety of her room, the memory of her mother came to her with equal longing and resentment. Three months in the ground; three months Alice had spent evading her father. From her window, Alice could see the forest. Somewhere beneath the trees was the spot where they had buried her mother. As far away as Miller could get without exciting tongues; far enough, he thought, that she wouldn't haunt him and dog his conscience, far enough that he could forget her and take refuge in his daughter's flesh. His daughter with her mother's face.

Alice remembered her mother's face, thinner than her own, pale skin, bloodless lips, eyes bruised with sickness, and a hand fluttering to draw her daughter close. Alice had stood back, believing her mother chose to go, thinking love was something corporeal that existed only as long as the body in which it resided lived. She refused her mother's final gift, her kiss, and ignored the dying woman who cried that she must pass a secret to her daughter. When her mother's sobbing ceased there were cold tears on Alice's cheeks. Angry and afraid, she stood at the door, refusing her mother's last kiss even as she lay: still, silent, and growing cold.

Now there was only her father, who watched her, day in, day out.

"Where's your daughter, old man?"

The uniformed men were impatient. Halfway between the mill and the house the four soldiers had reined in beside him; Miller stopped in his tracks. His bruised cut showing a week's worth of fading, Miller was in no mood to argue.

"Alice, get out here!" he roared. Squinting at the lead soldier, he asked, "What do you want my Alice for?"

"Word of her has reached the king," said the captain.

"Who's been talking about her?"

"You, Miller. His Majesty was very interested to hear that your Alice spins gold from straw. Got all those empty coffers at the palace, he has. Maybe your Alice can fill 'em. And an empty bed, too. Maybe your Alice has something he can fill in return."

"Alice!" cried Miller as his daughter appeared, her cornflower blue dress and white apron very bright in the sunshine. Alice moved with grace, raising her eyes to meet those of the captain, ignoring her father as if she knew what he'd brought upon her.

"Your father says you can spin gold," said the captain, dark eyes raking her.

Alice eyed her father. Her cold contempt was unveiled for the first time and he shrank to the size of a child.

"If my father says so."

"The king has commanded you come with us."

"If the king says so."

"Is there anything you wish to take with you? Is there anyone you wish to bid farewell?" He shifted in his saddle.

Alice touched the small gold locket at her throat, then dropped her eyes to the thin ring on her finger. Both her mother's. All she needed of her old life. She shook her head. The captain reached down and she grasped his hand, swinging up behind him. The last Miller saw of his daughter she was clinging to the waist of the dark captain, eyes straight ahead, her rigid back the only farewell he would ever have.

The castle appeared like a faded starburst on the hill. The captain had told her over and over that the king was poor, yet Alice had been unable to comprehend a king with no fortune until she saw the faded grandeur of a palace no one could afford to maintain. They rode through the gates of a ruin as utter as her own.

Paint crackled on the walls as if to draw attention to its plight; anything gilt had been stripped; tapestries were threadbare; furniture was held together with spit and spider webs; windows, greyed with dirt, cracked under the force of a gaze. The crown jewels, once a wondrous collection of fiery gems, were reduced to a single crown, resting on the king's brow, set with a single diamond.

The king was handsome enough. Tall, muscular, black-haired, and black-bearded. During her journey she had wondered if she might tell him the truth: that her father had lied. Perhaps he might find her beauty enough to stay his hand, but seeing this poverty she knew he could afford to forgive nothing. He would kill her and send the captain and his men to slaughter her father. While she had no objections to her father's demise, she had no desire to quit her own life.

Avarice and need ran through this man's veins. There was no safety for her here. The king's need for gold was a flood inside him, and she would be swept up and drowned by it unless she found a way to negotiate the current.

"My father," said the king when the niceties were over, "was a spendthrift, and long-lived. In thirty years he managed to impoverish what was once one of the wealthiest kingdoms in the land. When I came to the throne there was just enough money for the coronation."

The corner of Alice's mouth lifted wryly. Perhaps he saw in her face that she thought the money wasted.

"Now my problems are at an end. Come." He gestured for her to follow him out of the dingy throne room, along a dimly lit corridor, down chipped stairs, until at last they stopped at a wooden door, pitted and pock-marked, dark with age. "This should be no challenge for you, Mistress Alice." The king threw open the door.

From flagged floor to cobwebbed ceiling the room was filled with straw. Some bales had split and the yellow lengths spilt onto the floor like so much hope gone wrong. A spinning wheel sat, waiting for failure. Alice surreptitiously wiped her sweating palms on her white apron. The king caught the gesture and his smile broadened, dangerous and hard.

"You have one night, Alice. This night. Spin it all into gold and release me from my reduced circumstances."

"If I don't?" Her voice was stronger than she expected.

His eyes darkened as he drew close to her, his large hand slipping around her throat. He closed his fingers in a motion that was half-threat, half-caress.

"You have a very thin neck, Mistress Alice."

She held her breath until he released her and left the room. The sheer volume of impossible straw made tears heat the back of her eyes and she clenched her hands, digging her nails into the palms, hoping the pain would stop the panic. She was steel for a moment, before she threw herself to the floor, to the hated straw, and wept, wishing she could die on the spot.

Near her hand, one of the flagstones moved. She scrambled back in fright, almost burying herself in the straw. The flag moved again, jumping once, twice. A hand appeared in the crack between the stones. It was a small hand: white, smooth, almost feminine. It pushed the flagstone aside with surprising force as a man heaved himself up through the hole in the floor.

He was ordinary, so very ordinary. Not tall, but not short. Face round, unlined, not old but not young; hair neither blond nor brown. His clothes were neat, plain, and unremarkable; the kind of man she might pass in the street and not notice. He turned his eyes upon Alice. "Nasty."

She shook her head. "Pardon?"

"Nasty way to enter a room, nasty way to move about—under the floor. Always dirty and dark, especially in poor places like this." He brushed imaginary dirt from his clothes and looked at her again. "Fancy, a king with no money."

"Just fancy," said Alice bitterly.

The man's eyes took in the straw. "Straw into gold?"

Alice nodded.

"What will you give me to do it?" he asked.

She sneered. "You can't. No one can. Go back under the earth and leave me to die in peace."

"Rude, but understandable given the circumstances." He smiled a little. "What if I can? What will you give me?"

Alice looked down at her hands and saw her mother's ring. Better the thin ring than Alice's thin neck. She pulled the band from her finger and held it out.

"My mother's ring."

He took the ring and tossed it from hand to hand as if considering. His eyes were sly when he next looked at her.

"A mother's gift is very valuable. It holds magic. It's like a touch, or a kiss."

"How much magic has it brought me thus far? When my mother died she left me to my fate. If the ring buys me one more night of life, then it will have served its purpose well enough." Alice stood—she was taller than the man, but not by much.

"Fair enough," he said, pocketing the ring. He pointed to a corner of the room. "Go to sleep. All will be well."

"How can I trust you?"

Sitting at the spinning wheel, he grabbed a handful of straw and began his task. Within moments the straw had become gold, long strands of it, like wool. Alice felt its cold weight. She stared at the little man and nodded. "Thank you."

"It's business. Go to sleep."

Alice curled up in the corner, wriggling in the straw to get comfortable. Soon enough she drifted off to the whirring of the spinning wheel.

"Clever. Clever, clever Alice."

The king's voice woke Alice from a dream of her mother, slipping away from her. She sat up, noticing that even her pile of sleeping straw had disappeared, spun into wealth as she slept. Standing, rubbing her eyes, she pretended not to be surprised. The gold had been spun into thread and coiled into balls—unconventional, but legal currency all the same. She gave the king a haughty look that made him laugh. He called a courtier. Alice was to be rewarded: she could bathe, eat, sleep, take in the gardens, if she wished. She was to be dressed as befitted the king's favourite—in fact, she could do anything she wished except leave the palace grounds.

As the day passed, Alice noticed a great army of tradesmen trooping up to and around the castle. Repairs had begun. Hot on their heels were merchants with fabrics, gems, tapestries and all manner of the expensive frippery royalty are rarely without.

In the evening, Alice—bathed and dressed in new finery, her hair washed, curled, and set with ribbons—was led to another room by the king. Inside was an even bigger pile of straw and the same spinning wheel. Her stomach swooped and her head spun. She wanted to weep, but made fists behind her back.

"Was last night not enough for you?" she asked.

"Thirty years is a long time to exhaust a fortune. There must be more. I'll make you a deal: one night for each decade. Two more nights, Alice, and your future will be assured." He stroked her cheek. "You will never spin again."

"And if I fail?"

"You still have a very thin neck, Alice." He kissed the base of her throat, just above her mother's locket, and departed.

Alice slumped against the wall and waited. And waited. And waited. After an hour the tears came, the floor opened, and her saviour pulled himself out of the depths once more. "Hello, Alice. Was His Majesty happy?"

"Ecstatic. Alas, he's also greedy," she lamented. Her hand rubbed at the locket, as if to smooth away any marks in the metal.

"This is a much bigger room, certainly. What will you give me tonight?"

"My necklace," she answered and pulled hard on the chain until the links parted and it came away from her neck.

"No hesitation, Alice. You are decisive."

"No, little manikin, I just have a very thin neck." She took herself off to the corner. "Do your work."

"Sweet dreams, Alice."

Once again the spinning wheel sang her to sleep.

In Alice's dream her mother wept quietly. *You're giving me away,* she cried. *You're forgetting me.* Alice put her hand out to touch the pale skin of her mother's face, but the woman receded into darkness and left her daughter alone.

A hand grasped Alice's shoulder and shook her roughly. She started, and opened her eyes to find the king kneeling beside her, excited, stunned, amazed. He kissed her cheek and hauled her to her feet.

"Astonishing! Alice, you are really the most amazing woman." Cupping a hand to her face, he smiled. "Fit to be a queen. One more night, Alice. Make me the richest king in the land and tomorrow you'll be my queen."

He pushed her toward her chaperone of the previous day, with instructions that she was to be treated like a queen. Alice left the room, her heart heavy with the knowledge that one more night remained. She had nothing left to give.

"What will you give me tonight, sweet Alice?"

The little man's tone was amused and not a little cruel. He knew she had nothing. They stood in the biggest room yet, surrounded by Alice's yellow hell. As close to freedom as to death. There was nothing, Alice realised, that she would not do to escape the executioner's blade. One more night and she would be queen. Never again the smell of flour, nor fear of her father, nor planning how to escape the hole of her existence. For that freedom she was prepared to do anything. She fixed the little man with a determined stare and began to raise her skirts.

"You can stop right there, pretty maid. You have nothing I want. You're too old."

"I have nothing else!" she raged, tears streaming down her face. "You have already taken everything I valued. I'm a miller's daughter—what kind of riches do you think I am heir to?"

"Nothing, then. Only your potential," he mused.

"What do you mean?"

"Tomorrow you'll be the queen. He'll marry you, crown you, and bed you. Soon you'll have a child." He leaned in toward her hungrily. "I want that child, your first-born."

Alice rocked back on her heels. The glitter of freedom blinded her. She couldn't imagine wanting any child as much as she wanted to live. She nodded. The little man cackled happily, dancing a jig around the room. When he finally calmed, she pointed to the spinning wheel.

"Now spin."

"Indeed. Sleep, Queen Alice. Your future is assured."

Alice slept. She dreamt of empty places where mist and darkness reigned; her mother would not answer her calls.

The child had split her like a ripe fruit.

She lay in bed for seven days before the bleeding stopped and the physicians finally believed she would live. The child was a daughter, a mix of light and dark. The king doted on her. He doted on his wife, too; he had become fond of her and, through wise investment, had managed to increase the fortune Alice had made him. He honoured his promise never to ask her to spin again.

As she hovered between deeply drugged sleep and wakeful pain, she watched him sitting beside her bed, the baby in his arms, making faces at the child and occasionally glancing warmly at his wife. She hated him. And the child; she hated the child most of all.

She didn't want to move, she didn't want to speak, she didn't want to feed the child, although her breasts ached with unused milk. She wanted them all to go away and leave her be.

One night she woke with a start. Perhaps it was the sound of stone scraping on stone, of a small man walking lightly to the crib, or the sound of him speaking softly to her daughter. She sat up with a sharp intake of breath as her stitches pulled. The little man stood by the crib, her daughter in his arms, his face alight with hunger and happiness.

"Thank you, Alice. She's beautiful."

"Get away from her," she hissed as he held the hated child. He made a moue and tutted.

"Now, Alice. Remember our deal." He approached her bed, jiggling the now-crying baby. Alice reached out, an unfamiliar ache uncoiling in her chest.

"Give me my daughter."

Reluctantly, he complied. "I will take her, Alice. In three days I will take her away from you."

"I will give you anything else. Take whatever you want in my kingdom, just leave my daughter with me." Alice thought her chest would explode. Was this love? Was this what she was supposed to feel?

"You have nothing else I want."

"Anything."

"Alice, you're not listening. You have nothing to bargain with. You had nothing after you gave away the last piece of your mother. You forfeited her protection. The only thing you have of her now is your blood." He smiled. "I knew your mother, you know.

"Beautiful like you, but smarter. I offered her gold once, in exchange for you. She refused, but she was kind. Didn't teach you much, did she? Since I'm a fair creature, I'll give you one last chance. For her sake."

For a moment, Alice saw beneath his skin to a sharp-toothed, gnarled little beast squirming with excitement.

"What do I have to do?"

"Guess my name. Guess my name and the deal is void. You have three days, sweet Alice."

He clambered down through the hole in the floor and pulled the stone to cover his exit. Alice held the child all night, too fearful to sleep and too fascinated to look away from the tiny face that, mere hours ago, she could not bear to look upon.

"I have nothing left but my mother's blood."

Alice was out of bed, pacing. She would let no one near the child. The king was concerned. The ladies-in-waiting feared she would harm herself or the princess but no one could get near enough to separate them, and no one dared manhandle the queen.

It was the morning of the third day. Alice knew that as soon as daylight faded her tormentor would appear. She had neither bathed, nor eaten, nor slept. Alice had no idea of the little man's name. She had wracked her brain, going over his words, knowing there was something there, though she could not unravel its meaning.

She passed a table. Her robe brushed against a goblet and sent it tumbling to shatter on the flags. As she crouched to pick up the pieces, Alice cut her hand and began to weep. The baby began to cry, too. Alice lifted her daughter from the cradle. Blood trickled from her hand to the child's forehead, and Alice's attempts to wipe it away merely spread the crimson stain. Rubbing her own brow, Alice marked herself as she had her child.

She sank to the floor, huddling there, eyes closed, feeling the baby calm. Their breath slowed and joined; their shared pulse synchronised, a river of blood linking them, stretching back through time, mother to daughter. There, though, Alice sensed an end—a permanent ebb in the flow—an ebb that she had caused. She wept bitterly.

There was no sound, no door opening, but she felt a presence, a hand touched her shoulder, soft as silk, soft as breath. Without opening her eyes, she knew it was one who shared her blood. Her mother smoothed the hair from Alice's face. She breathed deeply, taking in the scent of her child and grandchild. A pale hand stroked her granddaughter's face and the child sighed, comforted. Alice felt her mother's lips against her ear and heard whispered words, light as mist, heavy as hope.

Wrapped tightly against the cold and tied to her mother's breast, Alice's child was silent. The rhythm of the horse's gallop was unfamiliar, but she didn't complain. Alice had chosen the king's favourite hunter. A gigantic chestnut, he whickered when she approached, snorted in annoyance when she saddled him and rode him out into the cold night air, but he did not falter.

The sun rose just before they entered the darkness of the forest. Alice knew the path as surely as she knew her own heartbeat. Along the barely visible trail, between the two biggest trees, down the slippery slope, across the stream, then up the bank and on to the rise where her mother lay beneath a small cairn.

Alice dismounted, unstrapping the child and laying her gently on her discarded cloak. The cairn she kicked away before she dropped to her knees and, not having thought to bring a shovel or spade, began to dig at the earth with her soft, pale queen's hands.

By the time she reached her mother, her hands were bloody, the nails broken back to the quick and aching. The simple coffin was easy enough to tear open, the cheap wood soft and rotten from the damp soil. Tenderly she unwrapped the shroud she herself had sewn, her blood soaking into the fabric. She saw her mother's hands, crossed on her chest, the dark dress she had been buried in, and, finally, her mother's face.

Even thinner than before, eyes sunken beneath their lids, a white mould covering the once-smooth skin, but it was her mother's face. And the one gift she had not accepted still resided there. Without hesitation, without disgust, with nothing but love, Alice leaned forward and kissed her mother's cold, damp lips.

A breath passed between them and, in that breath, a word, and in that word, salvation.

Back in her apartments she sat in a chair, the child on her lap, both of them still wearing their blood. Eyes closed, Alice felt the sun disappearing, like a slowing pulse. A cold breath, as something from under the earth gathered around them. Opening her eyes, she found him crouched not far from her, grinning.

"You've made a mess. I shall have to give her a bath. Yes, that's the first thing we'll do when we get home. I'll give my little princess a bath."

"No."

"Still think you can win? Your daughter's flesh is mine now. No one above ground knows my name, sweet Alice."

"No," she agreed. "But those who sleep in the earth know. The dead know."

He stood suddenly, almost losing his balance. Alice rose, too, her grace restored. The child rested quietly, safe in her mother's arms.

"You weren't quite right. There wasn't only my mother's blood left to me. But a kiss *is* a gift. It was enough, Rumpelstiltzkin."

He screamed. He raged. But he could not come near her. He stamped his foot and it cracked the stones. He stamped again and wider cracks ran across the floor, almost to where Alice stood. He jumped up and down with such force that the floor erupted, showering Alice with shards of stone. She turned away, barely in time, to cover the child. Her back was pitted with rock, and blood dripped from her cheek where flying flint had made a wide cut.

When at last she turned back, he was gone. The hole was large, the edges scorched black, and the shattered stones jagged as teeth in a dead mouth. Pain crept across Alice's flesh. She would be scarred but he was gone. And her daughter was safe.

THE COFFIN-MAKER'S DAUGHTER

THE DOOR IS A RICH RED WOOD, heavily carved with improving scenes from the trials of Job. An angel's head, cast in brass, serves as the knocker and when I let it go to rest back in its groove, the eyes fly open, indignant, and watch me with suspicion. Behind me is the tangle of garden—cataracts of flowering vines, lovers' nooks, secluded reading benches—that gives this house its affluent privacy.

The dead man's daughter opens the door.

She is pink and peach and creamy. I want to lick at her skin and see if she tastes the way she looks.

"Hepsibah Ballantyne! Slattern! Concentrate, this is business." My father slaps at me, much as he did in life. Nowadays his fists pass through me, causing nothing more than a sense of cold ebbing through my veins. I do not miss the bruises.

The girl doesn't recognise me although I worked in this house for nigh on a year—but that is because it was only me watching her and not she me. When my mother finally left it became apparent she would not provide Hector with any more children, let alone a son who might take over from him. He decided I should learn his craft and the sign above the entrance to the workshop was changed—not to *Ballantyne & Daughter*, though. *Ballantyne & Other*.

"Speak, you idiot," Father hisses, as though it's important he whisper. No one has heard Hector Ballantyne these last eight months, not since what appeared to be an unseasonal cold carried him off.

The blue eyes, red-rimmed from crying, should look ugly, unpalatable in the lovely oval face, but grief becomes Lucette D'Aguillar. Everything becomes her, from the black mourning gown to the severe, scraped back coiffure that is the heritage of the bereaved, because she is that rare thing: born lucky.

"Yes?" she asks as if I have no right to interrupt the grieving house.

I slip the cap from my head, feel the mess it makes of my hair, and hold it in front of me like a shield. My nails are broken and my hands scarred and stained from the tints and varnish I use on the wood. I curl my fingers under the fabric of the cap to hide them as much as I can.

"I'm here about the coffin," I say. "It's Hepsibah. Hepsibah Ballantyne."

Her stare remains blank, but she steps aside and lets me in. By rights, I should have gone to the back door, the servants' entrance. Hector would have—did so all his life—but I provide a valuable service. If they trust me to create a death-bed for their nearest and dearest, they can let me in the front door. Everyone knows there's been a death—it's impossible to hide in the big houses—I will not creep in as though my calling is shameful. Hector grumbled the first few times I presented myself in this manner—or rather shrieked, subsided to a grumble afterwards—but as I said to him, what were they going to do?

I'm the only coffin-maker in the city. They let me in.

I follow Lucette to a parlour washed with tasteful shades of grey and hung with white lace curtains so fine it seems they must be made by spinners with eight legs. She takes note of herself in the large mirror above the mantle. Her mother is seated on a chaise; she too regards her own reflection, making sure she still exists. Lucette joins her and they look askance at me. Father makes sounds of disgust and he is right to do so. He will stay quiet here; even though no one can hear him but me, he will not distract me. He will not interrupt *business*.

"Your mirror should be covered," I say as I sit, uninvited, in a fine armchair that hugs me like a gentle, sleepy bear. I arrange the skirts of my brown mourning-meetings dress and rest my hands on the arms of the chair, then remember how unsightly they are and clasp them in my lap. Black ribbons alone decorate the mirror's edges, a fashionable nod to custom, but not much protection. "All of your mirrors. To be safe. Until the body is removed."

They exchange a glance, affronted.

"The choice is yours, of course. I'm given to understand that some families are delighted to have a remnant of the deceased take up residence in their mirrors. They enjoy the sensation of being watched constantly. It makes them feel not so alone." I smile as if I am kind. "And the dead seem to like it, especially the unexpectedly dead. Without time to prepare themselves, they tend to cling to the ones they loved. Did you suspect your husband's heart was weak or was it a terrible surprise?"

Madame D'Aguillar hands her black shawl to Lucette, who covers the mirror with it then rejoins her mother.

"You have kept the body wrapped?" I ask, and they nod. I nod in return, to tell them they've done only just enough. That they are foolish, vain women who put their own reflections ahead of keeping a soul in a body. "Good. Now, how may I be of assistance?"

This puts them on the back foot once again, makes them my supplicants. They must *ask* for what they want. Both look put out and it gives me the meanest little thrill, to see them thus. I smile again: *Let me help you.*

"A coffin is what we need. Why else would you be here?" snipes Madame. Lucette puts a hand on the woman's arm.

"We need your services, Hepsibah." My heart skips to hear my name on her lips. "We need your help."

Yes, they do. They need a coffin-maker. They need a death-bed to keep the deceased *in*, to make sure he doesn't haunt the lives they want to live from this point on. They need my *art*.

"I would recommend an ebony-wood coffin, lined with the finest silk padding stuffed with lavender to help the soul to rest. Gold fittings will ensure strength of binding. And I would affix three golden locks on the casket, to make sure. Three is safest, strongest." Then I name a price—down to the quarter-gold to make the sum seem considered—one that would cause honest women to baulk, to shout, to accuse me of the extortion I'm committing.

Madame D'Aguillar simply says, "Lucette, take Miss Ballantyne to the study and give her the down payment."

Oh, how they must want him kept under!

I rise and make a slight curtsy before I follow Lucette's gracefully swaying skirts to the back of the house.

I politely look away as she fumbles with the lockbox in the third drawer of the enormous oak desk her father recently occupied. When she hands me the small leather pouch of gold pieces, her fingers touch my palm and I think I see a spark in her eyes. I believe she feels it, too, and I colour to be so naked before her. I slide my eyes to the portrait of her dearly departed, but she grasps my hand and holds it tight.

Oh!

"Please, Hepsibah, please make his coffin well. Keep him *beneath.* Keep us—keep me—safe." She presses her lips to my palm; they are damp, slightly parted, and ever-so-soft! My breath escapes me, my lungs feel bereft. She trails her slim, pink cat's tongue along my lifeline, down to my wrist where the pulse beats blue and hard and gives me away. There is a noise outside in the hall, the scuttling of a servant. Lucette smiles and steps back, dropping my hand reluctantly.

I remember to breathe, dip my head, made subservient by my desire. Hector has been silent all this time. I see him standing behind her, gnarled fingers trying desperately to caress her swan's neck, but failing, passing through her. I feel a rage shake me, but control myself. I nod again, forcing confidence into my motions, meeting her eyes, bold as brass, reading a promise there.

"I need to see the body, take my measurements, make preparations. I must do this alone."

"Stupid little harlot." Hector has more than broken his silence, again and again, since we returned to the workshop. I have not answered him because I sense in his tone *envy.*

"How hard for you, Father, to have no more strength than a fart, all noise and wind."

If he were able, he would throw anything he could find around the space, chisels and planes and whetstones, with no thought for the damage to implements expensive to replace. The tools of our trade inherited from forefathers too many to number. The pieces of wood purchased at great expense and treated with eldritch care to keep the dead *below*.

I ignore his huffing and puffing and continue with Master D'Aguillar's casket. It is now the required shape and dimensions, held together with sturdy iron nails and the stinking adhesive made of human marrow and boiled bones I'm carefully applying to the place where one plank meets another to ensure there are no gaps through which something ephemeral might escape. On the furtherest bench, far enough away to keep it safe from the stains and paints and tints, lies the pale lilac silk sack that I've stuffed with goose down and lavender flowers. This evening, I will quilt it with tiny, precise stitches then fit it into the casket, this time using a sweet-smelling glue to hold it in place and cover the stink of the marrow sealant.

We may inflate the charge for our services, certainly, but the Ballantynes never offer anything but their finest work.

I make the holes for the handles and hinges, boring them with a hand-drill engraved with Hector's initials—not long before his death, the drill that had been passed down for nearly one hundred years broke, the turning handle shearing off in his hand and tearing open his palm. He had another made at great expense. It is almost new; I can pretend the initials are mine, that the shiny thing is mine alone.

"Did you get it?" asks Hector, tired of his sulk.

I nod, screwing the first hinge into place; the dull golden glow looks almost dirty in the dim light of the workshop. Soon I will light the lamps so I can work through the night; that way I will be able to see Lucette again tomorrow without appearing too eager, without having to manufacture some excuse to cross her threshold once more.

"Show me."

I straighten with ill grace and stretch. In the pocket of my skirt, next to a compact set of pliers, is a small tin, once used for Hector's cheap snuff. It rattles as I open it. Inside: a tooth, black and rotten at its centre and stinking more than it should. There is a sizeable chunk of flesh still attached to the root and underneath the scent of decay is a telltale hint of foxglove. Master D'Aguillar shall enter the earth before his time, and

I have something to add to our collection of contagions that will not be recognised or questioned.

"Ah, lovely!" says Hector. "Subtle. You could have learned something from them. Cold in a teacup—it wasn't very inventive, was it? I expected a better death, y'know."

"It wasn't a cold in a teacup, Father." I hold up the new hand drill. "It was the old drill, the handle was impregnated with apple seed poison and I filed away the pinion to weaken everything. All it needed was a tiny open wound. Inventive enough for you, Hector?"

He looks put out, circles back to his new favourite torment. "That girl, she doesn't want you."

I breathe deeply. "Events say otherwise."

"Fool. Desperate sad little fool. How did I raise such an idiot child? Didn't I teach you to look through people? Anyone could see you're not good enough for the likes of Miss Lucette D'Aguillar." He laughs. "Will you dream of her, Hepsibah?"

I throw the hand drill at him; it passes through his lean outline and hits the wall with an almighty metallic sound.

"I kept you wrapped! I covered the mirrors! I made your casket myself and sealed it tight—how can you still be here?" I yell.

Hector smiles. "Perhaps I'm not. Perhaps you're so lonely, daughter, that you thought me back."

"If I were lonely I can think of better company to conjure." But there may be something in what he says, though it makes me hurt.

"Ah, there's none like your own family, your dear old Da who loves your very skin."

"When I have her," I say quietly, "I won't need *you*."

Ghost or fervid imagining, it stops him—he sees his true end—and he has no reply but spite, "Why would anyone want you?"

"You did, Father, or has death dimmed your memory?"

Shame will silence even the dead and he dissolves, leaving me alone for a while at least.

I breathe deeply to steady my hands and begin to measure for the placement of the locks.

"The casket is ready," I say, keeping the disappointment from my voice as best I can. Lucette is nowhere in evidence. An upstairs maid answered my knock and brought me to the parlour once more where the widow receives me reluctantly. The door angel did not even open its eyes.

Madame nods. "I shall send grooms with a dray this afternoon, if that will suffice." But she does not frame it as a question.

"That is acceptable. My payment?"

"Will be made on the day of the funeral—which will be tomorrow. Will you call again?" She smiles with all the charm of the rictus of the dead. "I would not wish to waste your time."

I return her smile, "My customers have no choice but to wait upon my convenience." I rise. "I will see myself out. Until tomorrow."

Outside in the mid-morning sun I make my way down the stone front steps that are set a little too far apart. This morning I combed my hair, pinched colour into my cheeks, and stained my lips with a tinted wax that had once belonged to my mother; all for nought. I am about to set foot on the neatly swept path, when a hand snakes out from the bushes to the right and I'm pulled under hanging branches, behind a screen of sickly strong jasmine.

Lucette darts her tongue between my lips, giving me a taste of her, but pulling back when I try to explore the honeyed cave of her mouth in turn. She giggles breathlessly, chest rising and falling, as if this is nothing more than an adventure. She does not quake as I do, she is a silly little girl playing at lust. I know this; I know this but it does not make me hesitate. It does not make my hope die.

I reach out and grasp her forearms, drawing her roughly in. She falls against me and I show her what a kiss is. I show her what longing is. I let my yearning burn into her, hoping that she will be branded by the tip of my tongue, the tips of my fingers, the tips of my breasts. I will have her here, under the parlour window where her mother sits and waits. I will tumble her and bury my mouth where it will make her moan and shake, here on the grass where we might be found at any moment. And I will make her mine if through no other means than shame; her shame will bind us, and make her *mine*.

"Whore," says Hector in my ear, making his first appearance since yesterday. Timed perfectly, it stops me cold and in that moment when I hesitate, Lucette remembers herself and struggles. She steps away again, breathing hard, laughing through a fractured, uncertain smile.

"When he is *beneath*," she tells me. A promise, a vow, a hint, a tease.

"When he is *beneath*," I repeat, mouthing it like a prayer, then make my unsteady way home.

I stood in the churchyard this morning, hidden away, and watched them bury Master D'Aguillar. Professional pride for the most part. Hector stood beside me, nodding with more approval than he'd ever shown in life, a truce mutually agreed for the moment.

"Hepsibah, you've done us proud. It's beautiful work."

And it was. The ebony-wood and the gold caught the sun and shone as if surrounded by a halo of light. No one could have complained about the effect the theatrics added to the interment. I noticed the admiring glances of the family's friends, neighbours, and acquaintances, as the entrance to the D'Aguillar crypt was opened and four husky men of the household carried the casket down into the darkness.

And I watched Lucette. Watched her weep and support her mother; watched them both perform their grief like mummers. When the crowds thinned and there was just the two of them and their retainers to make their way to the black coach and four plumed horses, Lucette seemed to sense herself watched. Her eyes found me standing beside a white stone cross that tilted where the earth had sunk. She gave a strange little smile and inclined her head just-so.

"Beautiful girl," said Hector, his tone rueful.

"Yes," I answered, tensing for a new battle, but nothing came. We waited in the shade until the funeral party dispersed.

"When will you go to collect?" he asked.

"This afternoon, when the wake is done."

He nodded and kept his thoughts to himself.

Lucette brings a black lacquered tray, balancing a teapot, two cups and saucers, a creamer, sugar boat, and silver cutlery. There are two delicate almond biscuits perched on a ridiculously small plate. The servants have been given the afternoon off. Her mother is upstairs resting.

"The house has been so full of people," she says, placing the tray on the parquetry table between us. I want to grab at her, bury my fingers in her hair and kiss her breath away, but broken china might not be the ideal start. I hold my hands in my lap. I wonder if she notices that I filed back my nails, made them neat? That the stains on my skin are lighter than they were, after hours of scrubbing with lye soap?

She reaches into the pocket of her black dress and pulls forth a leather pouch, twin to the one she gave me barely two days ago. She holds it out and smiles. As soon as my hand touches it, she relinquishes the strings so our fingers do not meet.

"There! Our business is at an end." She turns the teapot five times clockwise with one hand and arranges the spoons on the saucers to her satisfaction.

"At an end?" I ask.

Her look is pitying, then she laughs. "I thought for a while there I might actually have to let you tumble me! Still and all, it would have been worth it, to have him safely away." She sighs. "You did such beautiful work, Hepsibah, I am grateful for that. Don't ever think I'm not"

I am not stupid enough to protest, to weep, to beg, to ask if she is joking, playing with my heart. But when she passes me a cup, my hand shakes so badly that the tea shudders over the rim. Some pools in the saucer, more splashes onto my hand and scalds me. I manage to put the mess down as she fusses, calling for a maid, then realises no one will come.

"I won't be a moment," she says and leaves to make her way to the kitchen and cleaning cloths.

I rub my shaking hands down my skirts and feel a hard lump. Buried deep in the right-hand pocket is the tin. It makes a sad, promising sound as I tap on the lid before I open it. I tip the contents into her empty cup, then pour tea over it, letting the poisoned tooth steep until I hear her bustling back along the corridor. I fish it out with a spoon, careful not to touch it with my bare hands and put it away. I add a little cream to her cup.

She wipes my red hot hand with a cool wet cloth, then wraps the limb kindly. Lucette sits opposite me and I hand her the cup of tea and give a fond smile for her, and for Hector who has appeared at her shoulder.

"Thank you, Hepsibah."

"You are most welcome, Miss D'Aguillar."

I watch her lift the fine china to her pink, pink lips and drink deeply.

It will be enough, slow acting, but sufficient. This house will be bereft again.

When I am called upon to ply my trade a second time I will bring a mirror with me. In the quiet room when we two are alone, I will unwrap Lucette and run my fingers across her skin and find all the secret places she denied me and she will be mine and mine alone whether she wishes it or no.

I take my leave and wish her well.

"Repeat business," says Father gleefully as he falls into step beside me. "Not too much, not enough to draw attention to us, but enough to keep bread on the table."

In a day or two, I shall knock once more on the Widow D'Aguillar's front door.

By the Weeping Gate

See, here?

This house here in Breakwater, this one, by the Weeping Gate where men and women come to wait and weep for those lost to the sea. This house is very fine, given the notoriety of the canton in which it resides; indeed, given the notoriety of its inhabitants.

The front stairs are swept daily by the girl who tends to such things (more of Nel later); the façade is cleverly created, a parquetry of stones coloured from cream through to ochre, some look as red as rubies, all creating a mosaic of florals and vines (the latter use malachite tiles).

There is nothing like it anywhere else in the port city and there are uncharitable souls who whisper its existence is owed solely to the artisans' truck with magic. The windows are always clean and shine like crystals, but none may see inside due to the heavy brocade drapes hung within.

Come to the door, look at its intricacies, all carved from ebony, bas-relief mermaids and sirens, perched upon jagged rocks with the sea throwing itself against those ragged angles. The knocker is surprisingly plain, as if some tiny attempt at good taste was made; it's merely brass (highly polished, of course), with a slight ripple pattern so it looks something like a piece of rope.

The house was not built by its current occupants—they have shifted into it, grown like a kind of hermit crab into a new shell—but by a sea captain who quickly made then lost his fortune to the ocean and its serpents and pirates, its storms and violent eddies, its whirlpools and deceptive coasts with rocks sewn just beneath the surface. After that, another man purchased it, an ill-famed prelate with no flock, who spent his days delving into dark mysteries, talking to spirits and trying to create soul clocks so that, if he might not live forever, he could at least access another lifetime. His departure from the city was encouraged by a nervous populace. The abode lay dormant and lonely for several years until this woman came along.

Dalita.

Tall and striking with jet-black hair, skin the colour of wheat, and eyes like brown stones. She dragged behind her three small daughters, their features enough like hers and distinct enough from each others' to say they had different fathers. No one knew whether she bought the property or simply set up shop there—a lawyer did descend a few weeks after her presence was noticed, but by then her business was well-established (it took only a week).

The solicitor rapped the knocker, peremptorily, a look of displeasure on his face and entered when the door was whisked open. He came out some time later, features quite changed and set in what seemed an unfamiliar arrangement of happiness. He walked somewhat stiffly, now, but this did not seem to bother him at all. He became a regular visitor and was content to leave Dalita to her affairs (and her offspring, who continued to increase in number), and if his wallet was a little heavier and his balls a little lighter each time he left, then so much the better.

For all its decorative glory, the house does not have a delightful marine aspect. Perhaps that is unfair. By peeking out one window, inching one's body sharply to the left and pressing one's face hard against the glass, one might see, through the tight arch of the Weeping Gate, a sliver of water. It is, it must be said, a strip of the peculiarly unclean, slightly greasy liquid that lines the port, infected by humanity and its waste. But then, no one who ventures this far comes for the sea view.

The house has no wrought iron fence, nor tiny enclosed garden; it simply sits cheek by jowl with its street, which is muddy in times of rain, dusty in times without. The cries of the gulls are not faint here, nor is the smell of fresh, drying or dying fish.

Once inside, however, incense and perfume, a heady opiate mix, negates any piscine odours (and others more personal, leisure-related), and anyone setting foot in the spectacular red entrance hall will immediately lose hold of their fears or concerns. The richness of the decor and the beauty of the girls, their charm, their smiles, their voices (coached to pitch low and light), combine to wash away all imperatives but one. After a single visit, even the most nervous of trader, wheelwright, tailor, sailor, princeling, or clergyman—in short, anyone who can scrape up Dalita's hefty fee—will be content to wander the requisite dark alleyways to the house by the Weeping Gate.

And in truth, with time the locale became strangely safer—mariners keen to earn extra coin were easily recruited to run interference in the streets. Thieves and ruffians learned quickly not to trouble those walking in a certain direction with a particular gait, lest they find themselves faced with consequences they did not wish to bear. The longshoremen were known on occasion to shift some of the more inconvenient street-side debris further away from the house. No need to scare the punters.

Gradually, Dalita's clientele increased, and soon enough she took fewer habitués herself, becoming fussier, more miserly, with her favours. But as each daughter came of reasonable age, so too did the number of employees of the house; firstly Silva, then the twins Yara and Nane, then Carin, next Iskha, then Tallinn, and finally Kizzy.

Asha was kept aside, held back for finer things.

And Nel, too, was kept aside, banished to the kitchens.

Iskha, taking her fate in her own hands, ran away and should not have been seen again.

Nel has never feared the streets. They always felt more welcoming than the woman's house—she does not think of Dalita as her mother, possibly because she has never been encouraged to do so.

Nel is plain, astonishingly so—perhaps Dalita might have forgiven her if she had been ugly, for that would have been one thing or the other, but as plain as she is, Nel seems almost . . . nothing. A blank upon which looks did not imprint. Perhaps this causes the most offence—the other daughters all have some version of their mother's allure, enhanced cunningly with pastes and powders, dresses and corsets, all to make the best impression in the eye of the beholder.

But Nel . . . on the occasions her sisters tried to make her up, make her over, it seemed as if the colours they layered upon her face had no effect at all, merely sat on her skin effecting no more of an impression than the merest hint of a breeze. The lacy pink tea gown dangled listlessly on her as if it, too, could find nothing on which to take. Her hair, similarly, would neither kink nor wave even after a full night wrapped tight in rag curlers. When let loose, it simply hung to her shoulders in thick straight lengths, neither brown nor black nor blond, but an unremarkable mix of all three. Of middling height, with middling grey eyes, she was a middling sort of girl and blended into her surroundings as well as a chameleon might.

She'd found in the avenues, the alleys, the seldom-used thoroughfares, the hidden ways through, a kind of home and a kinship with those who inhabited those places. Similarly invisible they recognised a fellow shadow. Some took the trouble to help. Not attracting the eye meant not attracting attention and there was safety in this. Mother Magnus, the cunning woman, showed her smidges of magic to help dampen the sound of her footsteps, to make darker shades cling to her as camouflage. Lil'bit, the cleverest thief, taught her how difficult locks might be encouraged to open, even though she did not indulge this new-found talent for nefarious purposes. Every little bit of knowledge was stored away, if not used immediately.

But the streets had become less welcoming in the past few months, the gloom seemed darker and deeper, the night silences heavier, and she was never sure now what she might find when she went abroad, either on ways of packed earth or cobbles.

Nel had found the first girl.

She'd gone to buy the week's coal, dragging the newly cleaned little red tin wagon behind (Dalita always insisted it be pristine no matter that the coal filthed it up within moments). Nel was always there earlier than Bilson's Coal Yard opened, but she knew how to subvert the lock on the rickety wooden gates, and Mr Bilson was happy for her to leave the small bag of brass bits and quarter-golds in a tiny niche beside the back door of the building.

Nel let herself in, every bump of the wagon on the ground making a loud protest against the quiet of the dawn, but it kept her company. She made her way over to the huge scuttle (the height of one man, the length of two and the width of three) with its metal lid and rolled the thing open to find a face staring back at her. As she looked harder into the dim space she could see a body carelessly laid across a bed of black, bare but for its dusting of coal, an expression of eternal bewilderment on the dead girl's face.

The Constable, fat and red-faced, was terribly cross with Nel because she couldn't tell him who had done this thing—which was going to make his job difficult. He normally dealt with nothing more than theft, and drunk and disorderlies, He studiously ignored runaways, vowing that they would return whenever hungry enough. He quietly took his bribes from those who ran the underbelly of the city—they were terribly good at self-regulation, which he appreciated. Any bodies that were the result of the criminal machinations tended to disappear. He did not have to deal with them. This . . . this was something new.

"I didn't see anyone," she said for the third time. "I just found her."

"And what are you doing out so early?" he demanded.

She rolled her eyes. "Buying the coal for the house; and Madame Dalita will be looking for me by now."

At the mention of her mother's name, the Constable had realised that he didn't need to detain her any longer.

Everyone hoped this murder was simply an aberration, but no. There had been five others since—or, at least, five who had been found. Nel had seen two of them, but only from a distance as they were hastily taken away to avoid public panic. One from the fountain in the city square (which was round), one from the garden at the bottom of the old Fenton House (deserted for many years), another in the orchard belonging to the widow Hendry on the outskirts of the city, yet another on the steps of the city hall and the final one tied to the prow of the largest ship in port, a caravel belonging to the Antiphon Trading Company. The young woman was wrapped around the figurehead as if holding on for dear life.

The girls were all poor, mostly without family, but very, very lovely, once upon a time. It didn't matter, however, when they were lifeless and lying on the marble slabs of the Breakwater Mortuary, wrapped in black cloth so their souls couldn't see to get out. All waiting for the coffins paid for by the city council—penniless girls, yes, but nothing puts more of a fright into folk than the idea of the restless dead. Those who in life had been destitute and dispossessed, when improperly buried, seemed to be more disagreeable, disgruntled, and disturbing as revenants. So the council of ten, made up of four members of the finest families, three of the richest traders, two of the most vociferous clergymen, and the Viceroy, reached into their deep pockets and stumped up for properly-made coffins and decent burials.

The Viceroy began to make noises, after girl number two, found in the fountain—people drank that water!—and so the Constable was given two helpers to aid in his investigations. Unfortunately, the need to spend time in taverns asking questions also meant the under-constables found themselves unable to resist the temptation of drinking whilst working and managed, by sheer effort, to not help very much at all. The Constable traipsed daily to the Viceroy's office, a hang-dog expression on his face, head sinking lower and lower into the setting of his shoulders, so much so that people wondered if it might simply disappear and he would cut peepholes in his chest so he could see out. He stood quietly while the Viceroy yelled.

Nel had watched with interest some of the Viceroy's performances.

He was in his seeming mid-forties, a handsome blond man with a poet's soft blue eyes. Tall and well-made, he dressed with care and splendour, which set him apart from the previous Viceroy. He raged at the Constable. He ranted at the council members. He looked splendid doing it. He spoke gently to those who had lost daughters and paid out a blood-price to those who asked, even though, as people commented approvingly, it was not his place to do so. And he attended at the funerals of the murdered girls, eulogising each and every one, warmly praising the power of their youth and beauty, and lamenting their loss.

When Nel had first appeared at the door to the council chamber bearing her mother's initial missive, he had paused in his tirade at the

Constable and given a vague smile. Now he did not bother, as if her plainness made his eyes slide away and he could no longer notice her. She wondered if he thought the notes floated to him all by themselves. Indeed, her approach excited so little attention that she often watched him unheeded, caught his unguarded expressions and was surprised by those times when it seemed his face was not his own, but a mask set loosely atop another. Nel would shake her head, knowing her eyes deceived her.

She would clear her throat and he would stop what he was doing—whether it be reading, writing, making decrees or fiddling with the large yellow crystal he sometimes wore as a pin in his cravat—stretch forth his very fine hand with its manicured nails for her to place the letter onto his pale, lineless palm. That fascinated her, the blank slate of flesh, as if he had neither past nor future. As if he had simply appeared in the world as he had appeared in Breakwater, six months prior, bearing all the right letters with all the right seals. Accompanied only by two potato-faced men, who spoke seldom and then in monosyllabic grunts, he tidily ousted the incumbent Viceroy—a man known for his indolence, drinking, fondness for young flesh and payments made under the table—in a coup that had delighted and surprised the citizens.

He was terribly good at organising things and wonderfully talented at shouting down opposition, so the city began to run smoothly for the first time in many a year. Grumbles about his dictatorial style gave way to admiring nods as the mail began to arrive in a timely manner, providores were obliged to clean up their kitchens, and slack or shoddy workmanship incurred painfully large fines.

When Dalita initially sent her on this errand (having waited in vain for the new Viceroy to attend her establishment), Nel wondered at the woman touting for business. She thought perhaps Dalita feared the man's next target would be to root out moral corruption and the like—he seemed the type. How else could one explain his absence from the house by the Weeping Gate? Dalita's product spoke for itself, attracted buyers and created its own momentum, and would have done so even without the little bewitching touches such as enchanted whispers blown across a crowded marketplace, and tiny ensorcelled chains of love-daisies slipped into pockets and baskets.

Eventually, though, Nel realised that this was something more than a simple marketing ploy; this was higher stakes. Dalita was offering something for a more permanent purchase, not merely a short-term rental.

Dalita was planning to move up in society.

At the outset, Nel simply waited for the Viceroy to sniff and snort, and send her out of the chamber with laughter echoing in her ears; but he did no such thing. He read the note, opened the locket which had weighted down the billet-doux and stared at the miniature portrait of Asha for a while, then gave a nod, and the words 'I will consider this proposition.'

She duly reported to her mother, who sat back on a padded recamier, with a well-satisfied look and a gleam in her eye. The speed with which this business-like courtship has proceeded surprises no one.

Now Nel visits the Viceroy every second morning or so with some wedding-related query. He does not give her a direct answer, but sends one of his men with a written reply in the afternoon.

What he does give Nel are his traditional sennight gifts for the bride-to-be (whom he has never met), one for each day of the week before the wedding.

These are strange, gaudy things that seem to have begun life as something else. A rusty iron coin, set in a fine filigree and hung on a thick gold chain. A rag doll dressed in a robe of impossible finery and carefully crafted miniature shoes, but the doll itself smells . . . wrong, musty, a little dead. A bracelet of old, discoloured beads, restrung on a length of rope of wrought silver. A brass ring with a piece of pink coral atop it. A shard of green, green glass set in a gilt frame as if it is a painting. A mourning broach dented and tarnished, the hair inside ancient, dry, and dusty, but a new stout pin has been affixed to the thing so it won't fall away. And finally, today, the earrings.

They are large, uncut dirty-looking diamonds, stones only an expert would recognise (and Dalita is such a one).

They hang from simple silver hooks.

They are ugly and the Viceroy insists his bride wear them for their upcoming wedding.

The attic stretches the length of the house. It is populated by six beds, narrow wooden things, but with fat soft mattresses and thick eiderdown duvets, satin coverlets and as many pillows as might be accommodated. To one side of each bed is a free-standing wardrobe, plain yellow pine lightly lacquered, barely able to be closed for the wealth of attire stuffed within: day frocks, evening gowns, costumes for clients with more particular needs, wisps of peignoirs for those who prefer fewer hindrances to their endeavours. To the other, bedside tables overflowing with jewellery, hair decorations, stockings, knickers, protective amulets, random votives, powders, paints, and perfumes. Nel's thin pallet is in the kitchen, piled high with her sisters' cast-off quilts.

There is a space, too, where bed, wardrobe, and table no longer reside, but the marks of their feet are still visible. A gentle reminder of Iskha who always talked of running away and one day did. A space haunted by the glances the other girls give it, and by the presence of one of whom they now speak rarely and then only in whispers for fear their mother might hear. A space filled with yearning.

The wooden floors are covered with rugs of thickly woven silk—only naked feet may tread on these, so all the footwear for the ladies of Dalita's establishment is kept in the room, which takes up half the tiny entry hall to the attic (the other half is a curtained-off bathroom), and is lined with shelves stashed with rows and rows of all manner of shoes: slippers, boots, heeled creations, sandals of gold and silver leather, complex constructions of ribbons and bows that must applied to the foot using an equally complex equation of order and folds to ensure the wearer can walk.

Against the back wall of the long room is the shrine: one large bed with four posts, big enough to accommodate three fully-grown adults, and hung with thickly embroidered tapestries to cut out the light when beauty sleep is a must. On either side of the bed rests a wardrobe, mahogany these, also tightly packed. To the left of this suite is a dressing table, complete with a stool, cushioned lest the buttocks of the chosen one be bruised. On the tabletop, rows and reams and streams of necklaces, bracelets; droplets of earrings, and finger rings, all a'sparkle like a tiny universe of stars carelessly strewn. And amongst this are pots and bottles (carved of crystal in various shades), palettes and brushes to apply all the colours required to highlight eyes, emphasise cheekbones, give lips more pout than Nature intended, and an oil (expensive, rare) to make black hair shine like wet obsidian.

This is the space laid out for Dalita's special darling, her most beautiful child, the loveliest of them all; the one, Dalita believes, who most resembles her.

Asha's mane falls below her waist, its ends tickling the tops of her thighs when she stands; Nel, when she is not in the kitchen, spends many hours washing it, rubbing oil into it, washing it once more, then brushing it, brushing it again until it glistens.

Asha's eyes are just a little too large (like a doll's), and hazel, and in the company of men, frequently cast down as Dalita has taught her. Her skin is the colour of butter with a marked sheen—again, Nel spends many hours rubbing this skin with creams that contain tiny flecks of gold and silver. Asha's face is the shape of a heart, her nose pert and straight and her mouth an inviting purple blossom, lips always moist. She is secure in her position, in the knowledge that she's destined for something more. It does not make her unkind.

She is Dalita's gem, her pearl, her sole unspoiled child, for Dalita has greater plans for this daughter. Asha remains untouched and unbroken, a prize to go to the highest of highs. And at the moment, she is not in the room, which is awash with the noise of young women waking and dressing, bickering and bonding.

"Don't pull so!"

"Oh, hush."

"You're never so rough with Asha," whines Nane. Yara, sitting opposite her, nods, "No, never so rough."

"I'm not rough," protests Nel, "but you will let clients mess up your hair like this. Honestly, it's a bird's nest—what do they do?"

"Naught you'll ever know about." Nane laughs and pokes her tongue out. Nel catches sight of it in the mirror and tugs harder on the black tresses, smiling when her sister howls. Yara sniggers and earns a kick from her twin.

From one of the beds comes a growl. Silva sits up and glares. "Shut up, you lot. Some of us are trying to get our beauty sleep.'"

"Some need it more than others," replies Tallinn silkily and a barrage of giggles and pillows explodes from Silva's bed. Her aim is excellent and her ability to throw in more than one direction at once is impressive. Only Nel is safe. As if the sisters know Dalita's treatment of the plain one is more than enough torment for anyone, they are always tender to their kitchen sister.

"There." Nel draws the silver-backed brush through the now-smooth locks one last time, smiling at their lustre with contentment. "Hurry, Yara, you're next, before Asha comes."

"Oh, yes, Asha's big entrance. Gods forbid she ever slip quietly into a room." Kizzy rolls out of bed and slides to the floor, a look of discontent painted on her porcelain face. She is rounder than her sisters, scrumptious and cuddly, and the youngest; as such she instinctively knows she should be the one who is spoilt, but Asha's pre-eminence has deprived her of this and she she resents it daily.

Yara slips into the spot vacated by her twin, and lets her eyes close, feline, as the brush begins its work. Yara is as neat as Nane is untidy; with their faces so alike it's hard to believe that their natures are so different. Nane is robust, hoydenish; Yara is sleek, almost virginal (something truly precluded by her occupation, but the impression is more than enough to satisfy a particular kind of client).

"Someone help me with these stays," howls Carin. "Gods, Nel, can't you be more careful when you wash these things? You've shrunk my corset!" She struggles with the garment, tugging it this way and that, straining the tying ribbons until they threaten to snap. Nel puts down the brush and makes her way over the wildly struggling sister.

Calmly, she bats Carin's hands away and adjusts the corset, shifting a fold of fabric here, straightening a caught-up hem there, and finally pulling the ties into alignment and deftly doing them up. She pats her sister's face and kisses her cheek.

"I think you'll find the corset is the same size and you're one who's changed. How long since—"

"Oh, no!" Carin wails. "Not again."

"You're so careless," says Tallinn, rippling a frilly green day dress over her head. "Mother will make you keep this one—she said so last time."

Carin slumps to her bed, head hung low, face covered with her hands. But she doesn't cry—none of Dalita's girls are given to tears for they redden eyes, puff up faces, coarsen complexions, and fill sinuses with unpleasant fluids; no one looks charming thus.

"Maybe," she mumbles through her fingers. "Maybe it wouldn't be so bad?"

"And what life for it?" snarls Kizzy. "What life?"

Nel looks at the youngest and frowns, putting a finger to her lips. "Hush now, hush, Carin. We'll take care of it, don't worry. Dalita doesn't need to know."

"Maybe," says Carin, "Maybe I could find Iskha?"

Carin's expression of hope hurts Nel's heart. She wonders if her other sisters suspect. "I could go to stay with her? Do you think, Nel? Could we find her?"

"I think I'll make the appointment for next week. Mother Magnus will take care of it. Just keep your food down for a few more days, and give me one of those broaches the fat little Constable gave you last week.'"

"What for?" demands Carin, affronted that any of her trinkets might be taken. Nel rolls her eyes.

"You have to pay for her services somehow and what money do you think I have?" she asks tartly. Carin subsides and reaches into the top drawer of her bedside table to pull out a square mother-of-pearl container filled with things that shine. She hands Nel a cameo, engraved with the head of Medusa, lovely and serpentine, then insists, "Could you find her, Nel?"

"I think she wanted to get away and if she doesn't want to be found, she won't be." Nel pats her shoulder and returns to Yara's hair, which she gives a final cursory brush and twists into a tightly elegant chignon. "Now, all of you, neat and tidy! Lest she come looking and find you wanting."

As if summoned, Dalita appears, with all the imposing poise of an empress. Her eyes sweep the room, finding nothing to complain about, all daughters dressed and coiffed, paints applied to faces, potions and perfumes to skin. In her hands (strangely square, mannish, very capable, ruthless—what might those hands not do?) is a box, ancient, highly polished, yet with its wood cracking under the weight of years, a gold clasp holding it shut. It is almost four of the afternoon and the clients will soon come a'knocking, but first there is this to be done, this important thing before tomorrow.

Behind her stands Asha, quietly dignified, her wedding dress, a great white confection, glowing in a ray of last sun pouring through the skylight above. Taught by her mother, she knows how to always present herself in the best possible way; she knows everything there is to know about lighting, position, composure, posture, how to dominate a room from the moment you entered to the moment you left.

One senses, however, that she is not at full power, that she has dimmed herself for this practise run; she conserves her energy until she needs to glow.

The dress—the result of seven seamstresses sewing sleeplessly for seven nights—is rather like a wedding cake, with its lace and frills, its layers and embellishments. Shiny white, reflecting with so many hand-sewn crystals it almost hurts the eyes. It is the first time she's seen it and Nel thinks it looks like a suit of armour.

No one but Dalita is to have the honour of preparing Asha for her wedding day, for Dalita trusts no one but herself. She certainly knows her craft: Asha is breathtaking; her sisters, even Kizzy (slightly green) stare in admiration and longing, and not a little envy.

Upon Asha's hair—which has been carefully coiffed, bouffed, backcombed, woven, plaited, twisted, tied and knotted and sculpted like spun black sugar—is a fringe tiara, a framework of gold-wrought wire. From it flows a veil of silk gossamer, spider-spun, almost to the floor, but somehow incomplete. The headdress fans across the crown of her head like a peacock's tail, with seven fine, hollow spikes as part of the structure, yet there is no adornment, none of the gems one might expect.

Dalita looks over her shoulder, gives Asha leave to move into the centre of the attic so she is encircled by her sisters (not Nel, though; Nel falls back, knowing her place is not there, and stands against a wall, quiet as a shadow-mouse). Dalita's fingers clutch at the casket, fumble with excitement as she flicks the clasp.

"This box," she says, pauses, struggles. "This has not been opened for forty years, not since your grandmother wed. What is inside is a gift to the bride that only a family can give: protection and a dowry against the future."

She lifts the lid and offers the contents to Silva, then Tallinn, then Yara, then Nane, then Kizzy, and finally Carin; she herself retrieves the last item. Apiece, they hold what looks like a very long hatpin (the length of a hand), topped with a gemstone, each a different colour. Dalita takes her diamond-tipped pin and approaches Asha; carefully she inserts it into the middle spindle of the headpiece. "Long life to you, my daughter. Bring your family prosperity and pride."

All the sisters do the same, and soon a rainbow arcs across Asha's tiara: blue, red, green, purple, orange, pink, and the diamond, clear as light.

The earrings from Asha's betrothed hang like clumps of dirty water at her ears. Dalita adjusts her daughter's hair, just a little, to try to cover the offending ornaments. She frowns, making mental note to ensure the 'do is tweaked just-so on the morrow.

Dalita surveys her other daughters, does not speak, but merely waves a hand.

To a woman, they traipse out of the attic and down the stairs, past the two floors of the house where each bedroom is equipped with a sturdy bed, themed decorations, and a discrete bathing corner, down to the three parlours on the ground floor, where they will drape themselves over chairs and long sofas. Yara and Nane will pull back the curtains in the front windows and settle themselves on the padded seats to watch for oncoming visitors, and smile and wave, welcoming the regulars and drawing new customers in. Kizzy and Tallinn will ensure the drinks trolley in each room is fully stocked and all the heavy crystal glasses of varying shape and sort and size are ready. Silva will hover to open the front door upon the third knock (always the third, any less is too hasty, any more too tardy—three is just enough to sharpen a client's anticipation, but not enough to stretch his or her patience). Carin will wait with her, ready to take coats and hats and canes and carefully put them away in the walk-in cupboard by the door. Tomorrow, they will have the day off, but not tonight.

"You," says Dalita, pointing a finger at Nel, but not looking at her. Nel wonders if the woman suspects. "Take this to the Viceroy."

Nel nods, pocketing the letter.

"But first help your sister out of that dress." Dalita's need to control extends only to the construction, not the deconstruction, of an illusion.

Nel nods again, although she knows this is neither required nor expected.

Dalita turns, her burgundy gown whispering, and lightly touches Asha's creamy cheek. She catches sight of herself in one of the mirrors hung on either side of the doorway and pauses, struck. Nel wonders how many nights the woman spends before her own reflection, watching the years converge upon her skin and begin to decay her beauty. Dalita shakes her head, closes her eyes for a moment, then leaves. Both girls let their breath go as soon as they hear her heels on the stairs.

"Is it heavy?" Nel asks. Asha nods gingerly so as not to dislodge the work of art on her head. Nel begins with the headdress, unclasping the veil first of all and tenderly draping it across the nearest bed. Then the tiara, laid beside it.

"Is he handsome? Up close?" Asha asks unexpectedly.

Nel pauses in the task of unbuttoning the two hundred tiny pearl buttons running down the back of the gown. Nel wonders if she should tell her about the times when she fancied the Viceroy seemed other, but decides against it. "Yes. You've seen him from the window."

"But that's not close up. Is he nice? You've spoken with him."

"No, I've delivered things to him and that's different." She considers. "He seems . . . determined. He knows what he wants. He is polite."

Asha sighs. "I suppose it's the best I can hope for."

Nel hugs her sister, pressing her plain pale cheek against Asha's butter-rose one. They are silent then, knowing that Asha has already had the best that can be hoped for in the house by the Weeping Gate.

Mother Magnus works and lives in a long narrow room, a forgotten roofed area, a lacuna between two larger buildings. Her bed and washroom are at the back, her workshop and store at the front; a ramshackle kitchen divides the spaces. To look at, Magnus is anyone's idea of a witch, hunchbacked and bent, a shuffling gait, one side of her face a mess of scars, the other still quite smooth. Her hair, though, defies expectation; it is silver-white, long, soft, luxuriant, and hints at a different past. She smells like lavender.

Nel picks up bottle and jars, then puts them down. She flicks through the yellowed hand-written recipe and spell pages Magnus sells, stacked in boxes on a bench. She shifts back and forth impatiently while waiting, batting at the dried plants hanging from the low ceiling.

"Stand still before I hex you, child." The woman's voice is sweet, mellifluous and deep.

"I'll be late. Yet another letter to the bridegroom."

"Can't hurry magic, girl. Hurried magic is messy magic. Messy magic is dangerous magic." Mother Magnus points to the corrugated side of her face, then turns back to the mortar and pestle, attending to the task of grinding herbs with a particular intensity. Nel will ask her, one day, what happened, but she knows that now is not the time. The cunning woman's back is eloquent in its deflection of enquiries. There is a dry rustling as the crushed ingredients are shepherded into the neck of a small bottle, then a *glug* as a purple liquid is poured in after. Magnus stoppers the flask and seals it with black wax. She hands it to Nel, who, in return, counts five quarter-golds in her wrinkled palm.

"My thanks, Mother," says Nel. A tisane for Asha, to help with conception. Dalita is determined that her daughter will be embedded in the Viceroy's life as soon as possible.

Nel finds herself staring at the ruined side of Magnus' face and, without thought, she blurts, "Does my mother ever come to you?"

Magnus shakes her head. If the question surprises her she does not show it. "Never. Although if ever there was a woman I thought would seek me out, it's her."

"Why?" Nel thinks she knows the answer.

Magnus grins. "Why, for a cure against woman's mortal enemy."

"Time." Nel nods, smiles a little; is thankful she doesn't have to worry about having beauty to lose.

"If ever I thought there was a woman who would want potions—if ever there was a woman I thought would seek a soul clock or some such . . . "

"A soul clock?"

"Steals the life—the youth more particularly, and all that goes with it. Done right, it will give you another lifetime, perhaps."

"Perhaps?"

"I've never seen it done right." Magnus rubs at her own face and turns away. She will not say more. "Night, Nel."

Nel is out of the street and heading up towards the finer part of Breakwater, where the houses rest at the feet of the mountains, when she remembers she neglected to mention Carin and her needs. No matter. There will be plenty of time after tomorrow.

The Viceroy, in preparation for his wedding, is not at the council chambers this day. Running of the city has been suspended as the townsfolk anticipate the celebration to come and no one has any complaint. The taverns have opened their doors and libations are free—courtesy of the Viceroy's fat wallet—and the brothels similarly are offering their services gratis (not Dalita's girls, though—there is no promise of a change of life for them). There is much laughter in the streets and good-natured camaraderie; petty arguments have been suspended, debts and obligations forgiven and forgotten, at least for a few days. A carousing city relaxes, lowers its guard.

As the afternoon shades to an evening-lilac, Nel finds the iron gate of the Viceroy's mansion secured. From her pocket she draws out a lockpick (a gift from Lil'bit), and has the lock clicking merrily in a trice. She slips in and wanders along the path, which rises slightly as it makes its way towards the white plaster and granite edifice. A mansion of twenty bedrooms for a single man and his two men servants. And soon, Asha; and soon Asha will have children. Nel dreams that she might leave the house by the Weeping Gate and look after Asha's babies.

The trail winds its way through the overgrown grounds of the house, which are somewhat tropical; the air here is hot and damp. There is the smell of rotting vegetation and something else. Nel thinks the garden needs work and wonders that a man who so generously spreads his fortune across his citizens, who is so concerned with an organised and tidy city, takes no such care in his own home. In the foliage, behind the trees and bushes, things move and her spine twitches with the weight of gazes she cannot see. Nel picks up her pace.

The stone stairs of the mansion are off-white (no one washes and sweeps this stoop) and in places cracks make deep veins where dirt has infiltrated, looking like black blood. Nel tiptoes over them, and towards the front entrance. She raises her hand and knocks—which causes the door to swing open.

"Hello?" she calls.

There is only silence. She steps into the wide entry hall. The floor is covered with a black and white chess pattern of tiles; dual staircases climb the walls, to the left and right of a strangely placed fireplace, where only cold ashes shift in the slight breeze that has snuck in behind her. To her left and right are double doors, ornately carved, painted dove-grey with gold filigree decorations around the handles. Nel chooses the left. The parlour is empty, silent, and filled with stale air. She wanders through and finds another door, a single one this time. She pushes it open: a room lined with books and at the far end, two chairs (with curved armrests, slender legs and threadbare cushioning) wait, each with a large silver pan in front. In the pans is dust: two heaped piles of grey particles. On closer inspection, there is dirt, too, and what look like flakes of snake skin. On a delicate table between, two pewter ewers, filled with water and beside the chairs, a mound of clothes: the livery worn by the Viceroy's two attendants.

Nel slips a hand into her pocket and rubs at the thick paper of Dalita's note. Her heart does not hammer, but its rhythm has become more certain, like a punctuation of every second she remains here. She backs away, turns, and sees something she missed before: a curtained alcove. There is the sound of a latch rattling, a handle turning and now her heart kicks like a startled horse. Without a thought, she slips behind the hanging and holds her breath.

The space is small, containing only her, a slim crowded shelf and a chest, a sea chest, not closed, with fabric spilling out. Nel reaches down and pulls at one of the rags; it's a dress, aged, dirty, with smears of coal dust across the skirt. Another dress, and another. All old, well-worn, as if by someone who could not afford to replace it; eleven in all. On the shelf, bottles. Phials half the length of her hand; she counts twelve and only one is empty. The others swirl with a roiling red-grey mist that seems to push against the very glass as if to get out.

Her attention is drawn away by footsteps. Footsteps and muttering; nothing intelligible, but determined. She puts an eye to the split between the curtains and watches the Viceroy pace, his back to her, to the chairs and their pannikins and pitchers. He kneels, grunting and groaning like a grandfather and pours the contents of a jug into a pan, whispering all the while.

A mist rises, swirling into a tall tower that takes on the shape of a man. The Viceroy moves to the other pan and, while the first thing is coalescing and firming, begins the process anew. He lifts his head and Nel sees his face in profile: the Viceroy, yes, with all the peaks and valleys of the features she knows, but old, so much older than he has presented himself. Furrows in a skin blotched with age and malign intent. Nel, understanding her time is short, slips out of the alcove and through the open door.

Her mouth is dry as paper, her throat closed over as she sneaks from the house. A sudden breeze pulls the door from her numb grip and slams it. Nel is used to little magics, the tiny enchantments to help things along, the harmless brushes of conjuring; what the Viceroy has done—is doing—is beyond her understanding. She runs down the cracked steps, behind her she hears the front door pushed back against the facade of the house, and two sets of stumbling feet, as if their owners have just woken. Nel darts into the undergrowth, fear of what she knows is chasing her greater than that which she imagines might be lurking in the garden. She tiptoes through dank detritus, glances over her shoulder and in the process trips over an ill-covered lump, wrapped in a mouldering blanket.

The smell of something else is worst here, right by this thing, this cylinder-shaped thing that feels soft and giving beneath her shaking hands. Before she summons the courage to unwrap it, however, the sound of footsteps grows louder, more confident, rushing through the leaf-litter, following her tracks. The moment before they appear, the Viceroy's golems, there is a whisper and a sigh—no, whispers and sighs—and Nel is surrounded by grey, wispy women, made wan by death. Through them she can just make out the potato-faced minions, their heads moving back and forth, back and forth like confused bloodhounds. They cannot see her; the women have shielded her. The men servants shuffle off, back towards the path and the house.

Nel soughs her thanks, but the girls do not reply, merely watch her with sad, sad eyes. She glances at them, at the swirling number of them, trying to fix their features in her memory, until her eye lights on a face she knows too well. One for whom she packed a knapsack with warm clothing and food and drink; for whom, not six months since, she'd silently unlocked the door and watched as the other disappeared into the fog of the early morning. One she'd thought free of Breakwater and the house by the Weeping Gate.

She runs to her mother, not to the Constable, not any of the other council members. She runs to her mother, with the spectre of Iskha at her heels. To Dalita because she is the most powerful being Nel has ever known. No matter that there is no love there, Dalita loves Asha and Dalita will not allow her chosen daughter to be harmed.

Nel, propelled forward by the force of Dalita's large hands, keeps her balance until the final few steps. Then she trips and sprawls.

Her fall is broken by damp fabric; felt, soaked with water. There is the sharp, briny smell of salt.

"You will not ruin this for me!" Dalita howls like a cat impaled upon a hot poker. Her rage, her disbelief, when Nel told her what she had seen, what she feared, was something to behold.

At first Nel thought it directed towards the Viceroy, then a ringing blow to her head and a second to her face made her reconsider. While she was disoriented, her mother grabbed her by the hair and dragged her, half-crawling, half-walking through the house, then into the kitchen and down to the cellar. Nel was unsure what enraged the woman most: the idea that Nel might endanger the wedding or that she had helped Iskha flee.

"Liar! Ingrate! Knave! Bitch!"

Dalita threw open another door, in the floor—a sub-cellar.

And the terrible truth of this place is becoming clear, after Nel's drear hours in the dank dark room: this place is tidal.

There is a gap at the base of one wall, she can see, where the sea comes in, but there's no hope of escape: there is a crosshatch of bars across the opening. The water is rising, rising, rising.

Wailing and shouting have not helped—no one can hear her through the cold thick rock of the walls and ceiling. Anyway, her sisters are all a'flap with celebrations—there was no pause for them in the evening, business as usual, but today they wear wedding finery and act the dutiful daughters even though the streets will be filled with people who sneer and laugh at them behind their backs.

The hours have done nothing but make Nel colder, to bring her closer to despair; her teeth chatter, she shakes so badly she can no longer stand and beat at the wood of the trapdoor, which is sodden, but not soft, not rotten. Her hands are bruised and fingers bloody from that hopeless endeavour. There is no lock which she might finagle into compliance.

And the water has continued to rise mercilessly; inevitably; inexorably.

A wash of waves pushes Nel, and her bluish lips and nose scrape against the rock-carved ceiling. She tastes salt and metal; she smells mildew and death. In moments, the sea will replace the last tiny pocket of air and she will drown. It doesn't matter.

It doesn't matter anymore.

With this realisation she feels her body suddenly very heavy, her spirit suddenly very light. She ceases to fight, ceases trying to stay afloat, gives herself up to the water, and she bobs about, heedless as seaweed.

The tide pushes against her again, once, twice, thrice and she feels this is the end.

Hands.

Hands, strong and insistent, many of them; and voices, crying, angry, relieved. Many voices, all at once and Nel is hauled upwards. Behind her the trapdoor is slammed back into place, the bolt shot as loud as a lightning strike.

And her sisters, all her sisters but one—but two—gather around her, clamouring, demanding, groaning with fear and relief, wanting to know what happened, where has she been, was this why she missed the wedding.

And she tells them, choking on seawater and bile and vomit; shivering and shaking and desperately trying to pull her soul—which she so recently was preparing to let go—back into her body.

And they believe her; they believe her because she has never lied and because they know their mother and the length, breadth, and height of her ambitions.

Nel hopes Asha is safe, that there is time.

'The Viceroy insisted they pay their respects to the morgue dead after the ceremony, while the city feasts.'

The mortuary, thinks Nel, so full of lost souls and spent lives, of untapped power. And as they sit there, the seven of them, they hear in the distance the sonorous clang of the death-bell. Not a rhythmic beating, but a desperate clamour, a cacophony. A cry for help. It stills them, voices, faces, hands trying to dry Nel off. It stills their hearts and their minds for precious seconds. And then they run, all of them, even Nel in a halting, stuttering fashion.

They run up the stairs, through empty rooms. They tumble down the front steps like kittens released from a box; they process through the cobbled streets, fast and fleet and trailing diaphanous fabrics and long tresses behind them like banners. They run through the night streets like glorious, terrified ghosts, flashing past windows and open doors, glowing in the lamplight as they pass from shadow to light and back again.

Not far from their destination, the air is split by a rumbling and the lash of a whip; they are almost run over by a black carriage and four, ebony plumes waving in the air. In a blinking moment, Nel glimpses the Viceroy slumped inside, his white wedding attire bloodied and torn, his true age writ large upon his face. Then the conveyance is gone, on towards the city gates, and the sight gives wings to Nel's feet.

The sisters run until they merge with the gathering crowd outside Breakwater's black marble and cardinal brick mortuary, threading their way through folk who, minutes ago, were celebrating all unawares.

Upwards the girls rush, pushing past the fat Constable and his slack-jawed deputies, along corridors embedded with the smell of death: mortification and preservation. Finally they crowd into a room, the room where all will one day go, lined with alabaster tables, each bordered with gutters and silver tubes leading to channels in the floor, stained rusty with all the years of bodily fluids. A room laid out not unlike their own attic sanctum. A room with windows set very high in the walls so no gawkers might peek at the frailty of the dead.

A room with a roughly drawn scarlet circle laid out before them, a star etched inside it with a bottle at eleven of its twelve points. Bottles filled with a churning red-grey mist, some fallen on their side as if collateral victims of a struggle, but none of them broken; none but the empty one lying beside Asha, who is draped across one of the tables.

Her wedding gown is worse for wear, and her tiara is askew and missing some of its pins. As the sisters approach, they notice her makeup has smudged and run, the lip wax is smeared, the kohl and mascara lie in lines across her face, her eyes seemingly bruised by the mess of dark smudges. One earlobe is torn and bloody, its earring gone.

The others stop; these are steps they cannot take. But Nel continues, her feet bare and muddy (her shoes lost in the depths of the sub-cellar), her dress saturated and still dripping on the cold marmoreal floor. Her soles jerk with the shock of being cut—glancing down, she sees shards of yellow, the crystal the Viceroy once wore, now destroyed. She notices that her sister still breathes laboriously, crimson vapour travelling on the exhalation. Nel gathers her up, heedless of the heart's blood spilling from the tear in her chest. Nel leans close and catches Asha's last words, "I can see Iskha."

As her sister relaxes into death, Nel lets her lie back down. She arranges Asha's limbs and clothing, gently closes her lids over staring eyes, tries to tidy the wildly dishevelled tresses. Clenched in Asha's right hand is one of the missing pins, the diamond-tipped one. Its long thin shaft is covered with rapidly congealing blood. Nel does not believe this is her sister's and she wraps the spindle in a piece of fabric torn from the wedding dress and buries it deep in her own pocket.

She then notices, around Asha's body, an aura, a silver shimmer that pours off the dead skin; a voice in her head says no, but she ignores it and touches once more the morbid flesh.

There is nothing. No bolt of lightning, no arching pain, neither scream nor shout nor moan. Nothing, but a kind of itch, across her scalp and her own skin, her own face. Nothing that hurts, nor is even uncomfortable, but simply the sensation of a change creeping on, slowly.

"A soul clock," says Mother Magnus, her voice tunnelling through the dim front parlour of the house by the Weeping Gate. All the rooms have been dark for some weeks, all business dealings postponed, all noises hushed. Nel stands, staring out through the gap in the thick curtains. The view of the street has not changed, although there is a carriage waiting, not too fine, not too ordinary, simply one that will draw no attention. She lets the old woman reel out her explanation. Nel occasionally asks questions and wonders if the cunning woman should have—or did—notice the signs.

"Why girls? Why not boys?"

"Vanity? Convenience? Soft skin? Who looks for lost girls of suspect morals?"

"And Asha? Why Asha?" Nel's voice trembles but does not break.

"Who was more beautiful than Asha?"

Nel realises she is wringing her hands; she shakes them, stills them.

"He was aging—I saw him. I think he was getting desperate. He was getting sloppy, stopped bothering to hide them." Nel rubs her face, still getting used to it. "I wonder what he'll do now, where he'll go."

"Like I said, hen, you can track him with this, if it's his blood."

Nel nods, because she is sure. She wants to be sure. She takes the item from Magnus. "He won't recognise you, but it will be harder for you to hide."

"I know," says Nel, skin all goose bumps at the thought of being seen. "What about the other ones?" the old woman asks.

Nel turns. Mother Magnus is pointing to the eleven bottles, now empty. Nel hopes the wisps of souls will forgive her. It will not be long, she tells them in her heart, and prays Iskha will intercede for her.

"Home," she says. 'They went home.'

Upstairs, Nel can hear her mother's ruckus and she takes her leave of the cunning woman. Dalita, having disappeared after being given news of her darling's demise, was found hours later screaming at the Viceroy's mansion, yelling obscenities at the top of her lungs, banging at the doors and breaking the windows with anything she could find to hand. She has been a'bed ever since.

The first time she opened her eyes and saw Nel she recoiled, gibbering. Now she will take food only from this daughter's hands.

For it is Nel, but not Nel alone.

The plain daughter is transformed. She is not the great and terrible beauty Asha was, but something of the dead sister has passed over to her.

Her hair is now a decided black, her eyes are larger, but still grey. Her mouth has blossomed into something that demands attention, and her figure has filled out, hips and breasts growing wider, just a little, and waist pinching in without the aid of a corset. She is dressed in Asha's clothes for her own no longer fit.

She is a different girl, touched somehow by the magic left on Asha's skin. She is no longer a girl who can live in the shadows, and she feels this loss. Nel no longer feels safe for there is nowhere she can hide from the gaze of those who would drink her in.

This morning, dressed in a grey velvet travelling dress (once Asha's favourite), a beaded purse hanging from one wrist, and a black lacquer fan which, when open, shows mermaids and sailors, on the other, she gives instructions to Carin, who insists upon interrupting.

"And what do we do," asks Carin (now rounder than she was and determined to become rounder still), "when she asks for you? When she refuses to eat?"

"Mix a little of the valerian in her food, it keeps her calm. Tell her I am doing what I must and she needs to be patient." Nel pulls on kid gloves fastened with jet buttons.

"When will you come home?"

"When it is done."

Her single carpetbag waits by the doorway. When she is in the shadowy confines of the carriage, when she can feel the rock and sway of the vehicle and knows they are beyond the city's boundaries, Nel will take the diamond-topped spindle from her reticule. She will place it on her palm and wait to see which way it spins, until it finds the direction she must follow.

Nel takes a deep breath, steeling herself to step outside, to move through the world and be seen.

See here? See this girl?

She is a very fine girl indeed.

❦

St Dymphna's School for Poison Girls

"They say Lady Isabella Carew, née Abingdon, was married for twenty-two years before she took her revenge," breathes Serafine. Ever since we were collected, she, Adia, and Veronica have been trading stories of those who went before us—the closer we get to our destination, the faster they come.

Veronica takes up the thread. "It's true! She murdered her own son—her only child!—on the eve of his twenty-first birthday, to wipe out the line and avenge a two-hundred year old slight by the Carews to the Abingdons."

Adia continues, "She went to the gallows, head held high, spirit unbowed, for she had done her duty by her family, and her name."

On this long carriage journey I have heard many such recountings, of matrimony and murder, and filed them away for recording later on when I am alone, for they will greatly enrich the *Books of Lives* at the Citadel. The Countess of Malden who poisoned all forty-seven of her in-laws at a single banquet. The Dowager of Rosebery, who burned the ancestral home of her enemies to the ground, before jumping from the sea cliffs rather than submit to trial by her *lessers*. The Marquise of Angel Down, who lured her father-in-law to one of the castle dungeons and locked him in, leaving him to starve to death—when he was finally found, he'd chewed on his own arm, the teeth marks dreadful to behold. Such have been the bedtime tales of my companions' lives; their heroines affix heads to the ground with spikes, serve tainted broth to children, move quietly among their marriage-kin, waiting for the right moment to strike. I have no such anecdotes to tell.

The carriage slows as we pass through Alder's Well, which is small and neat, perhaps thirty houses of varied size, pomp, and prosperity. None is a hovel. It seems life for even the lowest on the social rung here is not *mean*—that St Dymphna's, a fine finishing school for young ladies as far as the world-at-large is concerned, has brought prosperity. There is a pretty wooden church with gravestones dotting its yard, two or three respectable mausoleums, and all surrounded by a moss-encrusted stone wall. Smoke from the smithy's forge floats against the late afternoon sky. There is a market square and I can divine shingles outside shops: a butcher, a baker, a seamstress, an apothecary. Next we rumble past an ostlery, which seems to bustle, then a tiny school house bereft of children at this hour. So much to take in but I know I miss most of the details for I am tired. The coachman whips up the horses now we are through the hamlet.

I'm about to lean back against the uncomfortable leather seat when I catch sight of *it*—the well for which the place is named. I should think more on it, for it's the thing, the thing connected to my true purpose, but I am distracted by the tree beside it: I think I see a man. He stands, cruciform, against the alder trunk, arms stretched along branches, held in place with vines, which may be mistletoe. Green barbs and braces and ropes, not just holding him upright, but breaching his flesh, moving through his skin, making merry with his limbs, melding with muscles and veins. His head is cocked to one side, eyes closed, then open, then closed again. I blink and all is gone, there is just the tree alone, strangled by devil's fuge.

My comrades have taken no notice of our surrounds, but continue to chatter amongst themselves. Adia and Serafine worry at the pintucks of their grey blouses, rearrange the folds of their long charcoal skirts, check that their buttoned black boots are polished to a high shine. Sweet-faced Veronica turns to me and reties the thin forest green ribbon encircling my collar, trying to make it sit flat, trying to make it neat and perfect. But, with our acquaintance so short, she cannot yet know that I defy tidiness: a freshly pressed shirt, skirt, or dress coming near me will develop wrinkles in the blink of an eye; a clean apron will attract smudges and stains as soon as it is tied about my waist; a shoe, having barely touched my foot, will scuff itself, and a beribboned sandal will snap its straps as soon as look at me. My hair is a mass of—well, not even curls, but waves, awkward, thick, choppy, rebellious waves of deepest fox-red that will consent to brushing once a week and no more, lest it turn into a halo of frizz. I suspect it never really recovered from being shaved off for the weaving of Mother's shroud; I seem to recall before then it was quite tame, quite straight. And, despite my best efforts, beneath my nails can still be seen the half-moons of indigo ink I mixed for the marginalia Mater Friðuswith needed done before I left. It will fade, but slowly.

The carriage gives a bump and a thump as it pulls off the packed earth of the main road and takes to a trail barely discernable through over-long grass. It *almost* interrupts Adia in her telling of the new bride who, so anxious to be done with her duty, plunged one of her pearl-tipped, steel-reinforced veil-pins into her new husband's heart before "Volo" had barely left his lips. The wheels might protest at water-filled ruts, large stones and the like in their path, but the driver knows this thoroughfare well despite its camouflage; he directs the nimble horses to swerve so they avoid any obstacles. On both sides, the trees rushing past are many and dense. It is seems a painfully long time before the house shows itself as we take the curved drive at increased speed, as if the coachman is determined to tip us all out as soon as possible and get himself back home to Alder's Well.

St Dymphna's School (for Poison Girls) is a rather small-looking mansion of grey-yellow granite, largely covered with thick green ivy. The windows with their leadlight panes are free of foliage. The front door is solid, a scarred dark oak—by its design I'd judge it older than the abode, scavenged from somewhere else—banded with weathered copper that reaches across the wood in curlicues.

Our conveyance slews to halt and the aforementioned front door of the house is opened in short order. Three women step forth. One wears a long black dress, a starched and snowy apron pinned to the front; her hair is ash-coloured and pulled back into a thick bun. The other two move in a stately fashion, ladies these, sedate, precise in their dress, fastidious in their person.

Serafine, too impatient to wait for the coachman, throws back the carriage door; she, Adia and Veronica exit eagerly. I pause a moment to collect my battered satchel, hang it across my chest; it puckers my shirt, adds more creases as if they were needed. I pause on the metal footplate to take everything in. There is a manicured lawn, with a contradictory wild garden ranging across it, then a larger park beyond and the forest beyond that. A little thatched cottage, almost completely obscured by shrubs and vines, hides in one corner, a stable not far from it, and the beds are filled with flowers and herbs. A body of water shimmers to the left—more than a pond, but barely a lake—with ducks and geese and elegant swans seemingly painted on its surface.

"Welcome, welcome, Serafine, Adia, Veronica, and Mercia," says one of the Misses, either Fidelma or Orla. I climb down and take my place in line with St Dymphna's newest crop, examining my teachers while I wait for their warm gazes to reach me. Both are dressed in finery not usually associated with school mistresses—the one in a dress of cloth of gold, the other in a frock of silver and emerald brocade—both wearing heavy gold-set baroque pearl earrings, and with great long loops of rough-cut gems twisted several times about their necks. Then again, were they ordinary school mistresses and this nothing but a finishing school, our families would not have gone to such lengths to enrol us here for a year's special instruction.

"Welcome, one and all," says the other sister, her heavy lids sweep great thick lashes down to caress her cheek and then lift like a wing, as a smile blossoms, exposing pearly teeth. In her late forties, I'd say, but well-preserved as is her twin: of the same birthing, but not identical, not the *same*. As they move closer, strolling along the line we've formed . . . ah, yes. She who spoke first is Orla, her left eye blue, the right citrine-bright. Neither short nor tall, both have trim figures, and peach-perfect complexions, but I can see up close that their maquillage is thick, finely porous, a porcelain shell. The cheeks are lightly dusted with pink, the lashes supplemented with kohl and crushed malachite, mouths embellished with a wet-looking red wax. I think if either face were given a swift sharp tap, the masque might fracture and I would see what lies beneath.

How lined is the skin, I wonder, how spotted with age, how thin the drawn-in brows, how furrowed the lips? And the hair, so thick and raven-dark, caught-up in fine braided chignons, shows not a trace of ash, no sign of coarsening or dryness. Their dresses have long sleeves, high necks, so I can examine neither forearms, nor décolletage, nor throats—the first places where Dame Time makes herself at home. The hands, similarly, are covered in fine white cambric gloves, flowers and leaves embroidered on their backs, with tiny seed-pearl buttons to keep them closed.

Orla has stopped before me and is peering intensely, her smile still in evidence, but somehow dimmed. She reaches out and touches a finger to the spot beneath my right eye where the birthmark is shaped like a tiny delicate port-wine teardrop. She traces the outline, then her smiles blooms again. She steps away and allows Fidelma—left eye yellow, right eye blue—to take her place, to examine me while the other students look on, perplexed and put out. Serafine's lovely face twists with something she cannot control, a jealousy that anyone other than she might be noticed. Orla's next words offer a backhanded compliment.

"*This*," she says severely, indicating the tear, "this makes your chosen profession a difficult one—it causes you to stand out even more than beauty does. Any beautiful woman might be mistaken for another, and be easily forgotten, but this marking renders you unique. Memorable. Not all of our alumni are intent upon meeting a glorious and swift demise; some wish to live on after their duty is done—so the ability to slip beneath notice is a valuable one."

I feel as if I have already failed. Adia laughs heartily until quelled by a glance from Fidelma, who says to me, "Never fear, we are mistresses of powders and paints; we can show you how to cover this and no one will even suspect it's there!"

"Indeed. You were all chosen for virtues other than your lovely faces," says Orla, as if our presence here isn't simply the result of the payment of a hefty fee.

At last, Fidelma too steps back and bestows her smile on the gathering. "We will be your family for the time being. Mistress Alys, who keeps a good house for us, will show you to your rooms, then we'll sit to an early supper. And Gwern," she gestures behind her without looking, "will bring your luggage along presently."

A man leaves the thatched cottage and shambles towards us. Tall but crooked, his right shoulder is higher than his left and his gait is that of someone in constant pain. He is attired in the garb of gardeners and dogsbodies: tan waistcoat, breeches, and leggings; a yellow shirt that may have been white; an exhausted-looking flat tweed cap; and thick-soled brown leather boots. A sheathed hunting knife hangs at his waist. His hair is black and shaggy, his eyes blacker still.

In the time it has taken us to arrive and be welcomed, the sun has slid behind the trees, and its only trace is a dying fire against the greying sky. We follow the direction of Orla's graceful hands and tramp inside, careful to wipe our shoes on the rough stone step. The last in line, I glance back to the garden and find the gaze of the crooked man firmly on me; he is neither young nor old, nor is his a dullard's stare, but rather calculating, considering, weighing me and judging my worth. I shiver and hope he cannot see inside me.

We troop after the housekeeper along a corridor and she points out where our classrooms are, our training areas. The rooms that are locked, she says, are locked for a reason. Then up a wide staircase, to a broad landing which splits into two thin staircases. We take the one to the right—to the left, we are told, leads to the Misses' part of the house, and the rooms where visiting tutors will rest their heads. We traipse along more hallways than seem possible in what is a such a compact abode, past statues and paintings, vases on pedestals, flowers in said vases, shiny swords, battleaxes, and shields all mounted on the wood panelled walls as if they might be ready to be pulled down and used at a moment's notice. Yet another staircase, even narrower than the first, rickety and not a little drunk, leading to a room that should be the dusty attic, but is not. It is a large chamber, not unlike the dormitory I am used to, but much smaller, with only four beds, each with a nightstand to the left, a washstand to the right, and a clothes chest at the foot. One wall of the room is entirely made up of leadlight glass, swirling in a complex pattern of trees and limbs, wolves and wights, faeries and frights. The last of the sun-fire lights it up and we are bathed in molten colour.

"You young ladies must be exhausted," fairly sings Mistress Alys in her rich contralto. "Choose your beds, and do not fight. Wash up and tidy yourselves, then come down for supper." She quietly closes the door behind her.

While my cohorts bicker over which bed covered with which patchwork quilt they shall have, I stand at the transparent wall, looking, taking in the curved backs of men hefting luggage from the top of the carriage, over the gardens, the lake and into the woods—to the place where my inner compass tells me the alder well lies.

The igneous colours of the afternoon have cooled and frozen in the moonlight and seem as blown glass across our coverlets. I wait until the others are breathing slowly, evenly; then I wait a little longer so that their sleep is deeper still. Exhausted though I am I will have no peace until I make my pilgrimage. Sitting up, my feet touch the rug, the thick pile soft as a kitten's fur, and I gather my boots but do not put them on.

One last look at the sleepers around me to make sure there are no tell-tale flickers of lashes, breaths too shallow or even stopped altogether because of being held in anticipation. Nothing, although I think I detect the traces of tears still on Serafine's face, silvery little salt crystals from where she cried prettily after being reprimanded by the Misses. At supper, I'd exclaimed with delight at one of the dishes laid before us: "Hen-of-the-Woods!" and Serafine had snorted contemptuously.

"Really, Mercia, if you plan to pass among your betters you must learn not to speak like a peasant. It's known as Mushrooms of Autumn," she said, as if the meal had a pedigree and status. I looked down at my plate, hoping for the moment to simply pass quietly, but both the Meyrick sisters leapt in and explained precisely why Serafine was wrong to make fun of anyone. It was kind but almost made things worse, for it ensured the humiliation endured, stretched agonisingly, was magnified and shared. And it guaranteed that Serafine, at first merely a bully, would become an adversary for me and that might make my true task more difficult.

I tiptoe down the stairs, and slip out the kitchen door which I managed to leave unlocked after doing the evening's dishes. Fidelma said we must all take turns assisting Mistress Alys with cleaning and cooking—this is no hardship for me, not the unaccustomed activity it is to my companions, whose privileged lives have insulated them from the rigours of housework. Orla instructed it will help us learn to fit in at every level of a household, and doing a servant's tasks is an excellent way to slip beneath notice—which is a skill we may well be grateful for one day.

Out in the spring air I perch on the steps to pull on my boots, and sniff at the heady aroma of the herbs in the walled kitchen garden; I stand, get my bearings and set off. Do I look like a ghost in my white nightgown, flitting across the landscape? With luck no one else will be abroad at this hour. The moon is crescent, spilling just enough illumination for me to see my way clear along the drive, then to follow the line of the road and, stopping short of the town, to find the well—and the tree, its catkins hanging limp and sad.

There is a small peaked roof of age-silvered timber above a low wall of pale stone and crumbling dark mortar and, on the rim of the well, sits a silver mug attached to the spindle with a sturdy, equally silver chain. Just as they—the Postulants, Novices, Sisters, and Blessed Wanderers— said it would be. I drop the cup over the edge, hear it splash, then pull its tether hand over hand until I have a part-filled goblet of liquid argent between my trembling palms.

The vessel feels terribly cold, colder than it should, and my digits tingle as I raise it. I swallow quickly, greedily, then gasp at the taste, the burn in my gullet, the numbness of my mouth as if I'd chewed monkshood leaves. The ice travels down, down, leaching into my limbs, taking my extremities for its own, locking my joints, creeping into my brain like icicles. My fingers are the claws of a raven frozen on a branch; my throat closes over like an icebound stream; my eyes are fogged as glass on a winter's morn.

For a time I am frost-bitten, a creature of rime and hoar. Still and unbreathing.

They did not say it would be like this.

They did not say it would hurt. That it would make me panic. That I would burn with cold. That I would stay here, dead forever.

They did not say it would be like *this*.

Then time melts, that which felt like an aeon was but seconds. My body begins to thaw, to warm and I feel new again, freshly born, released from all my ills.

This is what they said it would be like; that, in drinking from the alder well, I would feel renewed and refreshed, that I would view the world with clear vision and an open, receptive mind. And, having drunk of the wellspring, I would be ready, ready to join them—that those who had already partaken here, the Blessed Wanderers, would recognise the *flow* in me.

My exhaustion is gone, washed away. I stretch upwards, bathe in the moonlight, invincible, invulnerable, eternal—until I hear the crack of a fallen twig and I fold swiftly into a crouch. Trying to make myself small I peer into the gloom, my heart beats painfully, the silver in my blood now all a'bubble, seeming to fizz and pop. Through the trees I see a shape moving calmly, unconcernedly, tall but with one shoulder risen higher than its brother, the hair a shaggy halo around a shadowed face.

Gwern.

I hold my breath. I do not think he has seen me; I do not think myself discovered. He shifts away slowly, continuing on whatever night-time errand is his and his alone. When he is out of sight, I run, as swiftly, as silently as I can, back towards St Dymphna's. My feet seem to fly.

"While the folding fan may seem the least offensive thing in the world, it has been used in at least thirteen high-profile political and forty-five marital assassinations in the past three hundred years." To underline her point, Orla produces a black ebony-wood fan and opens it with a sharp flick of the wrist. The item makes quite a sound as it concertinas out and she beckons us to look closer. The leaves are made of an intricately tatted lace of black and gold, the sticks are wooden, but the ribs, oh, the ribs look slightly different—they are metal, perhaps iron, and with subtly sharpened points. Orla draws our attention to the guardsticks: with a long fingernail she flicks the ends and from each pops a concealed blade. One delicate wave and a throat might be cut, one thrust and a heart pierced. I cannot help but admire the craftsmanship as we sit on the velvet-covered chaises lined against one wall of the practise room, which is located in the basement of the manor, a well-thought-out and thoroughly equipped space.

In front of us is a chalkboard covered with diagrams of innocuous-looking fans of varying designs and substances (iron, wood, reinforced linen, nacre), with the names of all their component parts for us to memorise. To our right stretches the far wall, with four practise dummies made of wood and hessian and straw, red circles painted over the heart of each one. To the left are weapons racks filled with everything one might need, including a cunningly constructed sword that breaks down to its component parts, an orb that with the touch of a button sprouts sharp spikes, and two kinds of parasols—one that has a knife in its handle, the other which converts to a tidy crossbow.

Then there are the display cases which contain all the bespoke appurtenances a lady could desire: silver-backed brushes with opiate-infused needles concealed among the bristles; hairpins and gloves and tortoise-shell hair combs equally imbued with toxins; chokers and pendants, paternosters and sashes and tippets, garters and stockings, all beautifully but solidly made and carefully reinforced so they might make admirable garrottes; boots with short stiletto blades built into both heel and toe; even porous monocles that might be steeped in sleeping solutions or acid or other corrosive liquid; hollowed-out rings and brooches for the surreptitious transport of illicit substances; decorative cuffs with under-structures of steel and whalebone to strengthen wrists required to give killing blows; fur muffs that conceal lethally weighted saps . . . an almost endless array of pretty deaths.

Fidelma hands us each our own practice fan—simple lightly scented, lace-carved, sandalwood implements, lovely but not deadly, nothing sharp that might cause an accident, a torn face or a wounded classroom rival—

although at the end of our stay here, we will be given the tools of our trade, for St Dymphna's tuition fees are very grand. Orla instructs us in our paces, a series of movements to develop, firstly, our ability to use the flimsy useless things as devices for flirting: hiding mouths, highlighting eyes, misdirecting glances, keeping our complexions comfortably cool in trying circumstances.

When we have mastered that, Fidelma takes over, drilling us in the lightning fast wrist movements that will open a throat or put out an eye, even take off a finger if done with enough force, speed and the correctly-weighted fan. We learn to throw them, after first having engaged the clever little contrivances that keep the leaves open and taut. When we can send the fans spinning like dangerous discuses, then we begin working with the guardstick blades, pegging them at the dummies, some with more success than others.

There is a knock on the door, and Mistress Alys calls the Misses away. Before she goes, Orla makes us form pairs and gives each couple a bowl of sticky, soft, brightly coloured balls the size of small marbles. We are to take turns, one hurling the projectiles and the other deflecting them with her fan. As soon as the door is closed behind our instructresses, Serafine begins to chatter, launching into a discussion of wedding matters, dresses, bonbonniere, bunting, decoration, the requisite number of accompanying flower girls, honour-maids, and layers of cake. She efficiently and easily distracts Adia, who will need to learn to concentrate harder if she wishes to graduate from St Dymphna's in time for her own wedding.

"It seems a shame to go to all the trouble of marrying someone just to kill him," muses Adia. "All the expense and the pretty dresses and the gifts! What do you think happens to the gifts?"

"Family honour is family honour!" says Serafine stoutly, then ruins the effect by continuing with, "If you don't do anything until a year or two after the wedding day, surely you can keep the gifts?"

The pair of them look to Veronica for confirmation, but she merely shrugs then pegs a ball of red at me. I manage to sweep it away with my fine sandalwood construct.

"What has your fiancé done?" asks Adia, her violet eyes wide; a blue blob adheres to her black skirt. "And how many flower maids will you have?"

"Oh, his great-great-grandfather cheated mine out of a very valuable piece of land," says Serafine casually. "Five. What will you avenge?"

"His grandfather refused my grandmother's hand in marriage," Adia answers. "Shall you wear white? My dress is oyster and dotted with seed pearls."

"For shame, to dishonour a family so!" whispers Veronica in scandalised tones. "My dress is eggshell, with tiers of *gros point* lace. My betrothed's mother married my uncle under false pretences—pretending she was well-bred and from a prosperous family, then proceeded to bleed him dry! When she was done, he took his own life and she moved on to a new husband."

"Why are you marrying in now?"

"Because *now* they are a prosperous family. I am to siphon as much wealth as I can back to my family before the *coup de grace*." Veronica misses the green dot I throw and it clings to her shirt. "What shoes will you wear?"

I cannot tell if they are more interested in marriage or murder.

"But surely none of you wish to get caught?" I ask, simply because I cannot help myself. "To die on your wedding nights? Surely you will plot and plan and strategise your actions rather than throw your lives away like . . . " I do not say "Lady Carew," recalling their unstinting admiration for her actions.

"Well, it's not ideal, no," says Veronica. "I'd rather bide my time and be cunning—frame a servant or ensure a safe escape for myself—but I will do as I'm bid by my family."

The other two nod, giving me a look that says I cannot possibly understand *family honour*—from our first meeting it was established that I was *not* from a suitable family. They believe I am an orphan, my presence at the school sponsored by a charitable donation contributed to by all the Guilds of my city, that I might become useful *tool* for business interests in distant Lodellan. I'm not like them, not an assassin-bride as disposable as yesterday's summer frock, but a serious investment. It in no way elevates me in their estimation.

They do not know I've never set foot in Lodellan, that I have two sisters living still, that I was raised in Cwen's Reach in the shadow of the Citadel, yearning to be allowed to be part of its community. That I have lived these past five years as postulant then as novice, that I now stand on the brink of achieving my dearest wish—and that dearest wish has nothing to do with learning the art of murder. That Mater Friðuswith said it was worth the money to send me to St Dymphna's to achieve her aim, but she swore I would never have to use the skills I learned at the steely hands of the Misses Meyrick. Even then, though, anxious as I was to join the secret ranks, the inner circle of the Little Sisters of St Florian, I swore to her that I would do whatever was asked of me.

As I look at these girls who are so certain they are better than me, I feel that my purpose is stronger than theirs. These girls who think death is an honour because they do not understand it—they trip gaily towards it as if it is a party they might lightly attend. I feel that death in my pursuit would surely weigh more, be more valuable than theirs—than the way their families are blithely serving their young lives up for cold revenge over ridiculous snubs that should have been long-forgotten. I shouldn't wonder that the great families of more than one county, more than one nation, will soon die out if this tradition continues.

"You wouldn't understand," says Veronica, not unkindly, but lamely. I hide a smile and shrug.

"My, how big your hands are, Mercia, and rough! Like a workman's—they make your fan look quite, quite tiny!" Serafine trills just as the door opens again and Fidelma returns. She eyes the number of coloured dots stuck to each of us; Adia loses.

"You do realise you will repeat this activity until you get it right, Adia?" Our teacher asks. Adia's eyes well and she looks at the plain unvarnished planks at her feet. Serafine smirks until Fidelma adds, "Serafine, you will help your partner to perfect her technique. One day you may find you must rely on one of your sisters, whether born of blood or fire, to save you. You must learn the twin virtues of reliance and reliability."

Something tells me Fidelma was not far from the classroom door while we practised. "Mercia and Veronica, you may proceed to the library for an hour's reading. The door is unlocked and the books are laid out. Orla will question you about them over dinner."

She leaves Veronica and me to pack our satchels. As I push in the exercise book filled with notes about the art of murder by fan, my quills, and the tightly closed ink pot, I glance at the window.

There is Gwern, leaning on a shovel beside a half dug-over garden bed. He is not digging at this moment, though, as he stares through the pane directly at me, a grin lifting the corner of his full mouth. I feel heat coursing up my neck and sweeping across my face, rendering my skin as red as my hair. I grab up my carry-all and scurry from the room behind Veronica, while Serafine and Adia remain behind, fuming and sulking.

"Nothing fancy," says Mistress Alys. "They like it plain and simple. They've often said 'Bread's not meant to be frivolous, and no good comes of making things appear better than they are,' which is interesting considering their business." She sighs fondly, shakes her head. "The Misses got their funny ways, like everyone else."

I am taking up one end of the scarred oak kitchen table, elbow-deep in dough, hands (the blue tint almost gone) kneading and bullying a great ball of it, enough to make three loaves as well as dainty dinner rolls for the day's meals. But I prick up my ears. It's just before dawn and, although this is Adia's month of kitchen duties, she is nursing a badly cut hand where Serafine mishandled one of the stiletto-bladed parasols during class.

The housekeeper, stand-offish and most particular at first, is one to talk of funny ways. She has gotten used to me in these past weeks and months, happy and relieved to find I am able and willing to do the dirtiest of chores and unlikely to whinge and whimper—unlike my fellow pupils. I do not complain or carp about the state of my perfectly manicured nails when doing dishes, nor protest that I will develop housewives' knee from kneeling to scrub the floors, nor do I cough overly much when rugs need beating out in the yard. As a result, she rather likes me and has become more and more talkative, sharing the history of the house, the nearby town, and her own life. I know she lost her children, a girl and a boy, years ago when her husband, determined to cut the number of mouths to feed, led them into the deepest part of the forest and left them there as food for wolves and worms. How she, in horror, ran from him, and searched and searched and searched to no avail for her Hansie and Greta. How, heartbroken and unhinged, she finally gave up and wandered aimlessly until she found herself stumbling into Alder's Well, and was taken in by the Misses, who by then had started their school and needed a housekeeper.

I've written down all she has told me in my notebook—*not* the one I use for class, but the one constructed of paper scraps and leaves sewn into quires then bound together, the first one I made for myself as a novice—and all the fragments recorded therein will go into a *Book of Lives* in the Citadel's Archives. Not only her stories, but those of Adia, Serafine, and Veronica, and the tiny hints Alys drops about Orla and Fidelma, all the little remnants that might be of use to someone some day; all the tiny recordings that would otherwise be lost. I blank my mind the way Mater Friðuswith taught me, creating a tabula rasa, to catch the tales there in the spider webs of my memory.

"Mind you, I suppose they've got more reason than most."

"How so?" I ask, making my tone soothing, trustworthy, careful not to startle her into thinking better of saying anything more. She smiles gently down at the chickens she is plucking and dressing, not really looking at me.

"Poor pets," she croons, "Dragged from battlefield to battlefield by their father—a general he was, a great murderer of men, their mother dead years before, and these little mites learning nothing but sadness and slaughter. When *he* finally died, they were released, and set up here to help young women such as you, Mercia."

I cover my disappointment—I know, perhaps, more than she. This history is a little too pat, a tad too kind—rather different to the one I read in the Archives in preparation for coming here. Alys may well know that account, too, and choose to tell me the gentler version— Mater Friðuswith has often said that we make our tales as we must, constructing stories to hold us together.

I know that their mother was the daughter of a rich and powerful lord—not *quite* a king, but almost—a woman happy enough to welcome her father's all-conquering general between her thighs only until the consequences became apparent. She strapped and swaddled herself so the growing bump would not be recognised, sequestered herself away pleading a dose of some plague or other—unpleasant but not lethal— until she had spat forth her offspring and they could be smuggled out and handed to their father in the depths of night, all so their grandfather might not get wind that his beloved daughter had been so stained. This subterfuge might well have worked, too, had it not been for an unfortunate incident at a dinner party to welcome the young woman's paternally approved betrothed, when a low-necked gown was unable to contain her milk-filled breasts, and the lovely and pure Ophelia was discovered to be lactating like a common wet nurse.

Before her forced retirement to a convent where she was to pass her remaining days alternatively praying to whomever might be listening, and cursing the unfortunate turn her life had taken, she revealed the name of the man who'd beaten her betrothed to the tupping post. Her father, his many months of delicate planning, negotiating, strategising, and jostling for advantage in the sale of his one and only child, was not best pleased. Unable to unseat the General due to his great popularity with both the army and the people, the Lord did his best to have him discreetly killed, on and off the battlefield, sending wave after wave of unsuccessful assassins.

In the end, though, fate took a hand and the Lord's wishes were at last fulfilled by an opportune dose of dysentery, which finished off the General and left the by-then teenage twins, Fidelma and Orla, without a protector. They fled, taking what loot they could from the war chests, crossing oceans and continents and washing up where they might. Alas, their refuges were invariably winkled out by their grandfather's spies and myriad attempts made on their lives in the hope of wiping away all trace of the shame left by their mother's misdeeds.

The records are uncertain as to what happened, precisely—and it is to be hoped that the blanks might be filled in one day—but in the end, their

grandfather met a gruesome death at the hands of an unknown assassin
or assassins. The young women, freed of the spectre of an avenging
forebear, settled in Alder's Well, and set up their school, teaching the
thing they knew so well, the only lesson life had ever taught them truly:
delivering death.

"Every successful army has its assassins, its snipers, its wetdeedsmen—
its Quiet Men," Orla had said in our first class—on the art of garrotting,
"And when an entire army is simply too big and too unwieldy for a
particular task one requires the Quiet Men—or in our case, Quiet
Women—to ensure those duties are executed."

"One doesn't seek an axe to remove a splinter from a finger, after all,"
said Fidelma as she began demonstrating how one could use whatever
might be at hand to choke the life from some poor unfortunate: scarf, silk
stockings, stays, shoe or hair ribbons, curtain ties, sashes both military
and decorative, rosaries, strings of pearls, or very sturdy chains. We were
discouraged from using wire of any sort, for it made a great mess, and
one might find one's chances of escape hindered if found with scads of
ichor down the front of a ball or wedding gown. Adia, Seraphine and
Veronica had nodded most seriously at that piece of advice.

Mistress Alys *knew* what her Misses did, as well as did white-haired
Mater Friðuswith when she'd sent me here. But perhaps it was easier for
the dear housekeeper to think otherwise. She'd adopted them and they
her. There was a kind of love between them, the childless woman and
the motherless girls.

I did not judge her for we all tell ourselves lies in order to live.

"There he is!" She flies to the kitchen window and taps at the glass so
loudly I fear the pane will fall out of its leadlight bedding. Gwern, who
is passing by, turns his head and gazes sourly at her. She gestures for him
to *come in* and says loudly, "It's time."

His shoulders slump but he nods.

"Every month," she mutters as if displeased with a recalcitrant dog.
"He knows every month it's time but still I have to chase him."

She pulls a large, tea-brown case with brass fittings from the top of
a cupboard and places it at the opposite end of the table to me. Once

she's opened it, I can see sharp, thick-looking needles with wide circular bases; several lengths of flexible tubing made perhaps of animal skin or bladder, with what seem to be weighted washers at each end; strange glass, brass, and silver objects with a bell-shaped container at one end and a handle with twin circles at the other, rather like the eye rings of sewing scissors. Alys pulls and pushes, sliding them back and forth—air *whooshes* in and out. She takes the end of one length of tubing and screws it over a hole in the side of the glass chamber, and to the other end she affixes one of the large gauge needles. She hesitates, looks at me long and hard, pursing her lips, then I see the spark in her eyes as she makes a decision. "Mercia, you may stay, but don't tell the Misses."

I nod, but ask, "Are you sure?"

"I need more help around here than I've got and you're quiet and accommodating. I'll have your aid while I can."

By the time she returns to the cupboard and brings out two dozen tiny crystal bottles, Gwern has stepped into the kitchen. He sits and rolls up his sleeves, high so that the soft white flesh in the crooks of his elbows is exposed. He watches Alys with the same expression as a resentful hound, wanting to bite but refraining in the knowledge of past experience.

Mistress Alys pulls on a pair of brown kid gloves, loops a leather thong around his upper arm, then pokes at the pale skin until a blue-green relief map stands out. She takes the needle and pushes it gently, motherly, into the erect vein. When it's embedded, she makes sure the bottom of the bell is safely set on the tabletop, and pulls on the pump, up and up and up, slowly as if fighting a battle—sweat beads her forehead. I watch as something dark and slow creeps along the translucent tubing, then spits out into the bottom of the container: green thick blood. Liquid that moves sluggishly of its own accord as the quantity increases. When the vessel is full, Alys begins the process again with the other arm and a new jar which she deftly screws onto the base of the handle.

She pushes the full one at me, nodding towards a second pair of kid gloves in the case. "Into each of those—use the funnel," she nods her head at the vials with their little silver screw tops, "Don't over-fill and be careful not to get any on yourself—it's the deadliest thing in the world." She says this last with something approaching glee and I risk a glance at Gwern. He is barely conscious now, almost reclining, limbs loose, head lolling over the back of the chair, eyes closed.

"Is he all right?" I ask, alarmed. I know that when I lay down to sleep this eve, all I shall see is this man, his vulnerability as something precious is stolen from him. Somehow, witnessing this has lodged the thought of him inside me.

She smiles, pats his cheek gently and nods. "He'll be no good to anyone for the rest of the day; we'll let him sleep it off—there's a pallet bed folded in the pantry. You can set that up by the stove when you've done with those bottles. Shut them tightly, shine them up nice, the Misses have buyers already. Not that there's ever a month when we have leftovers."

"Who—what—is he?" I ask.

She runs a tender hand through his hair. "Something the Misses found and kept. Something from *beneath* or *above* or *in-between*. Something strange and dangerous and he's ours. His blood's kept our heads above water more than once—folk don't always want their daughters trained to kill, but there's always call for *this*."

I wonder how they trapped him, how they keep him here. I wonder who he was—is. I wonder what he would do if given his freedom. I wonder what he would visit upon those who've taken so much from him.

"Hurry up, Mercia. Still plenty to do and he'll be a handful to get on that cot. Move yourself along, girl."

When I hear a board creak, I glance at the two hands of glory, and notice that of the seven fingers I lit, only six still burn and my heart ices up. I have been careful, so careful these past months to quietly pick the lock on the library door, then close it after me, pull the curtains over so no light might be seen in the windows, before I kindle one finger-candle for each inhabitant of the house, then lay out my quills and books, the pounce pot, and open the special volume Mater Friðuswith gave me for this specific duty. Generations of St Florian's abbesses have asked many, many times for permission to copy *The Compendium of Contaminants*—rumoured to be the work of the first of us—yet time and again the Misses have refused access.

They guard their secrets jealously and this book is alone of all its kind. Their ownership of the only extant copy is an advantage they will not surrender, even though the Murcianii, the Blessed Wanderers, seek only to record and keep the information. There are to be found *fragments* of this greatest of poisoners' bibles, yes; copies with pages missing, edges burned, ink run or faded—but none *virgo intacto* like this one. None so perfect, so filled with recipes and instructions, magical and medicinal properties and warnings, maps of every manner of plant and where it might be found, how it might best be harvested and then propagated elsewhere, how it might best be used for good or ill, how it might be preserved or destroyed. Without it our Archives are embarrassingly bereft, and with only one single copy in existence, the possibility of its destruction is too great for us to bear.

And this is why I am here; this is my initiation task to earn my place among St Florian's secret sisters, the Murcianii, the collectors, the recorders, the travelling scribes who gather all manner of esoteric and eldritch knowledge so it might not pass out of the world. Folktales and legends, magic and spells, bestiaries of creatures once here and now long-gone, histories and snippets of lives that have intersected with our efforts, our recordings . . . and books like *these*, the dark books, the dangerous books, the books that some would burn but which we save because knowledge, *all* knowledge, is too important to be lost.

If I bring a copy of this book back to Mater Friðuswith then my position will be assured. I will *belong*.

But all that will be moot if I am discovered; if my betrayal of two of the most dangerous women of the day—indeed other days, long ago—is found out.

The door opens and Gwern stands there, clothes crumpled from his long sleep, hair askew, the marks of a folded blanket obvious along his jaw line. He sways, still weak from the bloodletting, but his eyes are bright.

"What are you doing?" The low voice runs through me. Part of me notes that he seems careful to whisper. He takes in the *Compendium*, propped on the bookstand, all the tools of my trade neatly lined up on the desk (as untidy as my person may be, I am a conscientious craftswoman), and the hands of glory by whose merrily flickering light I have been working.

And I cannot answer; fear stops my throat and all I can think of is Fidelma and Orla and their lethal ornaments, the choking length of a rosary about my neck, a meal infused with tincture of Gwern's lifeblood, a down-stuffed pillow over my face as I sleep. He steps into the room, closes the door behind him then paces over to lift me up by the scruff of the neck as if I am a kitten who's peed in his shoes. Not so weak as he seems, then. He shakes me till I think my head will roll off, until he realises I cannot explain myself if I cannot breathe. He lets me go, pushing me back until I sit on top of the desk and draw in great gasps of air, and he asks me again in that threatening tone, "What are you doing?"

And I, in fear of what might happen if two Quiet Women should find out what I've been doing, how I've been taking from them what they've refused—and hoping, perhaps, after what I'd witnessed this morning that he might not have much love for the Misses—I tell him almost everything.

And when I am finished, he does not call out and rouse the Meyrick sisters. He does not bend forward and blow out the glory candles, but rather smiles. He leans so close that I can smell his breath, earthy as freshly mown grass, as he speaks, "I knew it. I knew when I saw you that night."

"Knew what?" I demand, momentarily brave.

"That you were different to them; different to the others who have come here year upon tiresome year. When I saw you in the moonlight, I *knew*—none of the others ever venture out past the walls at night, certainly don't wander to the well and drink its contents down so sure and so fast. They don't make brave girls here—they make cowardly little bits who like blades in the dark, poison in the soup, pillows over faces." He straightens, rolls his uneven shoulders. "I knew you could help me."

"Help you do what?" I ask, mesmerised by his black gaze.

Instead of answering, he goes to one of the shelves and rummages, finds a slim yellow volume and hands it to me. *A Brief History of the Alder Well.* He says nothing more, but runs a hand down the side of my face, then leaves, the door closing with a gentle *click* behind him. I feel his fingers on me long after he's gone.

The alchemy laboratory is situated on the ground floor; it has large windows to let in light and equally large shutters to keep out the selfsame when we work with compounds that prefer the darkness. We each have a workbench, honeycombed with drawers filled with plants, powders, poisons, equipment, mortars, pestles, vials, and the like. On mine this morning, I found a rose, red as blood, its stem neatly sheared on an angle, the thorns thoughtfully removed; my heart beats faster to see it, that kindness. Indeed there's been a floral offering every day for the past three weeks, roses, peonies, lily of the valley, snowdrops, bluebells, daffodils, all waiting for me in various spots: windowsills, shelves, under my pillow, on the kitchen bench, in the top drawer of my bedside table, hidden among the clothes in my chest. As if I needed anything to keep their giver in my thoughts; as if my dreams have not been haunted. Nothing huge, nothing spectacular, no grand bouquets, but something sweet and singular and strange; something to catch my eye alone—no one else seems to notice them. Not even Serafine with her cruel hawk's gaze.

We have a new teacher for this sennight, who arrived with many boxes and trunks, cases and carpet bags, and a rectangular item neatly wrapped around with black velvet. When her driver seemed careless with it, she became sharp with him. It must be delicate, perhaps made of glass—a mirror? A painting? A portrait?

The poisoner is fascinated by Serafine. In fact, we others may as well not be here. She hovers over the sleek blond girl's work-table, helping her to measure powders, cut toxic plants, heat solutions, giving her hints that we may or may not hear and take advantage of. My copying of the *Compendium* means my cognizance of poisons and their uses is greater than my companions but I cannot show off; cannot appear to have knowledge I should not possess.

We are not working with killing venin today, merely things to cause discomfort—a powder sprinkled over clothing or a few drops of liquid added to someone's jar of night cream will bring up a rash, afflict the victim with itches and aches that appear to have no logical source. One must be careful, Hepsibah Ballantyne tells us in a rare address to the whole class, not to do things that disrupt a person's ordinary routine—that is what they will remember, the disruptions: the tinker come to a door selling perfumes, the offer of a special new blend of tea from a recent acquaintance. When you wish to injure someone, do something that rubs along with their habits, their everyday lives—blend into the ordinary flow and simply *corrupt* one of their accustomed patterns. No fanfare, no drawing of attention to yourself or your acts. Do nothing that someone might later recall as out of the ordinary—it will bring the authorities to you faster than you please.

Mistress Ballantyne arrives once a year to stay with the Misses and impart her venomous wisdom, although Alys tells me this is not her profession proper. She is a coffin-maker and most successful—she travelled here in her own carriage and four (the driver currently making himself at home in Alys's bed). Years and experience have made her a talented poisoner, although few know it and that's as it should be. I think she is older than she seems, rather like the Misses; in certain lights her face is as lined as a piece of badly prepared parchment, in others it seems smooth. She has short blond curls, and brown eyes that watched peachy-pink Serafine too closely from the moment she was introduced.

I take the apple seeds and crush them under the blade of my knife.

"How did you know to do that?" Hepsibah's voice is at my shoulder and I suppress the urge to jump guiltily. The recipe in front of us says to grind the seeds in the mortar and pestle, but the *Compendium* warns against that as weakening the poison—crush the seeds just once with a sharp hit to crack the carapace and release the toxin. I look into her dark eyes and the lie comes quickly to my lips.

"My mother. She learned herbcraft to support us after my father died."

Which is true to some extent: Wulfwyn did learn herblore at St Florian's after Mater Friðuswith offered her refuge, but our father had been well and truly gone for many years before that—or rather, my sisters' father. Mine hung around on moonlit nights, watching from the shadows as I grew. "She wasn't a poison-woman, but she knew some things, just enough to help get by."

Her gaze softens. I've touched a nerve; she's another motherless girl, I suspect. We are legion. She nods and moves away, telling me my labours are good and I show promise. Hepsibah gives Adia and Veronica's work a quick once-over and shifts her attention back to Serafine, resting a calloused and stained hand in the small of the other's back. I notice Serafine leans into the touch rather than away, and feel an unaccustomed wave of sympathy for her, to know she longs for something she will not be allowed to have.

Standing outside the library door, one hand balancing a platter of sweetmeats, the other preparing to knock and offer the Misses and their guest an evening treat to go with the decanter of winterplum brandy I delivered earlier along with three fine crystal snifters. A terse voice from inside the room stops me. I slow my breathing to almost nothing, stand utterly still; if I've learned nothing else here it's to be undetectable when required.

"Sweet Jesu, Hepsibah, control yourself!" Orla's voice, strangely harsh and raised in an anger none of us have yet witnessed in the classroom no matter how egregious our trespasses.

"I don't know what you mean," Mistress Ballantyne answers, her tone airy.

"I *saw* you in the garden this afternoon, busy fingers, busy lips, busy teeth," hisses Orla.

"Jealous?" laughs Hepsibah.

Fidelma breaks in, "We have told you that you cannot touch any student in our care."

"That one was thoroughly touched and not complaining, besides," retorts Hepsibah and I imagine a wolfish grin crossing her lips.

"Scandals! They follow you! It's your own fault—one then another, ruined girls, angry families and you must leave a city yet again." Orla pauses, and I hear the sound of a decanter hitting the rim of a glass a little too hard. "Lord, just find someone who *wants* your attention, who isn't already spoken for, and be content."

Mistress Ballantyne snorts and I imagine she shrugs, raising her thin shoulders, tossing her neat, compact head with its pixie features and upturned nose. She might fidget, too, with those stained fingers and her small square hands; she asks belligerently, "Where's the fun in a willing victim?"

Fidelma fairly shouts, "*He* has been seen. Not two counties away."

And silence falls as if a sudden winter has breathed over the library and frozen its inhabitants. It lasts until Mistress Ballantyne breaks it, all swagger, all arrogance gone, her voice rises to a shriek, "Has he been *here*? Have you *betrayed* me?"

Fidelma shushes her. "Of course not, you silly bint, but people talk, rumours have wings. Those who live long and do not change as much as others become the target of gossip. Those who do not hide, who do not take care not to draw attention—they are the ones who stand out, Hepsibah."

Orla sighs. "And you know he's been searching for something, something other than *you*—in addition to you. *We* do not live in a large city, Hepsibah, we do not live in a grand house and parade along boulevards in an open-topped landau, begging folk to stare and take note. Few people know who we truly are, fewer still that the wars our father fought ended a hundred years ago."

Fidelma: "It's a wonder you survived in the days before you knew he was hunting you. You've never learned the art of hiding yourself—of putting your safety ahead of your baser desires."

"You've had good service of me. I've shared my secrets with you, helped keep you young, taught your murderous little slatterns who think they're better than me." There's a pause, perhaps she worries at a thumbnail. "But if he's been seen, then I'm off."

"But you've still got classes to teach!" protests Orla.

Hepsibah shrugged. "Well, consider that I'm thinking of my own safety before my *baser desires,*" she sneers. "Get Magnus, she's a good poisons woman if you can find her. Last I heard she'd berthed in Breakwater."

There are quick footsteps and the door is wrenched open. I'm almost bowled over by Mistress Ballantyne, who shouts "Out of my way, halfwit" and charges off towards her room. The Misses stare at me and I hold up the tray of sweetmeats, miraculously not thrown to the floor as Hepsibah passed. Orla gestures for me to come in, then turns to her sister. "*You* see if you can talk sense to her. I'm not teaching poisons."

"You're the one who mentioned him. If it comes down to it, sister, you will."

Fidelma sweeps out, taking a handful of sweetmeats with her. Orla slumps in a chair and, when I ask if there's anything else she needs, she waves me away, not bothering to answer. On the small table beside her are three discarded vials, red-brown stains in the bottom.

I will not make my nest in the library tonight. Mistress Ballantyne will take a while to pack her trunks and rouse her coachman from the warmth of Alys's blankets. The household will be in uproar this night and I shall take the chance to have a sleep uninterrupted by late-night forgery at least; there will be no guarantee that I will not dream of Gwern. One night without copying the *Compendium* will not make much difference.

Orla's grace has deserted her.

All the patience and fine humour she's displayed in the past is gone, replaced by an uncertain and somewhat foul temper, as if she's been tainted by the subject she's forced to teach. The Misses, wedded to their schedule, decided not to try for the woman Magnus, and it is as Fidelma threatened: Orla, having caused the difficulty, must now deal with the consequences.

Open on the desk in front of her is the *Compendium* as if it might solve all of her problems. I wonder if Mistress Alys with her fondness for herbs wouldn't have been a better choice. I keep looking at the book, suppressing shudders each time Orla's hands—filled with a toxic powder, wilted stalk, or simple spring water—pass anywhere near it. It is unique, alone in the world and I feel it must be protected. Coiled, I wait to leap forward and save it from whatever careless fate Orla might bestow upon it.

The ingenuity and patience, which is so fully in evidence when teaching us how to kill using unthought-of weapons, has left no trace as Orla makes us mix concoctions, elixirs, and philtres to cause subtle death. She forgets ingredients, tells us to stir when we should shake, to grind when we should slice, to chop when we should grate. We are not halfway through the first lesson when our tutor swears loudly and knocks over a potion, which pours into an alabaster mortar and mates with the crushed roots there. The reaction is spectacular, a fizz and a crack and smoke of green then purple fills the alchemy room like a sudden, vitriolic fog.

I throw open the windows, shielding my mouth and nose with the bottom of my skirt, then I find the door and thrust it to—the smoke begins to clear but all I can hear are the rasping coughs of my fellow students and teacher. Squinting against the tears the smoke causes, I find them one by one and herd them out into the corridor, where Mistress Alys and Fidelma, drawn by the noise, are in a flurry. When Orla is the last one out, I dive back into the room and rescue the book—it tore at me not to save it before any mortal, but common sense prevailed and no suspicions are aroused. I hold it tightly to my chest as we are all hustled outside into the fresh air.

"Well done, Mercia," says Fidelma, bending down to pat her sister's heaving back. Orla vomits on the grass, just a little.

"There's no fire, Miss, just the smoke. It should clear out soon—there's a good enough breeze," I say.

"Indeed." She stands and surveys the lilac-tinged vapour gently wafting through the door behind us. "We are nothing if not adaptable. I think we shall leave the rest of our poisons classes until such time as Mother Magnus or a suitable substitute might be found—lest my sister kill us all."

Orla makes an unladylike gesture and continues coughing. Mistress Alys, having braved the smog, reappears with a syrupy cordial of black horehound, to soothe our throats and lungs. We swig from the bottle.

Some time later, order has been restored: the house has been cleared of the foul smelling fumes; pleural barks have been reduced to occasional rattles; Orla's dignity has been stitched together for the most part; and I have (with concealed reluctance) handed back the *Compendium* and been given by Fidelma a letter for Mother Magnus and instructed to deliver it to the coachman who resides in Alder's Well, begging him to deliver it to the poisons woman and wait for her reply—and hopefully her agreement to return with him.

I walk slowly there and even more slowly back, enjoying the air, the quiet that is not interrupted by the prattle of girls too silly to know they will be going to their deaths sooner than they should—too silly to know that now is the time they should begin mourning their lost futures. Or planning to run away, to fade from their lives. Gods know we are taught enough means to hide, to provide for ourselves, to change our appearances, to earn a living in different ways, to *disappear*. Sometimes I am tempted to tell Veronica about Cwen's Reach and the Citadel, about the Little Sisters of St Florian and how they offered my family refuge, and how, for a long time, no one found us, not even Cenred's ghost. How she could just as easily come with me and become one of the sisters or live in the city at the Citadel's foot as Delling and Halle do, working as jewel-smiths. But I know better. I know she would not want to lose her soft life even for the advantage of longevity; she will play princess while she may, then give it all up not for a lesser lifestyle, but for death. Because she thinks with death, everything stops.

I could tell her otherwise. I could tell her how my mother was pursued by her brother's shade for long years. How he managed somehow to still touch her, to get inside her, to father me well after he was nothing more than a weaving of spite and moonlight. How I would wake from a dream of him whispering that my mother would never escape him. How, even at her death bed, he hovered. How, until Delling did her great and pious labour, he troubled my sleep and threatened to own me as he had Wulfwyn. I could tell her that dying is not the end—but she will discover it herself soon enough.

I had not thought to go back by the clearing, but find myself there anyway, standing before both well and alder. They look different to that first night, less potent without their cloak of midnight light. Less powerful, more ordinary. But I do not forget the burning of the well's water; nor my first sight of the alder and the man who seemed crucified against it, wormed through with vines and mistletoe.

"Have you read it? The little book?"

I did not hear him until he spoke, standing beside me. For a large, limping man he moves more silently than any mortal should. Then again, he is not mortal, but I am unsure if he is what he would have me believe. Yet I have seen his blood. I give credence to things others would not countenance: that my father was a ghost and haunted my dreams; that the very first of the scribes, Murciana, could make what she'd heard appear on her very skin; that the Misses are older than Mater Friðuswith although they look young enough to be her daughters—granddaughters in some lights. So, why not believe him?

I nod, and ask what I've been too shy to ask before, "How did you come here?"

He taps the trunk of the alder, not casually, not gently, but as if in hope that it will become something more. It disappoints him, I can see. His hand relaxes the way one's shoulders might in despair.

"Once upon a time I travelled through these. They lead down, you see, into under-earth. Down to the place I belong. I was looking for my daughter—a whisper said she was here, learning the lessons these ones might teach."

And I think of the little yellow book, written by some long-dead parson who doubled as the town's historian. *The Erl-King who rules beneath has been sighted in Alder's Well for many a year. Inhabitants of the town claim to have seen him roaming the woods on moonlit nights, as if seeking someone. Parents are careful to hide their children, and the Erl-King is often used to frighten naughty offspring into doing what they're bid. My own grand-dam used to threaten us with the words "Eat your greens or the Erl-King will find you. And if not him then his daughter who wanders the earth looking for children to pay her fare back home." Legend has it he travels by shadow tree.*

"Did you find her? Where is she?"

He nods. "She was here then, when I came through. Now, I no longer know. She had—caused me offence long ago, and I'd punished her. But I was tired of my anger and I missed her—and she'd sent me much . . . tribute. But I did not think that perhaps her anger burned brightly still."

No one is what they seem at St Dymphna's. "Can't you leave by this same means?"

He shakes his great head, squeezes his eyes closed. It costs his pride much to tell me this. "They tricked me, trapped me. Your Misses pinned me to one of my own shadow trees with mistletoe, pierced me through so my blood ran, then they bound me up with golden bough—my own trees don't recognise me anymore because I'm corrupted, won't let me through. My kingdom is closed to me, has been for nigh on fifty years."

I say nothing. A memory pricks at me; something I've read in the Archives . . . a tale recorded by a Sister Rikke, of the Plague Maiden, Ella, who appeared from an icy lake, then disappeared with all the village children in tow. I wonder . . . I wonder . . .

"They keep me here, bleed me dry for their poison parlour, sell my blood as if it's some commodity. As if they have a *right.*" Rage wells up. "Murderous whores they are and would keep a king bound!"

I know what—who—he thinks he is and yet he has provided no proof, merely given me this book he may well have read himself and taken the myths and legends of the Erl-King and his shadow trees to heart. Perhaps he is a madman and that is all.

As if he divines my thoughts, he looks at me sharply.

"I may not be all that I was, but there are still creatures that obey my will," he says and crouches down, digs his fingers firmly into the earth and begins to hum. Should I take this moment to run? He will know where to find me. He need only bide his time—if I complain to the Misses, he will tell what he knows of me.

So I wait, and in waiting, I am rewarded.

From the forest around us, from behind trees and padding from the undergrowth they come; some russet and sleek, some plump and auburn, some young, some with the silver of age dimming their fur. Their snouts pointed, teeth sharp, ears twitching alert and tails so thick and bushy that my fellow students would kill for a stole made from them. They come, the foxes, creeping towards us like a waiting tribe. The come to him, to Gwern, and rub themselves against his legs, beg for pats from his large calloused hands.

"Come," he says to me, "they'll not hurt you. Feel how soft their fur is."

Their scent is strong, but they let me pet them, yipping contentedly as if they are dogs and they are, his dogs. I think of the vision of the crucified man I saw on my first day here, of the halo of ebony hair, of the eyes briefly open and so black in the face so pale. Gwern draws me close, undoes the thick plait of my hair and runs his hands through it. I do not protest.

I am so close to giving up everything I am when I hear voices. Gwern lets me go and I look towards the noise, see Serafine, Adia, and Veronica appear, each one trailing a basket part-filled with blackberries, then turn back to find Gwern is gone. The foxes melt quickly away, but I see from the shifting of Serafine's expression that she saw *something*.

"You should brush your hair, Mercia," she calls slyly. "Oh, I see you already have."

I walk past them, head down, my heart trying to kick its way out of my chest.

"I suppose you should have a husband," says Serafine in a low voice, "but don't you think the gardener is beneath even you?"

"I'd thought, Serafine, you'd lost your interest in husbands after Mistress Ballantyne's instructive though brief visit," I retort and can feel the heat of her glare on the back of my neck until I am well away from them.

Alys is rolling out pastry for shells and I am adding sugar to the boiling mass of blackberries the others picked, when Fidelma calls from the doorway, "Mercia. Follow me."

She leads me to the library, where Orla waits. They take up the chairs they occupied on the night when their nuncheon with Mistress

Ballantyne went so very wrong. Orla gestures for me to take the third armchair—all three have been pushed close together to form an intimate triangle. I do so and watch their hands for a moment: Orla's curl in her lap, tighter than a new rose; Fidelma's rest on the armrests, she's trying hard not to press her fingertips hard into the fabric, but I can see the little dents they make on the padding.

"It has come to our attention, Mercia," begins Fidelma, who stops, purses her lips, begins again. "It has come to our attention that you have, perhaps, become embroiled in something . . . unsavoury."

And that, that word, makes me laugh with surprise—not simply because it's ridiculous but because it's ridiculous from the mouths of these two! The laugh—that's what saves me. The guilty do not laugh in such a way; the guilty defend themselves roundly, piously, spiritedly.

"Would you listen to Serafine?" I ask mildly. "You know how she dislikes me."

The sisters exchange a look then Fidelma lets out a breath and seems to deflate. Orla leans forward and her face is so close to mine that I can smell the odour of her thick makeup, and see the tiny cracks where crows' feet try to make their imprint at the corners of her particoloured eyes.

"We know you speak with him, Mercia, we have seen you, but if you swear there is nothing untoward going on we will believe you," she says and I doubt it. "But be wary."

"He has become a friend, it is true," I admit, knowing that lies kept closest to the truth have the greatest power. "I have found it useful to discuss plants and herbs with him as extra study for poisons class—I speak to Mistress Alys in this wise too, so I will not be lacking if— when—Mother Magnus arrives." I drop my voice, as if giving them a secret. "And it is often easier to speak with Gwern than with the other students. He does not treat me as though I am less than he is."

"Oh, child. Gwern is . . . in our custody. He mistreated his daughter and as punishment he is indentured to us," lies Orla. To tell me this . . . they cannot know that I know about Gwern's blood. They cannot know what Mistress Alys has let slip.

"He's dangerous, Mercia. His Ella fled and came to us seeking justice," says Fidelma urgently. Her fingers drum on the taut armchair material. Whatever untruths they tell me, I think that this Ella appealed to them because they looked at her and saw themselves so many years before. A girl lost and wandering, misused by her family and the world. Not that they will admit it to me, but the fact she offered them a lifeline—her father's unique blood—merely sweetened the deal. And, I suspect, this Ella found in the Misses the opportunity for a revenge that had been simmering for many a long year.

"Promise us you will not have any more to do with him than you must?" begs Orla and I smile.

"I understand," I say and nod, leaning forward and taking a hand from each and pressing it warmly with my own. I look them straight in the eyes and repeat, "I understand. I will be careful with the brute."

"Love is a distraction, Mercia; it will divert you from the path of what you truly want. You have a great future—your Guilds will be most pleased when you return to them for they will find you a most able assassin. And when your indenture to them is done, as one day it shall be, you will find yourself a sought-after freelancer, lovely girl. We will pass work your way if you wish—and we would be honoured if you would join us on occasion, like Mistress Ballantyne does—did."

The Misses seem overwhelmed with relief and overly generous as a result; the atmosphere has been leached of its tension and mistrust. They believe me to be ever the compliant, quiet girl.

They cannot know how different I am—not merely from their idea of me, but how different I am to *myself*. The girl who arrived here, who stole through the night to drink from the alder well, who regularly picked the lock on the library and copied the contents of their most precious possession, the girl who wished most dearly for nothing else in the world but to join the secret sisters. To become one of the wandering scribes who collected strange knowledge, who kept it safe, preserved it, made sure it remained in the world, was not lost nor hidden away. That girl . . . that girl has not roused herself from bed these past evenings to copy the *Compendium*. She has not felt the pull and burn of duty, the sharp desire to do what she was sent here to do. That girl has surrendered herself to dreams of a man she at first thought . . . strange . . . a man who now occupies her waking and slumbering thoughts.

I wonder that the fire that once burned within me has cooled and I wonder if I am such a fickle creature that I will throw aside a lifetime of devotion for the touch of a man. I know only that the *Compendium*, that Mater Friðuswith's approval, that a place among the dusty-heeled wandering scribes are no longer pushing me along the path I was certain I wished to take.

"Here, you do it!" says Mistress Alys, all exasperation; she's not annoyed with me, though. Gwern has been dodging her for the past few days. Small wonder: it's bleeding time again. She pushes the brown case at me and I can hear the glass and metal things inside rattling in protest. "Don't worry about the little bottles, just bring me back one full bell. I'm going in Alder's Well and I'll take the Misses Three with me."

"But . . . " I say, perplexed as to how I might refuse this task of *harvesting*. She mistakes my hesitation for fright.

"He's taken a liking to you, Mercia, don't you worry. He'll behave well enough once he sees you. He's just like a bloody hound, hiding when he's in trouble." Alys pushes me towards the door, making encouraging noises and pouring forth helpful homilies.

Gwern's cottage is dark and dim inside. Neither foul nor dirty, but mostly unlit to remind him of home, a comfort and an ache at the same time, I think. It is a large open space, with a double bed in one corner covered by a thick eiderdown, a tiny kitchen in another, a wash stand in another, and an old, deep armchair and small table in the last. There is neither carpet nor rug, but moss with a thick, springy pile. Plants grow along the skirting boards, and vines climb the walls. Night-flowering blooms, with no daylight to send their senses back to sleep, stay open all the time, bringing colour and a dimly glimmering illumination to the abode.

Gwern sits, unmoving, in the armchair. His eyes rove over me and the case I carry. He shakes his head.

"I cannot do it anymore." He runs shaking hands through his hair, then leans his face into them, speaking to the ground. "Every time, I am weaker. Every time it takes me longer to recover. You must help me, Mercia."

"What can I do?"

He stands suddenly and pulls his shirt over his head. He turns his back to me and points at the base of his neck, where there is a lump bigger than a vertebrae. I put down the case and step over to him. I run my fingers over the knots, then down his spine, finding more bumps than should be there; my hand trembles to touch him so. I squint in the dim light and examine the line of bone more carefully, fingertips delicately moulding and shaping what lies there, unrelenting and stubbornly . . . fibrous.

"It's mistletoe," Gwern says, his voice vibrating. "It binds me here. I can't remove it myself, can't leave the grounds of the school to seek out a physick, have never trusted any of the little chits who come here to learn the art of slaughter. And dearly though I would love to have killed the Misses, I would still not be free for this thing in me binds me to Alder's Well." He laughs. "Until you, little sneak-thief. Take my knife and cut *this* out of me."

"How I can I do that? What if I cripple you?" I know enough to know that cutting into the body, the spine, with no idea of what to do is not a good thing—that there will be no miraculous regeneration, for mortal magic has its limits.

"Do not fear. Once it's gone, what I am will reassert itself. I will heal quickly, little one, in my true shape." He turns and smiles; kisses me and when he draws away I find he has pressed his hunting knife into my hand.

"I will need more light," I say, my voice quivering.

He lies, facedown, on the bed, not troubling to put a cloth over the coverlet. I pull on the brown kid gloves from the kit and take up the weapon. The blade is hideously sharp and when I slit him, the skin opens willingly. I cut from the base of the skull down almost to the arse, then tenderly tease his hide back as if flensing him. He lies still, breathing heavily, making tiny hiccups of pain. I take up one of the recently lit candles and lean over him again and peer closely at what I've done.

There it is, green and healthy, throbbing, wrapped around the porcelain column of his spine, as if a snake has entwined itself, embroidered itself, in and out and around, tightly weaving through the white bones. Gwern's blood seeps sluggishly; I slide the skean through the most exposed piece of mistletoe I can see, careful not to slice through *him* as well. Dropping the knife, I grasp the free end of the vine, which thrashes about, distressed at being sundered; green sticky fluid coats my gloves as I *pull*. I cannot say if it comes loose easily or otherwise—I have, truly, nothing with which to compare it—but Gwern howls like a wolf torn asunder, although in between his shouts he exhorts me not to stop, to finish what I've started.

And finally it is done. The mistletoe lying in pieces, withering and dying beside us on the bloodstained bed, while I wash Gwern down, then look around for a needle and strand of silk with which to stitch him up. *Never mind*, he says, and I peer closely at his ruined back once more. Already the skin is beginning to knit itself together; in places there is only a fine raised line, tinged with pink to show where he was cut. He will take nothing for the pain, says he will be well soon enough. He says I should prepare to leave, to pack whatever I cannot live without and meet him at the alder well. He says I must hurry for the doorway will stay open only so long.

I will take my notebook, the quills and inkpots Mater Friðuswith gave me, and the pounce pot Delling and Halle gifted when I entered the Citadel. I lean down, kiss him on his cool cheek, which seems somehow less substantial but is still firm beneath my lips and fingers.

The manor is empty of Alys and the girls and the Misses have locked themselves away in the library to mull over Mother Magnus's refusal, to work through a list of suitable names that might be invited—begged— to come and teach us poisons. I shall sneak through the kitchen, tiptoe past the library door, snatch up my few possessions and be well on my way before anyone knows I am gone.

All the things I thought I wanted have fallen away. The *Compendium*, the Citadel, the Murcianii, none of that matters anymore. There is only Gwern, and the ache he causes, and whatever mysteries he might offer me. There is only *that*.

All well and good, but as I step out from the kitchen passage into the entry hall, I find Orla and Fidelma standing on the landing of the main staircase. They turn and stare at me as if I am at once a ghost, a demon, an enemy. Time slows as they take in the green ichor on my white apron—more than enough to tell a tale—then speeds up again as they begin to scream. They spin and whirl, pulling weapons from the walls and coming towards to me, faces cracked and feral.

"What have you done?" screeches the one—Fidelma carries a battleaxe. Orla wields a mace—how interesting to see what is chosen in fear and anger, for slashing and smashing. None of the subtlety we've been taught these past months. Not such Quiet Women now. Angry warriors with their blood up.

I turn tail and hare away, back along the passageway, through the kitchen and breaking out into the kitchen garden. I could turn and face them. I still have Gwern's knife in my pocket, its blade so sharp and shiny, wiped all clean. I could put into practice the fighting skills they've taught me these past months. But how many have they put beneath the ground and fed to the worms? I am but a scribe and a thief. And besides: in all they've done—to this moment—they've been kind, teaching me their art, and I've repaid them with deception, no matter what I think of the way they've treated Gwern. I would rather flee than hurt them for they have been my friends.

I cross the lawn and launch myself into the woods, ducking around trees, hurdling low bushes and fallen branches, twigs slashing my face. At last, I stumble into the clearing and see the well—and the alder, which is now different in its entirety. The ropes and ribs of mistletoe have withered and shrunk, fallen to the ground, and the tree shines bright as angel wings, its trunk split wide like a dark doorway. And before it stands . . . before it stands . . .

Gwern, transformed.

Man-shaped as before, but almost twice as tall as he was. A crown of stripped whistle-wood branches, each finial topped with rich black alder-buckthorn berries, encircles his head. His pitch-hued cloak circles like smoke and his ebony-dark hair moves with a life of its own. His features shift as if made from soot vapour and dust and ash—one moment I recognise him, the next he is a stranger. Then he sees me and smiles, reaching forth a hand tipped with sharp, coal-black nails.

I forget my pursuers. I forget everything. And in the moment where I hesitate to take what Gwern is offering me—what the *Erl-King* is offering me—in that moment I lose.

I am knocked down by a blow to the back—not weapon-strike, thankfully, but one of the Misses, tackling me, ensuring I don't have a fast, clean death. That I will be alive while they inflict whatever revenge they choose. I roll over and Fidelma is on me, straddling my waist, hoisting the battleaxe above her head, holding it so the base of the handle will come down on me. I fumble in my pocket, desperate and as she brings her arms down, I jam Gwern's knife upwards, into her stomach. I am horrified by how easily the flesh parts, sickened by the doing of something that until now has been an *academic* concern. There is the terror of blood and guts and fear and mortality.

Fidelma's shock is apparent—has no one ever managed to wound her in all her long years? She falls off me and rolls into a ball. Orla, slower on her feet, shoots out of the trees and makes her way to her sister. The mace and chain swings from one hand as she helps Fidelma to her feet.

I look upwards at the pair of them, past them to the cloudless blue sky.

Fidelma spits her words through blood, "Bitch."

Orla, raises the mace with determination.

I am conscious, so conscious of the feel of the grass beneath me, the twigs poking through the torn fabric of my grey blouse and into the bruised flesh of my back. I turn my head towards the alder tree, to the where the split in the trunk has closed; to the empty spot where Gwern no longer stands. I watch as the trunk seems to turn in on itself, then pulse out, one two three, then in again and out—and out and out and out until finally it explodes in a hail of bright black light, wood, branches and deadly splinters sure as arrows.

When my ears stop ringing and my vision clears I sit up slowly. The clearing is littered with alder and mistletoe shards, all shattered and torn. The well's roof has been destroyed, the stones have been fractured, some turned into gravel, some blocks fallen into the water. The next Murcianii pilgrim will have difficulty drinking from this source. I look around, searching for Fidelma and Orla.

Oh, Fidelma and Orla.

My heart stops. They have been my teachers, friends, mentors. I came to them with lies and stole from them; they would have killed me, no question, and perhaps I deserved it. They stole from Gwern long before I came, yes, kept him against his will; yet I would not have had them end like this.

Fidelma and Orla are pinned against the trees opposite the ruined alder, impaled like butterflies or bugs in a collection. Look! Their limbs so tidily arranged, arms and legs stretched out, displayed and splayed; heads lolling, lips slack, tongues peeking between carmined lips, eyes rolling slowly, slowly until they come to a complete stop and begin to whiten as true age creeps upon them.

I look back at the broken alder; there is only a smoking stump left to say that once there was a tree, a shadow tree, a doorway for the Erl-King himself.

He is gone, but he saved me. And in saving me, he has lost me. I cannot travel through this gate; it is closed to all who might recognise it.

I will go back to the house.

I will go back to St Dymphna's and swiftly pack my satchel before Alys finds her poor dead girls. I will take the *Compendium* from its place in the library—it can be returned to the Citadel now the Meyricks will not pursue it. In the stables I will saddle one of the fine long-necked Arabian mares the Misses keep and be on the road before Alys's wails reach my ears.

Shadow trees. Surely there are more—there must be more, for how else might the Erl-King travel the land? In the Citadel's Archives there will be mention of them, surely. There will be tales and hints, if not maps; there will be a trail I can follow. I shall seek and search and I shall find another.

I will find one and let the shadow tree open itself to me. I will venture down to the kingdom of under-earth. I will find him and I will sleep in his arms at last.

By My Voice I Shall Be Known

If I still had a voice, I would cry out.

The fabric is thick and my needle blunt—I should have sharpened it before now—so I put too much weight behind my thrust and forced the point. Not only the quilt, but also my finger is impaled. I do not wail, though I long to, determined not to make the hideous grunt that is the only noise left to me. In my memory, I still hold the sound of my voice, but each time I *bellow* it lessens, chips away at the timbre so lovingly preserved in recollection. Slowly, carefully, I draw the thread fully through, then pull my injured digit off the silver shaft. A scrap of spare cloth is wrapped around the glistening blue-ruby drop, then the needle itself is assiduously cleaned. I set the bulky bundle of material aside and limp, my legs stiff from hours of sitting, to the basin in the far corner of the tiny room Mother Magnus has given me. Washing the injury, applying a salve, then bandaging the deep wound; I look out the window, not really seeing so much as remembering what is there before me.

Bellsholm sprawls along the banks of the wide Bell River, loose-limbed as a sleeping giant; a rough crescent with its northern tip truncated by the bulk of the Singing Rock. In the foothills that hug the edge of the town some few ramshackle houses have crept, not too high, and certainly nothing up on the majestic outcropping of the promontory. At the furtherest boundaries there are farms to supply the markets and businesses best located away from the centre of town, such as the carriage maker, the foundry, the marble worker's studio, three carpentry and joinery firms, and Ballantyne's Coffin Emporium where the strange woman employs four apprentices and, rumour has it, keeps a locked room filled entirely with mirrors. There is also the hostelry, where travellers with no interest in the hamlet can rest, eat, exchange their tired horses for fresh ones, then continue their journeys. Down by the river are the docks, brimming and bobbing with great ships from afar filled with all the finest things a prosperous place requires, and small local boats that bring in fish and travel up and down the reaches too narrow for the caravels and barques.

I can hear, dimly, the melodies of the *rusalky*, wafting up from the base of the Rock, where they laze daily (except Sundays when the sound of church bells sends them into hiding) and serenade anyone who will listen. Murdered maidens, those unfortunate in love, gather their spirits to sit on the rocks, dangling luminescent toes in the water. The weak of will may traipse too close and fall in. Some drown. The locals are, by now, mostly inured to the strains and are all brought up to swim like eels—indeed, Léolin will tell you that as a young man only his strong stroke saved him on the day when he was distracted by a particularly lovely ballad. The greatest danger is to travellers, on ships and on the roads, unfamiliar with our ladies.

My finger aches and throbs and drags me back to the four-walled space with its thin-mattressed brass bed, ancient velvet-covered chaise, stand of drawers, and the single lantern to brighten my nights. I must ignore the pain and get back to my work. To the quilt, the wedding quilt; the wedding quilt that should have been mine.

Adlai made his money on the ships.

I cannot say when we first met, for it seemed he was always there beside me as we two orphans made our way in the world—but our whole time together, reason tells me, could not have been more than three years. So, perhaps we met soon after I first came here, hoping to find a home. I had a voice then. A voice with which to sing and shout, speak and chant, to laugh and sometimes lie. I had a voice to say "Yes" when he asked me to lie with him, to say "Aye" when he begged "Marry me," to say "Please" when asked if he should read to me that which I could not for myself, and to bid him "Farewell, fair winds" when he sailed off on his very first journey. He—*we*—had scrimped and saved, set aside the money for his passage and the funds needed for the silks and velvets, the barathea and the bayadere, the cashmeres and organzas he would bring back to Bellsholm.

We had not married—all our meagre capital went towards this endeavour, towards *establishing* Adlai—but it was, he assured me, only a matter of time. The first trip was a happy success; the exquisite bolts of cloth were demanded by *modistes*, interior stylists, furniture makers, and craftsfolk whose living lay in creating elaborate curtains and cushions and bed linen for those with more money than sense. We made a profit, some of which was set aside and the rest reinvested in his next buying expedition.

Adlai's apprenticeship to a gentlemen's costumier did not satisfy him. He did not see any way that he might *rise*—even were he to inherit the business from his master some way down the track, he would not reach the heights he desired for himself. There would be no grand house in the Vines district (itself a tiny created island, surrounded by a diverted channel of the river, and accessed by six tidy bridges), no closed fiacre in red and black, no servants, no piles of money gradually accruing interest in the Bellsholm Bank, and—did I but know it—no well-bred wife to admire it. All that life guaranteed for him was continued servitude to those above, measuring coats and breeches, cutting waistcoats from splendid cloth he himself would never wear.

As funds accumulated, so our accommodations grew finer—or rather, so *his* grew finer. From the garret atop the gentlemen's outfitter, to a small room in Mrs Xavier's Rooming House, thence to a larger chamber, then to a suite with two rooms, then three, then four, until finally he purchased a tall house in Lady's Mantel Court. It was three-storeys high and, by all accounts, equipped with five bedrooms, an attic with space to store seven servants, a subterranean kitchen, and a large tidy garden out back. The facade was smoothed plaster, painted apricot and white, with shimmering filigree touches on the window and door fittings. A high wrought iron fence, black, with gold and silver finials on each spike, kept the common riff-raff on the street where they belonged. A riot of well-tended flowers bloomed in the front garden.

Adlai then handsomely paid those very same furniture makers and interior designers, curtain and linen and cushion makers, who had sought

his wares so avidly, to decorate his new home. The perfectly serviceable
fittings and furnishings left by the former owners (an importer of wines
and his wife and sons, fallen on hard times due to the predations of pirates)
were thrown out on the streets, and quickly snatched up by those with less
cash and more cunning. The old drapes were piled beside padded chairs,
sets of drawers, myriad duchesses and chaises; these textiles, hardly faded,
disappeared rapidly, only to reappear not many days later as dresses for
girls and exuberant sailor suits for boys. Wallpaper, that had clung vertical
for barely twelve months, was scraped off and burned in the basement
furnace. Everything, it seemed, must be *new*.

In the end, the abode at Number Six Lady's Mantel Court outshone
its neighbours. Adlai Alveson's social status climbed as well—prosperity
turned his humble origins into a mere bagatelle, easily overlooked. He
became a member of the chamber of commerce, of the town council,
and gained in short order a reputation as something of a philanthropist
with donations to the orphanage and the home for sailors' widows. His
betters (some still in full possession of their affluence, others rather
impoverished but with breeding in spades), soon turned speculative eyes
toward him. Few things open doors like a rapidly expanding fortune.

Why did I not move in with him as his lodgings changed? I asked—
oh, I did ask!—and was assured it would happen, but not yet, not at *that*
precise moment. He promised most faithfully that it should come to pass,
but for the sake of propriety, it would only be after the wedding, the date
of which seemed to shift like the horizon each time I enquired. And I did
not push, for after all, wasn't Adlai the one doing all the work? Wasn't he
the one who travelled and travailed to ensure our future? So I remained,
faithfully, steadfastly, in the attic room above my place of employ, Sally
Sanders Quality Quilts, sewing counterpanes for people's weddings,
stitching in tiny spells and good luck charms to help happiness, fertility,
and longevity attach themselves to a couple's life together. Putting aside
the money I made—for I wanted a wedding dress worthy of the name—
and making my own quilt out of the lovely scraps my mistress let me
harvest from the leftovers of the bedspreads I made for other women.

Adlai would visit, bringing gifts: kid gloves of deepest red, embroidered handkerchiefs, hats so light they seemed made of gossamer and wishes, a thimble, sharp scissors so beautifully crafted they appeared art rather than implement, and an enamelled brooch in the shape of a lovers' knot, which disappeared almost as soon as it arrived—Adlai said its clasp was loose, he would have it fixed, but it never again came into my possession. These presents, when they ceased, were soon replaced by small piles of coin before he left of a morning—or an evening—but I did not recognise them for what they were: payment for services rendered. He told me fewer and fewer of his dreams, rarely reading to me, never mentioning the time when we would marry and I would join him in his grand home.

Still and all, I welcomed him with open arms each and every time, greeted him with patience and trust—although truth be told I ignored the things that gave me pause. The fear of being alone was too great in those days, of being set aside—if I did not look directly at it, I felt certain I would not see it and if I did not see it then surely it could not exist. So I blinded myself quite willingly, showed him the designs I'd drawn for our wedding quilt, told him of the enchantments and charms I'd created just for us. How this would be my finest work, and we would be bonded more strongly than any lovers had ever been. I did not notice, then, how he changed the subject, nor how he failed to answer questions that pertained to our future. I filled the silences, the gaps between us with mindless chatter, busy useless noise. Had I but known my voice had only a short time to remain, I'd have chosen my words more scrupulously, used my breath more wisely, said things of importance, rather than babbling inanely.

I creep to the edge of the water, hang out over the bank like a weeping branch. The current is fast, the surface touched by a light cold mist that floats up towards me—it will burn off when dawn breaks properly. In the weak pearly light, I can see my quarry, dozing on a horse-shaped rock but a long leap away.

In sleep, the *rusalka* has lost some of her form. In the sunlight, when they know they're watched, they are careful to keep the shape they had in life; slumbering, they grow forgetful and let the changes wrought by experience and death come to the fore. The skin has a greenish tint, the hair a life of its own—not a gentle undulation as if shifted by eddies, but an angry serpentine motion. I can see, if I look closely, the holes in her body where the rot has eaten through.

I select a pebble from the ground and take careful aim. The thing on the rock jerks awake when hit, all grace lost to surprise; she hisses, her teeth sharp, and eyes backlit by an unholy light. I shudder, just a little, but I do not show fear when her glare lands on me. I straighten and begin my dumb show. She calms as she realises there is a deal to be made, and relaxes back into her daylight aspect: long-limbed, golden-haired, smiling, teeth as neat and white as pearls, gaze as blue as a summer sky.

I tap at my eyes, so she knows where things start, then my fingertips patter on my cheeks, miming rain. She cocks her head to the side, lifts an eyebrow; she knows what *I* want, but wonders what I will give in return. From the pocket of my apron, I draw an embroidered swathe of white cambric and slowly unfold its layers so she may view what lies therein. Her eyes go wide, and I hide a smile, knowing I will get my way in this thing. I look down at the long, thick plait of auburn-rose hair curled around and around, all three yards of it, thick as a baby's arm. The length that once hung down my back. I brushed it one hundred times to make sure it shone like richest cinnabar, then carefully plaited it before Magnus, protesting at the loss, cut it carefully off with the large, sharp scissors I reserve for shearing through thick fabrics. Magnus swore the murdered maids would find it irresistible, and I would need something irresistible if I was to gain the first ingredient.

The *rusalka* nods, this bargain too good to refuse, although I cannot imagine what she will use the tresses for; I do not care.

I pull a golden vial from my apron and carefully toss it towards her; she snatches it from the air, quick as a snake. She appears to concentrate and then, as if on cue, she weeps. No actress treading the stages of the great cities could do better. Sluggish silver tears creep down her cheeks and she holds the ampoule up to catch them, first one side, then the next. She cries freely, generously. When she is done, she pushes the stopper home, making sure nothing can escape, then slips down the rock and swims to me in a flash of white skin-now scales, flashing feet-now tail. She reaches up and offers me the vial; I reach down and give her the coil of hair; we swap our treasures at the same moment.

We both smile, each certain that she has gained the better part of the bargain.

On the day the *Revenant* docked, I was placing the last stitches in *my* quilt, the silver thimble he'd brought me all the way from Lodellan shining on my pointer finger. Pure damask, a double wedding ring pattern embroidered in argent threads. Between the two internal layers of padding I had sewn a series of tokens: tiny sterling horseshoes, miniature bags containing sprigs of apple blossom, yet others of althea and balm of gilead, cardamom and clove, rose and lavender; love knots and bows, four coins (one for each corner), and seersucker clovers.

And it was white, so white, white as snow, white as bone.

I finished my task, dexterously folded the coverlet, wrapped it in a laurel green cloth, tied it all together with a silk ribbon, then gently placed it in the box of reinforced hunter-coloured brocade decorated with gold lace trim. The box with the tiny stain in one corner that was ruined for customers, but which Mistress Saunders was more than happy to let me have. I wonder now, as I did not then, why I was so willing to accept second best things.

Outside, the air was fresh and intoxicating after a morning of being cooped up in my attic room. I wandered down to the docks, thinking to buy some of the sweet small fish Léolin kept aside, perhaps a fresh loaf of bread, which would be delicious today and passable tomorrow. As I neared, I could hear the sounds of ships creaking against moorings, of men shouting to one another, of cargo and baggage being hefted to and fro, and, beneath it all, the carillon peel of *rusalky* voices on the breeze. Salt aromas clung to hulls that had known the seas but days before, and I daydreamed of voyages I would take alongside Adlai.

"Careful, hen, or you'll fall in the drink. C'mon, pay attention now." Léolin's rough voice was belied by the kindness in his tone. He was tall and broad, blond and bearded, with skin red and rugged. He made a good living, but smelled like fish. "You're looking pleased with yourself, and your feet are barely touching the ground."

"I've finished my quilt, laid the last stitch," I fairly sang, and his face darkened.

"You'll be looking for your man, then," he observed, and shook his head, began adjusting the shiny grey bodies all lined up on the bench of his stall. "Wait; I'm sure he'll have business hereabouts."

He lifted his chin and I followed the direction of his gaze.

The *Revenant* was a clipper from Breakwater; it plied the seas then crept up rivers like ours, to despatch passengers and some cargo—mostly high end, expensive and small, cargo and passengers both—and it was a vessel on which Adlai had taken passage more than once. A party of five was tripping down the gangplank. A pretty pink miss with large eyes led them, with a parasol to protect her, an ecru and lapis dress with bustle and gold lace cuffs, her caramel-coloured hair all caught up in a net with the sheen of spider silk covered with morning dew, and a teeny-tiny hat perched on the crown of her head, tilted ever so slightly to the left. She was accompanied by an older woman, grey-haired, grey-gowned, with a black mourning veil wrapped tight about her face as if her private grief might never be allowed to escape; two girls—the Miss's sisters? cousins?—not yet in their twenties, who looked like twin roses in coral dresses and white gloves; and there was a man, old, serious in appearance, with the air of a majordomo about him—a man used to organising affairs.

I watched and listened as arrangements were made for their effects to be decanted from the ship as soon as possible and delivered, post-haste, to the house at Number Six Lady's Mantel Court. As I pondered this there was the sound of a carriage clattering to a halt; a fiacre, shining with red and black lacquer and gold fittings, drawn by four night-coloured horses, each with ebony leather trappings studded with brass bits and fastened with brass buckles. The conveyance pulled up and Adlai, lithe and resplendent in pale fawn breeches, hand-crafted square-toed shoes, brocade tailcoat with emerald buttons, white silk shirt, golden cravat, and a magnificent waistcoat of cream and cerise and wheat, stepped forth. He bowed so deeply to the lady at the centre of the party that I thought his fine tricorne hat (in shades of chocolate) might fall from his cinnamon curls. But no; it was judged perfectly, his obeisance, like all things Adlai had done—had *learned* to do—all the things that drew him further from me.

When he straightened, he was bold—but just the right amount—stepping in close to the pretty girl, one hand on her elbow, the other around her waist, his lips to her ear, almost touching, and I could see the wet glimmer of his tongue as he spoke words no one else could hear, but which I suspected I knew, for he had told them to me enough times. But to her—to her he would mean them. On her left hand glistened a fat sapphire set in gold, a piece I recognised. He had shown it to me and promised it would be mine, one day. And I noticed at that very moment, the flash of enamel at the join of her prim collar, twisted in the shape of a lovers' knot.

The *rusalky* chorus, which had been as steady a rhythm as an untroubled heartbeat, seemed to swell at that moment, impossibly high. Penetrating the air between their rocky domain and the docks, shocking all who heard it, making eardrums ring. Or perhaps that was simply my perception.

Then Adlai broke contact, and time moved again. He greeted the governess, the twins, the majordomo, and bustled them all towards the fiacre, which would be snugly packed, but he would sit so close, so close to the pretty girl, perhaps she would be almost in his lap—propriety suspended a little, after all, they were affianced and such a man could surely be trusted with a lady's honour. Certainly with a *lady's* honour. Not that, though, of a stupid illiterate quilter.

I watched. He was the last to climb into the carriage and he must have felt the weight of my gaze, for he turned and found me, standing in my faded lavender dress, with its made-over sleeves, patches, and many-times-repaired hem, the white lace applied to make it seem not so poor. For I spent no money on clothes, setting it all aside at first for his voyages then later when he stopped needing it, for our wedding, *our* life. For all the things that would never happen.

He smiled at me, sadly, nervously.

I wondered how long he'd thought he could get away with it. Not even I could tell myself she was a guest, the daughter of a business partner simply passing through, being offered hospitality. Perhaps I would have tried, had it not been for that *look*, that last look as he turned his head and hauled himself into the carriage and I saw him seated beside the pretty girl, one hand lightly laid over her pale two.

Léolin's paw was heavy with sympathy on my shoulder and, did I but realise it, hope. I heard him say my name and it occurred to me, finally, that Adlai had not used it for some time.

After the sun had set and good folk were sitting down to their evening meal, I took one of the bridges to the Vines District. I was unsure what I would do. Whether I would knock on that pastel door, ask to speak to the master of the house. Whether I would simply stand on the corner cloaked in twilight and watch the windows as people moved past them, carrying tapers to light lamps and candles. Whether I would take one of the stones I had placed in my pockets and hurl it at those very same windows, purely for the joy of hearing the shattering of their expensive glass and the high-pitched shrieks of well-bred women.

As it transpired I had no chance to do anything.

From behind, hands grabbed me and pulled me into deeper shadows. A cloth came over my mouth and nose, stinking of belladonna. Sleep was swift.

I run a finger across the stump of my tongue. It no longer aches, the scars are smooth now with the stitches removed and the blood-crusts gone. Despite the absence I still sometimes think it yet remains—a phantom tongue to match my phantom voice.

Setting aside the quilt, I stand—this *new* quilt is all but ready, the two halves finely made, some strips and scraps of my old wedding quilt worked in, so that skerricks of lost hopes and broken dreams will cling to it. It needs only to be pinned and sewn together, then the pattern I have chosen stitched, but the second ingredient is needed.

From beneath my bed, I draw a cup of water. Last night it was clean and clear when I placed it there. Now it is black and churns of its own accord, filled with the nightmares that would otherwise plague me if I did not employ this simple piece of magic to draw them away and trap them. Carefully, I add it to the contents of the stout earthenware jar Magnus gave me. I slide the flat copper disk into place then heat the stick of red wax, and seal the container, blowing gently to cool and set it quickly. I move into the sitting room, which is filled with light from the large windows and thence to the lean-to which runs off the kitchen. This is where Magnus grinds her herbs, mixes her potions, and casts her spells; a small area, cramped, its shelves over-laden, and hanging from the ceiling are bunches of dried plants waiting their turn to be made into something *else*. I place the jar on the workbench where it will be ready for her when she returns, and hidden from Léolin when he arrives.

Mother Magnus is a hedge witch. She is not shunned, nor is she embraced. She is, however, accepted as an essential part of Bellsholm's life. Her magic can shade from white to black, should she choose and should her clients pay enough. Her cottage, neat and tidy, is just at the edge of the town, just before the earth begins to climb, to roll up to the Singing Rock. There are no other dwellings nearby. This, perhaps, was why Léolin brought me here.

In the grey dawn, Léolin out in his dory, noticed what seemed a lavender sack floating downriver; then he recognised the rags of white lace, then the red hair stretching out like waterweed. When he pulled me aboard, I coughed and he had a brief hope, for it was a sign of life— but with that cough came a great gout of blood and a sound—oh, a sound he swears he never wishes to hear again. Something told him not to take me back to the town, not to try the doctors there, the doctors who socialised with Adlai. He made his way to the shore, then carried me to Magnus and begged her to save me.

And save me she did, although for a long while I would not have thanked her for it. She healed the cuts, helped the bruises fade faster, set the breaks in my arm and ribs, and stopped me choking on my own blood where they'd cut out my tongue. Léolin has told me since, somewhat unwillingly, that that particular part of me was taken as proof of my death, presented to my erstwhile beloved. I was fortunate; I suppose that they were too lazy to try for the heart as well. These are the rumours he collects, the whispers from the docks where worlds mix and mingle and good folk might hear terrible things about what has been done and covered up.

Magnus has tried, too, since that day, to mend the breaks in my spirit, but I did not respond until she began to stoke the strange and terrible cold fire of revenge. She knew, I think, that it was the only way to keep me alive, the only way to keep me from sliding into the apathetic darkness of death—for I was determined to walk that path for the longest time.

"Do something," begged Léolin as he sat beside my bed in those first days and weeks. "Do anything."

I wonder if he would have said the same thing if he knew what Magnus dangled before my dimly flickering soul in order to pull me back.

There is a knock, politely tentative. I wait and then the door opens, as always, and Léolin ducks his height under the lintel. He can stand straight inside, but must watch his head. He carries a posy of lilac roses and windflowers; the townsfolk surely must think he is courting Magnus. He blushes to see me and smiles. No matter that he plucked me from the river, that he saw me at my lowest, that he has seen me more in the past few months than he ever did in the time I lived in the town, that he has lain with me, he still flushes like a lad whenever he arrives.

"Hello, my dove, I like your hair." He fingers its sheared edges in wonder. We do not kiss but we do all the other things a courting couple might. Léolin makes plans for us.

"When you're quite better, hen, we'll leave. I have enough for us both. There's anywhere in the wide world we can go; put your finger on a map, choose a compass point and that's where we shall be."

I smile as he speaks and I listen. I wonder sometimes if this was how I sounded to Adlai. Léolin does not know how ruined I truly am.

After he leaves, Magnus discretely returns, her basket filled with medicinal blooms and newly-dug roots, a rabbit or two to feed us for the next few days. She has been trying to teach me my letters. I try, I do, but I cannot help but feel it is merely a distraction—that, having shown me a path, she now wishes to divert me from it.

Magnus is tall, her hair ash-white, but her face belies that colour, the skin smooth and creamy, a wide plum of a mouth—she has not yet crossed over that boundary into the shadow-land where women become invisible. Her figure is fleshy but shapely, her eyes the colour of honey, and her smile is ready.

"I saw Léolin," she says, "on the road."

I simply watch her. We have had this one-sided conversation before and I do not imagine its direction will change.

"He would take you, you know. Take you elsewhere, uproot his whole life all for your sake. You don't have to do what you've planned."

We have made ourselves understood with signals and signs these past weeks and months. When I first came to her, it was she who offered me solutions, with me accepting and refusing alternatively with nods and head shakes. It was she who suggested the option I ultimately chose and now she asks if I am *sure*? I don't even nod, merely lift an eyebrow and look towards the bench in the lean-to, where she can see the earthenware jar awaiting her attention. Awaiting her ministrations so I might have my second ingredient.

I need her and her wide-reaching, her all-encompassing magics—the tiny spells I have always known are white as white can be. They are *good*. But what I need now must be black as the cat curled by the cold kitchen hearth. I pay Mother Magnus in nightmares, in *aqua nocturna*. All I ask in return is a little dust.

"He doesn't know, does he? You will not tell him?"

I shake my head and look away, find the cat regarding me with large green eyes.

"Are you sure?" she asks. "Certain this is the path you wish to take?"

I nod, and stare at her so she cannot mistake the answer. She blows out a heavy breath and I think she deflates a little, seems to age, to bow and bend; then the moment is past and she inclines her head.

The bottom half of the quilt lies across my bed. I have covered my mouth with a cloth, as per Magnus's instructions, so I don't breathe in any of the dust made from the water of my nightmares. "Do not waste a speck," she said. Attentively, I upend the black pouch and sprinkle its contents over the fine white felt I have used as a warm lining. I make sure it is evenly distributed and as I watch each particle worms its way into the fabric, disappearing, embedding itself into the fibre and the future. When I can no longer see the argent-grey gilings, I lay the top half over and pin it in place. Then I pin the pattern that I will quilt, much as I did when I made my own, but this time I make a forest of trees, which a careful eye might note is actually a nest of serpents, but I make their long bodies look like trunks, their heads and tongues seem like flowers, all so intertwined that only the most alert, the most perspicacious might notice the malice sewn there. I place stitches with a silver thread, spun by Magnus from the *rusalka's* tears.

When I am finished, my eyes and hands ache. I show the coverlet to Magnus. "Just in time," she says, fingering the border thoughtfully.

While the inhabitants of Bellsholm are either at the wedding of Adlai and the girl I now know to be Edine, daughter of a rich Breakwater merchant, or celebrating it in one of the taverns, I will set foot in the house at Number Six Lady's Mantel Court for the one and only time. Covered and cloaked, I have wandered and stalked, meandered and crept through the town's streets and byways so many evenings these past months, moving like a spectre unseen and unsuspected. Magnus gave me a pair of soft slippers, their soles enchanted to muffle any noise I might make.

Now I move towards the Vines district in the dimness of dusk, my gift carefully wrapped and bundled on my back like a pack; I sidestep revellers and avoid any who might be sober enough to peer under my hood, perchance to recognise my face. And I slide through the tiny lane behind Lady's Mantel Court, where there is a back gate for deliverymen to use. I sidle up the gravel path, making not a sound, and thence inside through the servants' entrance, left unlocked so those preparing for the happy couple's return might enter and exit with ease. Up the stairs to the second floor, along the corridor towards the front of the house, where there is only one door—the master bedroom runs the width of the building.

The room is a symphony of grey-blues and creams, and all the furniture is of white oak: a roll-top desk, dresser drawers, a vanity complete with cushioned stool, two matching armchairs and a chaise longue placed around a delicate low table inlaid with mother-of-pearl. A walk-in dressing room and bathroom are at one end, and at the opposite, a canopied bed.

Upon it already lies a quilt. I look it over, wasting precious moments with professional contempt. The stitching is shoddy, the design mundane—flowers and rabbits—it may well be the work of my former Mistress; she had not sewn since I began to work for her and it seems her skill has deserted her. I yank the spread away, rolling it tightly and pushing it under the bed, where the layers of ruffled valance will hide it from prying eyes. I replace it with the coverlet of my making. It is perfect; even if anyone should notice the change, no one will remove it—not so close to the wedding night when another might not be found, and certainly not when it is as exquisite as this.

When I leave, the eiderdown is lying inert, snowy and lovely, waiting for the third ingredient.

Back at the cottage I help Magnus prepare. We both know Bellsholm will not be safe after this night; we fill carpetbags with all the possessions she refuses to be without. I do not know why she aided me at such cost to herself. Perhaps she simply felt it is time to move on; perhaps her outrage at what was done to me is what made her act; perhaps, as she tended me when I first woke and voiced a sound to make the Devil weep . . . perhaps she cannot live here without hearing it over and again. We load the small sturdy buggy and harness the tall horse, then she says once again, hopelessly, "Go to him. Now. He is a good man. He will take care of you."

I hug her hard and let her go; she climbs into the buggy with a sigh. The black cat is perched on the seat beside her, eyeing me wearily. Mother Magnus slaps the reins and the horse, somewhat startled, moves forward with a snappy gait. I watch until they disappear into the darkness of the bend that accommodates the insistent bulk of the Singing Rock, then I go inside. Enough of her things are left in the cottage that any folk who seek her out, who believe her behind what will happen, will not think her fled. They will wait here for her to come home, and by the time they realise she is gone, pursuit will be futile, and I—I will be beyond them too.

As the dark hours creep by, I sit sewing pointless, shapeless samplers, using up threads and scraps, listening in vain for the great swelling arias and canticles floating from the *rusalky* damozels, the sopranos and contraltos, with the altos winging between. But they will not sing again until daybreak. Sometimes I make flowers, other times animals, yet other times geometric shapes layered on top of one another. I work thus until I doze upright in the armchair. With no glass of water beneath the bed my dreams run riot, but this night they are different; they transport me, it seems, to the bridal chamber, to unwillingly watch as Adlai takes Edine as gently as a husband might a new bride, he with soft caresses, she with noises all reluctant that are given lie by her heavy-lashed gaze and the hearty wet kisses she bestows on him. Then there is the moment, when she cries out, surprised that he has hurt her, surprised that the pleasure has ended in pain, in tearing, in the blood her governess warned her about but to which she had not truly given credence.

I wake when the maids by the Rock begin their vocal exercises, an acrobatic warming of throat and voice, and I have but half an hour at best. I wrap the cloak about me once more and run.

I am breathless by the time I reach Lady's Mantel Court, and the morning light grows brighter. I stand on the pavement across from that house and watch the windows, listen intently until there is a scream, muffled by glass and thick curtains. Moments pass like breath as folk throw off their slumber, then a male voice, a grunt, and a howl. Adlai sees his bride, but not as he expected, not as he had seen her last night. I wonder at the horror I have created, for all my dreams since Adlai's men took my tongue and left me for dead have been of a spliced woman, her torso female, her lower half a serpent's tail. All it required was the third ingredient, which only the bride could provide: blood—so much better if it was virginal—to seal the spell, to make the nightmare dust and tear-threads come to life.

More bellows and cries now—they sound so like me! Servants

waking, rushing, seeing Edine's shame—I am sorry for her, she did me no intentional harm, but she was the means to my end. Now she's a fine bride for a seafaring man.

I turn on my heel and pace steadily, smartly across the bridge opposite the one on which I came. I walk with my head held high, a smile on my face. If I could, I would sing—part of me wants to do it anyway, but I know all I would produce would be a caw even a crow would disdain. In my head, my voice, my true voice sounds, a rich contralto, exultant. In my head, others hear me and turn to listen for as long as they can. I pass people as I go; they take second glances as they recognise me, recoil as if they've seen a ghost. I keep moving until I achieve the edge of the town, then begin to climb the steep winding path to the Singing Rock. The songs grow louder as I approach. I wonder if I will join them, the *rusalky* maids, when I am done. I recognise now that I've held this wish in my heart, refusing to look at it for fear it might be taken away. Now I admit it, acknowledge it, hope to find a place I belong.

I reach the peak and the breeze is strong—I can smell the brine, even though all I can see is the wide river snaking along, a green-brown band cutting its way through sometimes mountains, sometimes flat pasture, sometimes marshlands, sometimes land riven by many, many streams. I cannot see the ocean, though; it is too far away.

What I can see, when I turn my head, is the bright golden halo of Léolin's hair, far below as he knocks upon the cottage door. I hope he will be well, that my betrayal will not break him as I was broken by Adlai. I do not wait to watch him find the place empty.

I step to the edge. The drop is sheer, broken only at the bottom where the *rusalky* have their day nest and recline on stone couches. I can see shining hair in all hues, white blouses and long, long skirts in silver and gold. Perhaps there are bare feet flashing pale and pink or perhaps those are fish. I will be close enough to see soon enough. The wind picks up, buffets me. I wonder idly if Adlai was at all touched by the horrors my nightmares bred or does he stride freely as a man with a crippled wife must? A smile lifts the corners of my mouth. How will he like his Edine now?

How long before she, too, chooses the water?

I take a few steps back, then run, throw myself out into the sky.

I plummet for such a short time, but I do not hit. That is not what stops me. I open my eyes. The songs from beneath rise, knit themselves together, catch at me as a golden net. They pull me down slowly, slowly, gently towards the surface of the river. I hover above it, unable to move either up or down, thwarted utterly, as the murdered maids watch me sadly.

"You have no voice. You cannot join us," says the one, then the other, then another, then all the voices threading and weaving one into the next to make a chorus of the same words. The same ribbons of sound, wrapping around and around me, telling me that there will be no welcome here. One of them watches me with a spiteful gleam in her bluer-than-blue eyes, as if she knew my hopes and bided her time until they might be crushed; around her shoulders is a cloak woven of auburn-rose locks, lined with the tiniest chips of stars. Then the net is gone, that wonderful thing of light and sound disappears like a puff of smoke, and I am dropped into the Bell River. The current picks at me, the waters fill my skirts, making me heavier and heavier, pulling me *beneath*, and out towards the sea.

My nose and mouth fill. I give myself up to the flow—for a moment— then there is drowning and darkness and the actuality of a slow death and I begin to fight. I rip at the catch of my skirts, fingers numb, finally tearing at the band; the buttons wetly give way and all that complexity of petticoats, old lace and weary gingham fall away, down, a'down, into the depths of the Bell. Then my jacket is gone too, and the broderie blouse, and the clever, quiet slippers carelessly discarded after such good service. And here I am naked but for a shivering thin shift, a skin of muslin plastered to me by the press of the tide, which lifts me up and carries me downstream. Towards Breakwater, towards any of more than a dozen tiny places identical to Bellsholm, towards the open sea.

SISTER, SISTER

THE FINAL HYMN IS BEING SUNG OFF-KEY and I suspect the choir-master will not be pleased. I smile, imagining his scowl as he tries to locate the culprit amongst those angel-faces. Imagination is all I have at this distance, there's very little to see from the arse-end of the Cathedral.

Pillars, posts, baptismal fonts, and other members of the faithful all ruin the landscape. My kind are tolerated in church, but only just. This is not the view I used to have; once, I sat in the pews up front, those with little gates on the side to let everyone know how special we were.

Once, I was *on show*.

I still am, I suppose, but now it's looks of pity, occasionally of contempt. Always curiosity. I'd have thought that after six months it would have died down, but apparently not. I hold my head high, meeting cold stares with one even frostier until *they* turn away. But I tolerate this, continue coming back once a week for my daughter's sake. Just because I've lost faith doesn't mean Magdalene should be denied the possibilities of its comfort; besides she loves the theatre of it as only a child can. When she is older she can decide for herself whether there is something genuine to be had.

The archbishop lifts the chalice, makes his final flamboyant gestures, bows his head, and bids those within range of his voice to go in peace. This much I know from memory. Those in the front rows rise and I think I see the flash of Stellan's golden hair and a hook twists in my gut; but I could be mistaken. No sign of the other one though. The flock rises with the rhythm of a wave. One advantage of our lowly seating is its proximity to the door. We, the inhabitants of the inn, are out in the sunlight before the exulted few have managed to move two yards.

Magdalene's hand creeps up to twine fingers with mine, her grip tight and clammy. In the shade of the portico at the top of the steps sit the archbishop's six hounds. Grey and silver in the shadows, insubstantial until someone with ill intent crosses the threshold, then they become suddenly-solid, voracious and vicious. No one wants a resurrected wolf hunting them down. I have explained, over and over, to my little girl that they will do *her* no harm, but there is a core of fear in her that not even her mother can touch.

From across the square comes the sound of a carriage and four. It is the white ceremonial one I rode in on my wedding day. The sheer curtains are drawn but I think I see pale blond hair as the occupant peeks out. Polly, who has yet to attend a church service in all her time in this city. My sister makes no pretence of religious zeal.

Behind us the wolf-hounds growl and Magdalene wails, climbing up my skirts like a terrified monkey. She holds me so tightly I can barely breathe. Grammy Sykes pats her back and talks in a low voice to the wolf-hounds. They react to her tone, settle back to sit in the shadows, the exiting crowd giving them a wide berth. I look at them, wondering who among the press of bodies set the beasts off. Grammy pokes me to move along and we head for home.

The inn is old, so old that if you cut into the walls you might find age rings like those in the great trees of the forest beyond the city walls. The wood panels have been darkened by years, hearth smoke, sweat, tears, and alcohol vapour. If you licked them (as the children sometimes do), you'd taste hops as well as varnish.

The bar itself, where Fra Benedict serves the drinks, is pitted with the marks of drinking vessels slammed down too hard, the irresistible will of dripping liquid, and the musings and graffiti carved by the bored, the drunk, and the lonely when the barman is distracted. The glassware gleams, though, as do the metal fixtures and the bottles behind the bar are kept clean (although it's not as if they stay undisturbed long enough for dust to settle). There are booths with seats covered in balding velvet, and the hiss-hum of the gas lamps (lit low for daytime) is a constant comfort.

Things are quiet at the moment, Sunday afternoon, most of our clients still pretending their piety after Mass this morning. There's only Faideau in a corner booth, his breeches slung low and his shirt stained with wine. He's a poet, he says; drinks like one at any rate. He snores loudly. Fra Benedict will go through his pockets soon for the money he owes, then roust him to move on, to spend at least a few hours out in the sunshine.

In one corner is the crèche, where we whores and wenches leave our children (those of us who have them) under the tender, watchful eyes of Grammy Sykes and her half-wolf, half-something-or-other, Fenric. The small space is scattered with books and toys, which miraculously stay within a reasonable radius. Two little boys, and three girls, one of them Magdalene, three years old and still clad in her red Sunday robe. My little girl, the only reminder that I was once loved.

In the kitchen I can hear Bitsy dropping pans. A few seconds later Rilka chases her out, swearing mildly, which is about as angry as anyone can get with Bitsy, who now stands in the middle of the room, unsure what to do next. Fra Benedict makes his particular peculiar noise to catch her attention, jerks his head for her to come and sit at the bar. He is mute, his tongue having been torn out many years ago in some monastery brawl. Bitsy hoists herself onto one of the high stools and sips at the weak ale and blackberry shandy he pours for her.

Bitsy is a little older than me: her face bears the blankness of youth and her long straight hair is a white blond. She used to be a doll-maker. Not all of them go the same way; she made a special kind of doll, putting tiny pieces of her soul into them. Beautiful dolls, they were (I saw some in a museum, once), but each one left her emptier.

Now she's touched, little more than a doll herself, with just enough wit to sometimes take drinks to tables, wash dishes, and lie still when a client with no need for a real response climbs aboard and lets her giggle beneath him. Fra Benedict is kind to her; I think they are distant cousins.

Rilka's dark head pops out of the kitchen. "Finished with them peas yet, Theodora?"

I shake my head. "Soon, Rilka."

She disappears with a profanity. Rilka was a nun, in her better days.

Now she's just like us. Some men pay extra for her to lose her spectac-ular temper and hurt them. Her special gentlemen callers, she says with a laugh. Tall and muscular, cedar-skinned Rilka doubles as cook.

Kitty thinks Rilka killed someone, tells how she talks in her sleep.

Kitty mends our dresses, sitting in the corner, working on one of those I brought with me, taken apart and made over to fit others. I had no further need of finery. Kitty pulls hard on her final stitch, makes a knot then cuts the thread with her teeth, etching more deeply the tailor's notch in her left front tooth. Her hair is brassy-bright, a touch of red, a touch of gold; it's beautiful and distracts clients from the scars on her face: two running parallel across the bridge of her nose before dropping down her left cheek like deep gutters, relics of an unkind husband. Her eyes are blue and sad.

She holds the dress up for me to see: the green and gold brocade is now short enough to show off Livilla's fine legs, and tight enough around the waist to push her breasts up so they will spill from the top of the bodice. I nod approval just as we hear one of Livilla's loud sighs floating down from an upstairs room. A few seconds later there is a satisfied, bellowing grunt from her client. She has earned her fee for the day.

Fra Benedict and Grammy Sykes, his common-law wife, don't make us take all comers. Most of the men are regulars who know Fra and Grammy keep a fair house with clean, cared-for girls. Sometimes there are women, too, anxious for something soft and gentle as a welcome relief from their husbands' violent prongings. We need only bed one client each day, any after that are up to our discretion. The fee here is high enough and the need for us to work as bar wenches outweighs the pull of the money to be made in excessive bed-sports. One of the advantages of Fra and Grammy's lax policy is that men are anxious to have what might be refused them, so we always have clientele, banging on the doors, hoping to pay for our favours.

Grammy Sykes was a whore once herself; she remembers what it was like, the constant line of hard, demanding cocks. I think she prides herself on being kinder to us than anyone ever was to her. Livilla whispers that Grammy was a great beauty in her day, although there is scant evidence of it now.

Grammy and Fra will both tell you how many of their girls have gone on to better places, indeed, *so* many of their old girls are now the wives of rich and influential men that upper-class dinner parties sometimes resemble a whores' reunion; can't throw a silken shoe without hitting some woman who used to earn her living horizontally. The comfort of a prosperous future is for the other girls. They don't tell me this story.

I finish shelling the peas then turn to polishing the silverware Grammy keeps for the private parlour. I hear the front door open behind me, see the sunlight flare in momentarily before the door closes and the cool dimness is restored. I don't turn around until Fra nods to indicate that the customer is waiting for me.

Prycke was, still is, the Prime Minister. He wanders the capital with minimal guards as if he is still as unimportant now as he was when he was born in the lower slum areas, out near the abattoirs in the furthest, poorest quarters of the city. He's not overly tall, has a stern sallow face, but his eyes are kind. Clad in dark colours, you might not realise how fine the fabrics of his breeches and frock coat are unless you look carefully. The buckles on his shoes catch the light of the gas-lamps and it seems he has stars on his feet.

"Have you a moment, mistress?"

I nod, feeling the precarious pile of dark curls on my head sway; one long tendril breaks free and snakes down my neck. He watches it fall. "My time costs nowadays, sirrah."

He is taken aback, reaches into a pocket and draws forth two gold coins. I raise one finely plucked brow but say nothing. I remain silent until he has extracted seven gold coins, then tell him to pay Fra Benedict.

Prycke follows me upstairs. I choose the room with blue velvet curtains hanging around the four-poster bed and a view of the city, an expanse of roofs and, if you look straight down, the Lilyhead fountain and children playing in its greenish waters. I tug at the loose stays of my dress with one hand and at the single clip in my hair with the other; the russet velvet falls to the floor and torrents of hair tumble down to my waist, obscuring the jut of my breasts. I sweep the tresses back so he gets his money's worth.

He gulps, removes his shoes first (so sensible! So practical! So strategic!), then his coat, and unbuttons his breeches, letting them drop. His legs are pale, hairy, strong. The tip of his cock peeps from under the hem of his shirt, shy, not quite ready. He didn't expect this encounter, I'm sure, at least not this *kind* of encounter.

I lie on the bed, splayed like an open flower, and wait for him.

When we are finished, he avoids my eyes. He slips, calls me *Majesty*. I laugh long and hard at that.

"Would you come back, Ma—madam? If you could?"

"Even if I wanted to, I would not, could not. Another sits in my place." I fix him with a stare, blue and cold.

"Your step-sister, madam, she never sets foot in . . . "

"My *sister*, Prycke, neither step nor half. Only full-blood can hate so well."

"Your husband sent me."

"My *husband* heard me called 'whore' and believed it. My *husband* heard his daughter called 'bastard' and believed that, too." I hiss the words at him, spittle gathering at the corners of my mouth and curse that I still *feel* anything. "Five years together and I gave him no cause to doubt me, but the moment my sister *swears* to him that I had taken lovers he believed her."

"Madam, I was not in the city when it happened. I would have counselled him otherwise," he stammers. He feels badly for *me*. But he did nothing for me.

"For all the good it would have done. My husband brands me *whore* and takes my sister to his bed. So, I embrace my new title, Prycke. I am whore to whoever pays for me." I sit up, step into my gown, lacing it tightly for I have earned my keep for today and tomorrow.

He dresses quickly, a handy skill. "Madam, your sister has a strangeness about her. She is peculiar . . . she does not attend . . . "

I raise my hand. "No more, Prycke. No more." He reaches for the doorhandle. "Prycke?"

He turns back, face hopeful.

"Tell the archbishop I will see him on Tuesday, at our usual time."

"Illustrious company we're keeping," snipes red-haired Livilla, but it's a half-hearted dig. She's feeling generous after her early earnings.

Fra Benedict gives me a grin and flips me a gold coin. I more than double-charged Prycke and the spare is mine.

"My thanks, Fra." I smile at Livilla, then take pity on her and snap the coin down the middle, along the little groove meant for such making of smaller change. Livilla, for all her ill liver, has stood me well in the last six months; this is a small price, to share with her.

"Pippet, moppet, dolly-doll-doll!" Bitsy sings from the crèche, where Magdalene has crawled onto her lap.

"Watch yer childer," slurs Faideau. "Watch 'em after dark."

"Shut up, you sot," Livilla throws in his direction.

"Childer going missing, mark me." Faideau subsides back to his stupor.

"Man at his finest," sneers Rilka. "What a wonderful husband he'll make."

Livilla shrieks with laughter.

"When I remarry," says Kitty dreamily, "I want that fancy bread they make. Queer shapes and all."

"The girl, Emmeline's her name, don't do that no more and she's the one you want. She moved in with some rich fella, the one whose wife choked on *their* wedding bread." Rilka sniggers. "Sure that's what you want?"

I had Emmeline's breads at my wedding, but I don't tell them that.

Kitty tosses her curls. "I want what rich folk have. Her mother still makes the fancy bread; not so good, but still it's the best can be had."

Grammy finishes the argument. "Stop yer yammers. Time to get ready, my girls, clients be here soon, almost five of the after."

We troop upstairs to tidy ourselves. Those who've already earned their horizontal fee taking a little less care than those who have not.

Livilla and I will wench this eve; one of Rilka's beaters is expected, Kitty and Bitsy have no appointments and so will take whoever they like.

～

Restless, I leave my bed and sit at the attic window.

Through the frost-dimmed glass I can see square after square after square, all the way up to the giant square that is the epicentre of this city. All the way up to the Cathedral with its vaunting spire and gothic towers, flying buttresses—as if all possible styles were thrown together with no thought for taste. Right next to the Cathedral lies the Palace, my once and former home.

A small palace but respectable nonetheless, perfectly appropriate for the size and wealth of our city, with sufficient halls and ballrooms and bedchambers and kitchens and wine cellars to ensure we were not embarrassed by the standard of our Palace. Gilt and glass and crystal in all the right places, the chandeliers kept shiny and bright, the wood panelling polished to a warm, rich finish, the brocades and tapestries thick and elaborate. Just the right number of winding staircases, deserted towers, and hidden passageways.

Above it all flies the full-faced moon, soft and cold.

I look at Magdalene, curled into our bed like a kitten. This is the child I did not want. She was the change in my life that was utterly undesired. Stellan, though, he wanted her, wanted an heir, proof of his potency. I spent my pregnancy in a stew of discontent, resentful of being subject to the rhythms of another organism, of a heart beating not quite in time with mine. It was Stellan who would rub my swollen belly, caress the hot distended skin and whisper to what grew within.

He made plans for her, told her about the little city that was her inheritance. He created a future for her then forgot it just as quickly.

In truth, for me it did not happen with speed, the change of heart. I resented her as much in the first few weeks of her life as ever; I shudder to think on the bitter milk she drank from me. I do not believe there was a single moment when it changed: I simply found myself going willingly to her one day, craving the serenity of the times when she fed and I simply sat, we two in our tranquil little bubble. And Stellan stood outside where he was prey to others, although I did not know it at the time.

Bitsy and Livilla and Livilla's sons sleep in the room on one side of us, Rilka and Kitty and their respective daughters in the room on the other;

they will hear her if she wakes. I drop a kiss on her sleep-damp forehead then slip a long black woollen dress over the top of my night-gown and pull on a heavy coat, belting it tightly around my waist.

Under Bitsy's door I can see a splash of light—we have candlelight up here, only gas on the floors below. I tap lightly and go in. Bitsy is in bed, wrapped around a large doll with red hair. Livilla sits in a rocking chair, half-moon glasses balanced on her nose while she reads a scandal-sheet.

"Listen out for Magdalene? I'm going for a walk."

"Bring her in here?"

"Only if she wakes."

"Cost you half a gold coin." She grins wickedly.

"I'd say I'm in credit."

I hear her low laughter as I close the door. My boots I carry downstairs lest I disturb the others. Grammy Sykes is sitting by the fire, asleep, Fenric at her feet. Fra has gone to bed, leaving her to doze. He used to wake her up but sometimes she has fearful dreams and one night she almost took his right eye out, thinking he was one of the things that hunted her in sleep.

"Cold to be going outside, Theodora," she rasps, surprising me and Fenric, who growls grumpily, rolls over, farts, and goes back to sleep.

"Got the wanders, Grammy, itchy feet, bed doesn't feel right." I sit next to her, basking in the warmth of the fire, trying to store up its heat as I put on my boots. "Livilla is listening for Magdalene."

"Watch yourself on the streets. Not just children that go missing."

"I'll be careful. We're not in the worst parts, Grammy, I can handle myself." I lift the knife from the pocket of my jacket, its curved silver length gleaming.

She nods. "Beware all the same. There's a little girl needs you to come back."

I kiss the salt and pepper hair peeking out from under her white cap. "I promise."

The cold steals the breath from my lungs, the winter nights far worse than the days, when we get sunshine to take off the chill. I walk up the middle of the street, trusting that I will see or hear anyone moving in the shadows. I make my way quickly along the cobbles, accompanied by the sound of my own footsteps, the occasional feline yowl, the barking of a stray dog, the rumbling anger of households in turmoil. I feel the houses reaching up, towering over me. I can see under entryways through to the courtyards at the heart of each block, all with a well or a fountain, some with dark gardens and sculptures, some as bare as a newborn.

Soon the Cathedral is in front of me, crouching like one of the gargoyles that embroider its roof. The doors are open, and lights burn inside although it is well after midnight. The archbishop likes his house of worship to be open at all hours; and he trusts that the wolf-hounds will discourage any vandalism. I hold my hand out to the closest one. A shiver passes through me as it pushes its wet, ghostly nose against my palm, and whimpers for a pat I cannot give. I call it sweet and handsome and it settles back to its post. I walk through the great double doors.

Up the aisle, then to the left of the enormous altar, into the small Chapel of the Thirteenth Apostle hidden by a rich tapestry depicting the growth of Saint Radagund's very fine beard. Behind the elaborately carved *prie-dieu* my fingers find the catches carved into its underside and pull. Stone scrapes across stone and a hole appears in the floor at my feet, flagstones whirling aside like a child's puzzle. I take a torch from the wall. The steps are familiar under my boots; the skeletons sleeping in the wall niches feel like old friends.

This passage leads into the Palace, into the rooms I once called my own, before my sister took my place. Specifically, into the fountain room, *my* fountain room. A misleading name, really, as it's actually a bathroom, a marvel of white and blue marble, gold and silver tiles, and crystal and nacre inlays. The roof is made of a continuous sheet of rock crystal, so it seems open to the sky; it's especially beautiful at night.

My boots make a lonely noise as the steps begin to rise, and so I go on tiptoe. I open the hidden door and step out from behind a screen of gold, engraved with a fairytale pattern: Hansie and Greta and their adventure in the cottage made of sugar.

My footsteps sound hollow in this place where once I used to tread so confidently. There are fountains to decorate each corner, cushioned couches and benches, a small wooden hut for steaming oneself, hot and cold plunge baths, and a big swimming pool right in the centre of the room; I stop at its shallow end. The water is dark in spite of the moonlight, almost dirty, thick as blood or treacle. I can see ripples, though, sluggishly coming toward me. I suck in a sharp breath and retreat, back to the shelter of the screen, peering out through the tiny pinpricks in the metal.

It heaves from the depths and shambles up the pool steps to stand in the milky-white moonlight. I can see it clearly: tall but hunched and twisted, straggly black hair, hooked nose, wrinkled skin, long fingers and teeth razor-sharp, empty dugs half-way down its chest, and a great shaggy pubic thatch at the junction of its thighs.

A troll-wife come out of the forest and into the city.

It sniffs the air, treads toward my hiding place with deliberate paces. I don't want to take my eyes from it, but feel my bladder threaten to fail me. At last I look away and slam myself through the doorway; the panel clicks shut behind me with barely a whisper.

I rest my forehead against the cool stone, try to steady my trembling legs. On the other side I can hear cold, hungry breathing, sense uncertainty; sometimes they have trouble knowing how fresh a scent is but they have been known to follow an old one for days, to finally track a meal down, some unwary traveller who thought himself safely home.

There's a low growl that becomes a laugh: knowing and ugly. I turn tail and run.

"Mama, you're hurting me!" I've clung to my daughter so tightly that I've woken her. Morning light trickles in, grey and grim.

"Sorry, my love." I roll onto my back and stare at the ceiling, at the intricacies of the thatch-work that keeps us dry and safe from the weather but nothing more sinister. Magdalene falls back into a doze.

Downstairs, Faideau still snores in his corner; Fra must have given up trying to wake him and send him home. I pour out a measure of mulberry brandy and wave it in front of his nose, a treat. The smell wakes him as surely as frizzling bacon wakes Fenric and makes him dance on his hind legs.

"Breakfast?" I offer.

Red-eyed, he takes the pewter mug and tosses back its contents without a pause. I wince on his behalf but he seems to neither need, nor notice, my sympathy. He lets loose an eye-watering belch and I try to wave the fumes away, but the stench is stubborn.

"I swear your breath comes straight from Satan's arse, Faideau."

"Language, Your Majesty," he waggles a finger.

"You'll hear worse soon if you don't drop that." I tap the back of his hand to get his attention. A map is tattooed there. "Faideau, you said yesterday that children were going missing."

He nods, sombre, if not sober, as a judge. "Six months or a peck more. From all the squares—but mostly from the poorer ones—families as don't have much food and too many small mouths lining up for it. Sometimes they mind and report to Prycke's Peelers, sometimes they don't."

"Any children from around here?"

"Not yet. Mind the inn's childer, Theodora."

I tip another generous slug of brandy into his mug and am rewarded with a smile. "Keep an ear to the ground, Faideau?"

He nods, asks: "Do you know anything, Theodora? Only you look afraid this morn and you never looked afraid the whole time I knowed you."

"I . . . I think there . . . no, Faideau." I shake my head. "I don't *know* anything." I turn toward the kitchen to begin the day's breakfast, look back to him. "Faideau? Are you really a poet?"

His index finger rises and taps at the side of his nose. "Poets are folk what can't write full sentences," he says.

"After this, madam, just one more payment," says the stocky man, handing me a scrappy receipt. "The house is in good repair, and the estate around it. You can hire labour from the village."

"No need for that," I tell him, tucking the scrap into the deep pocket of my skirt. In return I give him a pouch heavy with gold coins, the third such in the past few months.

"Thank you, madam." He hesitates. "I must say I had no idea your particular line of work was so lucrative."

"It's amazing how much men will pay." True, but also true is the fact that I have gradually sold off the gems and jewels I had sewed into the stomach of Magdalene's favourite toy fox when I sensed trouble brewing in the Palace. And of course I have other means of funding our escape.

"One more payment, madam," he repeats. "May I ask when . . . ?"

"Soonest, Mr Spittleshanks, soonest." I stand, take a look around his study as I always do. "Your business is doing well, sir. I see another volume of Murcianus's treatise on folk tales."

He beams that I've noticed. Even a fallen princess is a princess.

"Perhaps madam would like to borrow something to pass the time?"

I laugh. "What a kind offer, but I have plenty to occupy my time, Mr Spittleshanks." He reddens and I add, not unkindly: "Perhaps soon, sir, when my life . . . changes."

We part on good terms. I go to his house for our transactions, entering by the back garden—I prefer no one to know my affairs, there might be questions—and we deal only about the house I am buying. None of my usual "commerce" gets done with him. If I thought it would decrease the cost of the house I would have no compunction, but Mr Spittleshanks is a canny businessman, with a plump, comfortable wife. I suspect he fears anything more—energetic—with me might stop his heart and he would certainly not think bed-sports worth a discount on a property.

I pass through the market at Busynothings Alley and buy the fruit and vegetables Grammy asked for, and a loaf of fancy bread shaped like a fine shoe to amuse Kitty and the girls. Some brittle sugar candy for the children takes care of the last of the pennies in my pockets, but there is always more can be earned so it bothers me not. The sunlight makes me feel happy, safe; I can almost forget last night.

I don't go through the front door into the main bar, but pass under the archway into the courtyard where Fra's two superannuated black horses stand with their heads over the half-doors of their stalls, hoping for a pat. I pull two carrots from the string bag and offer them up to eager teeth and tongues. I note that there are already fresh carrot and apple fragments on the cobbles. "Greedy."

In through the back door to the kitchen, where Rilka is waiting impatiently.

"About time, Theodora."

I poke out my tongue, dump the groceries on the large scarred table. I put the candy there, too, and point. "*That's* for the children."

She makes a rude noise. I pick up the bucket and go back out to the courtyard to draw water from the well in the centre. The bucket drops down faster than it should and there is a scrape and a splash. I draw it back up, and look into the water to make sure it looks clean enough.

Distracted, I examine my reflection. Still beautiful, strangely un-marked by my recent trials, only the eyes are cold now, pain frozen and held there.

Another face appears beside mine in the liquid mirror. I push away from the well, the pail falls and its contents splashes all over my visitor's fine shoes.

My sister does not look pleased.

Did she ever move so silently when we were small?

"You've ruined my shoes, Theodora."

"They were probably mine in the first place, Polly," I say.

"I've long since finished with your cast-offs." She reconsiders. "Well, except your husband. I'll keep him a while longer."

"You're welcome to him, sister." I circle away from her, uncertain why I am so unsettled, our recent history notwithstanding. Beyond the archway I can see the coach that brought her here, and two liveried footmen as well as the driver. I never used a coach in the city, I walked or rode my own horse. I smile in spite of myself; of course Polly would choose all the trappings, she thinks they make her legitimate.

Around her neck is the diamond necklace Stellan gave me on our wedding night. Strictly speaking, it's part of the crown jewels so it was never *really* mine, but it still sickens me to see it on her. Its entire length is set with diamonds and the central stone is a ruby the size of a bantam's egg. I tear my eyes from it. I have not truly seen her since the day she ruined my life. Prosperity agrees with her. Her face is plump, pink; she looks well-fed.

She takes a step to follow me.

"No. You will not enter here," I tell her. "This space is mine."

She shrugs as if it is no matter. "I came to ask a favour of you, Theodora, and you are being so rude to me."

"Ask and be gone and consider yourself lucky when you leave."

She pouts. "The archbishop."

I say nothing.

"The archbishop is an especial friend of yours."

I shrug.

She stamps her foot, small and damp, and water squelches. "He will not grant your husband a divorce."

I laugh and laugh. I laugh until tears run from my eyes and my jaw aches. Her face, pale as her white silk dress, turns an angry red.

"And so you can't marry him!" I say. "Ah, sister, you are just as much a whore as I."

"If you ask the archbishop he will consent," she almost shouts, remembers to be ladylike and lowers her voice—I'm sure my husband has yet to see one of her rages. "If you ask it of him, then I will be able to marry."

"Oh, you idiot. You still think you can get your way as you did when we were children. Throw a tantrum and wait for everyone to give in." I breathe deeply. "Polly, there's no one here to make me give in to you now. No mother or father begging for a quiet existence. Let what you've already taken from me be enough."

"I want to marry! I must marry! If I marry—" she stops herself, reeling the secret back into her mouth.

"What, Polly?" I scoff, unable to fathom this need of hers. "You'll live happily ever after?"

Her blue eyes, paler than mine, narrow. "Do you like your daughter? Do you love little . . . Magdalene, is it?"

As if summoned by her name, my daughter appears at the open kitchen door. She stops when she sees the snowy vision that is my sister, her little face uncertain.

I stand so close to Polly that she can feel the heat of my breath on her face and the spittle that flies from my mouth. "If you so much as say my daughter's name again, I will kill you, *sister*, have no doubt of that."

"You've made your choice then," she says flatly.

The clients have gone but the inn's residents are awake late this night, children included, so we sit by the hearth downstairs, drinking warm goats' milk made sharper by Fra's home-made whisky. The children have straight milk and some crumbly butter biscuits. We are a strange little family, but a family nonetheless.

Kitty is singing: a soft, sweet song about a disappeared lover and his forever-faithful woman when the fire wavers and almost dies. The room goes cold and a frost creeps across the mirror behind the bar. We are silent, listening hard.

There's a snuffling at the front door. The handle rattles but it has already been locked. Fra throws the sturdy bar down across it. The wooden shutters on the windows have been long-since pulled-to to keep the heat in. Whatever is outside grunts angrily, shakes the door again. Fenric growls but does not move; he is afraid, his fur in such sharp peaks that he looks like a large hedgehog.

"The back door!" hisses Kitty and Rilka bolts through to the kitchen.

We hear a thump as the bar slides into place there. The upper windows are out of reach.

We all cower by the fireplace, clutching our children and each other. It's quiet. I creep to the front door and put my eye to the small hole Fra drilled there so we can see who comes a-calling. A yellow eye stares back at me. I scream, scaring the thing as much as it scares me. It stumbles back and I can see all of it, and know it's the troll-wife come to sniff me out. It turns and shambles back up the street, away from the inn. It was hoping for surprise, to find me alone in my bed, asleep and vulnerable, not safely locked up with friends. It won't risk confrontation with a crowd.

"It's gone," I say, voice shaking. Magdalene climbs into my arms and I sit by the fire; it takes me a long time to get warm.

Grammy asks: "What is it?"

"Troll-wife," I answer. "I saw it last night. It's got my scent."

Grammy is quiet for a while. "Are you sure that's all?"

"What do you mean? What more can there be?"

Fra hands me another cup of warm milk, but I can't taste the milk for all the whisky he's put in. Grammy begins to rock in her chair.

Fenric sits close, careful his tail does not get caught under the rockers, but close enough that Grammy can bury her hand deep in his thick, syrup-coloured fur and soothe him.

"I mean, Theodora, that everyone knows *your* story. A woodcutter father who took a runaway princess to wife. The girl who freed a lost prince from a wolf-trap and captured his heart so he brought her here on his gleaming white charger."

"It was black, actually," I say.

"A happy princess, wife, and mother you were until your sister arrived. We know your story, Theodora, but," she pauses, rocks hard, "what's your sister's story?"

"That thing isn't my sister," I protest. "She's mean and spoilt, but . . . "

"Yes?"

"She stayed behind in the forest with our father when I left, to take care of him. I said they should come with me, but they both refused. My mother has been dead for . . . " Something comes to me, drifting up from the depths of memory. "When we were small—I was three, she just a few months old—our mother was washing clothes by the stream. I was playing with a doll and Polly was sleeping in her basket. Mama turned away for just a moment and Polly was gone, basket and all. She stayed gone for the better part of a day, all the while mama held on to me and screamed and shouted.

"We found her, though, further downstream, in a place we'd already looked. One minute she was gone, then back, no different."

Grammy speaks slowly, pulling old knowledge out of a deep well.

"Trolls will take human babies and leave their own offspring in place, re-shaping their children's flesh and putting a binding spell on to hold it for sixteen, seventeen years, or until the troll-child is about to come to adulthood.

"Some troll-parents will come looking for the child. Sometimes not, and the troll-child has to find its own malicious way."

"What happens to the human babies?" asks Kitty, holding her little girl close.

Grammy purses her lips. "Some are kept as slaves under the earth. Most times they're eaten as tender treats. When it's grown the troll-child learns to change back to troll flesh. Some choose to stay like that, retreat to the forests and mountains and caves and live out their long, miserable lives. Others choose to stay with humans, but some things they just can't hide—even in human form, stepping on hallowed ground makes them sick as sick can be. And they don't lose . . . their appetites."

"All the missing childer," moans Faideau from his corner. We jump, having forgotten he was there.

I shake my head. "No, Grammy, no. She's mean but not . . . not my sister," I finish lamely.

The Treasury is situated, contrarily, in one of the worst parts of the city. I like the irony, though, of the treasurer and his attendant parasites, bankers and moneylenders, daily making their way through a sea of honest thieves and pickpockets.

It is a newer building but that doesn't mean it's without hidden ways. I take the secret tunnel from deep in Bingle the wine merchant's cellar. When I was princess, Treasurer Pinchpen entrusted me with the city's finances—at least in word if not in deed—it was more for the sake of form, to honour the history of the thing, the princess's purview has always been holding the city's purse strings. Pinchpen didn't show me the passages, I found them for myself, pushed by boredom into exploring on the days when all I had to do was wait for the clerks to count taxes, balance books, and the like, so I could stamp the seal into the hot wax gobbet on the records.

The passage comes out somewhat inconveniently behind a book-shelf in an antechamber, not directly inside the vault. In the dark, when I generally undertake these trips, it's not a problem.

Today, in the light of the afternoon, it *is* a problem because my husband stands at the tall French window that looks out onto the grubby street. I catch my breath and he turns.

"Theodora," he says, the sunlight hits his blond hair and his tanned face gleams as if coated with gold dust. But he looks unwell. There's something grey under his skin, dark shadows beneath the green eyes.

"Hello, Stellan." Nothing for it but to brazen it out.

"You're here. I haven't seen you in so long."

I give him a look that says quite plainly he's an idiot and he has the good grace to seem ashamed. I don't want to prolong this but still I say, "What are you doing here?"

"End of the month book balancing. I have to do it now you're . . . "

I am thankful, for once, for his self-centredness, which means he doesn't think to ask me what *I'm* doing there. "I must go," I say and turn on my heel, away from my goal, cursing silently. It will have to wait, until darkness falls and I must risk the streets.

"I sent Prycke to speak with you," he said. I'm willing to bet Prycke didn't tell him the details of our negotiations. "Was I wrong, Theodora? Was I wrong to listen to her?"

I stop. "If you need to ask, Stellan, then you know the answer."

He grabs my arm, forces me to face him. Between his pearly white teeth he hisses: "Theodora, there's *something* in the Palace."

I cannot shake him off. "I *know*. I know."

He drops my arm. "Why didn't you tell me?"

I laugh. "And how would I have done that? Since you banned me from my former home? Should I ask my loving sister to take a message to you? For her to whisper it in your ear at night as you lie together? Is she sweet and tender and loving?" I lower my voice. "Don't you wonder that there are nights when she does not come to you? Does she go to the Cathedral with you, Stellan, every Sunday?"

His mouth moves but nothing comes out. His eyes are filmy with tears. How could I have loved him? How could I have thought him brave, charming, strong? I should have left him in the wolf-trap.

"How is Magdalene?" he whispers.

I step away. "*Don't* you speak her name. You have no daughter and you have no wife. You have a city that's losing its children, a palace that's haunted, and a foul creature in your bed." I don't hate him anymore, there's just a kind of sad, hollow pity. "I wish you joy of them, Stellan."

"Hold her tight, watch her close." My words circle around in my mind like confused birds, the words I spoke to Bitsy when I entrusted Magdalene to her earlier.

In the stables, Bitsy lies, torn from groin to sternum, innards spilling out onto the fresh straw. The black horses stand as far away as they can, both trembling. The air in the dim, enclosed space is rich, fœtid, choking.

There is no sign of Magdalene.

I told Bitsy to look after my daughter, and I condemned her to this, because Bitsy would never have let Magdalene go without a fight.

Kitty is frozen next to me, staring at our dead friend.

"Who came?" I ask, unable to breathe.

She doesn't seem to understand. I grab her shoulders, shake her violently, unfairly. "Who came?"

"Your sister!" Two voices, Kitty and Rilka together, Rilka at the entrance to the stables, her shadow long, making Bitsy's corpse almost invisible. "Your sister came."

"I saw the carriage," says Rilka, "but she didn't come in."

"Must have gone around the back," gulps Kitty, tears starting. She falls away from my hands, sinks to her knees beside Bitsy.

"Where's Magdalene?" I ask, and they both turn pale, even Rilka under her cedar skin. I moan, hold my head, feel sick, but I don't indulge for long. I can't.

I run, pushing through waves of people who seem to have materialised just to slow me down. My breath sounds loud to my ears and I'm sure everyone can hear the thud of my heart, matching time with the clacking of my boots on the cobbles. The knife in the pocket of my skirt thuds rhythmically against my thigh. The spire of the Cathedral comes into view, looming over other rooftops. I round the corner and cross the square, lungs aching, take the steps to the portico two at a time, ignore the shimmering shapes of the bored wolf-hounds pacing there.

Up the aisle, past silent, wide-eyed parishioners. Into the chapel, anxiously waiting for the stones to shift aside, not fast enough, not fast enough. Along the tunnel through cold, damp air, the flame of the hastily-grabbed torch flickering, guttering with my speed, but staying stubbornly lit.

I don't know, I don't know where they are, but this is the place I will start, the place where I first saw the troll-wife, the only place I can think of.

The panel to the fountain room slips aside. Heedlessly, I throw down the torch and without caution step from behind the screen.

Magdalene sits on one of the benches, nervously swinging her little feet, face pinched and pale, bright curls damp and darkened with sweat. One of her shoes is missing and there is a tear where one of the sleeves meets the rest of her dress. She sees me, face lighting up.

"Mama!"

"Oh, my heart." The distance to her seems so long. I kneel down, hold her tight, blink away the burning tears. I pick her up, and discover why she did not come to me when first she saw me. A rope runs from her left ankle to the leg of the bench, which is embedded in the floor.

"Oh, how sweet! What tender motherly love! How delightful a reunion." Polly's tone is poison. She steps out from behind the little steam hut and stalks towards us. Her dress is pale pink, silky, her tooled leather shoes a matching hue. Around her neck is the diamond necklace, the master stone lying snugly just below the hollow of her throat.

"Polly," is all I can manage.

"No, no, don't thank me." She gleams at me. "Really."

"That was hardly the thing on my mind." I push Magdalene behind me. She clutches at my skirts, tiny terrified hands pinching at me.

"I have tried so hard, Theodora. That is what you don't understand." She sighs. "What I am—what I was born—I have tried to escape, to change. If I try hard, ever so hard—if I live as a human, then perhaps I can *become* a human. Live a normal life, keep my human skin tight around me. Marry a human. Then maybe, just *maybe* it will rub off on me."

Here is the heart of my sister's desire: humanity. I push my daughter further behind me. "I'm taking my child, Polly, we're leaving the city."

"Oh no, not good enough. I've been thinking, sister dear, divorce really isn't good enough at all. You'll still be in his thoughts; he'll always wonder if he was right about you or not. He'll think about his little girl and how she's growing up without him." She smiles and it brings a cold rush of air into the fountain room. "Missing is better. Dead is best."

She begins to change, to elongate, to increase in bulk; her skin loses its sheen and firmness, darkening and corrugating; her bright hair dims, becomes thin and black, writhes like snakes; her eyes grow wider, turn yellow and bloodshot; her teeth, no longer uniform pearls, grow sharp and brown; hands lengthen and nails turn into talons.

When her slender dress begins to split, I am released from my horrified fascination and pull the knife from my pocket to slice through Magdalene's bond.

"Run," I tell her, pointing to the gold screen and give her a push. I turn back to Polly, who is now half a human taller than me and looking at her new hands, flexing them, listening to the sound of her over-sized knuckles crack. She laughs and lunges.

I sidestep and jam the knife into her stomach. She roars and stumbles. The silver handle protrudes from her belly, black blood wells where the hilt meets her flesh. I am backing away. She looks at me, and quite deliberately pulls the knife out, slowly. The blade is gone, eaten away by the substance of her troll blood. I lose my nerve then and flee, gathering up Magdalene at the mouth of the tunnel, hitting at the lever to shut the door and running blindly down the steps into the darkness.

I hear a grunt behind me and risk a glance. Polly has jammed her hand into the gap between the panel and the doorframe and thrust the panel back. I keep running as my sister's shape fills the doorway and blocks out the light.

I am thankful, in some tiny, screaming part of my brain, that my feet know this passage, have the memory of it embedded in their soles.

I do not stumble.

Magdalene clutches tightly to my chest like a limpet.

I move through the tunnel, imagining hot breath and long, reaching fingers at my back. Soon, I see gentle light slowly seeping down to light my path. I swear I fly out through the opening, I swear I grow wings in that moment, until I trip, my foot catching at the top step just as something tugs at the hem of my dress from the darkness below.

I keep hold of my daughter, twisting in mid-air as I fall so as not to crush her beneath me. I slide along the smooth flagstones and watch as the troll-wife leaps from the hole, the remnants of Polly's pink gown hanging in tatters on the grotesque form, the diamond necklace tight around the troll-wife's much bigger neck, almost embedded in the flesh. She is all hunger, no caution, seeing only me.

She takes three thundering steps towards us before she falters, stumbles a little, senses something is wrong. Her eyes goggle around and she howls when she realises we are in the Cathedral. She tries to throw herself forward to get at me. She should have gone back down to the tunnel while she still could. Her fearsome noise is drowned out by the growls of the archbishop's hounds.

They've become solid, substantial, heavy in the presence of the troll-wife. And they are *hungry*. All six wolf-hounds leap and knock her to the ground.

I hide Magdalene's eyes.

It takes them a long time to eat Polly. She is alive right up until the end as they shred her flesh, gnaw on her bones, tunnel through her rib cage to get at her large, meaty heart, and slurp on her steaming, stinking innards.

In the end there is only lank black hair, and sad pink strips of silk on the floor of the Cathedral. The wolf-hounds lick up the blood and, sated, begin to assume their usual ephemeral outlines. One coughs, seeming to choke, but as his form softens, becomes smoky, the object drops through his insubstantial throat and jingles on the flags at my feet.

The diamond necklace. I pocket it as a ruckus begins at the front of the Cathedral.

The archbishop will be pleased to see how well his hounds earn their keep. I do not think my husband will recognise his mistress.

Night has fallen and Stellan is waiting outside Spittleshanks' house as we exit. Magdalene hides behind my skirts. She remembers her father, she simply does not like him. I refuse to leave her behind ever again. I hope we will soon be able to sleep the night through. Untroubled slumber is the balm I long for; for nights when Magdalene does not wake and whimper, and when I do not clutch at her in my sleep, terrified of finding her flesh changing in my hands. And I pray for nights when I do not dream of my sister, my *real* sister, dead or worse, toiling underearth, never seeing the light of day.

"Will you come back to the Palace now?" My husband is crying. "Come home, be with me. We will be a family once more."

In the carriage under the street lamp my other little family waits: Grammy and Fra and Rilka and Kitty and Livilla and all their children and Bitsy's doll, so we never forget, are wrapped up in warm coats and scarves. The windows of the inn are now dark. Faideau will not come: he says he is afraid of trees; I have left him a stack of gold coins to keep him in food and drink.

Within my grasp is my past, my former life. It slips and slides under my fingertips like treacherous silk. And here once again is my husband, who is beautiful still for all his flaws. Memories of *before* conjure rich flavours: Stellan *before*, our love and lust *before*; luxury and leisure, never knowing want or hardship. If I just stretch out my hand it can yet be mine. But there is a sour aftertaste; there is what happened, and what was done. There was loss and betrayal and it can never be erased.

I shake my head. "No. Better we take our chances among the whores and thieves. They're more honest, more loyal." The deed parchment and the remaining half of the diamond necklace sit solid in my coat pocket.

I take my daughter's hand and turn away, setting our feet on the wet cobblestones, shining like a path to a better place, to the dark coach that awaits to take us far, far away.

THE BADGER BRIDE

THE TIP OF THE QUILL scratches its way across the parchment, a sound that sets my teeth on edge.

One might think I'd be used to it by now. The black marks it leaves in its wake make no sense to me—indeed the entire book makes no sense—then again, I am a mere copyist and mine's not to question why. Although I do.

Frequently.

Much to my father's despair.

When he brought me this commission, I turned the tome over and over—a difficult enough task, for the thing is heavy, aged, and fragile, the ebon cover tacky to the touch, the pages brittle—and a smell rose from the skin of the thing that was quite unpleasant. The name of the author and the title of the book were utterly obscured, a thick stygian gum had been smeared across them and it was hard to perceive whether this application was intentional or the result of mere carelessness. The inner leaves confirmed intent—no extant title page waited therein, merely the remnants of a folio torn from the binding, tiny sad folds of paper with ragged edges remained.

So, an anonymous book.

"Who is the client?" I asked my father, Adelbert (former Abbot of the monastery of St Simeon-in-the-Grove), who rolled his eyes and bid me *Just do the job*.

"But, Father, it is very old, very frail, the ink is faded—indeed fading as I watch if my eyes don't deceive me." I manoeuvred the article in question so he could better see. "Is it the last of its kind? Who is the owner? What does he expect?"

"He expects, like your father, that you do not ask questions, little prying thing. That you take this volume and copy it as quickly as you might!" He took a deep breath and roared, "Else I'll put you out in the cold, Gytha!"

I harrumphed, and left his study. He will not put me out; he will do no such thing. I am the only child in Fox Hollow House who earns her keep, after all. Aelfrith spends her days draped across the couch, sighing for a husband, and Edda spends hers exercising and grooming the six horses in the stables. I alone understood and adopted the scholarly arts Father had tried to teach us; and I alone I adopted the trade he learned in the monastery—and at which, he freely admits, was terrible. People come from all around, from as far away as Lodellan, to have me copy their books, their precious, unique, failing books; to have me adorn and enhance them, to add vines and flowers and strange animals in the margins; to change the existing illustrations they cannot bear (modestly clothe a naked Eve, paint out grandmother's warts on her nose, give uncle a chin that does not slope so straight from lower lip to clavicle). Copy, edit, amend, ameliorate, augment, and occasionally, if the pay is right, forge.

I will make a book what you want it to be, either more or less itself.

So many since I was very small—so small that Father had to lift me onto the stool piled with two firm fat cushions that I might be able to sit at the tilted desk and reach the inks and shafts, the paints and tints, the papers and parchments that required my attention.

My fingers are stained from the mixing of hues of slate and blue, flashes of umber and gold, red and green; the same fingers are scarred, fletched with nicks from sharpening my very fine goose feather quills. When I work, I wear white cotton gloves, each pair washed in the hottest of hot water after use. I have spectacles, thick half-moons of polished glass to magnify the things I must discern and craft; these perch on the end of my nose only when I am mid-copy. Aelfrith says I look like someone's granny, for all my smooth skin and dark hair.

"No one," she taunts, "would ever believe you young."

Edda merely grunts at that and adds that I need to get out more—

that both Aelfrith and I need to take in the healthful air, and exercise that she regards as she does. We three have different mothers, so we are more like to be dissimilar than if we shared a maternal imprint. Fathers have so much less influence.

The scratching of the nib, which has almost hypnotised me, has a rival: the tap-tap-tapping of a bare frozen branch from the wild cherry tree by the side of the house.

With a tiny bed cupboard in one corner, my scriptorium is located on the second floor, in the room with the most windows so I might steal all the light I can. The cherry tree is naked and frosted; it looks dead, as if it will never bloom again. The cold coming from the glass panes may just convince me this is true—this place cannot be too warm, so I may have only the smallest of fires, banked low in the grate, which is why I prefer to not work in winter.

I have spent the day copying this wretched thing, stopping but once to read a couplet aloud, hoping that speech might add some meaning, but it remained nonsense. Looking up I blink hard until my eyes stop watering at the change in focus, and watch the thin branch as the wind pushes it this way and that; any moment now, any moment, it will snap. But no, the thing is hardier than I would have thought. It endures.

I stand, stretch, arching my back until I hear the four distinct cracks that say my spine is aligned once more. I take stiff steps over to the window, where a cushioned seat awaits, draped with shawls, and survey the garden, white as white can be, its purity broken only by the shadowy things there's not *quite* enough fall to cover: the chopping block, the wood pile, the swing we use only in summer and only when we are feeling particularly frivolous. And at the edge of the lawn, a dark mobile thing the size of a small dog or a large cat, is inching its way forward, terribly slowly, shaking the snow off its gentleman's coat quite determinedly.

A badger; no creature should be left to suffer in this weather.

All stiffness is gone from my limbs and I fly from the room, down the staircase with its carved banister and hideous newel post (the head of a green man, but not as cheerful as it should be), making a great commotion that brings my family from various directions. I don't even worry about a cloak, but fling open the door and charge out into the white.

For precious moments I'm lost, blinded, then I catch sight once more of the determined lope—almost a waddle, with his limbs so chilled—of the black fur and the hoary streak down his back. I stumble through the cold powder and catch up the poor creature. He is heavy; he smells strongly, oh so strongly; he looks at me with bleary-eyed distrust.

"There, there," I croon, stroking one hand over his head and face as I trudge towards the front door, where Father and my sisters wait. "You're safe here, little brock, little badger."

And the poxy little whoreson bites me.

Not viciously—it was merely a warning nip—and only on the one finger but still he breaks the skin and it wells red and stings. Then he snuggles against me, smugly content.

EDDA WASHES and salves my would. While she applies a bandage to the two sharp punctures, I glare at the animal, curled snug in a blanket-lined basket by the kitchen fire.

His eyes are closed, his breathing is even and he is making a deep throaty noise somewhere between a grunt and a purr. One lid lifts, a brown orb stares at me, then is slowly sheathed again. In a bowl in front of a hastily emptied basket are slices of preserved apple and cherries, tepid milk, porridge, and honey. His left hind foot is bandaged; a deep cut slashed its fat pad. The cold had stopped the bleeding, but once inside, the flow started again. He let us bathe the limb with warm water and apply a rosemary salve to it before Edda swaddled him like a baby. He didn't bite *her*.

"He must have gotten lost," says Aelfrith, admiring his coal coat. He is a young male, not a cub, but not a fully grown boar. The streak of white from his snout to his tail is clean as clean can be. All things considered he is a very *hygienic* badger; well, except for the smell, which is not unpleasant, merely strong and musky.

Edda nods. "Yes, he's wandered away from his sett."

"Or perhaps he's been driven out—old boar and new boar can't live in peace," I say, flexing my finger in hope of loosening Edda's tight wrapping. "Especially as he seems to be a biter."

"He only bit *you*, Gytha."

"I'm sure it was just to say *hello*," laughs Aelfrith.

I give my sisters the look they deserve and am about to serve up a retort when Father's bulk hoves into view. "Still fussing with that confounded animal?"

"*O God, how manifold are your works!*" I quote.

"*In wisdom thou hast made them all,*" follows Edda.

Aelfrith chimes in with, "*The earth is full of your myriad blessed creatures.*"

"*Yea, blessed!*" we chorus, our mockery taking on the ring of a hymn.

Adelbert regrets (many times daily, I suspect) teaching his daughters scriptures, for we have ended up with firm beliefs, but also varied means of arguing with him on his own terms.

"Gytha, don't you have work to do? You know the client expects that book by season's end."

"And yes, I've been meaning to talk to you about this, Father. Winter work and no say to me in the deadline! It's not acceptable." I frown.

He sees that bluster and bullying will not get him far this day, so he softens his tone. "Gytha, I am sorry, but this is a special job. No more like this, I promise—but with the coin from this one commission, we need not work for two whole years!"

"*We* don't work, Father. *I* work," I grumble, but turn on my heel and stride from the kitchen.

In the scriptorium, the fire has gone out and I have only a few more hours of usable light left. I poke at the embers and stir them up until flames lick at the twigs I throw on. When it is crackling, I defiantly throw on a larger log than I normally would and watch it catch with satisfaction.

I rub my hands together until they warm, carefully massage the fingers, then sit down to begin once more. Page ten: a drawing of a young woman, who seems to be sleeping, but for the fact there is a great tear over her heart; and words in a language I do not understand, but which make me nervous nonetheless, are written around her corpse.

I manage the rough outline of the body before there is a scratching at the door.

I curse and pull it open. No one is there. Then: a furry weight as Master Brock crosses the threshold and treads over my feet, to sit himself on the rug in front of the fire.

We stare at each other for a moment, until he closes his eyes.

I shrug and return to my desk.

I come down to a scene of high circus the next morning, the badger limping at my heels. I stop in the kitchen doorway and he peeks out from behind my skirts.

"The cheese is gone!" Father shouts.

"The cheese?" I ask.

"All the cheese!" says Edda.

"All our lovely, lovely cheese," wails Aelfrith.

"The cheese?" I repeat, thinking perhaps I am not awake, but still dreaming. I did not sleep well, and the welt on my finger throbbed throughout the night.

Father looks at me as though I am an imbecile. "The cheese has been eaten. Our entire winter supply. Gone."

Father is fond of his cheese.

"And no sign of a thief. No doors unlocked, no windows broken," says Edda knowingly.

"Well, don't look at me." I traipse down the narrow stairs to the cellar, which is a surprisingly small room, half the size of the kitchen, and lined with shelves laden with bottles of preserved fruit and vegetables from last summer, wrapped parcels of salted fish and pork, sacks of flour and sugar, small jars of salt and ground pepper, three kegs of Father's cider, one of his brandy, and a distinct lack of the five large wheels of cheese I set there at the beginning of winter.

I look closely at the walls, the floor, as if I might find a secret passageway heretofore unsuspected, then I shake my head. It's probably Aelfrith, wandering in her sleep again and now feeding her frustrations by eating. She'd best stop or we'll be well out of food before the snows end. Turning to go back up, I find myself pinned by a dark gaze in a curious face. I narrow my eyes and wonder at the badger sitting patiently at the top of the stairs. The cheese was on the highest shelf, my head height, and badgers are not known for their climbing ability, nor for their love of dairy. I shake my head once more and return to the kitchen, wondering how to phrase my suspicions of Aelfrith politely.

But this drama, it seems, has passed and another, quieter one has taken its place. Father is nowhere to be seen, and my sisters have moved themselves to the parlour, where they sit expectantly. Aelfrith, in particular, is preening.

"Where's Father?"

"In his study and not to be disturbed," says Edda.

Aelfrith nods. "He's with a client—*the* client." She takes a deep breath, which she exhales with words riding upon it, "He's ever so handsome, Gytha!"

Even Edda nods and I've not seen her enthused about the appearance of anything but a horse for many a year. Then again, we don't get too many men passing by, only the occasional monk, old friends of Father's, random clients, and tinkers. Certainly none from the burnt-out bones of Southarp village.

I make a move towards the door and Edda leaps up, terribly distressed and barring my way. "Oh, no! You mustn't disturb them—Father said so."

I narrow my eyes and stomp off to my workroom. Honestly, she doesn't know me at all. I sit at the window seat and watch, noting the absence of either horse or carriage. It doesn't take long before I hear the front door open and see a figure step out from beneath the storm porch, firmly settling a tricorne hat upon thick golden hair.

He gets a good head-start while I fight with the frozen casement latch and eventually clamber down the stout limbs of the cherry tree. I follow his tracks, deep footprints, and huddle against the shawls I threw hastily around my shoulders. Soon, I'm into the woods; icicles hang where leaves should be, and the patches of sky glimpsed through the bare tangle of branches are grey and unwelcoming. If I do not find him soon I will give up—I'm no fool. He will visit again and I will be waiting;

next time I will charge into Father's study and take the golden-haired man's measure.

I'm cold and shivering. The moment I turn around, there he is, grinning like a wolf.

I see none of the handsomeness Aelfrith was mooning over, merely appetite and a will to do whatever he wishes. In his hands, a knife, long and thin, a stiletto blade; his knuckles are white around the ivory handle.

"The book," I blurt and his expression alters. Ah! Here it is, that beautiful mask. But I've seen what it covers and I will not be deceived. "I wanted to ask you about your book."

Smoothly he hides the knife in the sheath at his belt, tucks it out of sight as if it might be easily forgotten. He is richly dressed, his coat lined with ermine.

"My apologies—I could only hear someone following me and thought to defend myself from footpads. I did not mean to frighten you." He points and I follow the direction of his kid-gloved finger. "My coach is there."

And so it is, on the road above where we stand in a hollow. Black and shiny as ebony, with four black steeds, a driver and a footman, both blank faced as they peer down at us. I find myself shaking and will it to stop. I clear my throat.

"The book—I was wondering if you knew its name and author? Only—I've been wondering. Professional curiosity," I say, trying to look scholarly and serious.

He gives me a brilliant smile and shakes his head. "Afraid not, Mistress Gytha—it is Gytha, yes? My copyist? I am—a collector—the book took my fancy; its value is purely ornamental and sentimental. It reminds me of someone very dear. But its ink is fading, the cover is derelict. I require a copy."

"But I can re-ink the text, clean the cover, fix the bindings."

"No, no. My memory hinges on the contents, not the container. New is best." His expression tells me that he does not like old things; he is one of those who prefer possessions to be pristine and unused when they come to his hand. An old book is not the artefact for him—the knowledge therein is what he wants, but he desires it in a splendid new repository. I notice his clothing—blue breeches, gold and cream waistcoat, white silk shirt, silver-grey frock coat and highly polished boots—not one item seems overly worn. Indeed, there is no sign of anything having been worn before at all; there is no fading of colour, nor weakening of nap, no hint of threadbare at the collar and wrists, and certainly no wrinkles or folds that might come with habitual attire. This man likes his things *shiny*.

"Where did you find it?"

He smiles again and does not answer, effortlessly striding up the slope to his conveyance. He tips his hat and climbs in. He leans out the window and says, "I shall return in the spring, Mistress Gytha, to claim my book. I trust you'll not disappoint me."

I stand shivering for some time after he is gone.

St Simeon-in-the-Grove is a small monastery, all things considered.

A mere twenty monks, aged from twelve (two boys left on the doorstep some years before) to ninety-five (the librarian).

Edda has let me take our oldest horse, a tall beastie, with feathered feet and a mane like a blanket. Hengroen moves slowly and surely—it's a bit like being on a very sturdy boat, his gait is almost floating, which makes me feel both safe and seasick after an hour on his broad back. My rear protests as I dismount and I groan loudly. The young monk who comes forward to take Hengroen looks astounded as I tip back the hood of my thick travelling cloak—obviously he has been brought up to believe women are crafty creatures, both fragrant and evil, but not given to terrible bodily noises. He should hear Edda after a meal of beans.

"Larcwide will see me," I say, before he begins the speech about how my kind are not allowed in the monastery. A rule instituted since—in fact because of—my father's tenure. "I'm bringing a book."

Of course, I'm *assuming* he will see me as he has done before—that he will not remember that little fracas a few years back. This young man knows the librarian collects tomes, is consulted on them regularly, is an authority on things that hold words in one place. I'm banking on the very good chance that he has been terrified by at least one of the old man's tirades, and will be too afraid to refuse me.

"Don't worry," I say, and pat his hand. He shivers the way a horse does when a fly lands on its hide. "I'll take the side entrance so as not to cause a fuss."

I'm rewarded with a flash of relief and he nods, leading my great mount to the stables for a rest. I dart across the rectangle of snow that in summer is a patch of green, keeping my head down, but I needn't bother—most of the brothers are at prayer this time of day. At the base of a tall tower—not the one with the bell in it, the one opposite—there is a small slender door, overgrown with winter ivy (which in this season looks deceased, as if the wall is shedding its skin), but a sharp eye will note the dry grey handle twisted about with dead vines, almost invisible. I get splinters, but the ingress opens with relative ease. Inside there is a set of black stone steps curving around and up. The air is dry and cold, but warmer as I rise. I can smell ink and paper, and old man.

The librarian is shuffling back and forth between cases, twitching folios from the shelves which line the walls, muttering, sliding them back into place or shifting them to another spot. In the centre of the tower is a series of platforms, weighted down with even more tomes, reached by a sort of elevator and pulley system, that creaks above. As I watch a thin monk steps onto the third platform, nimbly balancing an armful of volumes. Larcwide glares upward as dust particles drift down.

"I told you," he yells, "to clean your shoes! And did you? Did you?"

There is a muffled and indecipherable reply from aloft, and the old man swears softly.

"Father Larcwide?"

He swings around in surprise and squints at me. He won't rant about me being a woman, although he may well rant about my incursion. He shared in many of my father's adventures, but his continued presence at St Simeon is testament to both his inability to produce offspring and to his unassailed position as bibliognost. By virtue of his irreplaceable knowledge, his transgressions could be overlooked. Unfortunately for

Adelbert's career, anyone can be an under-enthused abbot and mediocre copyist.

"Father Larcwide, I need to talk to you," I say and hold up the satchel hanging at my side. His eyes sparkle and he gestures for me to come closer.

He peers at my face and recognition dawns. "Adelbert's girl? The clever one."

I grin and nod. "Gytha. I need you to look at something."

"Why me?" he grumps, contrary for the sake of it.

"Because there's none like you." His ego, duly stroked, allows him to lead me along a maze of shelves to an alcove just big enough for a writing desk and two chairs. He sits and invites me to do the same. I draw the thing out of the bag, and unwrap it from the layers of shawl, then place it on the table between us. Larcwide leans forward to read the now-visible title. I have been working at it, testing out a variety of oils and soft cloths, trying to wear away at the black mess. It was slow toil: if I used too much of the lubricant, too much pressure as I rubbed, the stuff would have simply eaten its way through the cover. It is a capricious mix, with a peculiar personality all of its own, bought from the strange little man who travels in spring and summer and brings me supplies of the things that are hardest to find. One letter at a time. So carefully. So very carefully, until:

Murcianus. A Book of Craft.

Larcwide's hands shake as he reaches out but does not touch the tome. His fingers are blue and brittle, stained with age spots. They hover over what I have so painstakingly cleaned.

"Do you know what this is? Of course you don't," his voice quivers. Then, "Where did you get this?"

No, I don't know, although, I have a suspicion, have had since I reached a page I recognised: a drawing of a hand with candles set in the tops of all the fingers and the thumb. A hand of glory. But I choose to act the innocent and answer only his second question. "A client. A commission my father took on."

He shakes his head. "Oh, Adelbert. Will you never learn?" He closes his eyes, no more than a blink, but he looks exhausted when he opens them again.

"What is it?" I ask.

He nods. "A *grimoire*. A book of craft. And this one . . . " He finally picks the thing up and rubs his fingers on the back cover, in the right-hand bottom corner, finding what I already know is there: the subtle relief of an embossment, *M*. He almost drops the book, so great is his surprise. "Belonged to *him*!"

I want to poke and prod, extract the information swiftly, but I wait. He looks at me dubiously, then with judgment. I don't know who *he* is.

"Murcianus. This is the Bitterwood Bible."

And I stare blankly at him and Larcwide's expression rolls into utter despair.

"Murcianus, one of the greatest encyclopaedists ever known. Well, of the arcane and the eldritch specifically. He wandered the world, recording and compiling every strange ritual, every bizarre being, every spell, curse, myth, legend, enchantment, magical locations . . . " the monk seems to run out of words. "Everything!"

I remain silent.

"Those books, nowadays, are so rare you barely find one outside of a private collection—or with those bloody women at Cwen's Reach," he mutters. "They are wonderfully illustrated, most erudite and informative, filled with wisdom and wit and scholarship." He turns my tome over in his hands. "But there are other volumes, Gytha, like this one, written in the language of witches, comprehensible to only a few, this one is a rarity. Full of knowledge best left unknown, things too dangerous to be writ down. There are places, Gytha, where his works are banned; where those who carry them are burned, their ashes scattered."

His face reddens and he looks away, remembering to whom he speaks; remembering at last our argument when I asked him for information my father refused. The one occasion I managed to extract the name of my mother from Adelbert, he was in his cups. He'd called her *Hafwen* and told me she had been so briefly beautiful, then burned. She was his final indiscretion, the one that sent him from the monastery, lucky to leave with his life. That is all I was able to get from him before he passed out; he woke the next day with a sore head and foul temper, and would tell me nothing more. When I asked Larcwide about it, tried to get an answer, he banned me from coming to see him. I'd hoped the intervening years and his age had dimmed the memory.

"And the book. Where would *this* have come from?"

He shrugged. "Lost? Left behind? Stolen? Who knows. All I know is this isn't some harmless thing you're working on, Gytha." He pauses, suddenly suspicious. "You haven't read from it?"

I would like to deny it, but my blush makes a liar of me. Larcwide goes pales and pushes the book at me, insistent. "What did you read?"

Flicking carefully through the pages I find the relevant one, with the drawings of wheat sheaves and other plants. The old man's dark eyes skim the words and they seem to make sense to him as he sits back and puffs out a sigh of relief. "Transformation, but it's just a season spell. Not much harm in it."

"What's that?"

"To work change for a few months only, to make an animal change its shape."

"Not a person?" I worry at the bandaged finger, which has not healed these past weeks, but itches still.

"Oh no," he flicks through the pages and points to a couplet. "Here: this one will work on a person, but only one who is willing. A resistant subject requires far more effort, instruments and ingredients." He rubs his hands together. Larcwide seems to know rather more about magic than he should, I think, but do not say. "But you have no ability, so I shouldn't worry about it. Just don't do it again—some spells are so powerful they need only be spoken, without intent, for them to effect a metamorphosis, unwanted or otherwise. You should know, though, that every bit of magic leaves a trace, Gytha, no matter how small. Even the tiniest skerrick may rub off, leaving the potential for alteration in its wake."

"Thank you, Father." I take the book from him and begin to wrap it up once more. He leans across the table, grasps my wrist and says, "What will you do with this?"

"This is a commission, I cannot simply make it disappear." I lower my voice. "And I fear this client, Father, I fear him greatly. I will not risk my life nor that of my family by refusing to give him what he has demanded."

"But, child, it's too dangerous. If you will not listen to sense, I shall have to tell the Abbot."

"And if you do so, there's every good chance I will be burned—it won't matter that this book is not mine, it will simply matter that it is in my possession." I hold his gaze for a long moment. I do not think he would like to see me as ashes.

"What will you do?" he asks quietly once more, defeated.

I shake my head. "I'll think of something."

I WIPE MY HANDS on a rag, then wash them with hot water and Edda's whortleberry soap, massaging the cramps and the smell of ink and oil out of them. Passing my desk I survey the work: the replica is almost done. I am exhausted and my eyes ache; I have been copying by the light of the fire and as many lanterns and candles as I could find without leaving my family in darkness. Outside the black mirror of the window, the air smells of spring. The days have grown longer, warmer, but I have spent an eternity inside, slaving over this damnable book. The time is fast approaching and although I have not slept well since the client's last visit, it is not the sole reason for my sleeplessness.

The doors to the bed cupboard are open, just a little, and inside I can make out blankets and coverlets heaped up, mounded over the form of a slumbering young man with the thickest, blackest hair relieved only by a streak of white down the middle. He snuffles and snores, his hands curled like paws, batting at the pillows as he stirs, then stilling as he settles once again.

I struggle with the buttons of my dress, then drop it to the rug, half-undone. Crawling in beside him, I fit myself into the half-moon of his body and breathe deeply. He smells musky, slightly sweet. I close my eyes, nestling as his arms come around me.

"I want peaches," he mumbles, breath warm in my ear.

"You ate them all, remember?" That was how I found him, in his night-time shape, late on the evening I returned from St Simeon-in-the-Grove, crouched on the floor of the cellar, struggling with a bottle of preserved peaches. His hands seemed not to know quite what to do, and he dropped the bottle, which smashed impressively. He merely gave a grunt and neatly picked slices of the preserved fruit from the glass, carefully examining it for shards, then elegantly chewed it in tiny bites.

"It doesn't stop me wanting them," he points out, in a reasonable tone.

"Ordinary badgers don't eat peaches."

"Well, I'm no ordinary badger, obviously," he says, and shrugs, a movement that takes his whole body, not just his shoulders.

Badgerish.

"You ate plenty this evening. I cannot believe how much food you put away—and Aelfrith insists upon feeding you twice a day. You won't fit in my bed soon."

"Get a bigger bed." As he cuddles comfortably into my back. I take hold of one of his hands, weave our fingers together.

"At least there's no cheese left."

"Oh, that cheese! Terrible cheese. Awful constipation."

"An ordinary badger doesn't eat *cheese*. Or indeed, spend his winter in a girl's bed."

"An ordinary badger doesn't get hit by stray magic." He nuzzles my neck, pauses. "How long will this last, do you think?"

I shake my head, feeling dizzy as if I am dangling over a terrible pit where all the loss in the world resides. "I don't know." I squeeze his hands. "What do you think about, in the day? When you're . . . "

"Four-legged and furred? Badgerish things: about food and warmth, staying safe, about spring and blackberries and wild cherries and windfall apples." He wiggles against me to suggest the time for talking is done and other activities should be considered.

Here is the problem with raising daughters so far from suitable mates: it makes them prey to roaming, transformed badgers. It makes their hearts easy pickings, like windfall apples.

~

I keep my eyes downcast, but watch through lowered lashes. Adelbert is trying to hide his surprise at my seeming modesty. He is also trying to hide his look of mistrust. We sit in his study, all three of us on separate over-stuffed armchairs.

The client has my work in his hands. He is appreciating the fine red leather cover I've added. It is different to the old one, but I see that I was right: this pleases him, this newness. There is neither title nor author on the front.

"Your workmanship is exquisite, Mistress Gytha. I commend you." He tosses my father a heavy bag of coins, and Adelbert's eyes go soft, like a drunk seeing his first drink of the day. "And the original?"

"I burned it," I pipe up and two pairs of eyes turn on me. I hold up a small box and shake it gently. "The ashes. The book—the ink was almost unreadable by the time I finished and I did not think you would care, sir. It was old and not new."

The man stares at me for long moments, then nods and brings out a smile. "Yes, you're right, Mistress Gytha. Although, such a decision I would have liked to make myself."

He does not care the original is gone, he merely cares about my high-handedness. I offer the box and manage to sound sincere, "I apologise, sir. Would you like . . . "

He shakes his head dismissively and I nod. "I *am* very sorry, sir."

"No matter, no matter," he smiles and waves his hand. He places the book into a leather case he has brought specifically for the purpose. "I shall take my leave."

Father sees him to the door, then returns to the study. Through the open windows comes the warm air of the first day of spring. I watch, just as I watched him that first occasion, as the client appears around the side of the house, then disappears into the green of the woods. I do not pursue him this time. I watch until the trees swallow him, until I am sure he is nearing his carriage waiting up on the road, waiting far from us so no one will know he has been here, has brought something here, so no one will question and perhaps hunt here, or suspect him of whatever he is doing.

"Well done, Gytha," says my father. His good mood cannot be contained, despite the loss of part of our fee, and it makes me wonder if all this has been about more than mere money. He moves around the room, laughing and joking, pouring us both a glass from the last bottle of the summer-berry wine. He counts out my coin into a smaller purse and gives it to me. I sit opposite and stare at him until he becomes uncomfortable. "What is it?"

"Who is he, Father? How did he come to us?" I ask now because it has occurred to me at last that Adelbert did not tell me how this client found us. It is his usual habit to go into great detail about who they are and what drew them here, who referred them on. That I've only just thought of this is a sign of my distraction.

Adelbert gives a kind of half-hearted shrug. "I knew him long ago, in my days at university. Before the seminary, before St Simeon's."

"He looks too young," I point out and he shrugs again.

"Some age better than others. Perhaps his life has been easier." He scratches at his chin. "As I said, I knew him before."

"Before Hafwen?" I do not say "my mother" for she has never been that, only ever an absence to whom I was able to put a name a few years ago. He makes a sharp sound and jerks his head to one side before bringing his gaze back to me.

"Yes," he says.

"Well?"

"Well what?"

"Who was she?"

"A girl. Just a girl."

"Was she a witch?"

I have never seen such grief in my father, such a terrible thing clawing its way up from inside and painting itself across his face. He lowers his head so I cannot see, then slowly raises it once more. Everything is gone but an awful blankness. I will get nothing from him.

"Enjoy the spring, Gytha, while there are no new commissions," he tells me and looks away, staring resolutely out the window at the garden, but not, I feel, seeing it. His voice halts me at the door. "Gytha, all you need to know is that your work has paid a debt that will plague me no more. Never think me ungrateful, daughter, but never ask me about her again."

From the blanket box at the foot of my bed, I lift out several coverlets, folded winter dresses and shawls. At the bottom is the original Murcianus *grimoire*, its text and diagrams re-inked each day before I copied it. Each page has been dusted with a setting powder of my own devising. I run my fingers across the cover and wonder how long it will take me to learn the language of witches, to take the knowledge I need for my purpose. I wonder if Larcwide might be prepared to teach me. I wonder if I have any of my mother's blood in me to help.

I notice a four-legged absence. I look around for the badger. He is not in his usual spot, the rug by the hearth, but then as the days have grown longer he has been roaming about the house more, seemingly restless. Perhaps he is in the kitchen, begging food from Aelfrith. He will be so fat soon.

My sister is rolling out dough; a dozen apples sit on the bench, waiting to be peeled. Beside them, a bucket of blackberries, lush and dark. But there is no sign of the badger.

"Where is he? Where is Brock?"

Aelfrith looks at me in surprise. "He wanted to go out."

The kitchen door stands open. From the threshold I survey the green grass and the plants, growing thickly in the house-garden.

There is no sign of him.

No track, no trail, no hint.

I run out, to the stables. Edda has a curry comb and is grooming Hengroen.

"Have you seen him? Have you seen the badger?" I ask, uncaring that my voice is breaking.

She shakes her head, and *tuts*. "You knew he would go, Gytha. I know you're fond of him, but he's a wild creature. It's not as if he's a dog or a horse."

I knew the spell would end. I knew he would change back, but I thought he would stay. I thought he would wait. I thought I could find something in the *grimoire*, some means to make him transform for good, to keep him with me.

A breeze starts up but the dancing air does nothing to lift my spirits. I did not think his badgerish instincts would lead him away from me so soon. The itching of my punctured finger is all I have left.

It is only three days later that I see the client again.

I thought I would have longer. I had planned to leave when he'd collected his finished product, when I had both book and badger. I had planned to run and find another life, but with my love departed, I had fallen into a funk. I had lost the will to move. I lost any care that the golden-haired man might try one of his new spells and find it did not work. That he would try another and it, too, would not work. And another and another until he realised that I had copied each and every enchantment, each and every curse, incorrectly. Just a tiny detail in each, a line missing, an ingredient changed, a direction left out, an instrument added.

Sitting on the window seat in my room, I see the man breaking out of the woods, his long knife catching the sun, and I finally rediscover the will to move. I bundle the *grimoire* into a satchel and drape the bag's strap across my chest. I clatter down the stairs, run into Edda, who protests, until I put a hand over her mouth, the bandage still on the finger that will not heal.

"Sister, if you never listen to me again, listen now. Lock the doors. Do not let anyone in, especially not that man, the handsome man. Don't let him in, Edda, no matter what. Keep all the doors locked. I am sorry for whatever I may have brought down upon you."

I flee before she can answer. I tear out the door, creep around the corner of the house, then make sure the client catches sight of me. He gives a sound somewhere between a yell and a scream, but all rage, and pounds after me. It's the only thing I can do, to draw him away from my family. As I run, I feel myself pulled onward, my direction not as haphazard as I planned. My feet seem to have a plan of their own.

I know these woodlands far better than he. I know the paths both seen and hidden, I dart between trees, under hanging mosses, I hurdle over rocks and stiles and rills, but still he keeps on my trail. I think of the words I've practised these past weeks.

Then, all is silence. I stop, wait, turning, turning, turning, trying to see if he is anywhere in sight. From behind a huge oak, he lunges, the knife preceding him and slicing across my left side, not enough to kill, but to wound, to hurt. I swing the heavy satchel up at him and catch him in the face. He goes down like a sack of potatoes. I run.

I keep running, fleeing into the darkest, deepest part of the wood, bleeding, weakening, aching, my lungs burning, my legs shaking. Silently I mouth the spell, the spell on which I pinned my last hopes, try to feel it taking effect but there is nothing. In a green hollow, a spot dotted with mounds and slopes, I trip over a fallen branch and the breath *whumps* out of me. I hit my chin and bite my tongue and taste iron. Behind me I can hear the crashing, the swearing, the inexorable rampaging of the golden-haired man.

My injured finger tingles, twinges, burns. I hear a chittering, a squeak, a growl close by. Searching, I find the mouth of a hole and in that mouth a creature of black and white, a fine well-fed badger, who calls to me. At last I think *Make a noise, make a sound, if it cannot be heard it cannot be made!* and I finally I speak aloud the couplet Larcwide pointed out that day at the abbey. With a shaking voice I speak through blood that spatters the ground. I scramble up, try to stand, but my entire body convulses, arcs in on itself. The hand with the injured finger curls beyond my will, as does the other. They turn ebony with fur, the nails elongating, becoming hard horn. I drop on all fours and shudder as the transformation completes.

The boar's call changes, the noise more urgent. With the strap of the satchel still around my new shoulders, I scamper up the hillock, and follow my love down the tunnel and into the sett. The book is dragged along behind, getting caught now and then, but the corridors are wide enough for it to get through with a tug or two. We come to a large chamber filled with clean straw; the strap slips from me, the book's progress halting, pushing up a wave of the dry yellow covering that will eventually settle over it.

I can no longer hear the sounds aboveground of a man thwarted and driven beyond his patience. I cannot hear the raging and the cries of loss. I lie still and my mate snuffles at the wound in my side, licking it clean. He curves around me, our black and white fur a chessboard match. Even as I hope my family will be safe, I begin to forget Fox Hollow House. Ideas about books and inks and pages and covers all subside into a dim memory place. I begin to think of worms and beetles, of windfall apples, blackberries, and wild cherries. I begin to think badgerish thoughts.

THE TALLOW-WIFE

CORDELIA DOES NOT THINK about the things she has lost.

She does not think on the children, or her husband, or the fine house in Lodellan. She does not think on the jewellery, or the dresses, or the shoes. She does not think on her former status, on the Sunday afternoon teas, the Saturday morning bruncheons, or the Friday night balls. She does not think of her sister, or her friends, or the shades of her dead parents who surely grow even paler with shame. Nor of all the handkerchiefs with knots tied in them to ensure good luck, every one of which failed dismally to do its allotted task.

No, Cordelia thinks only of the lengths she must cut with the dull knife. Of the quantities she must measure so carefully to ensure neither wastage, nor excess. The turnkeys who appear daily at the barred window only ever hand out the precise amounts needed to create three dozen candles at a time.

Any less and there will be trouble. Any more will be an equal calamity, for it means she's skimped on the quality and girth, that the women who want these things will know they are lesser . . . women like she once was . . . and they will not buy them. Or, worse still, they will buy them, find them wanting, and return them, demanding their good gold back. Either way Cordelia will be punished.

She wishes the candles were of a much different sort.

But at night, after she extinguishes the tiny ceramic stove where she melts the wax, when she closes her eyes, when sleep will no longer be denied, when the groans of other inmates and creaks of the old prison ship recede, when the rock and pitch of the hulk is gentle as a cradle, then she dreams. When she fingers the raised edges of the scar on her shoulder, *traces the rough petals, the scabby stem. When she curls herself into a cold ball, settles her hands on the concave stomach that should by now have been convex,* then *she dreams of all she has lost. She dreams and it feels so real that she prays not to wake up. She prays that sleep will take her and hold her and keep her. She prays death will come while she slumbers so the memories she carries with her into darkness are those of life* before.

The front parlour is cold when Cordelia enters, and she glances immediately at the hearth, which is stacked full with logs, none alight. She rolls her eyes; the tweeny cannot take instruction, or refuses to do so. Not enough lightwood, again. Not enough care or attention paid when Cordelia has gone to the trouble of crouching beside her and showing her how to do it *properly*. The girl is sullen, or has been noticeably so for a sennight. Cordelia refrains from thinking *stupid*, for it seems unfair— she's seen Merry embroider some exquisite kerchiefs and shawls, make cutwork and bobbin lace finer than anything they've ever imported, sew the most sublime dresses and frockcoats. Not stupid, no, but perhaps merely resentful of things that do not revolve around her talents.

Cordelia sighs and kneels, removes the excess wood, replaces it with extra kindling: twigs, shreds of old broadsheet, and the tiniest length of char cloth. She breathes the prayer Mrs Bell taught her when she was little, an invocation to the hearth-sprites. She finds the flint and steel where Merry has discarded them, and strikes, once, twice, then the tinder takes. Soon delicate golden flames are licking at the larger pieces, seducing them, convincing them to burn. Cordelia smiles. This is her favourite task, though it's beneath her nowadays. She loves the simple ritual with all its power and import. So elementary, yet so essential.

She gives the blaze a last nod, a grateful thanks whispered, then stands, her palms rubbing against each other to remove any dirt or dust, finally smoothing out the cream and blue skirts of her dress, making sure no soot has impressed itself on the fine fabric. She won't speak to Merry, no, but she will tell the housekeeper, Mrs Bell—the tweeny's aunt—to tend to this chore herself. They have an understanding: Mrs B had worked for Cordelia's parents, tended the girl from her cradle, then accompanied her when she'd come to Lodellan to marry. Sometimes Mrs B still called her "dearling" when no one else can hear. Cordelia does not wish Merry removed or harshly berated—gods know she wishes the girl some happiness!—but she would like on winter days to come down in the mornings to warmth and a fire crackling sweetly.

Out in the hallway, there is a breeze, colder even than the unlit parlour was, and Cordelia frowns. She soon finds the source. One panel of the front double-doors with its frosted and etched crystal panes is wide open, chill pouring in and bringing with it the smell of newly baked bread wafting up from Bakers' Lane. She makes an exasperated noise—not a curse for that would be ill-bred—and bustles forward. Merry is too careless; with the recent robberies in their neighbourhood *this* is utterly reprehensible! Despite Cordelia's weakness for lame ducks and a belief that better human nature can always spring forth, given the right encouragement, she does have her limits. But when she steps onto the black marble stoop (which gleams—for all her faults, Merry keeps it brilliant, as well as rubbing coarse salt into it once a month to keep away ill luck), she loses impetus.

The clamour of carriages and horses masks Cordelia's footfalls, and Merry, whose attention is focused on the lad at the bottom of the stairs, does not hear her. The youth is tall, flame-haired, sapphire-eyed, milk-skinned. Cordelia recognises him only because she's seen him at Belladonna Considine's home. A footman Bella had apprenticed to the aging valet whose service was coming to an end. The boy would learn from and care for the old man at the same time, ensuring that the House of Considine was always tended by loyal staff. Cordelia had hoped for something similar with Mrs B and Merry, which is why Annie, the parlour maid, has been freed of several of her duties: so Merry might learn by doing. Cordelia believes strongly that managing can only be done when you understand a task fully through experience, and if Merry is to replace Mrs B in the fullness of time, she must be properly prepared.

This young man is certainly pretty to look at, definitely prettier than their own footman whose plainness of face is quite astonishing. But this one, oh this one! the breadth of his shoulders, the slenderness of his waist and hips, the length of his legs in the fitted trews, demand attention. Pretty, yes, but oh! Now Cordelia notices that Merry is shivering in her mint-green brocade frock with white lace at the collar and wrists. No, worse, more than shivering, this is a tremor, the girl is shaking from head to toe as if in the throes of a fever. Cordelia raises a hand, opens her mouth—

—the boy spies her and the shift in his gaze makes Merry turn. Cordelia feels all her annoyance drain away. The girl's face is deathly pale, her eyes red-rimmed, and tears have drifted down her rounded cheeks. Her dirty-blond hair is untidy as if she's run troubled fingers through it, and her bottom lip trembles. Cordelia is face-to-face with another's agony and it makes her throat seize up. And Merry, poor Merry does not wish to be seen like this. Her gaze at first burns with hatred and resentment to be found thus, then it softens as pain comes to the fore, overwhelms her pride.

At last Cordelia swallows, once, twice.

"Don't forget to lock the door when you come in, it's cold," she says quietly and Merry nods, as if grateful to have an excuse to cut short whatever is passing between her and the pretty boy at the bottom of the stairs.

Inside, Cordelia rests her head against the wood of the doorframe, listening carefully as if she might hear something from the mummers left on the stoop, but there is nothing, merely the noises of the street, strangely louder.

"What are you doing, Dellie?"

Cordelia jumps, pushes away, and moves down the hallway to where her sister waits at the entrance to the library. She doesn't want Bethany to see Merry's pain; she's been aware for some time now that the two do not get along. Nor do they need to, she supposed, Bethany isn't a servant and Merry is, but sometimes Bethany goes out of her way to be mean. Perhaps it is because they are closer in age, because Merry grew up in Cordelia's house and Bethany came to it somewhat, although not much, later.

Bethany's golden hair is several shades darker than Cordelia's, and her eyes a paler shade of green, but there is no denying they are sisters. Bethany is taller, despite being the younger; where Cordelia is buxom, Bethany is a willow; where Cordelia will pour oil on troubled waters, Bethany will often put a match to the oil purely for the sport of watching things burn. But not all the time; only when she's taken by a spirit of mischief. There's no true harm in her sister, thinks Cordelia.

"What are you doing, Dellie?" repeats Bethany, a novel in one hand, her burgundy skirts bunched in the other as if they are an impediment to movement, though the young woman is quite still. "Is it Merry mooning over that boy again?"

Cordelia does her best not to show surprise, but of late her sister has been different. She wonders if it's Bethany's age, though she herself was married and a mother by the time she was eighteen. Once they shared everything, now it seems Bethany keeps secrets and lets them out only when it will embarrass others. Cordelia has often thought this behaviour stems from her sister feeling untethered in the household and their best efforts, hers and Edvard's, to make it otherwise, appear to have failed. Or sometimes at least.

It's not as if Bethany's some penniless maid who must marry where she can for security. Cordelia and Edvard have always made it clear they plan to settle a considerable sum on her as well as a house—not one in the Cathedral Quarter, no, but certainly a more than respectable merchant's abode, something only Bethany will own—either upon her wedding or her eighteenth birthday, the latter event being but a few weeks away. The former is a different matter entirely: the marriage proposals, which once flew thick and fast, have become rarities. The bucks of the city initially thought Bethany a challenge, yet the sheer constancy, the unwavering tenor, of her refusals had beaten them down. Cordelia has heard her sister described as an unwedable, unbedable Atalanta, and worse, when the men who come to drink her husband's brandy and smoke his cigars think she cannot hear. She wonders if Bethany has heard them, too.

"I thought I would take the children to the fair after lunch, Bethany. Will you come with us?"

"I'm otherwise occupied, Dellie, I'm sorry." She smiles impishly, a child again. "But will you bring me a bag of sweeties? The hard sort, the rock that crunches between your teeth and makes your tongue fizz so! You know I love such confectionery."

Cordelia laughs; her concerns melt.

"Of course! I—"

A clamour comes from the floor above, from Victoria's bedroom by the sound of it. Cordelia's only daughter is shrieking, a sound so high-pitched she can barely discern any words at all—her tone, and projection demonstrate the singing lessons have not been wasted. In response Torben shouts he didn't take her precious brooch, and Victoria parries that *he did, he did, he did*. Whatever thoughts Cordelia might have expressed to her sister are lost, and she gently touches Bethany's shoulder in apology, then picks up her pace, mounts the gold and black coloured wrought iron staircase, girding herself for the battle.

The travelling show comes to Lodellan once a year, and Cordelia is sure she recognises faces amongst the older members of the troupe. The children look forward to the event, although Henry's expression is torn between excitement and embarrassment, as if he feels himself too told to enjoy such pastimes. But he did not refuse to accompany his siblings, and he has his arm linked with hers as they walk beneath the makeshift archway the travellers erect every year to claim their space outside the walls of the city. Merry, her expression serene and sweet as if nothing untoward occurred this morning, walks a little ahead with Victoria and Torben, one on each side, their hands in hers. Cordelia drops several coppers and one quarter-gold into the palm of the wizened woman at the entrance and her generosity is rewarded with a smile, no less genuine for its lack of dentition.

Around them is all manner of noise: laughter, shrieks of shock and delight, howls of terror from children who pretend to mislike strangeness, gasps from women and guffaws from men. The carnival is small, but takes up more space than it seems it should. Everything is rich and colourful, if a little worn in places; a maelstrom of movement and light, hue and shadow. The Parsifals pass stalls packed with impossible amounts of things: bottles of perfume and potions, tonics and tisanes; scarves and dresses, cheaply and sloppily made, but bright and pretty, items poor girls would be perfectly happy with if given as gifts by otherwise inattentive suitors. Cordelia wonders if Merry's ever received such things from the boy on the front stoop.

There are stands with sweet-smelling soaps, and flowers carved so finely the wood might be paper. Some merchants offer knives designed to deliver injury and cutlery for meals, plates of metal brightly polished. There are pots and pans, tobacco and cigars, pipes of ivory and horn and stone. One hawker shows jewellery she claims has magical properties, made by the hands of the finest jewel-smiths trained, she so swears, by those who once lived in the city of Cwen's Reach before the Great Fall of the Citadel—such women could have coaxed the sun and moon into something more lovely if they'd but taken the notion. Another stall has only boxes, but all manner of them, made of materials imaginable and otherwise: ceramic, glass, bone, quartz, skin (not animal), hair, silk, all stiffened and held in shape by strange means. This'un, promises the salesman, is made of naught but breath and wishes. Cordelia examines it as closely as she is allowed, but remains certain it's simply extremely thin-blown glass.

They pass from the merchants to the showfolk, and this is where the wonders are.

On a slapdash stage is a boy, a youth really, of middling height with blond curls, whose face is not his own. He remakes it at will into imagined creations or does a fair imitation of someone in the crowd—male or female—which is never quite right and guarantees a laugh. His cerulean velvet frock coat is very fine, embroidery creeping across the lapels: leaves in green, cherries or apples in red, creatures that begin as birds but flow into beasts, all picked out in silver that catches the winter sun whenever it peeks from behind the clouds.

Elsewhere is a man who juggles stone spheres in a three ball cascade. At the end of each circuit in the air, one of the rocks becomes a bird which flies into the sky, wings flashing with quartz, then returns to settle in a basket at the man's feet so he may reach in for new material. On another platform a woman swallows glowing coals, then spews forth great gouts of fire as if it is nothing out of the ordinary; beside her an old man drinks water from a bucket then farts out cubes of ice that clatter from his trouser legs and onto the stage. Yet another has two young women, scandalously under-clad in the cold, their breath steaming around their heads like dragons' exhalations; they throw frayed-looking ropes upwards, which become still and stiff and remain where they are put. The young women smirk at the observers and shinny their way up the strands, the sequins and fringes of their tiny frocks waving at the crowd as the girls reach a particular height and then evaporate, becoming pale mists of pink and purple.

"Oh! Fairy floss! Mama?" Torben is the one who shrieks, but Victoria's expression is equally avid.

"Don't spoil your dinner," Cordelia says automatically, but reaches into her reticule and pulls forth bits of coin. "Henry, you're in charge. Not too much."

Her eldest child gives a sweet smile and leads his siblings off to where two middle-aged women, their white aprons stained with the bright food colours they add to the candy cobwebs they make apparently from air. She senses Merry standing beside her, fidgeting as if unsure whether to follow the children or not; Henry is at that in-between age where he is being given more responsibility, but the bounds of it are as yet uncertain.

"Merry?" says Cordelia

"Yes, Mrs Parsifal?"

"Merry, are you happy here? With us, I mean, in Lodellan." The scene she witnessed this morning coupled with her own concerns about the girl's behaviour in past months, have sat heavy on Cordelia's mind. The girl gives her a blank sort of look. "I only ask because you've seemed out of sorts lately. If I can help in anyway, tell me."

The girl's lips open and close but no sound comes.

Cordelia is aware she's starting to feel foolish, which makes her annoyed at herself; her tone is clipped as she asks, "Do you need new things? New tools for your work? New things for you personally? Would you like to take a trip somewhere, perhaps to learn from the Master Seamstresses of Mistinguett's Lace, or somewhere else? We would be happy to send you, to pay your expenses . . . or do you . . . do you perhaps wish to leave us? Find a position elsewhere?"

"Whyever would I want to leave? Whyever would I want to leave you and my aunt and the kiddies?" Merry's pale hazel eyes fill with tears, as if she's astonished that Cordelia has asked. As if she's not considered the idea herself, not even once. And then, with dread, "Do you want rid of me, Mrs Parsifal?"

"Oh no!" Cordelia's distress is sharp, high-pitched. "I hope you never leave us! Even if you marry, I hope you'll stay with us, Merry." She grasp the other's hands, feels the calluses and places where needles and pins have left their mark over the years. "I only want you to be happy, Merry, and I feel as if you've not been. Never think I want you to leave or that I'm trying to get shot of you. Let us say no more of it, but you must promise to tell me if you think of anything that will make you happier?"

Merry nods, sniffs back her tears. Cordelia gives her a little push towards where Victoria and Henry are bickering over who gets which hue of floss. "Kindly deal with them, Merry."

The girl moves away. Cordelia takes a deep breath and rolls her shoulders to loosen the tension gathered there; she lacked the courage to ask about the boy. She closes her eyes for a moment, and another and another, only opening them when a voice grabs her attention.

"Difficult when there are so many paths in front of you."

Cordelia looks around, finds a woman to her left, tending a cart. The flat surfaces are stacked with candles every colour of the rainbow. The woman sits in front of it, on a low stool by a small fire, over which is suspended a pot. The woman holds a long white strand of what looks like string and every few seconds she dips it into the contents of the pot. With each immersion, the string comes out thicker, the blue of it intensifying.

Wax and wick, Cordelia realises. The woman is a tallow-wife, a candle-maker.

"Pardon?" Cordelia steps closer to watch the work.

"So many choices for you and yours at this moment. Who can know which is the right one?" says the woman pleasantly. She's got a cloud of ashen hair with small silver charms and favours woven through it; there are bells which give a tiny but clear peel when she sits up, stretching her back and allowing the candle a few moments for the latest layer to dry.

"My, what patience you must have." Cordelia looks at the range of the woman's wares, thinks they would be lovely in the sitting room and on the dining table for formal dinners with the Agnews and the Considines. "I'd never be able to wait for so long."

"Ah, we never know what we can do until need forces it upon us. What will you have, mistress?"

"The jade and the lavender, please," she says reaching into her purse, but the woman is shaking her head, her mouth pulled in a sad smile.

"Ah, they're not for the likes of you, the green and purple. The green is for fertility and I doubt you need that, and the purple's to make a woman cautious, but you're too far gone for that, my dear. There's blue to lift a heart, yellow to bring light into a life, and the reds make passion blaze. But you . . . best to take the black, they'll do what needs doing, they'll find out the darkness at the heart of your path."

Cordelia's hands begin to shake. What does this woman know of her? She doesn't appear to offer a threat, but her words imply she wishes Cordelia ill . . . or believes it will befall her. She is about to ask what is meant by the unpleasant words the old woman had uttered, when Victoria's voice carries clear to her: "Mama! Mama!" Primed for fear, prepared for the worst, Cordelia looks up, desperately searching for her children, but sees them precisely where they were, eating the coloured floss, Merry watching over them like a hawk, while a man stands beside Henry, speaking earnestly with him.

It takes a moment for Cordelia to recognise him. Mr Farringdale. Edvard's factotum, a man of many talents who acts (as his own father did, rather less successfully, for Edvard's father) as a mix of legal advisor, accountant, and personal secretary. Not, as Cordelia's momentary panic would have her believe, someone new, a stranger, a peril; the candle-maker has her at sixes and sevens.

Isambard Farringdale has been in the Parsifals' lives for so long they can barely remember a time when the short, dapper man was not there. As she watches, he hands Henry a leather-bound journal, Torben a model ship, then turns to Victoria and offers a doll; not one of the rag moppets suspended from various stall roofs and marquee support poles, or sat in the forks of trees. No, this is a porcelain treat with auburn curls and creamy kaolin clay skin, a dress of red and purple in satin and lace. Cordelia sees tiny black leather shoes with silver buckles peek out from beneath the hem as her daughter takes the doll with a delighted squeal. Cordelia says under her breath, "How kind."

"Come now, mistress, take 'em as a gift." The old woman's voice intrudes. "I don't often give my wares away. Only when there's need." In the woman's voice there is bitter amusement and sadness and Cordelia cannot think why. She only knows she wishes to be elsewhere.

"Thank you, but no," mutters Cordelia.

"Mark my words, there's fire and water and air coming for you, mistress!" But the woman sounds resigned now, as if she's done her best and a refusal is not her fault.

Cordelia moves away from the tallow-wife and stumbles towards her children. Unnerved by the candle-maker's words, her steps are less assured than she would like. She wonders if the woman makes more money from scaring people than her selling her candles, fleecing the gullible. Does she double as a fortune-teller or is her portrayal of a distraught prophet of doom merely part of her sales technique? What can that woman know of Cordelia and her life, her family, her future? Cordelia fixes a smile and holds her hand out so that Mr Farringdale might bend gallantly over it and press his thin lips to the cool kid of her gloves.

Although Edvard is some twenty years her senior, Cordelia has never truly felt the age difference, never thought of him as an old man, until tonight. In their shared bed with all its hangings and posts, high firm mattress and fine snowy linens, he is propped against pillows, a book in his nightgown-covered lap, eyes closed as if asleep. She regards him in the dressing table mirror as she brushes her hair, applies night-cream, and she can see from the rise and fall of his chest that he is still awake. That his breath has not yet settled into a rhythm of which he himself is unaware, yet she knows well from the hours she's watched him sleep and dream.

His features have not relaxed despite the shuttered lids; they remain taut, the muscles standing at attention. His brow is lined, the fine skin beneath his eyes dark and thin and dry; his lips, rough when he kissed her cheek earlier, are peeling as if from sunburn. Patches of grey have infiltrated the ruddy brown locks she loves so. He is a man under a burden, she decides, and though she does not know what it is, equally she *does* know he will not tell her.

Her husband's firm beliefs are as affected by change as the path of the sun around the Earth, which is to say not at all. Edvard holds that a marriage has two participants, two spheres of influence, and the captain of one shall never set a hand to the tiller of the other. In all their time together he has never confided anything to do with Business (and it is always *Business*, not merely *business*) to his wife. The responsibility for making money, ensuring they are financially secure, is his, and an entirely unsuitable thing for her to learn about; in his endeavour he is helped by Mr Farringdale. Her task is to tend their home and raise their children, ably assisted by Mrs B. In this way and this way alone does their partnership function.

When Cordelia was younger and braver, wilder, she tried on a few occasions to *adjust* his attitude. She'd reminded him, when they were first married, how her parents had given her charge of dealing with the buyers who came to the Singing Vine Vineyard as soon as she'd turned thirteen. How her presence and charm had ensured greater sales every year. She bid him remember that was how they met, that his order for the SV Rouge Felix was the largest there'd ever been. Edvard, far from convinced, had spent days voicing his disapproval of her father for allowing a child—and a girl-child at that!—to be exposed to commerce in such a fashion.

Cordelia let the matter drop, let his umbrage subside, learned to quietly do what she was allowed. Then, just after the birth of Henry, thinking that surely her husband would soften since she'd provided his heir, she tried to cajole Edvard into teaching her about import and export, the ships and their ventures, all the ins and outs of their shares in the Antiphon Trading Company in far-flung Breakwater. He'd refused, gently at first, citing her fragility. She, annoyed, pointed out that as she'd had the fortitude to push his gigantic son through a very tiny fundamental hole, she was certain she could weather the rigours of buying and selling. He'd been so offended by the coarseness that he'd refused to speak with her for a week and, only after she'd apologised in floods of tears, had he relented.

Her parents, when discussing dowry terms with Edvard, had frequently praised her biddable nature: *Cordelia has the habit of good behaviour,* they would say, though they did not mention she'd learned it through hours locked in a cupboard, with belt-stripes across her backside. She found in obedience a form of camouflage, and she'd taken refuge in it as soon as she'd discovered her husband to be no more flexible than her parents. Apart from the occasional moments of rebellion, which never lasted too long, she'd done her best to behave as a dutiful wife. Her mask was so effective that she managed to convince even herself, forgetting for long periods who she was, what she'd wanted.

In some ways the habit has stood her in good stead as far as a contented marriage was concerned, although it has blinded her to other matters, and given her a firm conviction that her abilities are limited, her capacity for suffering and pain minimal, and her resilience non-existent. She tells herself she does not resent Edvard for *she* made the choice to let the less docile aspects of herself go, to bury the knowledge of her own strength and resource. To let them wither, if not die. She could have fought, certainly, until their life together was a scorched earth; she could have won if she wished, but she made the decision to be submissive and that at least was her choice alone. Cordelia is nothing if not fair-minded.

"Are you all right, my love?" she asks quietly. He startles, as if he'd forgotten she was there, jerks his knees so the book in his lap falls, and stifles a curse. In the looking glass she sees the pages in brief flashes, numbers and columns, until the ledger hits the thick carpet with almost a sigh. There is a flare of annoyance on her husband's face, then he laughs and his eyes light up. He swings his legs off the bed, fine ankles on display, and bends to retrieve the tome, which he tucks into the top drawer of his bedside table.

"Of course, my dearest. Just mulling over some figures." He crosses the room to stand behind her, his hand caressing her waves of hair, smiling at the reflection of her green, green eyes. She smiles back, thinks how handsome he still is, and he slides his other hand over her shoulder, down to cup her breast, leans in to whisper, "Come to bed, my good wife."

Afterwards, when she knows he is sleeping, when she recognises the tiny catch that presages the loud snoring she has learned to block out, she rises, sweat cooling rapidly on her naked form even with the fire blazing in the hearth. She quietly extracts the ledger from the drawer. It's curiosity more than anything, a tiny rebellion; but she doesn't understand what she sees. So many digits, neat and tidy, most in black but some in precise red, which come more and more frequently the closer she gets to the last pages. All those ciphers so conscientiously written in Mr Farringdale's tight little script. She shakes her head, thinking with a small grief that she has left it too long to learn these things, has let her mind atrophy, let too much of her intellect run out with the breast milk she's given generously to their three children. Too much energy put into selecting weekly menus and daily dresses, planning parties, running a household.

Cordelia returns the book, careful to make sure it's in the exact position she found it. Her mind may feel stagnant, but she is no fool.

In Cordelia's dreams, Bethany is small, so small, nothing but a little girl, her parents' late bliss. The child she'd bade farewell to when she left Singing Vine to marry. The child she hardly knew, for such little folk are barely formed before they are five; the fifteen year age gap made her sister a beloved stranger, someone for whom she had affection as a result of obligation rather than any great knowledge of who Bethany truly was.

Cordelia conjures a time she knows only from Bethany's occasional tales, stories sobbed after waking from nightmares. Of the time when the Blight came, traipsed in on the boot of some traveller, or dropped from the beak or shit of some bird flying from one land to the next. How it came mattered not at all; that it happened is all that mattered. She dreams of parents who, she tells herself, are not the ones she knew, not the people who shared their good fortune with those who wandered, footsore and starved, from one place to another; whose prosperity enriched the town huddled at the foot of the hills upon which Singing Vine was set. She dreams of a man and woman who'd become thin and malnourished, their mouths sunken where teeth had fallen out, bellies swollen with hunger, hair falling in clumps as despair made its home in their hearts.

She dreams of the night when the Lawrences drank down the last of the vineyard's best reds, all liberally laced with a gentle poison that made them think themselves young once more. She imagines her sister, only ten, accepting but not drinking the draught offered by loving hands. She imagines Bethany watching their parents die. She thinks of the little girl found by neighbours unable to feed another mouth, who sent her off to an orphanage in Seaton St Mary. A little girl who, when finally located almost twelve months later by Mr Farringdale's exhaustive investigations, stared at her elder sister with a gaze so empty and old that she was barely recognisable as the golden-haired cherub who lived in Cordelia's memory.

Cordelia thought that child would never forgive her, but then Bethany had fallen ill with fever and spent nigh on a month in bed. Sitting beside her, night and day, almost ignoring her own offspring, Cordelia waited to see which side of the divide between life and death the girl would choose. When Bethany at last awoke, her eyes were clear and new, and she smiled at her sister as if she was the loveliest thing ever seen. For the longest time, though, Cordelia was roused by terrified screams as the nightmares rode Bethany hard, and there ever remained some questions about life at the orphanage which her sister refused to answer.

In the small dining room, not the formal one, Victoria sits beside Cordelia and glares at her younger brother. The brooch has not been found, nor has Torben admitted his crime. Unable to find any evidence of his culpability, Cordelia will not mete out punishment; she spoke quietly with him earlier, emphasising her disappointment if he *had* taken the trinket. Henry, at fourteen, has grown out of tormenting his sister, yet Torben, at seven, still finds joy in the act. However, he swore his innocence, green-brown eyes awash, and she chose to believe him.

Edvard, at the head of the table, has been discussing with Henry the next stage of his schooling.

"Whitebarrow, Father. Or St Isidore's Mount, at a pinch."

Edvard, as yet not convinced the boy truly wishes to become a medical man rather than a merchant, lifts a brow and suggests Pennworth. Henry, tall and handsome, already a copy of his father, manages to keep his expression neutral and nods consideringly. Cordelia frowns for the both of them: Edvard had agreed to abide by the boy's wishes. Pennworth is not noted for its medical curriculum, but commercial . . . that and the fact that it is known to be . . . *economical*, the sort of place people lower on the social scale than the Parsifals send their sons in the hope they'll learn to make money. Such an alma mater may well cost a young man certain positions, certain advancements. Henry's tutors have given glowing reports of his abilities, supported by the results of the entrance exams he'd sat some weeks ago, which showed he was more than capable of undertaking the studies at Whitebarrow.

Cordelia smiles at her son, encouraging, hoping he will remain strong, and not be swayed by another's wishes. Stronger than she has chosen to be. The problem with appeasing others, she thinks, is that it becomes a hard habit to break. Should she tell her boy this sooner rather than later, or point out to Edvard that he has three heirs, not simply one, if he would but open his eyes? Torben will settle, when he's older. Victoria . . . she gives her daughter a surreptitious glance and worries that she's made the girl too readily into what she herself has striven, by denial of self, to become. Is Victoria helpless, will she drift until she finds a husband to tell her who to be, what to do? Cordelia swallows the disquiet and resolves to speak with Edvard after dinner, to remind him of his promises; remind him if she must that, according to his own rules, the children are *her* purview and she will see them follow their hearts.

Bethany's place is empty but Cordelia gives Merry a nod to serve the rare roast she's been carving at the sideboard. Cordelia rubs her stomach surreptitiously; a new life is growing there. She wasn't certain until this morning, when her bloods failed to appear—she has been regular as the moon ever since her twelfth year—and now she knows. She is unsure how she feels: three children have done enough to drain the life from her. It's not that she doesn't love them, but she'd thought Torben the last. She has been looking forward to a time when she might convince Edvard to let her travel with him, to leave landlocked Lodellan and go thence to the sea. Perhaps even to make the journey *home*, up into the mountains to where the old vineyard lay, to see what might be salvaged, perhaps to try her hand at a new venture and see if her parents' sacrifices might still be worth something. She hoped, when the children were independent, but this . . . this would delay that at least another fourteen years.

She squeezes her eyes shut, keeps them that way until she senses someone at her elbow. Merry stares at her, a little moodily, a little concerned, the fresh pot of coffee in a pin-and-needle pricked hand. Cordelia smiles and nods for her to pour the steaming bitter brew. Edvard has always disdained her habit of drinking it with dinner, but he has ceased to comment. She adds cream, but no sugar, and sips; feels the thing in her stomach, however small—two months, no more—squirm and protest. All her children were thus, all objecting *in utero* to the beverage; to this day Victoria screws up her nose at the smell. And every day Cordelia bids her not to do so for the wind may change and leave her face all a'turn. Well, the girl would not need worry soon enough, for this new pup will curtail her mother's customs if she wishes to keep any food down at all.

She wonders if she might refuse to go through with it. She is thirty-two, almost thirty-three: hasn't she done enough? Hasn't her body done enough? How many more dark purple veins will pattern her hips and thighs? How many more crêpe-ripples will emboss her breasts, her belly? How much higher will her hairline reach, how much thinner will her hair get, how much will fall out this time? And will it recover as well? Will it regain its thickness, its sheen, its weight? *Who would I go to? Who might know of such things?* Nowadays the city is filled only by male physicians; the cunning women have been hunted, driven to ground, and are few and far between. Magic and old medicine have become elusive, rare, endangered. Even Mrs B's little habits and rituals, her acts of household magic—hanging a toadstone pendant around the children's necks when they were ill; putting little purses of graveyard dirt beneath pillows when a member of the household could not sleep; all the tisanes she brewed for any number of ailments—all are carefully hidden lest someone see and talk.

Her reverie is broken by Bethany's bright greeting, and she removes the hand from her stomach so no one might notice. Her sister offers an envelope to her, and an inky broadsheet to Henry. Cordelia recognises the lilac stationery and gold wax seal, and breaks into a relieved smile, which Edvard echoes. She barely notices her sister's excited glow as she sits beside Henry, hand lighting on the lad's shoulder so briefly. The boy buries himself in the news, while Bethany's attention is concentrated on Cordelia.

This missive is coveted in Lodellan: a summons, really, to the Winter Solstice Ball thrown by the Princess Royal. This is the second occasion in a row that the Parsifals have garnered such favour. To be invited one year and forgotten the next, replaced by newer, richer, more amusing callers, is to be dreaded! A second request means one automatically passes onto the repeat guest list. It is precisely the sort of invitation Edward spent so many years seeking—subtly, of course, without appearing to do so. He's rebuilt the family fortune his grandfather frittered on dancehall girls who were more expensive than one might have expected, racehorses that were slower than they should have been, and a variety of alchemical experiments meant to create diamonds and gems and gold by the molehill, by the mountain.

"What will you wear, Dellie?" asks Bethany, tone sly. "Though why I ask when you've spent so much of your time on this important decision . . . "

Cordelia chooses to ignore the dig, and toys with the envelope flap, reluctant to break the resplendent seal; then she carefully slips the length of her pink nail beneath and gently encourages the wax up, all in one piece. The small triumph makes her smile. "The purple, I think."

The dress has often felt like a daring, audacious thing, made in *hope*. Merry has been working on it for months and Cordelia watched the last stitches being placed in the hems not two days ago. She has worried, sometimes, that it has been too cheeky, a challenge to fate; others she simply revels in how lovely it is and that it is hers.

"A decision worthy of the intellect devoted to it," says her sister, as if it's a joke, as if there's no edge to her words, and nods at Merry. The girl brings the wine decanter, pours for Edvard and Bethany; a half-glass for Henry, which is then topped up with water. Cordelia shakes her head when the girl lifts the vessel in offer.

"Then this is the perfect time, my love," says Edvard. Cordelia concentrates on him, on his eyes, mouth, then glances at her sister's avid expression as she, too, watches Edvard. It makes Cordelia uncomfortable; it brings to mind this afternoon when she came upon her husband and sister, standing close and whispering, huddled like conspirators, Bethany's posture reminiscent of the women on Half-moon Lane, those not fortunate enough to have a place on Courtesans' Row. She pushes aside the fears that have crawled up her spine, have curled in the pit of her belly. She brightens her gaze, widens her smile.

In Edvard's hand is a burgundy velvet box.

"For you, darling, to ensure you are the belle of the ball."

Her fingers slip and shake as she accepts, and seeks the latch. By clever design, the lid flips open when the catch is released and inside, lying on a bed of dark red, is a necklace. Her sister smiles and claps with delight, but no surprise. *This*, Cordelia thinks with relief, is why her husband and sister have been speaking secretly. Her relief is too great, but she chooses not to examine what that might mean, and concentrates on the gift.

An enormous amethyst is the heart of the piece; it is glorious, cut many times over to give the perfect shape, to glean every bit of light from the candles, the fire in the hearth. It seems to have impossible depths, a darkness and a lightness dancing within and without its hallucinatory purple hue. It is surrounded by a band of alternating emeralds and diamonds, set in an opening lily of white-gold, each petal perfectly recreated. All hangs from a chain of tiny elegant interlocking silver spirals.

Cordelia drapes it around her neck, ensures it's secure. It feels warm against her flesh as she rises to stare at her reflection in the gilt mirror above the small fireplace. A few dark spots on her creamy skin distract her—a sure sign of a babe on the way; lemon juice solution will help. She attends to the necklace again, primps and preens, smiles at her second self in the mercury, the one who is free from all the burdens she bears, all the burdens she has consented to. Her smile dims when she recalls that the Winter Solstice Ball will be the last time she can fit into the dress for a long while. She touches the amethyst absently.

Edvard calls, "To the table, my love, and your dinner. You must eat, you need your strength."

And Cordelia realises, then, that he *knows*. His smile is too smug, his words too weighted. He won't mention it yet, will consider it something for her to announce, but his knowledge gives her no options, other than deceit. The thing around her neck turns cold as she recognises it as a bribe, a sop, a pretty thing to wear while she grows fat yet again. While all her chances for change disappear. Still, Cordelia is skilled at hiding her true self, and she smooths her expression until it is pleasantly bland, then takes her place beside her husband.

Merry brings out the first dessert and places it on the sideboard. The boys eat quickly and will be through their main course well before the rest of the family.

"Henry," Cordelia says, noticing the broadsheet beside his plate leaves smears on the snowy cloth. "Put that away, you're making a mess."

"The Agnews," he says sombrely, folding the pages and handing them off to Merry without even looking at her, as if she's not there. Cordelia is caught between reprimanding him for that small impoliteness, and preoccupation at his words. Preoccupation wins.

"What of them?"

"They've been murdered—Master and Mistress, Mrs Agnew's parents, the four children, and the three servants."

Cordelia's hand goes to her throat, finds the gem, grasps it. The amethyst curls into her palm as if it belongs there. She seems to feel the echo of her heartbeat deep in the stone.

"Do they know . . . " begins Edvard, unable to finish a question with so much potential, so many gaps, and mysteries, and lacunae, so many possible answers. The Agnews were one of the city's most prominent families, certainly one of the richest; not bad folk, generous to those beneath them, kind to their servants and those in their employ, charitable, philanthropic. The robberies have been bad enough, but now, *this*.

Murder.

And not a slaying in the road, not a battle of lowlifes, not a fight between tarts that's gotten out of hand, not an over-enthusiastic debt-collector, nor a constable taking his duties too seriously. But a killing in a fine house barely three streets away. A killing of a fine family who should have been touched by no more than time and the rigours of old age, not by violence. Not by something so . . .

Henry clears his throat, he is pale; he'd been friends with the oldest Agnew boy. "A robbery gone wrong. There was another body. They think someone interrupted the thief, who tried to eliminate all witnesses. Perhaps Mr Agnew managed to kill him even as he himself was dying."

"Who?" asks Victoria through her tears. She would no longer play with Ozanne and Oriel Agnew, her closest companions.

"An employee of the Considines', their valet-in-training . . . Japheth something or other."

Cordelia's twists in her seat, gaze going immediately to Merry, who has dropped the second dessert tray. Meringue and cream and fruit compote spread far and wide across the expensive silk carpet. The girl holds both hands to her mouth, face drained of all colour, and Cordelia thinks, foolishly, that she is quite lovely when not scowling. Merry's eyes are huge, the pupils so large there is almost no white left around the irises that at this moment look more green than hazel. Before Cordelia can go to her, the tweeny flees, sobs trailing behind her like black mourning ribbons.

The last notes of the requiem mass still hang in the air when the Parsifals leave by the great arched doorway of Lodellan's cathedral, passing by the six ghostly wolf-hounds—age evident in their fading outlines—that guard the holy house. The family is in the front half of the dolorous procession following the archbishop; the line of mourners snakes across the portico, down the stone steps, then along the footpath to where the lychgate breaks the walls surrounding the graveyard. Cordelia looks up at the elaborate roof and see shadows shifting in the steep angles there; then the moment is gone, and she is through the strange bottleneck and pursuing the safest paths. The ground is treacherous in places, the unwary who wander are likely to find themselves breaking through the crust of the earth and turning an ankle in an unsuspected grave, or worse. The trees, mainly yew and oak, are ancient, branches and roots entwine from one tree to the other, and thick bushes fill any space in between; beneath the canopy the shadows are cold, and Cordelia hears the chattering of teeth behind her. *One of the children*, she thinks, *Victoria*.

Ahead, she sees the flickering torch the archbishop carries to light his way into the Agnew vault.

The cortège sweeps past the graves of the poor, marked by simple white crosses or piles of stones. Next come the merchants' plots, which are tidier and larger, the slabs and headstones made of better material, more marble and granite, the statuary showing signs of artistry. There is Micah Bartleby's tomb, black quartz glistening in the skerrick of sunlight that's fought its way through, and here an angel leans drunkenly, its features all but erased by the elements and the only trace of a name left is *Hepsi . . . tyne*.

At last they come to the mausoleums, where Lodellan's richest and best lie, and the great snake of mourners splits around the pink marmoreal structure where the Agnews will take their final rest, and forms a line either side. No distant cousin or such can be located—the family has been utterly annihilated—so Belladonna Considine, wrapped in shimmering black bombazine, undertakes funereal honours. She wears a veil of netting so thick one can barely make out her features.

How must she feel? wonders Cordelia. *Knowing her own servant visited such catastrophe on her dearest friends?* Belladonna takes the fat golden key from the archbishop's hand and inserts it in the lock, then gives the heavy door a good push. There is neither creak nor groan of hinges, for the structure is kept in good repair. Belladonna steps aside, into her husband's politely waiting arms, and the clusters of pallbearers trail the archbishop and his blazing brand down into the darkness of the crypt.

Cordelia is grateful she does not have to go beneath, to feel the blackness pressing in from all sides. She puts an arm around Victoria, who stands close, shivering. The cold on the girl's shoulders is so intense it bites through the leather of Cordelia's glove. She looks at her daughter and sees, to her left, in the space between Victoria and Torben, a pale white formless mist. Cordelia blinks, but is careful not to draw attention. She glances at the crowd then realises no one else can see the icy cloud; she manages a motion that is part-rub, part-wave, and her fingers pass through the thin fog, leaving traces and trails in the air. Soon it dissipates and Victoria's tremors ease.

Cordelia takes a relieved breath and finds Bethany, who holds Henry close, looking at her. Cordelia smiles and focuses once more on the mouth of the sepulchre, where the first group of attendants returns to the light, quickly stepping aside so the next can deposit their own burden. She'll not tell her sister about the mist or how it felt; Bethany needs no encouragement to laugh at her. She does not wish to be regarded as mad as well as weak, but Cordelia knows as surely as night follows day that around them, in the trees and foliage which weaves their way through the graveyard, there are things, other things, which move and watch, breathe and sleep, dream and desire. Things that the clever rich folk of Lodellan don't believe in for it is not *fashionable*. But those with less money and more sense still leave offerings on the graves; the sexton still plants lavender over the common burial pits where the indigent and unloved lie, in hope of ensuring they rest in peace; and mothers in the slum quarters still warn their children not to listen to the sound of the jingling copper bells hanging from some of the yews and oaks in the bone orchard. Though she's told no one Cordelia has seen them on occasion, the things that shift and threaten, when she's come to visit the grave of one friend or another. She holds her daughter closer.

Later, at the wake at the Considine house, Cordelia finds herself alone with Belladonna. A small bubble of quiet, of suspended time, forms around them; outside it there is well-mannered noise, conversation, people attired in haute couture black weeds moving in a strange kind of dance. Cordelia touches her friend's hand gently and says how sorry she is. Belladonna pauses, tugs at her veil and shows her face. The transformation is terrible: the once-silver eyes are dead grey ice; the elegantly high cheeks are hollowed and the skin drawn tight, with a yellow tint; the pouting mouth is slack, the lips strangely thin, and poised as if a howl might force its way between them at any moment. There is such guilt and such burden.

"How can I go on? Knowing we—*I*—harboured a viper in our bosom?" Belladonna's voice is so low that Cordelia can barely hear. She squeezes the other woman's arm tightly, hoping for sympathy and strength to flow into her. She thinks, although she tries not to, how Bethany told of the boy Japheth's body: thrown onto the midden heap outside Lodellan's walls. While she can understand the urge, she still considers such an act vindictive and short-sighted: no carefully constructed coffin to either help him rest easy or keep him from haunting the city until the last trumpet sounds.

"My dear Bella, you have no need of guilt. You did not employ him in an ill house, did not subject him to evil influences. However his heart and mind were turned, the cause was not here. Not you." Cordelia lightly strokes the other's sleeve. "Mourn your friends by all means, but you had no role in their deaths, please set aside that woe."

Tears flood the other woman's eyes, as if the kindness is unbearable. She pulls from Cordelia and flees, to the upper levels of the house, covering her face as she goes. Cordelia feels empty, bereft. She shakes her head; her mind is adrift, her emotions high with the tragedy striking so close to home. She just needs time, as does Bella, to recover, to feel as if the ground is solid beneath them once again. Blinking, Cordelia turns to the ballroom—the only room big enough to hold the crowd—now hung with black crepe and wreaths of lily and rowan, acanthus and asphodel.

Henry, Victoria, and Torben will be in one of the auxiliary parlours, playing in desultory fashion with what pass for friends amongst the children of the rich. Across the room Cordelia spies Edvard, part of a group of sombre-looking men. Their expressions are carefully maintained, but she suspects she knows what they hide: a combination of judgment and fear. Judgment of Leon Agnew, that he did not protect his family, and fear that he *could not* do so. Fear that there but for the grace of God went each and every one of them. Edvard has spent the past few days ensuring weapons are hidden throughout their house, that Henry knows where they are and so do the coachman and footman. Not Cordelia, though, nor Victoria nor Bethany, nor Mrs B, nor Merry, for if the menfolk failed to defend them, what could women possibly do?

One of his companions says something and Cordelia watches as Edvard's face pinches, sours. His reply makes the other man wither and shrink, and she wonders what has lit her husband's serene temper so quickly. She senses someone beside her: Bethany, pale and lovely, hair beneath an ebon lace mourning bonnet, her dress of charcoal satin with tight pintucks that Merry's clever fingers took hours and hours to achieve. At her breast is an oval broach, glass-fronted, showing the coil of blond hair that belonged to their mother. By rights it should have been Cordelia's but it was the sole possession Bethany managed to keep during her stay at the orphanage and Cordelia never had the heart to insist when her sister had already lost so much.

"What do you think he said?" she says idly, wistfully. "What are they discussing?"

"Surely, sister, you've enough gumption to find out?" Bethany's tone is sharp and it cuts. Why don't you ask him yourself? Keep at him until he answers?"

Cordelia knows her shock and hurt are writ large on her face; Bethany shows no sign of caring, and continues, "Why do you insist on being wilfully ignorant? I swear, Cordelia, you were never such a fool when we were small."

Cordelia thinks that unfair; Bethany was so young when her older sister left Singing Vine. What recollections could she possibly have? She has the uncomfortable feeling, though, that Bethany is right; as a child and young woman Cordelia was outspoken and inquisitive, insistent, and always, always gained the knowledge she wanted, needed. She did not dwell in ignorance, and no one ever told her certain things were not her concern. How did she become as she is now? Did she give up all at once? Or bit by bit, unaware of how she was changing? *Lessening* just to make life easier? She turns her mind from the idea of growing dim, of diminishing. It seems too hurtful, too fearful. She blinks, feels Bethany's hand on her arm.

"I'm sorry, sister, I should not have spoken so. It is . . . the grief." Bethany bats away tears or so it seems. "They speak of men's matters, of commerce and the like. They will discuss Agnew's failure as man and husband, protector and guardian of his family. They'll opine how terrible a monster that boy must have been to do this thing, to overcome one such as Leon. Then they will grow quiet and discomforted until someone mentions a mistress to break the tension, the residence he keeps her in on Courtesans' Row, the clever things she does, and how happy it makes him to know she is his refuge from a demanding wife and puling offspring."

Cordelia wonders if Edvard is one of those men, if he visits another woman in a tall house that she can imagine all too vividly: red velvet drapes, luxurious sofas, beds hung with silks and fine netting, walls decorated with erotic frescos from which inspiration might be taken. Cordelia shakes her head; Mrs Bell sewed a swan's feather into Edvard's pillow the day of their marriage, a sure way to ensure fidelity she'd said. Cordelia feels quite unstable already without the weight of Edvard's possible secrets tumbling onto her. She absently pats Bethany's cheek and moves off before her sister can say something even more disturbing; she feels, yet again, that she no longer knows the girl she raised as her own. *It is her age*, she thinks, *she is finding herself*. It will settle, eventually, and they shall rub along nicely once more.

Cordelia tries to change the direction of her dreams, encourage them back towards happier terrain; she knows, though, that they will not obey her entirely, or indeed for long. But still it seems she succeeds as the days before the Winter Solstice Ball run together. In her sleep, she could swear the fire is real, that the scent of burning wood and roasting chestnuts tickle her nostrils. She picks pleasant scenes as she once did the sweetest cherries from a bowl. She is sure she can hear the crackle and snap of twigs, the small avalanches of cinders and glowing coals through the grate, that she can hear the laughter in the house. She turns in her slumber, enjoying the warmth, the memory . . . yet that changes once again all too soon.

The air in the house is thick with mourning. Cordelia finds it hard to breathe, harder still to see the expressions of shock on her children's faces. They've never been faced with loss or grief in their short lives; she feels she has failed to prepare them. Edvard's parents were long-dead by the time he married, and her own parents' deaths occurred when Henry was very small. Their world has been intact, hermetically sealed from heartache, and she searches desperately for a way to make them smile again. Cordelia leaves Merry at home, does not even mention that they are going out. The girl has been heavy-eyed, inattentive, hard of hearing since news of the Agnews and their murderer was heard; she has refused to discuss the matter though Cordelia has tried to offer comfort. Even Mrs B has failed to draw anything from her, or so she has told Cordelia. Cordelia wonders if the girl has been outside the city walls, walking the paths that have been worn through Lodellan's great midden heap by scavengers who go on two legs as well as four, looking for the body of the boy she loved.

Yet taking the children to the carnival the morning of the Ball is a mistake, which she understands only as they step beneath the archway entrance, and she once more trickles coin into the toothless old woman's hand. This is the final day, the crowd is thin, and the troupe are already packing up: there are fewer toys and gewgaws on the stalls, most of the makeshift stages have been pulled down and only the girls who climb the enchanted ropes are performing. Their air is one of boredom, barely concealed impatience; they're the last act, thinks Cordelia, the one most likely to attract attention. Does this happen every time the show moves on or is there a ballot and the girls drew the short straw on this occasion?

Her offspring remain listless, indeed their languor seems to increase as if infected by the apathy of the dying carnival. Cordelia sighs heavily and Bethany, strangely compassionate, takes her arm as they wander aimlessly through the partially deconstructed landscape. Torben, Victoria, and even Henry amble in front of them like lambs. Bethany does not even rouse herself to make disparaging remarks and Cordelia is grateful her sister has at last developed some kind of restraint.

The sight of her babies so passive, so downhearted, is depressing. Normally she would have to shepherd them, drag them back into easy reach, or have Merry do it. The longer she watches, the heavier the oppression becomes, but she fights it until she sees the cart with the coloured candles—much fewer than last time, whether due to sales or packing she cannot know—and the woman who makes them, the tallow-wife, who stares at her with an unfathomable gaze. That is when she feels her chest compressing, compacting, growing tighter; finds the air harder to pull into her lungs no matter how deeply she breathes.

"Take care of them for me, Bethany," she gasps, pulling away from her sister. "I must walk."

And Bethany nods and lets her go, as if recognising what Cordelia needs most right now is solitude, not worry nor sympathy.

Cordelia pushes and shoves her way through the dwindling crowd as if she's a fishwife on the docks of some town that actually has an ocean, has something more than the river that's become sluggish and brown over the years. It's all she can do to keep from breaking into a run. She's out now, beyond the enigmatic gaze of the tallow-wife, gone from the press of bodies; the noise and chatter diminish behind her as she walks faster and faster and her ladylike shoes beat a desperate rhythm of escape along the main road.

Farther away from Lodellan, she feels she can breathe again, and she slows, stops. Between the trees is a building, a low dilapidated affair of wood bruised by time and weather. Cordelia moves toward it; the roof has fallen in at some point, a tree grows through the western wall, the door hangs by one tenacious hinge alone, and the windows have long been shattered. She searches her memory and finds something at last, snags it, draws it up. Tales of a woman many years ago, the city's finest coffin-maker though none recall her name. Her demise was murky and led to whispers and rumours about her true goings-on, though Cordelia cannot recall precise details try though she might.

She looks at the tumbledown structure, at the wreckage of what someone sought to build. She thinks of her parents, of the Singing Vine and what its loss meant to them. She thinks of the Agnews, how their lives were lost but their possessions remain, to do no good to anyone. She thinks that the destruction of *things* should not mean the ruination of a life.

Cordelia looks over her shoulder, looks at the road that leads away, is struck by the scandalous idea that she could simply keep going.

Then she remembers the child that grows inside her, remembers the children she has already birthed, recalls Mrs B and Merry, Edvard and Bethany. She thinks on the pillars of her existence and is ashamed she could contemplate such cowardly flight. Cordelia turns on her heel and returns to the carnival.

The old woman on the gate lets her through, waving away the coins she offers. More, she points the direction in which she might find her family. Cordelia gives the candle-maker a wide berth.

She espies the children at a tiny petting zoo. Victoria and Torben seem more animated as they fuss over the baby animals: there's a bear cub, a pony, a lamb, a calf, and a wolf pup; kits of snow fox and badger. Henry kneels, with no thought for his expensive kerseymere breeches, beside an exotic kitten with fur of black and orange stripes, which eyes the other animals as if they might provide its luncheon.

For a few moments she cannot see Bethany and anger begins to boil at the perceived lack of responsibility. Then she is there, her tall slender sister with her golden curls held in place by fine black netting, wearing yet another exquisite black mourning gown made by Merry's clever, miserable fingers.

Bethany is gesturing at someone Cordelia cannot see until her sister moves aside and there is Mr Farringdale once more, this time gripping a magnificent bouquet of flowers: red roses, asters, carnations, daffodils, daisies, forget-me-nots, and hyacinths . . . in fact so many blooms that are out of season Cordelia wonders how he got them and how much this tribute cost. This token of his affection, however, goes unnoticed, uncollected, unaccepted, and Cordelia is pierced by the expression of loss on the little man's face.

Oh, poor Mr Farringdale, to hold a torch for such as Bethany. Bethany, who's refused the richest, handsomest, finest bucks of Lodellan. What chance could he possibly think he might have?

And her sister turns then, as if she senses Cordelia's presence, her thoughts. And in that moment Bethany's face is naked: Cordelia doesn't recognise this girl whose expression is so fierce and feral, shows too many wishes and wants, too much greed, lust, abandon, arrogance, and pride. And in that moment Cordelia feels as though there is more, much more than an age gap between them . . .

. . . then Bethany sees her and grins; she is herself again, sweet though mischievous, sometimes cruel but never too much so, a little bold, but not too bold, eyes warming and dancing. She is Cordelia's little sister once more, not a woman standing on the precipice between light and shadow. Cordelia tries to smile, finds her lips stiff and unwilling, for the memory of her sister's changed face is too fresh, too raw; it leaves a residue of fear that Cordelia cannot comprehend. She forces the corners of her mouth upwards; dismisses the moment for it is too unreal.

As she approaches, Mr Farringdale scurries away, no doubt to nurse his heart with the aid of the mulled cherry wine and blackberry port of which he is so fond. Cordelia will speak to Bethany, yes, but not today, not tonight. Tomorrow, after the Ball. There has been enough unpleasantness, and Cordelia is determined to rebuild her family's happiness. They will stay here as long as the children wish, as long as she can see their joy returning if only in some small measure, for it is a start.

And Mr Farringdale, poor Mr Farringdale . . . she will make enquiries and investigations. There will be women in Lodellan who would welcome his suit, who would see him as a good, solid investment, someone who would appreciate their kindness and wifely efforts on his behalf. Someone who would mend what Bethany in her youth and hubris has injured.

Tonight is the winter solstice: the longest night. Tomorrow will be a time of new beginnings, the day to start over. Yes. Everything can be fixed.

The dress is exquisite, a raw silk that contains within its warp and weft all possible variations of purple: lavender, lilac, fuchsia, violet, amaranthine, magenta, periwinkle, mulberry . . . every tone and shade and hue. It skims Cordelia's trim-for-now figure perfectly, though Merry has had to let it out twice in the fortnight before the ball. She has done so with lips pursed, gaze judging, as if Cordelia has been overeating, doing it on purpose. Alas, all the adjustments—and Merry's grieving inattention—have left one of the appliquéd roses, which encircle the waist and trail down the skirt like a cascade, somewhat loose. A few quick stitches are required before Master and Mistress Parsifal depart.

Cordelia's hair is swept up onto the crown of her head, pale sunlight curls tumbling artfully, although it took more than two hours to get them to look so casual. The gown shifts and changes its colour and mood with every movement, and the necklace, oh the necklace! It is pure magnificence. There will be nothing like it at the Ball.

Merry's room is at the top of the stairs, a large attic space fitted with rugs and hangings to keep out the winter chill, a comfortable bed with a richly embroidered quilt full and fat with goose down. Part of the area is set aside for the girl's sewing: there are three tailor's dummies, a workbench for cutting patterns and material, a series of shelves with skeins of silk, and drawers wherein lie needles and pins and scissors of various size and shape and sharpness, each intended for a different purpose. But of Merry herself there is no evidence, which makes Cordelia puff an exasperated breath. Yet she'll not entrust this small task to Annie the parlour maid's ham-fisted efforts.

No matter. A tack or two is all that's needed, a service she did for her own mother many years ago. As long as she is careful not to prick herself and bleed on the fabric, it will be a simple task. She eyes the range of threads and finds the correct hue, then opens the drawers one after another seeking the right gauge of needle. In the last compartment something catches her eye, a flash of silver and green and nacre, a small brooch in the shape of a spray of lilies. The one she gave Victoria for her thirteenth birthday, on the eve of her Presentation Ball, the item the girl wore on the pearl organdie gown with argentella lace. The very brooch Torben has been accused of stealing.

And it is *here*.

In this drawer.

In this room.

In the possession of this girl . . .

Cordelia's throat tightens as she thinks of having this girl, this dangerous girl, this sullen, angry, moody girl in her house, near her family. This girl . . . this girl whom she'd welcomed when Mrs B had taken in the orphaned niece as a baby, who'd been raised beside the Parsifal children, to whom she'd given a position, a wage, and much patience. The thought that this girl should so requite her kindness in a petty dishonest manner, that this girl had been associating with a killer . . .

Her fear makes her angrier than she might otherwise be; it washes reason and kindness away. Deliberately, Cordelia reaches into the drawer and finds a tiny silver pin. Her hands shake as she fastens the wayward rose in place, and it's only by sheer force of will that she completes her task without drawing blood. The she picks up the brooch, all her anger, her fear, her umbrage, pooling, roiling and boiling as she makes her way downstairs to the basement kitchen.

Once again there's no sign of Merry, but Mrs Bell is tidying after supper, grey-gold tendrils peeking from under her mob cap. She smiles as Cordelia enters, eyes lighting up, expression fond as fond can be, but finds no answering grin. Cordelia holds out her fist, fingers opening like petals to show the spray of gilded lilies there. Mrs B is perplexed.

"Where did you find it, madam? Did Torben—"

"It was in Merry's room," says Cordelia tightly.

Mrs Bell stares, then shakes her head. "She's a good girl, Mrs Parsifal. I know she's had a hard time of it and she's been a challenge for you, but she's a good girl for all that."

"She has to go." Cordelia's tone is arctic, and it chills the housekeeper who's never heard such a sound from her mistress's lips.

"Perhaps Miss Victoria misplaced the brooch when she was in for a fitting . . ." The excuse is weak even to her ears: Victoria hasn't had a new dress in months. "You've known Merry all her life, Mrs Parsifal. She's not bad, no more than Miss Bethany's ever been. I'm sure . . ."

The older woman's pain begins to crack Cordelia icy determination, but she steels herself: she will not be defied. Not in this. The house is the one sphere over which she has control. Her husband keeps secrets from her; her sister is becoming a stranger; this is the sole change she can enforce.

"Make sure she's gone by the time we get back tonight, Mrs Bell," orders Cordelia, blinking hard to keep the tears confined. They cannot be allowed to run or they will take the black lash powder and eye-paint with them, cut swathes through the glimmering pearl foundation powder, drop onto and ruin her dress. "I'm sorry, but I really must insist."

"There's no bad in my niece, Mrs Parsifal." Mrs Bell wrings her apron with dry, red hands. "I beg you to reconsider, my dearling."

"Not much good either it seems," snaps Cordelia, fighting the effect of her childhood nickname, then watches as Mrs B's aspect freezes. All her affection drains from it. She speaks quietly.

"If Merry goes, then so must I, Mistress," says Mrs Bell, her own tears utterly unfettered, pattering on the white of her apron front. Cordelia is stunned, hurt, possibly as stunned and hurt as Mrs B, but this doesn't occur to her, nor will it for weeks to come. Her face burns while her heart closes—that her old nurse would choose such a girl over her!—and she draws herself stiff and straight.

"Do what you must," says Cordelia, breaking a lifetime's bond too easily, and spins about, hurries up the stairs into the hall where Edvard waits impatiently. Annie, beside him, has her mistress' fur-lined cloak waiting. She drapes it around Cordelia's shoulders as she gently draws on the lavender silk gloves that are meant for show, not warmth; then Annie disappears, subtle as a ghost. Cordelia keeps her head down so Edvard cannot see her expression, will not ask what is wrong and delay their departure. Had she but taken the time to steal a glance at *him* she would have observed his distraction, his pallor, and the fact that his eyes do not quite light upon her at all, as if she is simply an amorphous thing on which he cannot focus. But, caught up in her own web of upset, she does not notice that her husband is distressed to the point of inattentiveness as they step outside to where their coachman awaits with a carriage and four.

~

In her sleep, Cordelia imagines the baby is still inside her. She feels it turning and twisting, making her stomach bubble as if in the grip of terrible indigestion. As if a small sea creature does somersaults in the very pit of her. She could swear it's real, could swear it's solid and true—though it's months since her belly carried anything but hunger. She imagines that when she wakes it will be to the sweet, demanding cry of a newborn seeking milk, of a child wanting the comfort of its mother's arms, the warmth of her familiar flesh.

She dreams that the unwished-for child is still hers to have and hold.

The coach takes them the short distance to the palace, pulls up outside the grand wing which Armandine, the Princess Royal, has made her own since her brother's marriage. Though the Prince of Lodellan will not be in attendance tonight—he seldom partakes in his sister's soirées—his wife will be, for this is the woman with whom Armandine herself was, and still is, in love.

Some whisper the prince's bride has no aristocratic lineage at all, that she was selected for her peasant heartiness, the width of her hips, the generosity of her breasts—for her perceived fecundity. Thin blue blood, fussy breeding habits, and limited marriage pools have failed the ruling family, and the days of large broods are done with. It is said that Princess Armandine gave up her lover only in the daylight hours when propriety still held some sway, that she and Ilse yet meet on all but those nights when the royal physicians deemed her most likely to conceive. As a result, Ilse is round, set to provide the longed-for, much-needed heir, an heir with his mother's robustness, born of a woman whose bloodline has not been weakened by its *purity*.

But Cordelia doesn't think of the rumours. She doesn't think on the importance of this invitation, of the culmination of Edvard's ambitions, of the beauty of her dress and the splendour of the necklace lying cold around her throat. She thinks only of Merry and her betrayal, of Mrs Bell and her ill-placed loyalty. She thinks of a home without Mrs B's warmth, of the absence of a woman she only now admits she loves better than she ever did her own icily beautiful mother; the woman who protected her from the worst of her maternal parent's rages and punishments. She shakes herself as the footman rolls out the metal steps, and Edvard helps her from the carriage. She makes a concerted effort to forget all that's happened, to concentrate on the Ball, on being Edvard's fine wife, on doing him justice.

They sweep in through the first set of doors, wood and fittings faded by the elements, up stone steps covered in a red carpet for this eve only, along a phalanx of men-at-arms in shining livery, and join the receiving line waiting outside a second set of doors, great arched things of highly polished ebony banded with gold. Cloaks are taken by maids and whisked away. When their turn comes, Edvard offers the pale purple leaf to the chief doorman, whose expert eyes scan the contents. Satisfied it's no forgery, he gives a nod to the lesser doormen, who push open the panels and let them through. Their card returned, they step inside, onto a landing high above the ballroom floor. A herald, now, takes the invitation and reads out their names at the top of her lungs, so all heads swivel to look, to see, to judge.

Proceeding down the red marble staircase they are engulfed, briefly, by friends before joining the next section of the receiving line. Cordelia notes, amongst the already-arrived, already-welcomed guests, Belladonna Considine in an exquisite sable gown covered with shimmering jet beads. Her very public mourning is tasteful, understood, yet no one would expect her to forego the Winter Solstice Ball. Cordelia fixes a smile for her, part greeting, part sympathy, and flutters her fingers to catch the other woman's eye. Belladonna's lips begin to lift in answer, then stop, her glance hooked and caught by . . . something. Cordelia wonders if she's been found somehow unfit, her dress has been compromised by errant snowflakes, stained or marked in the kitchen during her confrontation, but a downward glance reassures her.

Belladonna moves off, swiftly. *Is she embarrassed by her outburst at the wake?* Before Cordelia can comment to Edvard they are swept onwards to a raised dais where the Princess Royal, platinum-blond locks carefully braided into a crown studded with gem-encrusted pins, awaits on a high-backed chair. Beside her, on a chaise longue set slightly lower, lounges a woman with fiery red hair and bored yellow eyes that glitter at the sight of Cordelia's gems. Her cheekbones are broad, her head quite round but for the sharp little chin, and a heavy belly presses against the fine chiffon underskirts displayed through the slit of her amber high-waisted outer gown. It's all Cordelia can do to resist the urge to touch her own stomach in sympathy.

Edvard bows and Cordelia curtsies. The Princess Royal's appreciative glance takes in the dress and necklace. She offers her hand, long and pale fingers weighted down by many rings. First Edvard, then Cordelia, bow over them, kissing the cool stones and even cooler flesh. One of the diamonds catches Cordelia's bottom lip, just a little and she feels a tiny cut, and a minuscule spring of ruby red. She licks it away and raises her head to meet Armandine's gaze.

"What a delightful ensemble, Mrs Parsifal. You must tell me the name of your seamstress."

"A girl of our household, Your Highness," she replies, the lie heavy in her mouth.

"You must let me borrow her," says the princess.

Cordelia nods. "Of course, Your Highness." She does not know how she will make this happen.

"And come visit with us, take tea." She waves a hand at the thin woman in green standing behind her chair, book and pencil in hand. "Rada, make arrangements for next week."

The clerk nods, and the Parsifals are moved on. No one bothers to introduce them to the woman with auburn hair and yellow eyes. The woman who is ostensibly the reigning Princess of Lodellan, the mother of the city's next ruler.

Now they are free to mingle in the to-and-fro of the crowd's waves, to shift and dance across the mosaic floor of gold and gem tiles that shows scenes from the city's history, good and bad: the miracle of the twice-born prince; the queen who let a dark woman lead the violet-eyed royal children astray and ended her days walled into her chamber; the troll-wife who almost stole the crown and her defeat at the hands of the unloved princess; the archbishop who raised the new cathedral yet disappeared before its completion; the lost children turned to wolves by the bite of a grieving widow; the bakeress whose creations caused more trouble than they should . . . all this and more collected in the stones beneath them, now ignored by heedless feet whose owners no longer find miracles and magic fashionable.

The Parsifals gravitate towards a group of friends—two groups, really, the men and women forming separate circles close enough that they might each hear the others' conversation, but not take part. While she chats with the wives, Cordelia begins to relax, almost forgets the drama leading up to this point. She basks in compliments about her dress and necklace, although part of her is dedicated to listening to her husband's discussions, determined to learn any way she can the things he keeps hidden. Determined to prove Bethany wrong.

"The profit we made on that latest Antiphon expedition has equipped three more ships!" bleats one youngster, hair black and thick as a fleece, but with no discernible moustache or saving sign of a beard. A son of one of the merchants, too foolish and wrapped up in himself to keep his boasting more private.

Edvard frowns. "You turned a profit?"

The gentlemen around him nod. He seems confused. "But we *lost* money on the deal."

The others, older and wiser, look elsewhere so he might not see their pity. Their lack of comprehension. He shakes his head and the young cumberground laughs loud and spiteful. "Forgotten how to count, old chap? I'd find a new accountant if I were you."

And Cordelia watches as the blood leaves her husband's face and he shakes as if suffering a sudden palsy, as if a terribly misplaced trust has been revealed. She tries to go to his side, but a hand grabs her arm, nails scratching the skin. She turns and meets the eyes of Belladonna Considine, filled with hatred and grief so palpable that Cordelia feels the gaze almost as a physical force. Then she notices the men-at-arms on either side of the woman, stern-faced, implacable.

Belladonna points at Cordelia, at her throat. "That's it. Odela Agnew's necklace, Leon had it made especially for this ball. She showed it to me not two days before the murders."

Cordelia says gently, though her voice trembles, "No, Bella, you are mistaken. My Edvard gave it to me."

Belladonna shouts, "Do you think I wouldn't know it? Do you think I'd not recognise it? How dare you? How dare you do this and come here wearing the spoils of your evil labours?"

"There must be some mistake. Edvard, tell them . . . " Cordelia looks to her husband for support, but sees he is in the custody of two guards, taller even than himself, as though specially chosen for his apprehension. "Edvard, tell them!"

But though he struggles, though he tries to throw off his captors, though he shouts their innocence, their outrage, no one listens. The crowd around them simply grows, as if the Parsifals form the vortex of a whirlpool from which there is no escape; in which the couple will be dragged a'down.

Finally, one of the guardsmen, tired of Edvard's dissent, draws back a meaty fist and hits him square in the mouth. There is blood, a tooth flies across the gathering to be lost in a sea of shoes, and her husband crumples so he must be carried from the ballroom. Cordelia, dragged along behind and protesting all the way, finds herself drained of sympathy. She wants to shout at him, to rail, pull a response from him, but he has left her to face this shame on her own.

As they pass through the crush, people step away as if a stench has attached itself to the Parsifals. Cordelia hears the whispers, the snippets that cut like cold winds, like sharp knives: *financial problems*, *lost his edge*, *murders*, *living beyond their means*, *thieves*, *shame*, *driven to it by her demands*.

And then out the doors they'd so recently entered in triumph, taken across the courtyard with its frozen air, marched over the uneven flagstones to the entrance of the palace gaol. Snow and sleet come down hard, chilling them, marking them. The dread iron gate is opened, then closed behind them with a terrible clang, and in a dingy chamber rough men strip them of all belongings but their clothing. The cool absence of the necklace makes her flesh burn. Next it is down, down, a'down into the dungeons that stretch beneath the city. It is barely warmer here than in the winter wind outside. They are delivered to separate cells so far from each other that even if he would answer her cries, Edvard could not hear them.

It is almost a week before Cordelia sees anyone other the gaoler and his hateful wife. That woman brings her stale bread, stew that smells richly of ferment—of which Cordelia eats no more than she must—and water that is sometimes fresh, most often not, but cannot be ignored. Though she isn't supposed to talk to the prisoner, Mistress Lamb does for the first few days, taking time to spout spite as she shoves the food through the bars, happy to see someone like Cordelia fallen so far, so fast.

The pieces have been put together, she says with glee. *The broadsheets have traced the coincidence of the Parsifals' waning finances with the spate of robberies. No one, of course, believes* her *guilty of being but an accessory— anyone who knows Cordelia Parsifal swears she's too dim to think up anything so devilish clever. But then equally*, the woman continues, *no one believes she did not know what he did. No one believes a husband wouldn't confide his deepest failures, his darkest solutions, to the woman he loved, and their devotion is well known*, sneers the gaoler's helpmeet.

But why? asks Cordelia when she can get a word in edgeways, *Why would we do all this and then flaunt the spoils in such a stupid manner?*

Oh, she says, *the penny-papers know that's where they ran aground! The necklace was new, assumed unseen by anyone but the dead. Edvard rashly, arrogantly, presented it to her. How fortuitous that Mrs Considine— wonderful woman, devoted friend—had been shown the thing by poor Mrs Agnew!*

Where are my children? asks Cordelia, over and over, never getting an answer, but it does not stop her asking again.

By the third day, though, the goodwife has worn out her bile, and even in her malicious stupidity she realises that Cordelia's hurt bewilderment is not an act; no mummer, this sad and terrified captive. She has stopped spitting in the water and simply hands over the meals, although their quality remains unimproved. And still Cordelia has seen no one, no lawyer, no representative of the courts, no friend or acquaintance, no priest to offer succour or damn her soul, not even Mr Farringdale—who could surely clear up any financial questions!—has come. No one has formally presented the charges to her, though she cannot help but know of what she is accused. She's wondered if all matters have simply been addressed to Edvard, if she's been wrong in her anger towards him; if her husband is negotiating—nay, fighting for—their futures. Their lives.

On the sixth day, when the gaoler's wife brings the morning repast, she also leads in Bethany and Cordelia dares to hope.

"Bethany! Are the children all right? Are they safe?"

"They are safe, sister, never fear. I have the care of them."

The tears she's held in—even two days ago when she began to bleed and cramp, and knew the child—suddenly, strangely precious—was gone—spring at last. Cordelia's heart, so battered and bruised, leaps, certain somehow that she is saved.

But Bethany's mournful expression tells her soon enough that *this is not over*. They hold hands through the bars, and sink to sit: Cordelia on filthy straw, Bethany on cold stone flags. The goodwife watches for a few long moments, then shuffles away. From her beaded velvet purse, Bethany pulls a wrapped napkin and passes it over. Knowing that the children are in no danger makes Cordelia ravenous, and she wolfs the smuggled pastries so quickly that she feels sick.

"Have you seen Edvard?" she asks, watching greedily as Bethany hands her another napkin, more pastries. "Has he spoken to the lawyers? To Mr Farringdale? How much longer will this misunderstanding go on? I simply don't understand, Bethany, how it happened, why Bella would say such a thing."

"Dellie, you must prepare yourself. Life is going to be very different."

"It will take a long time for us to live down the humiliation, certainly. But once we're released, once people realise this has all been a terrible mistake . . . " she takes a sharp breath. "A trial . . . "

"There will be no trial, Cordelia," Bethany says. "There will be no public shaming—or at least nothing worse than there has already been."

"We may be grateful for that small mercy then."

"But they say there must be seen to be a reckoning."

"But we are innocent! Bethany, you know we are!"

"Yes, sister, I know you are. But . . . "

"What of Edvard and Mr Farringdale? Are they not mounting a defence? Edvard was with me on the night the Agnews were killed."

"Ah, but you would say that, wouldn't you?" Bethany's eyes are weirdly bright, then she looks away. "Or that is what *they* will say—and the newsmen have already judged you—what dutiful wife wouldn't lie for her husband? And they consider you a dutiful wife, Cordelia, if a stupid one. They think you merely obeyed your master's wishes."

"But what about Edvard? What has he told them?"

Bethany pauses, as if choosing her words carefully to spare feelings, then realises that there is no gentle way forward. "Dellie, my dear, your Edvard is dead."

Seeing incomprehension, she goes on, kindly, "He took his own life, hung himself." She points to the wall behind Cordelia where there are metal shackles set high, but not so high that a man of Edvard's height couldn't reach to loop his own belt, then wrap it around his neck and lean forward slowly, oh so slowly, until all his breath was gone in a terrible, slow asphyxiation. "It's as good a confession as anything, Cordelia. He gave up his right to defend himself—and you."

Edvard is gone. He's left her alone, alone in this hole, in this morass. Her husband, her *protector*, the man who could not bear to allow her a speck of independence, is no longer here—by his own choice.

"He was weak, sister, like they all are: with fortune frittered away, he was a failure as businessman, husband, and father." There is a flash of contempt, quickly covered, as if she realises now is not the time. "And all the humiliation of the past days, having everyone who counts think he's a thief and a murderer . . . "

"But you do not, do you?" asks Cordelia quietly.

"Of course not. But with his money gone through bad investment, wasted on foolish ventures it certainly makes him look guilty. For God's sake, Dellie, he was the only man not to make a profit from the Antiphon venture!" Bethany says in disgust and the comment hooks into Cordelia's memory; she begins to think, trying to swim through the numbness. She is not really listening.

"I have some money put aside, I can take care of the children. Henry can still go to university. I will teach Victoria to be self-sufficient. And Torben will learn to grow up soon enough."

"How did you know about Antiphon?" asks Cordelia.

Bethany pauses, thinks, answers, "Edvard told me."

"No, he didn't," Cordelia says. "He didn't. He didn't tell me, he certainly wouldn't have told you. I heard them talking at the Ball: everyone else made money, but he seemed to think we had not."

Bethany remains silent.

"The woman here tells me we'd been having financial problems, problems Edvard never mentioned."

Her sister's face freezes, as if she's deciding what to do, then she finally smiles: the deception is no longer worth her effort. The mask peels away, leaving the true Bethany utterly unveiled before her, the Bethany Cordelia has only glimpsed as if in a bad dream.

"Oh, sister," she pleads, "what have you done?"

"What I wanted to."

"Why, Bethany? We never refused you anything!"

"I lived as a beggar in your house! Everything I had I had to ask for—you gave me nothing of my own! Always let me live on your charity."

Cordelia's mouth moves, but no sound comes.

"So I started taking what I needed at first, then what I wanted. Others have been willing to help . . . and those who were not were easily enough disposed of."

"That boy . . . "

"A pretty distraction, useful until he got squeamish, until your Merry maid gave him a conscience. He didn't want to . . . " says Bethany, almost reluctantly. She looks at Cordelia, shakes her head, and repeats, "He didn't want to hurt them. Wasn't averse to stealing, but he lacked the backbone to kill, even though leaving them alive would mean our discovery. Men are weak like that."

"You gave Edvard the necklace. You stole it from the Agnews, murdered them . . . "

"He told me to find something *special* for you. Fool. Didn't ask where I'd found it, didn't question the amount I demanded."

"He set aside his pride, asked for your aid. He opened his home to you and you . . . " Cordelia seems to feel the sticky warmth of Odela Agnew's blood on her neck where her jewellery had once sat. "How did you . . . how did you take *our* money? He'd not have asked your advice about investments . . . "

"Mr Farringdale can be most accommodating when given the right incentive."

"Mr Farringdale . . . "

"I have found, sister, that once you discover someone's secrets you hold their heart in your hand."

Cordelia thinks of Mr Farringdale and his spurned suit, his hopes and heartache; how long has Bethany strung him along? What promises has she made that he would betray his employer? "My children—"

"—will be safe so long as you are compliant. I have enough money to save the house, indeed, to buy up all those buildings Edvard owned and rented out to butchers and bakers and candlestick makers!—they will be sold cheaply to get rid of them, to wipe out the shame. Mr Farringdale will kindly see to that."

"Why would he—"

"Have you ever been to an orphanage? Have you visited the one in this fair city?" Bethany rocks back a little as if easing the stiffness of sitting on the floor. "Oh, I know Edvard gives—gave—regular donations, but I don't think either of you ever actually went to see the conditions. Of course, it is considerably better than the place you left me for over a year."

"We came and got you! As soon as we knew what had happened we came! As soon as we could."

"But you didn't, did you? *You* didn't come. You sent Mr Farringdale, didn't you? Thin, yearning Mr Farringdale, with his darkest of desires, desires that could only be sated on a child . . . but you sent *him*." She gives a bitter laugh. "Oh sweet sister, how innocent you are. Now consider Victoria: she's older than I was when he came for me . . . perhaps she'll be safer." There is a moment when every particle of Bethany's hurt, her agony, shows in her eyes, and Cordelia thinks the girl might cry; she reaches a hand to her sister, all scratches and grimy nails. Bethany pulls away, straightens.

"Bethany, I'm so—"

"Don't say you're sorry, sister, it's far too little, too late," she quietly says, then hisses, "Bad enough you left me with Mother in the first place! Bad enough you took Mrs Bell with you when you left, took away the only person who might have protected me!"

Tears pours down Cordelia's cheeks, washing through the filth. She thinks on her own hours locked in the cupboard by their mother, learning hard lessons that made her only too glad to escape . . . not caring who she left behind, not caring that whatever she escaped would be visited on her sibling. She takes in the change in Bethany's face, the expression that says her sister is an empty shell hollowed out by her past, eternally washed through by need and greed; a shell that can never be filled. There is a light in her eyes that says her steps across the precipice have been taken, that she's chosen the dark over the light.

"And when—oh when, sister!—I at last arrived here what did I find but that you'd all but adopted Mrs Bell's bastard daughter! Don't look like that, Dellie. What an idiot you are: can you not see it in their faces? Their eyes? That little nose with its tilt? Oh, you're so blind you deserve everything that happens to you!" Bethany sits back from the bars, shaking, and Cordelia isn't certain whether it is from laughter, sadness or hatred, or perhaps some strange mix of all three. "You'd taken in that little accident, that stray, that base-born by-blow, and left me to the tender mercies of Mother, then Mr Farringdale!"

"Oh, Bethany, I'll tell. I'm going to tell." But Cordelia is trembling, rocked by her sister's revelations and betrayal, by her own crushing guilt.

Bethany shakes her head a little sadly. "No, you won't, Cordelia. You really won't."

"I will shout until someone listens. Edvard still has friends, influential friends—"

"Edvard is dead, sister. He is a disgrace; all those friends have distanced themselves from you both." She smiles, as if reasonable.

"Mrs Bell—"

"Is gone, sister, as is Merry. Clever tarts, scarpering like that." She laughs, mirthless.

"The brooch . . . " says Cordelia, wishing she could apologise to Merry for every ill thought she'd ever had about her. Feeling the loss of her and Mrs B almost as keenly as that of her children.

Bethany's eyes are lit with malevolence as she answers obliquely, "Little sweet thing with her principles. The moment Japheth set eyes on her, spoke with her, he turned soft. He was as bad as you, setting me aside for Merry."

"It wasn't enough to take him from her?"

"It's never enough, sister!" shouts Bethany, spittle shooting from between her lips to splash hot on Cordelia's hand. Then she calms down, takes a deep breath. "You are utterly without allies. Everything you once had is mine. Now, think on this: what will you do to keep your children from harm?"

Cordelia says nothing, feels ice forming in her throat.

"Your husband took the easy way out. Perhaps you might do the same? A strip from the hem of your gown would be a tidy noose. No? Then as I said, there must be a public shaming, justice must be seen to be done. If you confess to being Edvard's accomplice, I will take care of your children. Keep your mouth shut, sister, and your babies will be safe."

Cordelia stares at Bethany, trying in vain to see the little girl who'd come to live with her so long ago. She thinks of Merry rubbing salt into the doorstep to keep wickedness at bay, all for naught when they didn't know the wickedness was already inside the house.

Bethany leans forward again, her voice soft. "One word out of place and I will drown the little darlings, I promise you. It won't matter if anyone believes you because by then your darlings will be dead, I swear."

She fixes Cordelia with a hateful glare and speaks in a clipped fashion. "The prince has agreed: one year in the Rosebery hulks if you confess. Not such a long time. One year and your sweetings returned to you. What do you think, Cordelia? Willing to risk it?"

Before dawn, Cordelia is woken and her dress, now a ruined purple rag, is taken and in its place she is given a bleached calico shift, rough and itchy, and a coarse woollen cape too short to offer any real warmth. Other women are led up from the depths beneath Cordelia's cell, and she is chained to them. Their ankles are fitted with shackles already speckled with rust and dried blood, which immediately bite into tender flesh, drawing new vital fluid to add to the old. Cordelia, eyes grainy with an excess of tears and a lack of sleep, not to mention the dust that rises constantly from the flaking stone walls and the straw on the floor of her cell, can feel only the sting of the rose tattoo they applied to her shoulder as soon as she gave her confession. Though the process took barely five minutes, the scarring burns constantly, as if the acid is daubed over and over.

The women, all twelve, are hustled out through the cobbled courtyard. As they wait to be loaded into an enclosed dray, Cordelia looks around, sees the portcullis, and in the voids between the metal latticework finds two faces, familiar and drawn: Mrs B and Merry. She'd know them anywhere though they've covered their bright hair with scarves and have thick travelling cloaks drawn around them. Both reach a hand through the bars as if to touch her, as if to throw something to her. Cordelia clasps her own hands and presses them to her heart; fights the urge to run to them, screaming questions, begging. Instead she nods, then the gaoler prods her in the back hard enough to leave a bruise, and she mounts the rickety stairs up into the body of the dray with thin wooden benches on either side, and only one window, set in the door, too high for any of the seated passengers to see much but the blue of the sky. Six a side, those at the farthest end must stretch their legs to accommodate the short reach of the shackles. Cordelia, at the end of the human chain and nearest the door, is spared that at least. The woman beside her has no front teeth and her breathing is harsh, the exhalations rotten. Two inmates across from her begin to talk, low voices, low words. They gossip because it makes them feel better, to know someone is worse off than they are.

"The rich ones got no guts, not strong enough to live through loss," one says, and laughs to show she too has no front teeth.

"Position's all they care about. When they lose their place on the ladder . . . " the other shrugs, looks at Cordelia as if she knows who she is, leans in to speak directly to her. "Well, they're brave enough to do their terrible deeds, but too weak to take responsibility for 'em."

Cordelia merely stares. She stares so long that they become uncomfortable, they shift and shuffle, avoid her gaze, stop talking.

And though she wants to, she still does not fight. She does not scream or shout or leap to her feet. She feels instead a stiffening in her back, realises it's the spine Bethany always said she'd lost. She knows pleas will fall on deaf ears, that no one will believe the tale she might tell. She does not fight because of her children, because in her silence lies their salvation.

So she says nothing, ignores the gibes and the acid-burn of the tattoo. She sways with the motion of the carriage, all the rattling, rolling, clattering way to Rosebery Bay. Three days with the other women and the smell they make, not allowed out for piss breaks except in the morning and the evening, fermenting in the back, the rank stench of body odour and shit and vomit.

All on the road to Rosebery Bay.

Cordelia dreams of the fire, of the warmth and the heat, of the sound of the logs as they crackle and burn and weaken, shifting as they become less solid. She dreams of the time that Henry once tucked chestnuts in the coals. In reality, they popped and exploded, giving all and sundry a fright. In her fancies one flies from the hearth, is propelled towards her skirt. The fine lace, highly flammable, takes the spark like a lover and the trail of flame speeds up her dress, up the bodice, then up the left sleeve. She uses her right hand to try to pat out the flickering red-gold, and succeeds only in burning her fingers. The dream-flames bite into her upper arm, her shoulder.

She does not like this fantasy—it is not the refuge she has come to expect, to desire, to need. She shakes herself awake and finds, much to her distress, that the flames have jumped the slender gap between sleeping and waking; she can see them through the barred window, an orange glow brightens her tiny cell despite the white-grey billowing in the passageway, trickling under her door. She has woken to shouts and cries and screams and coughs, but no sound of the turnkeys coming to release any of the women on this ship.

Cordelia curses, despairs that the smoke did not take her as soon as it could, that it did not kill her while nestled in the memories where she wished to lie. She backs into a corner, and the space she has just vacated is gradually filled again: at first there is ash, then cinders, then embers, and finally blackened and half-eaten planks as the ceiling caves in. She stares through the dust that shifts on the breeze, giving her glimpses of the open maw of the night sky, with its twinkling teeth of stars.

Freedom, above.

So far away.

Briefly she thinks of stepping into the smoke, breathing deeply. Or onto the flaming timbers that begin to crackle once again, slowly burning their way through the floor on which they've landed. Asphyxia or incineration are her only choices.

But no. Somewhere in the back of her mind she knows that if she's survived everything thus far, she will not give up lightly. She pulls the thin straw-filled sack of a mattress from the bed she's slept in all these months—not a proper bunk as she's in one of the last cells to be added to this ship, which does not sail anywhere, so no care has been given to ensuring beds are nailed down and secure—and exposes the slats she feels against her bony back each night. Cordelia throws the mattress-sack away; it lands on the pile of planks and the fire grows large with new fodder. She heaves the rickety frame onto its short end and prays it will be strong enough and long enough.

As she steps to the first rung, her skirt kicks back with the movement and brushes against the inferno of the mattress. The line of flame she'd only imagined becomes a reality, leaping up her poor calico gown, strangely focused as it moves to her left forearm, upper arm, shoulder, nibbles at her hair. She hears the creaking and complaining of the ship as its body is consumed and in the coldest part of her brain she knows that if she stops to swat the flares, she will surely die; she will lose her chance, her momentum, her precious few seconds to get out.

A burning brand of a woman, she scampers up her makeshift ladder, and scrambles onto the deck, which is beginning to tilt. The flames on her shoulder are eating, eating, eating at the rose tattoo that was put there to show her as a thief, a sneak, a convict, a murderer for all they said "accessory." It scorches like the acid used to etch the design there in the first place. She bats at the tiny, deadly flashes as her eyes take in the swaying masts, the last of the dirty canvas sails, that are orange then black, then crumble in the wind. She wheels and turns like a dancing doll, out of control, turning in a decaying spiral that finally sees her at the rails. She hits the strakes, loses her balance, and pitches headfirst over the side.

For moments she is free, she flies, the fire seems to pull away from her and her skin does not know that it's been hurt, then the waters of Rosebery Bay meet her, hard black glass. At first she is against it, then she is through it, and finally she is lost, travelling a'down, a'down, a'down, farther and farther from the dark sky and its starry teeth. Farther and farther, to where dreams no longer live.

A'down, a'down, a'down, and Cordelia Parsifal, wife, mother, sister, tallow-wife, lets go of all that she is, of all that she has been. She is free, suddenly light, spinning away as if a great pressure had been released . . . yet in a moment there is a change, vital and irresistible. She hears the voice of the woman in the prison coach, her sly dig that *The rich ones got no backbone, not strong enough to live through loss. Something finds her, pulls at her, drags her back to her body, insists her spirit remain.*

She does not have the energy to fight life anymore than she did death. The impulse will not let her go, it takes possession of her limbs, her aching arms and legs, and makes them move, kick and stroke, kick and stroke, kick and stroke.

Up and up and up. Above her the surface of the water is silver and midnight blue, where the moon sits and waits for her return. Waits for her to make herself anew.

WHAT SHINES BRIGHTEST
BURNS MOST FIERCELY

MR ISAMBARD FARRINGDALE KNEW he was being followed by someone well-versed in the art of not being seen.

He'd had the sense of it for some days now; it began as a kind of low-level itch at the back of his neck and grown as time passed, creeping across his scalp like a spider, slithering down his thin spine until it coiled at the base like a loving snake he couldn't shake. Yet every time he looked over his shoulder as he travelled the streets of Lodellan, either crowded or empty, there was nothing and no one in sight. He thought to become cleverer, more cunning, slipping swiftly around corners then peeking out to catch any pursuer unawares, but it never worked. All he managed was to frighten several servant girls on their way to the Busynothings Markets, to startle a costermonger who was understanding, and an ironmonger who was not.

This evening, though, the gentleman in question has shrugged off his disquiet and attended at his favourite private club for entertainment few folk would enjoy, or admit to, or even countenance. Mr Farringdale knows full well that his pastimes would draw, at the very least, opprobrium from upstanding citizens and he is careful to ensure the truest nature of his pleasures is kept under wraps. The kind of people who share his predilections are equally circumspect; and the objects of their intense interest . . . well, they are given no opportunity to complain.

Puffed with indulgence and warmed by copious cups of mulled cherry wine and blackberry port, Mr Farringdale steps from the unprepossessing doorway which hides Madame Arkady's House of Curiosities (a name unknown to all but its clientele) and into the cobbled back street that runs off Half-moon Lane. He draws himself up to his full height, all five feet two, does his best to stride in a dignified manner in the direction of his home. But the alcohol gets the better of him and the best he manages is a sort of strange listing canter, the heels of his buckled boots making a tap-tap-clack on the stones under his feet. He giggles. He giggles quite loudly and for quite some time, until the sense of being watched again starts to haunt him, and the spider-snake twitches awake. Isambard sobers a little, quickens his step, tripping more than he would like, until at last he is at his own door, fumbling the keys, forgetting to lift the latch so he panics, thinking himself shut out . . . then calms and does what needs doing.

Inside, he turns the lock with shaking fingers, shivers. He allows no servants to live in, so the hearths have been set but not lit in anticipation of his return. Mr Farringdale presses his forehead to the polished oak of the entrance and waits for his heartbeat to slow, for his pulse to stop thrusting against his skin; he swears he can see the thud and thump of it at his wrists where the veins are terribly blue.

The house—new, purchased with his ill-gotten Parsifal gains—is silent, so quiet. There is no noise at all. Nothing, no sound of drawn breath as a warning, nothing except the words, "Good evening, Isambard."

Mr Farringdale takes one great dancing, twisting leap to face his visitor. His eyes seek the shadows in vain until there is the scratch and spit of a vesta and a tiny light throws a halo on a round face. Soon illumination spreads through the rich front parlour where no one spends much time at all, the caller lighting lamps and candelabrum as he finds them, then finally touches the spark to the kindling in the hearth. Mr Farringdale's dark eyes follow his movements.

The guest is neither tall nor short, but somewhere in between. His hair is a mop of golden curls; someone has gone to great lengths to make their arrangement seem artless. His face is a series of soft circles, the rosy cheeks, the eyes, the mouth, even the tip of the nose, but not in a clownish way. All are well-formed, perfectly proportioned and pleasing, as if the features are constructed not to excite the least fear or concern: a visage with no angles, no edges, is far less threatening. Or Mr

Farringdale suspects he is meant to find it so, although he doesn't know where that thought comes from.

"Good evening, Isambard," repeats the young boy—youth? man?—and gives his unwilling host a smile meant to allay fears.

Mr Farringdale's fears remain firmly unallayed.

The boy's outfit says "affluence": the trews are a dark velvet (midnight blue? hard to tell in this light), his cream shirt sporting a frilled collar trimmed with golden thread, and his frock coat cerulean, velvet again, embroidery creeping across the lapels: leaves in green, cherries or apples in red, things that begin as birds but flow into beasts, all picked out in silver. His footwear, however, tells a different story. Although well-made, the boots are dusty and worn, the toes scuffed; they whisper of a life hard-lived, of steps taken on rough paths, many under trying circumstances. These boots give lie to the dandy's indolent air.

Then the youth's smile widens and he bends into a flourishing bow, his left arm sweeping back like a wing, the hand at the end of his right executing a detailed sort of dance. For a moment, he is a grandee of some great and mysterious court. Then he straightens and once more he's a misplaced jester or ringmaster, Isambard can't quite choose.

"My name is Jacopo," says the boy, "and I am come to offer you an exchange that will benefit us both."

Mr Farringdale raises a brow, feeling the sweat break from his sloping forehead, the tell-tale itch begin at the tip of his beaky nose, the surest sign that his fear has peaked and now he is planning for his own advantage. He relaxes slightly, his curiosity piqued at the thought of a bargain. Feeling less endangered, his bartering instinct rouses. He does not wish to be won over too quickly, appear too easily placated, but work has been thin on the ground since the unpleasantness. No one blamed him outright, but the people with money wonder how it was he allowed so much of Edvard Parsifal's to slip away, and no one has been willing to employ him since. Fortunately, he has reserves, many of them skimmed off the top of the Antiphon profits, but it won't hurt, he thinks, to have *more*.

"Were you following me? Was it you?" His voice is pitched higher than he would like, but the question is out, too late to change his mind.

The youth's face falls, his expression a pretty mix of shame and regret. His body moves, a tremor that transmits itself down through his torso, thence to arms and legs, hands and feet. As if a current has passed through him. Isambard is fascinated, although part of him wonders if it's an act designed to distract, to charm and disarm him. If Isambard's interest ran to boys, it might work.

"It was indeed, and I offer my humblest apologies if my observations caused you some distress. But as a man of intellect, not given to rash actions, you will understand my desire to make sure you were whom I sought. My employer bid me be circumspect. It would not be wise to approach the wrong individual with what I am offering—and I do feel now that you are precisely *the* man with whom I wish to deal."

In spite of himself, Mr Farringdale is flattered. "Your employer?"

The lad continues. "I'm aware that what I ask for is valuable—as is your time, which is also rare and irreplaceable—so I am prepared to offer something equally valuable, rare and irreplaceable. A one-of-a-kind *objet* in return."

The youth produces from his pocket a strange item: a chrysalis of a thing, translucent, transparent. It starts out the size of a pellet, then grows before Isambard's astonished gaze. An egg—chicken, goose, turkey, eagle—until it is an ovoid a foot high, about eight inches in circumference and takes up all the space between Jacopo's palms and threatens to overflow. Mr Farringdale shuffles closer and the boy turns so he might better regard what is being offered. The shell is glowing, pellucid: through it can be seen what lies inside.

It is a girl, like a smallish doll. Isambard makes out the dark golden hair, the high cheekbones, the rosebud mouth, the chin jutting forward, a little pugnacious and, when she opens her lids suddenly, the bright green of her eyes. He realises why she is so very familiar: it is Bethany Lawrence as she once was, so delicate and defenceless. Not his first, not by a long shot, but certainly his most desired, most earnestly yearned for, his most dangerous, and longest loved though she's grown well beyond his preferred *vintage*. She lodged inside him, though, and refused to leave; he wonders if it was some revenge magic of her own, or if he has, somewhere deep down, a conscience, guilt for all the pain he caused her. In part, it's why he could never refuse her anything, even the demands she at first couched as requests. To a certain extent, it is because he feared being exposed for what he was and what he'd done . . . and continued to do to others.

"She'll grow, but only so much. She'll never be any older than when she was *yours*, when you took her." The boy's voice trembles and Mr Farringdale looks at him, suspicious, but there is nothing in Jacopo's face to say he disapproves, that he judges. There is only a strange brightness that Isambard realises provides more of the light in the room than the lamps. But the girl in the chrysalis takes his attention again, her gaze meeting his and holding. Mr Farringdale's fingers stretch forth, almost touching the oval until, at the last moment, Jacopo pulls it away.

"She'll be yours again, on one condition."

Isambard is unsurprised but resentful to hear that this will not be free. Yet he knows himself well enough: he will have this thing. He will do whatever it takes to have her again as she lives still in his mind. His one love, did she but know it. No, he thinks, she knows it full well and uses it to her advantage; it's that she doesn't *care*. He doesn't dwell on the irony of the girl he so injured and possessed so very young, now having a grip on his soul.

"How do you know?" asks Mr Farringdale, dread limning his very being. "How can you know?"

"Ah, Isambard, my ways and means are my secrets, and that's how it shall stay. It's sufficient that I—and my employer—*know*, don't you think?" He waits until Isambard nods unwillingly. "So. You'll have your heart's desire on one simple condition. In exchange, Mr Farringdale, I ask for something that weighs nothing! Light as a feather, you'll barely feel it go: information."

Isambard shivers. He knows that substance is *not* light. It does not float. It is a thing to weigh one down. The right kind will drag a soul to the bottom of the sea and keep it there until flesh rots from the bones. Information, when it is known, comprehended, when it's value becomes obvious to the holder, then it is *knowledge*, and that is the most dangerous thing of all. He says none of this however.

"I need to know two things. Firstly, what happened to the necklace, the Agnew Necklace? Secondly, I need an address for Mistress Bethany and the children. I know she no longer resides in this fair city."

Isambard blinks; his mind darts from one thought to the other. He will tell one thing quite willingly, the other . . . he plays for time.

"The Princess Royal has the necklace." He hurries on, seeing Jacopo's disbelieving expression. "There was no one left, of the Agnews, you understand. The estate wound up in the royal coffers, as will happen when there are no heirs, and Armandine claimed the jewellery for her own."

He does not mention rumours of the effect this had on the royal household, of the discontent it sowed between Princess Royal and lover. He does not think it will matter to the boy. After a long moment, Jacopo nods, accepts what he's been told. Isambard can tell, though, that the lad is calculating some sort of odds.

"And the other matter, Isambard?"

"I cannot . . . You must understand: she put her trust in me."

"You can and you will." Jacopo holds the chrysalis in front of him so Mr Farringdale can better see the girl inside. She bats her lashes and smiles, pulls at his dark heart. The youth's tone changes, becomes less friendly. "She left you, Isambard, she left you here all alone. After everything you'd done for her."

The warning voice in Mr Farringdale's head becomes smaller, quieter as the other voice, the one that tells him he is the injured party, that he deserved better, becomes louder, more strident. Angry not at him, no, but at her, she who caused his misery, who complicated his life, who demanded and took so much, then left him. Here. Alone.

"Breakwater," he says, his voice catching even as his heart thrills at the betrayal and the thought of the girl in the egg.

Jacopo nods as if it is something he suspected. "I will need proof, of course."

For a moment, Isambard's mind is blank, then he remembers the letter, the one and only communication. He rifles through a drawer in the corner bureau, until he finds it, pressed between the pages of an old diary, finger marks visible as are port stains; he imagines there are tears, too, their ghosts blotting the onion-thin paper. The tears are his. It is all business, this epistle, but it contains the address to which he was to send the last of the household goods, and details of her new bank accounts for a final transfer of funds. He holds the sheet with a traitor's shaking hands, but the voice in his head assures that when he has the girl in the chrysalis, what need will he have of this cold folio?

His faltering steps bring him to within a few feet of the youth and he holds out the letter, which flutters only a little with his emotion. Jacopo takes it, barely glances at it and thrusts it into his pocket, crinkling it so that Mr Farringdale's heart aches. Then the boy says, as if an afterthought, "And the children? She took them with her?"

Isambard shivers, swallows. The girl in the egg nods at him encouragingly. "She took the boys."

"And Victoria?"

"Sent away some months before. To a cousin, Bethany said." But he knew now just as he had known then, there were no cousins. "I don't have an address, but I believe it was to Seaton St Mary."

Mr Farringdale thinks the boy blanches, his glow dimming briefly, then Jacopo nods again.

"Thank you, Isambard. I do believe you've played fair with me. But I am no fool. I must ascertain what you've told me about the necklace—what good would I be to my employer if I were easily duped?" He smiles. "I'll leave this here with you as a gesture of good faith, but be aware that she will not be freed—will not be yours—until I return and open this clever cage. If I do not find what I am looking for in the palace, I shall simply take her away. Do we understand each other?"

Mr Farringdale nods. He has told his truth, his only fear is that the boy will fail to find the jewellery, will think him a liar and refuse his prize.

Jacopo snatches a knee rug from the back of an armchair no one ever uses, to make a nest before the fireplace, then carefully balances the egg on it. He stands, dusting off the knees of his trousers as if Mr Farringdale's day-maid's labours leave much to be desired, then he points at the chrysalis.

"Build a fire, Isambard, it will benefit the egg. But don't touch it—the egg, I mean—it is not yours until I return and gift it to you, after I've tested the quality of your information." He gives a smile, as if between friends sharing a great joke, but Mr Farringdale notices how Jacopo's teeth show and how sharp they are.

There were other ways he could have taken what he needed from Mr Farringdale, but he didn't fancy swimming around in the man's memories. Didn't want to carry that with him. Besides, *she* was very specific about how he was to deal with Isambard; she was quite intent that things be done in this manner.

Jacopo pushes all other thoughts from his mind and concentrates on finding his way to the square, the great square. He is not familiar with this city, having only been here once with the troupe, and despite the past few days of following his prey, mapping his habits. Jacopo likes to know his mark as well as he possibly can. He's been in the house on more than one occasion, sometimes when its occupant was at home, sometimes not. He has flicked through the contents of wardrobes and dressers, walked around the special room with its rose-pink curtains and coverlets where the small visitors stay, however briefly, before they are inevitably found to be not quite right. Part of Jacopo understands Mr Farringdale's wanting and dissatisfaction, but no part of him understands the man's desires.

He steps out into the well-lit public space that flows around the cathedral like a moat. The building is huge, a vaunting spire, gothic towers and flying buttresses, yet all in a strange harmony. There are no guards, at least no human ones; around the portico of the cathedral he can see the smoky flashes of the wolf-hounds, the resurrected beasts who serve as ecclesiastical guardians of the structure. They are rare, these things, and old, the knowledge of their making lost to time. They harm only those with ill-intent, Theodora said when he was a little lad dandled on her knee. I've no ill-intent *here*, thinks Jacopo, and hopes his logic works; inside the palace things will change. He straightens his spine, stands tall and sturdy, and crosses the square, thinking determinedly of anything but what he plans to do.

Jacopo recalls Grandmamma Theodora's tales: of how she learnt the secret byways of the palace and cathedral through boredom and accident. Fated to stand around waiting while the treasurer tallied all the coin that might be counted as Theodora's in her role as Princess of Lodellan, she wandered and explored once a week while the money-rat concerned himself with other things until she was required to affix her seal to his ledgers. As he lost himself in the various coffers and caskets of gold and silver, crates and sacks of goods in kind, she meandered, and in doing so she found secret passages and false walls, hidden doors and staircases that went deep, deep, deep, joining the palace with the great cathedral and a variety of other buildings of varying degrees of salubriousness, mansions and public houses, dens of iniquity and shops frequented by the rich and richer. She'd wondered every time she saw the piles of coin—small avalanches that threatened to cover the feet and ankles of the treasurer's minions—how many children went hungry, how many families slept cold, how many farms and businesses failed all so Lodellan's prince and his treasurer and his archbishop might hoard all this like bipedal dragons. So that the few might be assured of yet one more ermine cloak, one more purple silk robe, one more golden-tassled cushion for the comfort of tender buttocks. Jacopo remembers how she told him she'd ensured the leftovers from the royal table always went to the orphanages, and to inns whose charitable staff gave the foodstuffs to the beggars who gathered at their back doors at night.

Four silver-grey shadows wait for him at the top of the steps. They are faded and he wonders how long it will be before they disappear entirely, remaining only as a disembodied bark, a sly nip, a cold shiver. Boldly, he moves forward, stops, opens his palms so they can sniff at him to their hearts' content. They are puzzled; he wonders if they catch a whiff of his grandmother, long dead, embedded in his being. More likely they think him a strangeling, something like themselves, although not reanimated; just *different*. With confused whimpers, they fall back, let him through, watching him pass over the threshold, their fine large heads tilted to the side, pale eyes questioning, teeth very white. If they notice how Jacopo shudders when he steps inside they give no sign.

There are things buried beneath, he can feel it; unhappy, exhausted things, used long beyond their intended years. The bones are cursed, and more: they are caught in place by their function, to act as a surety for the foundations; not even a pale shade can shuffle through the stones. He senses them, although they were never mentioned by Grandmamma Theodora in her tales, tales she told him so many times they've become like his own memories. However, he supposes this place has stood for a long time, longer than Theodora lived near it. She could have learned only so many secrets, for not all are spoken, not all leave a trace.

His footsteps echo on the flagstones as he approaches the monumental altar coated in so much gold that he is sure it could feed the entire city for a year or more. To his left is the tapestry hiding the entrance to the Chapel of the Thirteenth Apostle; he passes through, notes the arras is becoming threadbare, Saint Radagund's very fine beard looks thinned and in places he can see where the gleam from the lanterns glinting on the golden altar in the nave pierces it. There is the *prie-dieu*; looking closely he can see it's carved with a mix of sea monsters, wolves, and trees. Running his fingers along its underside—and gathering splinters as he does so—Jacopo locates the catch and pulls.

There are aching moments when nothing happens. When he wonders how best to proceed . . . but then comes a reluctant scrape and scratch of stone on stone and the flags before him whirl aside like a child's puzzle. At his feet there is a square of black, a mouth without teeth but no less daunting for that. *How long since anyone walked this path?*

Jacopo's glow increases as he enters the darkness, throwing out a light to show his way into the catacombs. He tries to ignore the feeling that the earth is closing over him, that the things beneath are stirred by his presence just as the dust is by his well-worn boots. The sense of the unhappily departed grows stronger; Jacopo feels juddering as a rhythm up and down his spine, a throbbing where the back of his skull meets the nape of his neck. He shakes his head, lets the motion become a shudder, and his radiance wavers.

For all the things Theodora had imparted, drilled into him, for whatever reason, all those years ago, she'd not mentioned the buzzing.

The angry vibration that began moments after he kindled his own luminescence, as if this sign of his difference caused offence in some unearthly quarter. At first it is simply a noise like a cluster of midges are pursuing him. He picks up the pace, conscious that his footfalls signal nervousness. He cannot help but feel that behind him something shifts and shuffles, its form summoned into being by sheer malicious will, but it is only when he feels a stab between his shoulder blades—not deep, but painful—that he can force himself to turn and face his demon.

Not far from him, drawing ever closer as the boy's glow diminishes from fear, is a man—or the remains of one at least. An old man in the rags of a white cassock trimmed with purple and gold; the brownish stains might once have been bright blood. A ragged cloak retains some evidence of a cobalt hue. The head is skeletal, the skin a thin canvas stretched tight over the frame of the skull, bare of all but a few clumps of yellowed hair. At the end of knife-thin fingers are nails long and sharp, almost waving at him.

For a dreadful moment, his terror is so great that his light goes out entirely, his flesh loses its gift, and he's plunged into darkness as surely as a drowning man goes through the ice in an unseasonal thaw. He stumbles over his own feet, goes down on his hands and knees, feels the scrape of his palms on rough earth. There is no sound, though, anything but his heartbeat's staccato: where is it? The spectre?

Theodora never mentioned such a thing! At the thought of his grandmother, the light in him stutters, flickers back into being. In its weak flare, the old man—dreadfully closer—flinches, hisses, scuttles away. Jacopo concentrates on memories of Theodora, reading him books, telling him stories, holding him tight, tucking him into bed, and the glimmer around him becomes stronger. His pulse calms when he sees the phantasm cringing. Jacopo climbs to his feet, his confidence bolstered. He's incandescent, the tunnel far ahead of him is illumined, and he notes that the ground begins to slope upwards, the coffin niches are filled with nothing more than skeletons and dust and cobwebs. He doesn't turn his back on the haunt, though, is careful as he walks with a strange sideways gait, that takes him forward but allows him to keep an eye on the strange wispy thing behind.

At the top of the stone steps, Jacopo locates the hidden door, which proves more stubborn than the entrance to the catacombs, and requires a shoulder to make it budge even after the lever is pulled. The panel pops out unwillingly and Jacopo steps into the magnificent fountain room, dimly lit by sconces, that always featured in Theodora's stories of the troll-wife. He almost slams the panel behind him, but the creature did not follow him up the stairs, had given up any serious pursuit when it realised he could not be intimidated; that he had good memories to serve him well. Yet his heart still hammers inside his chest, there is a cold sweat slicking his skin, and he clenches his hands into fists to stop the shaking. He'll not go back this way.

Jacopo lets his brilliance go low, until he is blinking to readjust to the dim chamber. The golden privacy screen Theodora always mentioned, of Hansie and Greta and the sugar cottage, is missing and he's disappointed; he'd waited so long to see it. The tiles are still of gold and silver with crystal and nacre inlays though, and the tubs, basins, fountains, and benches carved from white and blue marble remain. Jacopo sees the moon through the ceiling, a sheet of rock crystal. There is the tiny steam hut, the smaller pools—and the larger one. There is movement in its waters.

A woman rises from the night-dark liquid. Her hair, though damp, flashes fire. She is short, stocky, her hips broad, her breasts heavy, legs muscular. Jacopo is surprised; Grandmamma always said the Lodellan royal family were tall without exception, and slender, platinum blond. But this woman is . . . not regal. She walks with a determined, plain gait, there is no elegance in her stride. Her face is pretty enough but her expression's dissatisfied. Discontented. Sour. He wonders who she is, but in the end decides it doesn't matter. The palace has changed since Theodora's day, there are new rooms, new wings. She is what he needs at this moment.

He hitches his most charming smile to his lips, takes quiet steps— not silent ones for he does not wish to frighten her—and collects the deep red bath sheet that is lying on the bench closest to the pool. He holds it to cover his attire, so she will not realise immediately that he is not a servant. He need not worry, she sees him but pays no attention, takes his presence for granted, assumes he is here to tell her something, bring her something, do something for her. She walks into the towel, and this close he can see her eyes are topaz-hued, large. He wraps the thick fabric around her, holds tight for she is not much smaller than he and he suspects she has a peasant's strength. When it becomes clear to her that she's been swaddled, she looks askance at him.

"I'm sorry," he whispers, "I just need you for a little while."

And before she can struggle, he fixes his lips to hers and draws the very breath from her and with it all the knowledge she carries. Jacopo feels the transformation coming quickly, and he lays the woman on the bench before he falls.

Memories and emotions rush into him, pressing down on who he is, compacting everything that makes Jacopo, *Jacopo.* Sedimentary layers of feelings, years of yearning, hurt, thoughts of Amandine that *ache,* ecstasy and exaltation run like mercury through his mind—and his body is changing too. His cock shrivels and pulls up inside him, his hips broaden, his legs shorten, his chest is heavy with tits so big he doesn't know how the woman—Ilse, her name is Ilse, he picks that from the rising swarm of new information—manages to balance. A single drop of milk leaks from a nipple and Jacopo is dizzy with the thought she is nursing, knows it's the second child, not the first, that she's a breeder for the weak-blooded royalty of this great city.

When the changes are in place, when his own mind reasserts its dominance over the stray recollections, the new knowledge, then he stands. He finds her clothing, a dress of lilac and gold, crumpled on the floor not far away, next to a pair of bejewelled jiffies in soft leather. He puffs out a breath and undresses, folding his own garb neatly. He looks down at Ilse, surveys the fountain room, lights upon the steam hut; she must be hidden in case someone comes in looking, and he cannot have her form for too long, not beyond two hours or, disconnected from her own essence, she will perish.

The air in the hut is cool. The fire has not been lit, the rocks are cold; Ilse will be safe here, she will not be scalded or scorched, nor suffocated by steam. There is a mirror running along one wall and Jacopo pauses. He carefully examines his face, which is hers without a doubt. No one will suspect a thing. He takes a moment, picks through her scrambled memories, finds a thread and pulls it. Follows it. It will lead him to the place where Ilse's malcontent begins and resides.

Isambard sits cross-legged on the rug, an unaccustomed position he's not adopted since childhood. There's a grinding in his hips that he tries to relieve by rocking from side to side, a protesting tightness in his knee joints, and where his thin ankles touch the floor, pain radiates. He stretches both legs straight out, the heels of his buckled shoes hit the stone of the hearth and make a noise too loud in his empty home, one that startles him even though he knows its source.

Mr Farringdale looks around, embarrassed as if he might be watched, then giggles at his own absurdity. Perhaps there is still too much alcohol in him? He'd have thought it all frightened out in that initial rush of terror when the youth appeared, when he spoke of things he should not have known.

Isambard considers rising, searching through the drawers of his desk or bedside table to find one of the weapons he keeps for just such an eventuality: dealing with a thief. It's not really a threat he's faced much in Lodellan, not since the fall of the Parsifals, which ironically enough was when malfeasance went on the rise. Anyone inclined to criminal activity became quickly acquainted with Bethany Lawrence, and equally quickly came to realise she was not to be trifled with. Mr Farringdale, as her representative now she's relocated to Breakwater, is virtually untouchable—or thought himself so.

Now he wonders if he dare flee, take the egg with him, run back to Madame Arkady's House of Curiosities, beg her protection. But then . . . what might happen to the precious thing he's been promised? Its opening depends upon the boy's touch—or did he lie? Is there some magic in his skin? Or might any touch do? Dare Isambard risk it?

The suite of rooms, hung in shades of green, is decorated like a bower. Seats and tables are shaped like flowers, couches and chaises like velvet hillocks, scattered with cushions made to mimic floral spreads. The carpets are thick and deep as spring grass, the curtains are ephemeral things, veils of petals falling in a shimmery cataract of cleverly sewn fabric. There is a fountain, delicate and tall, shaped like a calla lily in shining mother-of-pearl.

In the very last chamber he finds the bed. It is round, wide, and above it is suspended a canopy shaped like a bluebell, but in a diaphanous olive. Its coverlet is the same colour, an overlapping series of tulip-shaped pieces, so they look almost like dragon scales. Bedside tables of rosewood sit to the left and right, their mirrored backs shaped like foxgloves. There is a slatted door leading into a dressing closet. One wall of the bedroom is taken up by a cabinet, a conglomeration of drawers and glass doors. Through the vitreous front, Jacopo sees the glitter of all manner of jewellery.

Chokers and pendants drape around busts of ebony. Bracelets and bangles dangle on hands of the same material. Rings drip from the branches of miniature trees made especially for this purpose. If this is what's on show, the youth wonders at what might be hidden in the drawers. Everything gleams by lamplight in the quarters of the Princess Royal.

And the thing he has come for is staring him in the face. It has pride of place in the centre of the magnificent repository; there would be no joy in hiding it away. *That* is the amethyst she described, there can be no other like it. Multifaceted, it drinks in all possible illumination, holding the rays in its depths so it seems to pulse and dance with both darkness and a lightness. The band of alternating emeralds and diamonds around it are perfect in the white-gold setting shaped like an opening lily, and the elegant interlocking spirals of the chain are starkly beautiful.

It is his for the taking. There is neither lock nor latch on its door, and in a trice Jacopo has his fingers on the strikingly cold necklace, feels the hardness of the gems, the nip of the precious metal. He retreats from the cabinet, the treasure hung over two fingers, dangling in the air, throwing watery colours around the bedroom. But, in his reluctance to crumple it like paper or fabric, he waits too long to hide it. And he knows it in the moment before a voice spears from behind him.

"Whore," someone hisses. He forgets for a moment who he is: not simply Jacopo with his charm and cunning, but now Ilse-Jacopo, with all the baggage of Ilse's loves and hates and hurts. He tilts his head forward, lets his shoulders slump in an attitude of distress; considers his options. They are few; all are brazen. He turns, settling his new features differently, consciously refusing the pull of the malcontent expression on Ilse's face when first he saw her, the one that has become her habit. He smooths out the disappointment, the dissatisfaction, the disaffection. He washes away the reproach—not guilt, no, but the blame she daily apportions to her husband and his sister, her lover, for the choices they gave her. As if she had no say in yea or nay, as if she had not grasped at what they offered—a choice of beds, property, glittering rewards when she produced the longed-for heir, the unassailable position of mother of the next Prince of Lodellan, and more rewards with each and every child she bore—with both greedy hands. All the things she had had, still had.

Instead Jacopo drops a veil of grief over his visage, softens his eyes, shows all the affliction and longing that are buried deep within her, all that she has hidden in her stiff-necked pride. He lets tears collect and bank precariously. His lips part, just a little, and his chin quivers with the force of his—her—pain. Her heart shows in his face; she is naked before her lover for the first time in long, long months.

And Jacopo sees the effect it has on the Princess Royal. Armandine is so struck, so pierced, it is as if she is staggering under a blow. Her own porcelain veneer of disdain cracks as surely as a teacup dropped on a marble floor. She reaches a hand to Ilse-Jacopo and follows through with a step, uncertain, then another and another, until the tall ethereal princess has her sturdy inamorata in her arms, in an embrace that is unbreakable. Jacopo has no choice, he gives himself up to this, to these sensations, to this love, this reunion. If he makes excuses, tries to flee, he will be caught. He does all the clever things to her that the gypsy girls taught him, all the clever things he hopes to do to Tove one day. He takes part, terribly conscious of the minutes ticking by, relieved, at last when Armandine falls away, exhausted, and begins to snore.

Swiftly Jacopo dresses once more, pocketing the necklace that had been discarded on the combined skirts of their fallen robes. He leaves the slippers behind, knowing his own bare feet will be quieter, and sneaks along the corridors, unerringly finding his way to the fountain room. He puts on his own clothes, drops the gown, then opens the door to the steam hut where Ilse sleeps deathly still.

His puts his lips—still tasting of Armandine—to hers and carefully breathes her back into herself. There are moments when he is sure he is too late, then she sighs, hiccups, and starts, eyelids flickering like butterflies. She stares at him and he gives his most reassuring smile . . . until she screams.

It is a high sound, a piercing shriek, and he knows it will have been heard by the guards. He slams the door of the steam hut and runs, darting as quickly as he can through the panel, shoving it closed, forgetting his earlier fear of the darkness, and bolting with only his skin to light his path. He has no choice: he must go back the way he came or risk being found by a mortal threat.

Mr Farringdale nurses his injured digit: the right forefinger was badly burned where he touched the egg and he'd cried out.

The pain made him weep, made him angry and vengeful. He would run, the prize be damned. He would have Madame Arkady send two of her largest hoodlums, the ones who'd hired themselves out of the Assassins Market in Breakwater, back here to wait for the youth. To hurt him as much as humanly possible, to get whatever he knew from him, before finally putting him down. And whoever had sent him would know that Isambard Farringdale, right hand of Bethany Lawrence, was not to be taken lightly.

But then he caught sight of the egg, of the lass inside pressed up against the translucent shell, her expression one of concern. And was that . . . a tear glistening on her pale cheek? Isambard held his hand closer, lost himself in the gaze of the girl in the oval, lost himself in how like Bethany she was. That expression, just like the first time he'd found her, the first time he'd loved her, and every time he was able to do so again before he had to hand her over to her sister, the uppity Cordelia.

That expression . . . not unlike the one on Mrs Parsifal's face several times in the weeks leading up to the family's grand disgrace. Did she suspect the pillars of her existence were being chipped away? By her nearest and dearest? Isambard feels, though he will not admit it, that the sting of his finger is minuscule compared to Bethany's and Cordelia's. He feels a fleeting guilt at his part in causing it, but reminds himself that both acts were done from his love.

The tiny girl in the chrysalis holds his gaze, her compassion and kindness are drugs to him; he thinks she appears poised to dance, like the ballerina in a jewellery box. All thoughts of flight subside as he watches, breathless with anticipation.

The haunt is waiting when Jacopo reaches the bottom of the stairs, drifting back and forth like a stalking wolf. There's a gleeful expression on its malicious face. Despite everything, Jacopo's heart becomes cold with fear and his light dims drastically.

This is what the spectre has been waiting for and it swoops at him. The boy falls backwards, cowers, cannot force even one greater glimmer from his skin, which flickers. He watches the creature come closer, closer, closer . . .

Then it stops.

It tries again, throwing itself forward and stopping just short of the prone youth. Jacopo is bewildered, yet grateful. He recalls the new item in his possession: the necklace. A thing the ghost cannot win against? His employer did not tell him its history, but perhaps it is steeped in sins or glory greater than this spiteful wisp ever committed? The apparition hisses in frustration, and over the top of that angry exhalation Jacopo hears the sound of many hands beating on the secret panel not so far above him. He rolls to his feet, his radiance flaring, making the spectre cover its eyes with those horrible hands, and the boy flees, runs for his very life.

Behind him are a splintering of wood as a door is broken down, many boots on stone steps, and then . . . and then . . .

And then screams.

Screams as the haunt of the catacombs finds victims who have none of Jacopo's protections. Can it go beyond the level of the dead, will it float up and go through the palace at its leisure? He thinks not, senses once again that it cannot. Then he shakes the thought away and concentrates on finding his way back to the cathedral.

Breathless, Jacopo enters Mr Farringdale's house. The owner had locked the door after his guest left, but locks are no barrier to Jacopo.

The first thing he gazes at is not the egg, but his host's hands, which hang loosely now, almost touching the floor as he sits cross-legged in front of the fire. The chrysalis remains in its tidy nest, resting between Isambard and the hearth. Jacopo scans the man's digits and lo! What he seeks is there: a sear mark on the soft pad of the right index finger, its existence given away by a slight glimmer, the same sort of luminescence that Jacopo emits. The youth smiles, secretly pleased to know he'd assessed the man so correctly. Mr Farringdale couldn't resist *touching*. Jacopo wonders how long it took between his departure and the moment Isambard's curiosity got the better of him. He wonders if the wound still throbs and aches. He wonders if the man realised that the thing is made of wax, that strange substance *the woman* has mastered and made her own.

"Couldn't help yourself, Isambard?"

The man's expression is studiedly neutral, but his eyes are filled with fear that this prize will be snatched from his grasp. Jacopo smiles to show he understands. That it's all right. That nothing has changed. That Mr Farringdale has not ruined his chances. The man's features relax, and for a moment he glows as if a little of Jacopo's shine has rubbed off on him.

"Did you . . . ?" Mr Farringdale's voice is raw.

Jacopo nods, draws his hand from his deep pocket. The necklace drips from his fingers, trailing light and colour.

Isambard catches his breath. He only ever saw it that once, when Bethany showed it to him, just before she gave it to Edvard Parisfal. She'd boasted then how new it was, that everyone who knew about it was dead—except its maker and she was too far away to make a difference—so it was perfect to fill her brother-in-law's request, to get him further into her debt. She got cocky, he thinks, and things had fallen apart so quickly, though he'd admired how smoothly she'd managed to shift all the consequences to others, to her foolishly blind sister. If she'd not, he was aware, he'd not be living a life that gave him such pleasure; yet he was also aware that she might have used him as a scapegoat, just as easily, had she not needed him for a little longer.

The boy shoves the gleaming thing back into his jacket and breaks Isambard's meditation.

"And so, Mr Farringdale, you have held up your part of the bargain." Jacopo kneels on the other side of the chrysalis and the flames from the hearth turn half of him red-gold, throwing the other half into darkness. He reaches out, his long fingers with their carefully tended nails touch the top of the oval, ever so gently, and a word leaves his lips though Isambard cannot hear it for it is only a whisper. The girl looks directly at him and the egg begins to grow.

His breath is trapped in his throat for so long that Isambard fears he may pass out. Just before the thing gets too large, just as he is about to doubt the lad's promise, about to believe she will get too big, too old, too mature, everything stops.

A crack forms at the top of the shining ovoid and zigzags its way to the floor. The girl raises a small fist and gives a single, sharp punch. The waxen shell shatters into pearly shards and the girl, his girl, *his* Bethany, steps out and away from the wreckage. Her dress is white, lace and satin, a child's frock. Her shoes, equally white, have silver daisies embroidered on the straps. Her hair hangs in two thick plaits of darkest gold and her eyes are glittering green, her mouth a rosebud of red-tinted pink.

A great sigh escapes Jacopo as he rises out of his crouch. Mr Farringdale had forgotten, for the slimmest of moments, that he was there. "Good luck, Isambard. You have certainly earned your reward."

He nods at his erstwhile host, pretends not to see the hand the man offers in farewell, and strides into the darkness. There is no sound of the door opening or closing, but Mr Farringdale does not notice. He turns back to the girl and reaches out.

He brushes one of her plaits and finds it adheres to his fingers. He cannot pull away. His other hand goes to the rescue of the first, and it too is caught in the spider web of her locks, and against the skin of her neck, which proves equally viscid. The girl makes a noise, something like a snicker, something like a snarl, and she winds her arms around him, pulls him closer and closer until they are body to body, and stuck thus.

No matter how he struggles, Isambard is held fast. The girl is adhesive, a wax baby, a tallow trap. From her very pores, from her mouth and nostrils, eyes and ears, pours forth a sticky substance. It bubbles up, over her owner's shoulders and down his back, his front, stomach, crotch, legs, until it meets up and covers him and her utterly, sealing both of them in. Or rather, Mr Farringdale alone, for the girl is gone, become a sea of waxy foam that has surrounded him, is in his mouth, his throat, his ears and nostrils, pushing against his eyeballs. Slowly but surely the new chrysalis begins to cool and tighten, to shrink, compressing Isambard, crushing him down and down and down, until there is only a shining pebble on the rug before the hearth.

Jacopo steps from his place in the shadows and pockets the strange stone with barely a glance. His own features have changed, no longer so round and inviting, that gilt sheen of his has dimmed, the face elongated, the jaw is harder and squarer, the cheeks angular, and the nose crooked, showing it was once broken. These features have been lived in, not borrowed; they are his and worn with pride, no longer secret. He is older, a young man, no longer a boy barely out of puberty.

Before he leaves he goes through the drawers and cupboards, liberating any and all valuables he can find in the house—his *employer* will welcome new funds for her endeavours; the necklace holds significance for her, he is sure, but ready currency is always appreciated. There is also a considerable stash of gold and silver, full coins and bits for change, Mr Farringdale had feathered his nest very nicely indeed. There are other things, however, things that obviously once belonged to some child or another, which he sets aside to deal with properly, respectfully: Jacopo sends them on their way in the hearth, blessed by fire and air so they might find their path home, back to the hands that loved them.

The Burned Woman, the Cinder's Sister, the new Tallow-Wife, will be pleased, he thinks, and the idea brings a smile to his lips.

BEARSKIN

TORBEN KNOWS HE HAS ONLY ONE SHOT. The crossbow shakes in his grip. There is a single bolt and even if there were more he has not the strength to reload for the weapon belongs to Uther, the woodsman, who has left the boy to wait in the small, smelly blind set between the trunks of three ailing alders. The walls are of woven rushes and withy. The flimsy roof fell in who knows when and Torben feels the drip-drip-drip of snow-melt from above—not that the weather's warming up, but it seems the unhealthy branches won't allow the ice to remain on their limbs much past daybreak.

The boy is cold in his pale wolf furs, despite their thickness. He never had a taste for hunting though Edvard, his father, tried to teach him. Henry, his brother, took to it like a duck to water, but Torben refused to attend what Edvard patiently told him. He has never learned the knack of willing himself warm, of wiggling his fingers and toes to keep the blood moving. Uther does not bother to instruct, or even to try, he simply slaps the boy about the ears each and every time he fails at one rough task or another. Torben suspects the man rather enjoys it and encourages missteps whenever he can. Edvard was always kind and tolerant, going over the same lesson time upon time, never punishing his youngest child's inattention. Perhaps that's why the lad suffers so now.

Thoughts of his father bring, as usual, hot tears which the boy wipes away—he does not want them to freeze on his face. He has learned that much. He bites his lip and steadies his aching heart. He dare not think of his mother.

Torben presses an eye against the matting, except there is nothing beyond but a vastness of white broken only by thin naked trees. There is no canopy above of evergreens to offer any cover. He squints, trying to see if Uther is returning, slinking through the forest, quiet despite his hulking size. Yet no, there is not even the icy comfort of Torben's gaoler on offer.

Gaoler. Not the word Aunt Bethany had used. *Guardian*. *Teacher*. Master to Torben's apprentice. He'd asked over and again *why*? Why did he need an apprenticeship when Henry had been allowed to go to University. There was plenty of money—all the problems his parents had caused were sorted—why was he not to be given the same chance? Wasn't that why they'd moved to Whitebarrow? So Henry could study medicine as he'd desired? It was a few more years, certainly, before Torben would be old enough, but his tutor said he was terribly bright for a twelve-year-old, that he had great prospects, great possibilities. It hadn't occurred to Torben then, though it had many times since, that his repeated interrogations were the reason he now found himself huddled in Edmea's Wood in the depths of winter, yearning for the company of a man he couldn't stand. A man whose face wore the scars of a bear attack. A man who'd grown so tired of Torben's stumbling and tripping, his barely swallowed whimpers, that he'd left the boy alone in the decaying blind with instructions to *Fecking wait* while he went and checked the traps on his own.

Torben sits back, tries to get comfortable; he can barely feel his feet and his backside has gone to sleep. Everything will hurt when he stands, when the blood flows back into his flesh and muscles—oh yes, he has muscles now, not big ones, but they've replaced the baby fat he'd had in copious store *before*. The physical labour, the sparse diet, have stripped the excess from his bones. He is constantly hungry, a gnawing in his belly day and night, but he doesn't dare steal. Uther is keenly aware of the quantity of provisions in the larder, and Torben is certain that the quiet, scrawny girl who keeps house for Uther would be unwilling to risk her master's wrath all for the sake of the plump little rich boy who came to them weeping eight months ago.

He listens carefully in case Uther is sneaking up behind to scare him so he pees his pants again. Torben would have thought that trick one to grow old quickly, but apparently not. All he can distinguish is the wind rattling branches, the creak of frozen wood, the whoosh of his own breath as it makes dragon's mist in front of his face. Put him in a library and he can identify the title of a book by the sound of its fall, but here . . . here he is lost. He clears his throat; it seems terribly loud in the sighing of the snow. A bird calls overhead, a melodic thing, and he thinks of Victoria, his sister, gone before him. That should have been a warning, he thinks, a sign that Aunt Bethany would brook no dissent no matter how much she professed to love them. Henry will be safe, Torben thinks, Henry has the habit of obedience and Aunt cares for him more, differently, strangely.

There is a noise outside, closer than it should be. Something has stalked him, gotten into proximity, and he all oblivious. To one side it shuffles and snuffles . . . his finger tightens on the trigger of the crossbow . . . whoever or whatever is there moves nearer . . . Torben's finger twitches and the bolt is released, punching through the withy screen. A thud, then a brief sigh-sob, then the sound of a small body falling to the snowy ground.

Heart in mouth, Torben scrambles up, fighting his way out of the blind; unable to find where the door latches, he tears it in panic. He falls through the rip and discovers that he has murdered a bear cub.

The cub is not especially large and his brown pelt is thick and matted. He should not have been out, thinks Torben in distress, he should have been sleeping the deep winter's slumber, not wandering about—Torben assumes it's a "he." He kneels and feels for a pulse, however, there is nothing. The barb is embedded right where the creature's heart should be. Blood has dripped, making crimson blossoms on the white carpet. The fur and flesh beneath Torben's hand are warm, so warm, but he knows the heat will flee soon enough. Copper eyes glazed over, bewildered, snout damp, teeth sharp beneath the sweet upper lip. The boy begins to weep and does not try to stop; tears drop like liquid stars onto the dark coat and stay there, held on the tips of the bristles.

He cries until he hears a new noise, a crashing and a thrashing somewhere amongst the trees of Edmea's Wood. Not Uther; the woodsman would never make such a racket. That is when Torben flees; he doesn't see anything but his imagination has always been worse than what might be real. He struggles through drifts, uncertain if he is heading in the right direction, driven only by the desire to escape whatever is behind. He doesn't care what punishment Uther will inflict on him for not staying put. He only knows he must run.

It is almost an hour later when he stumbles, more by luck than design, into the white-swept courtyard of the small stone house in the woods to which the woodsman lays claim.

Tove took pity on him when he threw open the door and staggered over to the roaring fire in the large front room. She handed him a mug of heated winter-plum brandy. It was liberally sweetened with molasses and made smooth by a knob of butter and took away what little breath he had left. But it warmed him and quickly, pressing life back into his extremities, even those he was sure had been frozen forever.

"Thank you," he croaks to the girl. She doesn't speak and he wonders, not for the first time, if she cannot or simply won't. He's never heard her answer Uther, nor have a conversation, not that their master was much of a one for such pleasantries. She watches everything though, he's noticed that. Her dark blue eyes seem everywhere at once, as if taking in all possible threats, all available exits and places to hide. Torben feels for the first time, as she refills his mug, that he may stare openly at her, at the fine dark blond hair, and the small stubs of antlers that poke through it on each side of her head. They are not fully formed and have not changed in the time he has been here. Tawny velvet covers them and he wants to run his fingers over it.

"I killed a bear cub," he says as she stirs the stew pot on the fire. She pauses, shoulders tensing, goes back to it, then speaks the first words he's ever heard from her.

"What sort of bear?"

"Brown. A brown bear."

"No, idiot. Was it a true bear or a one that's a bear only some of the time?"

"Is there a difference?" he asks, then wilts beneath her gaze, is burned by the contempt he sees there. His world is cracked open, his firmly held idea of who and how she is shatters. He wonders if this is why Uther does not touch the girl, does not abuse her. She's not his daughter, Torben knows that much for so the woodsman told him, said *No, she goes with the house.* But Torben thinks she doesn't go with the house at all, that she belongs somewhere else entirely and is just *here* for a while. He says, "I'm sorry."

She stills again, then relaxes, seeming to shrug away the tension. Her lips are no longer set in a sharp line and her eyes soften. "You're not to know, I suppose. City folk are ignorant."

That stings from this strange girl with her barely-born antlers, her silence. He blurts, "At least I'm not some stupid superstitious country clod. Bears are just bears, all the time. My parents—"

"Your parents?" she sneers. "What about them?"

He stops, wonders what she knows. Wonders what she's been told and by whom. Wonders if she knows how Edvard ended his life in gaol, and that his mother . . . oh, his mother. They stare at each other for long moments while the drink in his hand goes cold, and the stew on the hob, unstirred, becomes agitated, bubbles up and spatters on the flags. It breaks the spell, and he says softly, "What are you?"

But their brief connection is lost. She turns away and does not answer.

When Uther finally comes home a few hours later, a brace of fat bone-coloured coneys slung over his shoulder, he doesn't yell as Torben expected. Isn't angry at all, just curious. Strangely proud. He hands the catch to Tove, then eyes the boy.

"You kill tha' cub?" His voice is deep and raw, rough as elm bark looks.

Torben cannot find a reply so he merely nods from where he sits by the hearth, the aching cold almost out of his bones.

"Should ha' lugged it home," the man says, seating himself across from the boy. The fire plays shadow and light over his face, making the scars seem to dance. "Not much you can do with th' hide, but meat's sweet so young."

"I . . ." Torben croaks. "I heard something else after it, coming for me. I thought it might be the mother."

Uther nods. "Might ha' been. Mayhap she woke early too, found him missing." He leans forward to unlace his boots. "I'd ha' run too. You did th' smart thing."

Torben is surprised and disturbed, that the man has addressed unnecessary words to him, words of comfort and approval. Torben is distressed that the worst thing he has ever done, though it was an accident, is the one thing this man approves of, is the one thing that might make his life here easier if only for a little while. He cannot find it within himself to be glad, even a little. He swallows hard, nods so Uther will think they are in harmony however briefly, and will not suspect that the boy is so sickened by himself he's thrown up three times in the privy out back. That every time he closes his lids he sees those copper eyes staring at nothing at all.

"Ne'er fear. I brought it back. Skinned it afore I came in, meat's in th' smoking hut. He'll no go to waste." Uther rises, leaves his boots to dry by the flames, lands a heavy hand on the top of Torben's head, not in violence, but a kind of rough pat as he stomps to the washroom where Tove has heated water in the tub. *Good lad*, it says and Torben wants to weep again. His stomach rebels at the idea of eating such flesh, or indeed anything. The winter-plum brandy is long gone. His skin crawls to think of the hide made into shoes or a hood. He refuses the bowl of stew Tove wordlessly offers and makes his way upstairs to his small room under the eaves.

He was not allowed to bring any books, though he managed to smuggle a copy of Murcianus' *Mythical Creatures*, and it lies beneath the mattress. He limits himself to a single page each night to stave off the time when he must either beg Uther for a new volume or begin again. The lack still claws at him. He does not read this eve; he is exhausted. Sleep comes weirdly quickly, with dreams chasing its tail like nipping pups. His mother, Cordelia, sits at his bedside. Cordelia as he last saw her, not as Aunt Bethany said she'd become. Cordelia loving and laughing, telling him he was her sweetest, her best darling, her last child, and her only light. That he was special.

It's so long since Torben felt special.

He wakes himself before the dreams turns to nightmares, almost throwing himself from his mattress.

He stares out the tiny window into the darkness where nothing can be discerned until the full moon rises over the reaching fingers of skeletal treetops. Everything is bathed in silvered indigo. Torben looks down at the lean-to; he can just see the edge of the cub's skin stretched over the tanning rack. In the moonlight it's paler than he recalled, and it appears as if there are stars at the end of each bristle.

The stone house sits in a small clearing. To the left is a frozen rill, where Torben and Tove must hack at the ice to melt it for drinking and cooking and bathing. To the right is the lean-to and the outdoor privy. Behind is a barn-cum-stable where the jersey cow and two Clydesdale horses share straw with chickens, ducks, and geese. The front garden is dotted with rose-beds, the plants blooming all year round due to Uther's strangely green thumb. The coloured blossoms look like jewels against the moonlight-blue snow.

Torben's attention is caught by a hesitant movement at the edge of the clearing. A shape materialises, taking slow steps. At first he thinks it a bear, but the size is too small, the gait too elegant, and the owner walks on two feet, not four. The smudge resolves itself into a woman, her skin dark olive, her hair a blackish-brown running down her back, past her waist, to her ankles where it drags in the deep powder. She is tall, very tall, and heavy-boned, large around breasts and hips. Her face is gentle, her eyes flash amber. She raises her head and Torben sees how she sniffs at the air.

She drifts towards the lean-to, her hands reaching out to the cub's hide. Just before she touches it, she looks up as if sensing Torben's gaze. His tears have started again and course down his cheeks. He wonders if the woman can see them glinting. Her expression does not change, she merely stares at him for long moments, then helps herself to the fur, carefully unhitching it from the frame. She cradles it in her arms and returns to the forest.

For a long time Torben watches the space where she no longer is. When he's half-frozen again, he crawls back into the bed with its goose-down quilt and pillows, the only luxuries Aunt Bethany sent with him. He trembles with fear that the nightmares might overwhelm him, but his dreams when sleep will no longer be denied are empty, and he is safe.

In the morning, Uther finds bear tracks outside, where Torben had watched the woman walk.

"Did you see aught?" he asks, scars twitching, and the boy swears he did not.

Uther grunts and strides towards the barn.

Torben knows the woodsman keeps his great crossbow there—one Torben has no hope of lifting, let alone arming—and the bear traps, cruel things with steel teeth. He shivers in the cold as he looks down. The prints are huge, almost three times as long as his own foot. He cannot reconcile the woman he saw with the traces she left behind.

No, perhaps not her. Perhaps a bear came after he slept. Perhaps a bear followed the scent, hers or the cub's, and obliterated the woman's footprints. His heart constricts, then: what if the bear stalked the woman? What if it found her with her gentle face and wondering eyes? Neither woman nor bear deserve Uther's attentions, he decides.

He looks to the house and finds Tove regarding him from the back door. She stares, then retreats inside.

The girl's barely paid him any attention in almost a year, yet here is the second day in a row that she's met his gaze. That she's let him know again she disapproves. She sleeps on a pallet in the kitchen. He wonders what she saw through the window there, and if she'd even tell him if he asked. Torben opens his mouth but the only thing that comes is heated mist before Uther's shouts from the barn: "Hurry up, boy. We're hunting bigger game today."

He envies Tove that she gets to hide, even as he is afraid of what she might say if he spoke to her again.

~

It is late in the day when Torben catches the trail. The light is beginning to fade and they are deep in Edmea's Wood, where the trees, though leafless, grow oh so tightly together, and the shadows are lengthening. Torben has thrice been lost, but managed to right himself again before Uther realised and had to come and find him, swearing as he went.

The prints are strange, sometimes they disappear for large spans, with nothing to show how the creature got from one spot to another. Torben hopes every moment that the woodsman would not pick up the spoor again, but the man is tenacious, bloody-minded. The scars on his face, the memory of the claws that put them there, drive him. But this time . . . oh, this time, it's Torben who has found the tracks. He looks at the direction they lead, peers amongst the close trunks but sees no hint of the creature that left them. He spins on his heel as well as he can in the sluggish white and tramps back towards where he last saw Uther.

Breaking from a stand of singing winter grass that croons as he passes, he spies Uther on the other side of a clearing, heading straight towards him. The boy increases his pace, almost jogs, trying to ensure the man stays as far away from the evidence as possible. He is breathing hard when he reaches the woodsman, but it covers his nervousness about lying.

"Anything?"

Torben shakes his head. "Nothing." He pauses. "It's . . . it's not a normal bear, is it?"

For a moment he thinks the man will not answer, then he nods, a sharp jerk, says, "No."

"Was it . . . " Torben is stricken by his own audacity, raises his hand, points to his own face as if he is the marked one, " . . . the one who did that?"

"No. Tha' one's th' rug on my bed." Uther looks around, stares up at the greying sky that seems to deepen every second. "Home now. Light's going. Try again tomorrow."

On the journey back to the stone house, Torben's heart is light, his feet lighter still, and he does not feel weary though they have traipsed the length and breadth of Edmea's Wood for hours. There will be hot stew tonight and a warm bed, and perhaps he will allow himself two pages of the Murcianus, though he is already part way through *P*; the *Plague Maiden* awaits his attention. Relief leads his mind elsewhere, as if he's carefree once more. Perhaps Tove will forgive him, talk again; her voice was sweet.

TOVE REMAINS SILENT when they return, and it is only after Uther has clattered up to his bed in the master chamber that Torben is able to approach her. But when he tries to engage her she glares and calls him *lackwit*.

"Why?" he asks, bewildered.

"Because of the bear," she hisses.

"But, but . . . but I led him astray. Though I found the tracks, I did not tell Uther." He feels a tremor starting in his legs. Torben had expected something nicer, if not a kind word then at least not this spitting rage. "Won't it be enough?"

"You think that will be enough? He'll be out there tomorrow and the day after that, then the next. He won't stop until he's found her."

"Her?" His tone wavers though he knows she speaks truly, gives voice to what he suspected but did not wish to believe.

"And it's all your fault because you're a frightened little baby." She looks at him as though she hates him. He thinks if she had full antlers she'd do her best to impale him, and not regret it at all.

"I didn't ask to come here," he stammers, wanting to cry, but he will not let this hard girl see his tears.

"I would you hadn't," she hisses. "Why did you? Why did you come and bring this misfortune?"

He has no answer for her or none he wishes to give. How to say *My parents are dead? My Aunt has no love for me? Father killed himself in despair and Mother . . . oh, my poor mother. Mother burned to a crisp on a prison hulk right in the middle of Rosebery Bay? In all that water, Cordelia seared and smoked, scorched and singed, blistered until her skin split.* How to say *My Aunt told me all of this with a smile and a laugh?*

He swallows and settles on, "I ran away . . . I tried to find where my sister had been sent . . . but I didn't get far . . . was dragged home . . . I'm not very good at anything, really. I couldn't even run away properly."

He turns his back so she will not see the unshed tears. They are not friends. They will not be friends. The realisation is sharp. He crouches by the fire and does not move, not even when he hears her boots come close, then move away; even when he hears her return to the kitchen and settle on her thin bed there.

If asked, he could not tell what thought is uppermost for everything seems a maelstrom of emotions and images, of things long lost and desired to reappear. The flames die down as the hours pass and Torben becomes an invisible lump in the limpid, leftover glow. He only comes back to himself when he hears two things at once: a creak on the stairs, and the sound of something falling outside. Frozen by uncertainty he remains immobile. He's so still and small, so saturated by shadows, that Uther does not see him when he creeps past. The woodsman has the great crossbow held at the ready; the sight takes Torben's breath away.

Uther undoes the latch and slips out. Torben stands, his limbs throbbing painfully as his circulation speeds up. He follows the woodsman.

The lean-to is empty though the tanning rack has tipped over, and there are footprints, man and bear, leading towards the barn, where the door hangs open. Torben takes only a few steps before he hears a rumbling roar, and a man's shout. One of the building's walls splinters under the weight of an ursine charge, and a brown she-bear tears into the silvery night.

She streaks towards Torben, he can see fear in her copper eyes, and steps aside for he instinctively knows she will not slow down. Her one thought is of escape. She rushes by and he can smell musk and fear. Uther stumbles from the barn, dark marks on his winter furs where the bear's claws made their mark. He curses, then plants his feet apart, and lifts the crossbow into position.

The seconds seem long between the release of the bolt and when Torben steps into its path. He knows the she-bear will run in a straight line making her an easy target. He knows she has come here because of him, because he killed her cub. He left it for Uther to skin. He led her *here*. He knows this is the very least he owes her. Or perhaps he simply knows that if he remains, he will carry her grief as well as his own and it is a burden he does not want.

The angry thud of the missile into his chest pushes all air from his lungs, and he falls. He stares at the winter stars. The pain comes, and Torben finds it hard to breathe. The snow beneath him is soft yet brittle, melting slowly. He sweats, the droplets freeze, and soon he has a layer of ice over his skin. He prays that death will come quickly. Perhaps he will meet his mother again. He wonders if Cordelia wanders, looking for her children.

Then the sky is eclipsed as something huge soars over him. There is a scream which cannot possibly come from Uther, but must: high and terrified, and abruptly cut off as the sounds of flesh tearing and bones breaking become so terribly loud. Then heavy footfalls come towards Torben and, once again, the sky goes dark. Though he cannot make out the features above him, something wet and warm rains down on his face, a mix of blood and spittle. He manages to roll onto his side, though it hurts; he does not wish to see the yellowed teeth descending. He wonders if Tove is watching from the kitchen window, her breath making distressed shapes on the glass; if she nods, thinking *this is right*? The she-bear bends forward and takes the scruff of his fur collar in her mouth; a tooth sinks into him, pierces the fleshy part of the shoulder where it meets the neck. He cries out, but it is the least of his agonies.

Torben is dragged like a sack of meat from the yard, into the woods. He is so cold he barely feels it when he hits a rock or a log, when something sharp tears this clothing. He is part-pushed, part-pulled into a dim pungent burrow. He lands on something soft; as he grows warmer his wounds bleed afresh.

His lids flutter open and he sees the woman again. She has large hands, and brown furry feet; toes tipped with long claws peeking out from under the hem of her dun-coloured gown. She ambles about the burrow gathering things he cannot see, hunched over so her head does not scrape the roof where luminescent roots poke through from above.

There is the sound of mortar against pestle, and he ponders if perhaps he's been dreaming all along, if he dreams still.

The bear-woman holds his head and makes him swallow the powder she has ground. It's bitter, bitter, then sweet. He opens his lips to beg for water, and she spits into his mouth. Startled, he swallows that too, finds it is not foul, but quenches his thirst, eases his aches. Darkness begins to pull at him and he thinks it is death. He tries to say *I'm sorry* to the bear, to the woman, because he thinks it is important that she hear it. But his tongue is going numb and seems to grow; his teeth feel more numerous.

She pats his head and whispers *hush*, or at least he thinks that's what she says. Perhaps it is simply a bear noise that he interprets as he wants—needs—to. His failing gaze paints Cordelia's image on the bear-woman's face. His mother smiles and says *Hush, all will be well*, and Torben thinks he smiles. A hand brushes his hair, then he feels the soft thing beneath him being adjusted, wrapped tightly around him. The hands fall away but the fur rug does not. It grips him snugly and grows, along his limbs, up over his head, down his forehead, nose, cheeks, jaw, neck, over his chest . . . and Torben thinks he imagines it as he surrenders to what must surely be his final slumber. His last thought, with some regret, some relief, is of Tove. He will never know what she is, who she was; she's a mystery he will never solve.

Torben is surprised when he wakes. but he knows he has slept long.

He rolls over, finds himself changed, but is not overly concerned. On his back, he twists this way and that, trying to scratch the itch along his furry spine, enjoying the sensation more than anything he can recall in life. A tree, he thinks, outside there will be a tree with rough bark and he will rub the length of himself against it and it will be most satisfying. He rolls again, receives a gentle swat for his troubles, a warning not to wake his mother sooner than he must. She has had a busy winter, with her sleep interrupted.

He raises his large head, looks to where the snowfall had once formed a door to their den. It is gone now and in its place are puddles of melt, and beyond it the sight of Edmea's Wood, the trees bristling with new leaves, branches, and bright colours. Birdsong rings through, the sky is a warm blue. At first he thinks to bound forth, to try out his new shape, the four paws with their powerful claws, then another swat, a little less gentle, and he settles, curls back to back with the she-bear. There will be plenty of time to learn the world anew, he thinks sleepily; he knows what happens to cubs who stray from their mothers too soon.

AFTERWORD: AUTHOR'S NOTES

Sourdough

While I was doing my MA, I was reading a lot of fairy tales, then re-writing them, and also writing new ones. I had an idea about a girl who made bread into works of art; I thought about the fairy tale "Donkeyskin," where the princess puts her jewellery into food for the prince and I thought about what a silly, dangerous act that was. I'd read Margo Lanagan's tale "Wooden Bride" and the city she described gave me an oblique inspiration for Lodellan. I chose the name Emmeline for my protagonist because it means labourer and labour she does over the making and baking of her bread creations. I chose Peregrine as her lover's name because it means both a pilgrim and a wanderer, and he does indeed wander for a time. "Sourdough" was one of the tales that didn't make it into my Master's collection (*Black-Winged Angels*), but I'd sent it off with a query to a bunch of small presses, including Tartarus Press. The lovely Rosalie Parker replied to say they weren't interested in a collection, but she was very interested in taking "Sourdough" for *Strange Tales II*. This is also the tale I chose as a project with Kathleen Jennings, to turn into a graphic story.

Dresses, three

This story WAS commissioned by Mary Robinette Kowal for *Shimmer's* Art Issue in Spring 2008. I was given a piece of art by the amazingly talented Chrissy Ellsworth for inspiration: "Life as a Fashion Designer" had a woman with a dress of birds, feathers, and words. I thought about the fairy tale "Donkeyskin" (again; an inspiration for me on more than one occasion). The princess in that story demands three dresses from her father, one like the stars, one like the moon, the other like the sun. I knew I wanted an echo of that idea, but the dresses were part of a larger spell: one of peacock feathers, one of butterfly wings . . . but in the end I found I needed to chat with my sister about the form of the third dress. Shell helped me get the idea to crystallise: a dress of words. Of course! The story was short-listed for the Aurealis Award Best Fantasy Short Story in 2008.

Bluebeard's Daughter

Gerry Huntman contacted me to say they were doing a special fairy tale issue of *SQ Magazine* and would I contribute. I was pressed for time but said "yes," because: fairy tales. I sat down at the computer and this is one of the fastest stories I've ever written, all done in an afternoon. From the first line: "Here," she says, "have an apple." I had the story fully formed: ideas about bad dads (who's worst than Bluebeard?), stepmothers, teenage daughters, romantic crushes, and gingerbread houses all coalesced most obligingly. It's short, sharp, bitter, and I'm tremendously fond of it.

The Jacaranda Wife

This was another of my challenge stories—a friend had told me that Jack Dann was looking for tales for his *Dreaming Again* anthology. I'd sent him one of my MA stories (a version of "Little Red Riding Hood" called "Red Skein"). He liked it, but not enough and said, "What else have you got, kiddo?" I had *nothing*. But I'd had the idea of jacaranda women in my head for a while, just nowhere to put it. My study at that time looked out into the backyard where there was a giant jacaranda tree and one rainy day I was writing—or rather, not so much writing as staring out the window at the tree, which was in season and the bunches of purple flowers were so heavy with rain that they looked, well, pregnant. At last I knew what to do—a kind of weird selkie story—and added a personal connection to it: my mother's family came to Australia with the Second Fleet and initially settled in Port Macquarie. Their property was called Rollands Plain. The jacaranda has been transplanted all over the world—just like ideas and stories and fairy tales—and I like the sense of it not quite belonging, of a strangeness in the landscape, an Australian fable with its roots in a European fairytale tradition. This story was first published in *Dreaming Again* in 2008.

Light as Mist, Heavy and Hope

This story sprang from one of my stranger ideas. I'd been thinking about how to rework "Rumpelstiltzkin" while watching a crime thriller late one night, in which a character observed that paedophiles don't wear big signs or the mark of the beast to distinguish them from everyone else. The idea was that it was so damned hard to know who was safe and who wasn't. I'd always wondered about the little fairytale man's motivation—and since Rumpelstiltzkin has always creeped me out I just made him a bit creepier.

The Coffin-Maker's Daughter

Editor Stephen Jones emailed asking if I'd submit something to his *A Book of Horrors* anthology (Jo Fletcher Books)—the catch was that it had to be more horrific than what I usually wrote. So: I was casting about for ideas with a bit of personal terror; I don't really think of myself as a horror writer. My first effort was deemed "Good, but I think you can do better." After some fist shaking and howling (on my part), I went back to work. I was listening to Florence and the Machine's *Lungs* for the first time . . . when "My Boy Builds Coffins" came on, I imagined a society that regarded coffin-making not simply as a necessary service, but also as an art form. On top of that, it was an eldritch art form required to keep the dead beneath the earth. I wanted a story that had layers of unspoken secrets—and also different sorts of ghosts.

When I heard "Girl with One Eye," I got an image of Hepsibah: this thin girl standing in front of a heavy door. She had a short gamine haircut that was growing out and curling, and she wasn't overly given to worrying about her appearance. She wore a brown woollen dress, a bit Jane Eyre-like, with long sleeves, buttons up the front, and long skirts, and she had on a kind of baker boy's cap. At her shoulder was the spectre of her father, and Hector is a nasty piece of work. I could hear his voice and knew how adversarial their relationship was, but that no matter how much Hepsibah hated him, they shared some fundamental characteristics and that's why he was still hanging around. When I first drafted the story, the society was a kind-of mirrored Victorian setting but mixed with elements from the world of *Sourdough and Other Stories*.

Hepsibah is one of my favourite characters—she's a terrible mess of a human, but really fascinating. I wanted to give a reader one picture of her, then twist that around at the end and show that she wasn't as well-adjusted as she at first appeared. That she and her dreadful father had more in common than anyone might think. And she was very important because as soon as I'd written this story, I knew I had the start of a new collection—*The Bitterwood Bible and Other Recountings*—because she wasn't the sort of character who would just quietly go away. It also won me a British Fantasy Award for Best Short Story.

By the Weeping Gate

This story first appeared in Stephen Jones' *Fearie Tales: Stories of the Grimm and Gruesome* (Jo Fletcher Books). I was thinking about pirates and ports, bordellos and brides—as you do—and the name came to me to describe a place where you pass from land to sea and those who watch you go or wait for you to come back, weep. I liked the idea of a girl who is terribly plain amongst all her beautiful sisters, but the sisters aren't cruel to Nel. Her mother is, though: Dalita is a terrible woman, the epitome of a mother trying to relive her life through her favourite daughter. I have a whole history in my head for her—how she fled her family and marriage, and made her own way in the world, how it turned her tenacious nature harsh and hard, and how—even though she's got a strong idea of family— she sees even her own children as a means to an end. Except Nel, who isn't physically lovely, so she can't be used as Dalita's usual currency. Although Nel's plainness is a source of some distress, she finds a way to use it to her advantage—she's able to pass unseen when others would attract attention, so she can collect secrets as well. I love how Nel learns and changes and *becomes* something else in this story, how she takes her courage in her hands and goes out into the world to make things right, even though she is, at the end, someone who can no longer hide. This story later appeared in *The Bitterwood Bible and Other Recountings*.

St Dymphna's School for Poison Girls

The title for this story came from a friend's throwaway line about St Dymphna's Home for the Wealthy Insane (thanks, Dr Carson). I thought "No, St Dymphna's Home for Poison Girls," and my mind went off on its own and sat in a corner, conjuring visions of a boarding school like the one in Charlotte Brontë's *Villette* except with more murder and fewer French lessons.

I thought about finishing schools for young ladies and the sorts of girls who are sent there, and the kinds of families they come from. I thought about the strife between grand houses caused by matters of pride and honour (not to mention thefts), and wondered what might happen if the female offspring from those grand houses might be taught something useful, like the art of assassination rather than napkin-folding and the Minuet . . . which was then still misused by said houses. I wondered about the sorts of young women who might not think beyond what their families were sending them to do, who didn't say to themselves, "Sod this for a game of soldiers—I've just been taught these great and terrible skills by independent and terrifying women, why should I go off to die in the service of my family? Why shouldn't I too become an independent and terrifying woman?" That's precisely what Mercia does—even though her surrogate family has set her to do something dangerous, she's not one of the herd; in the end she follows a different path. This story first appeared in *The Review of Australian Fiction 2014* (Volume 9, Issue 3)—and won the Aurealis Award for Best Fantasy Short Story in 2015. It later appeared in *The Bitterwood Bible and Other Recountings*.

By My Voice I Shall Be Known

In "By My Voice I Shall Be Known," I wanted to combine elements that contained echoes of legends about the Lorelei Rock, the *rusalkas*, and Melusine, all wrapped up with a traditional kind of betrayal and revenge tale. The title comes, I think, from something I read about one of the sibyls . . . but unfortunately I can't quite remember which one and I don't seem to have kept a note about it. Bad writer. But I love the bold statement that her voice will be all she needs . . . even though it's been taken from her. My mother is a quilter and I find what she does absolutely fascinating and very beautiful, yet I'm not a person with any talent for crafting things with my hands—I tend to sew my shirt to my pants or craft-glue my fingers into my hair—so the endeavour does seem a kind of witchcraft to me. When I was writing, I remembered a comment by my friend, Alan Baxter, who'd said that watching his wife knit was like watching folk magic happen—and I thought that quilting was pretty much like that too.

Sister, Sister

"Sister, Sister" has its roots in my childhood: one of the books we had to read was an old collection of my mother's, a thin forest-green tome with silver lettering called *Norwegian Folk Tales*. I suspect she'd won it as a school prize—it's long since disappeared, though I found a later edition earlier this year and bought it. (Still not the same, just saying.) In it were all sorts of tales of hulders and trolls, of women whose back side was hollowed out like a tree trunk, and yet others who looked perfectly normal but for their cow tail . . . but the bit of information that most appealed to me and stuck over the years was that trolls were known to steal away human babies and leave their own nasty, mewling offspring in the cradles. Even at a young age I loved the idea of the changeling child—and even more I loved to torment my younger sister, telling her when she annoyed me that she wasn't really my true sibling, but a troll's daughter left in the crib to cause trouble. All this probably says more about me than my sister, but when I began to think about new stories for *Sourdough* I knew I wanted a troll tale and I knew I wanted to use the changeling child as a motif.

The Badger Bride

I love badgers—yes, I know all the arguments against them, the great list of their sins—but I love them all the same. I've also always loved transformation stories, but they generally run along the same lines: one character must be transformed from animal to human in order for there to be a happily-ever-after. That ending assumes that whatever was threatening the star-crossed lovers has been defeated; but, I wondered, what if it's not? What if the threat remains, blundering about, looking for its dearest, darkest desire? What might our heroes do in order to escape? The characters in this story are among my favourites. Gytha seeks answers no matter what the cost, and Adelbert the ex-Abbot and Larcwide the Bibliognost are direct products of my love for monastic libraries and the preservation of knowledge—due in no small part to Umberto Eco's *The Name of the Rose*, and my Uncle Rod, who's also a collector of books and no mean bibliognost himself. And I love the idea that sometimes, just sometimes, though you don't get what you think you want, you get what you *actually* want.

The Tallow-Wife

"The Tallow-Wife" began with a dream of a woman within a dark woman, waiting for I knew not what. All I knew when I woke up was that she'd been hard done by and suffered terrible losses . . . but that she had also survived and in doing so she would take her revenge. I talked with my husband about it to try and pull more information from my subconscious and he made a throwaway comment about someone using candles to change things. I looked at him and said, which set off a series of ideas in my imagination and the rest of the story flowed from there. She begins life in this tale as Cordelia, a wife and mother, ends it quite differently, but not without hope. "The Tallow-Wife" is a novella and the first story in *The Tallow-Wife and Other Tales*, which will eventually be the third Sourdough universe book. Remain patient! But please note that the last three tales in this book (two of them brand, spanking new) are a Tallow-Wife suite and will open the new collection—you're welcome!

What Shines Brightest Burns Most Fiercely

This is the second story in the Tallow-Wife series, and I wanted it to specifically connect the action of the novella to the tales in *Sourdough and Other Stories* because I envision this to be the final instalment in the Lodellan cycle. *Sourdough* is the second book, so it acts as a bridge between the first (*Bitterwood*) and second (*Tallow-Wife*) collections in the series, and I wanted to hark back to characters like Theodora, and show the bloodlines are still running through like threads. Jacopo is the son of the daughter Theodora had with Faideau, and his life is as strange as that of his grandmother; he's got the power of shifting his appearance, and he finds Cordelia when she escapes from the Rosebery Bay hulk, and they form a bond, and things begin to happen . . .

Bearskin

"Bearskin" is another of the tales from what will be *The Tallow-Wife and Other Tales* collection. It follows Cordelia's youngest child, Torben, after his parents disappear. He's been cosseted and protected all his life, and now he's under the supervision of a brute called Uther, who tries to teach him to hunt, and the only person who might be his friend, Tove, is angry at him most of the time.

Publication Data

"Sourdough," *Strange Tales II,* ed. Rosalie Parker (Tartarus Press, 2007).

"Dresses, three," *Shimmer Art Issue*, Spring 2008.

"Bluebeard's Daughter," *SQ Magazine,* May 2015.

"The Jacaranda Wife," *Dreaming Again*, ed. Jack Dann (HarperCollins, 2008).

"Light as Mist, Heavy as Hope," *Needles & Bones*, ed. Deena Fisher (Drollerie Press, 2009).

"The Coffin-Maker's Daughter," *A Book of Horrors*, ed. Stephen Jones (Jo Fletcher Books, 2011).

"By the Weeping Gate," *Fearie Tales: Stories of the Grimm and Gruesome,* ed. Stephen Jones (Jo Fletcher Books, 2013).

"St Dymphna's School for Poison Girls," *The Review of Australian Fiction*, Volume 9, Issue 3, February, 2014.

"By My Voice I Shall Be Known," *The Dark*, Issue 1, October 2013.

"Sister, Sister," *Strange Tales III*, ed. Rosalie Parker (Tartarus Press, 2009).

"The Badger Bride," ed. Rosalie Parker, *Strange Tales IV* (Tartarus Press, 2014).

"The Tallow-Wife" is published for the first time in this volume.

"What Shines Brightest Burns Most Fiercely" is published for the first time in this volume.

"Bearskin," *The Dark,* Issue 7, February 2015.